The Chieftains
of South Boston

by Stephen Burke

Published by:
Stephen Burke
www.chieftainsofsouthboston.com

The Chieftains of South Boston

—

In Loving Memory

Elizabeth Ann Burke
Leo James Burke
David Francis Burke

—

Chapter One
A Sort of Homecoming

Get me the fuck out of here.

That's what Matthew Mahoney thought on his wedding day. Not while taking his vows at First Presbyterian Church in Ipswich, Massachusetts. Nor during the ten-minute drive down Plum Point Road that brought Matthew and his wife, Anne, from the church to the wedding reception at the seaside home of Anne's mother.

It happened beneath the big blue tent pitched on an expansive back lawn, where the mid-September sun had made the day particularly warm despite a breeze from the nearby shore. The open tent held a collection of tables, each topped by a colorful bouquet of flowers. At one end of the gently billowing tent, a jazz band was finishing its first set. At the other end was an open bar, where two bartenders were mixing drinks.

The slushy sound of a martini shaker blended with a conversation about the upcoming season at the Gloucester Repertory Theater. Beside the bar, an old wooden rowboat had been perched on sawhorses and filled with shaved ice. Caterers were busy shucking oysters and cherrystone clams, arranging them in the ice along with rows of pink prawns.

As Matthew waited at the bar for drinks, he scanned the crowd of more than ninety guests. Most of them were from Anne's side of the aisle. He didn't connect with the faces and the voices and the strange way strangers have of laughing. But at six foot three, Matthew was tall enough to see across the crowd. He spotted his father at the other end of the tent, standing tall and solid, like a pillar. The familiar white shock of hair bristled from his father's head. The face, broad and blunt, was the face of a fighter. It was the white hair and combative style as a politician that earned him the nickname "Salty."

The sight of his father made Matthew want to leave the reception. It always happened when he came back to the East Coast for a visit, and it was why the visits were kept so short. He wished, as he had done before, that this would be the last time he ever saw his father.

Matthew now lived in Seattle. When people would ask him why he had left South Boston and moved all the way across the country, Matthew would sometimes say that it was to get away from his family. Not once did he ever say that he left South Boston to get away from his father. But that was the truth.

Matthew hated the man. He called it something else for a long time, but hate was what it was, for how he treated Matthew and his brothers when they were growing up, and especially for how he treated their mother. Matthew had never discussed it with his two brothers, but he hoped they both felt the same way he did. Not that it mattered much. Or that it would change anything. Or that they'd ever talk about it. It was just that he didn't want to think he was hating alone. Misery might love company, but hatred demanded it if you wanted to feel justified and get a good night's sleep.

Then Matthew felt a breeze brush his face, followed by the strong scent of the ocean. It was clean and refreshing. He hadn't gotten such a rich breath of ocean air in a long time. It was one of the things he missed about the place where he grew up. Seattle had Puget Sound, but that was nothing next to the open Atlantic.

When the smell of the ocean passed and his father disappeared from view, Matthew organized his collection of drinks from the bar. He tucked two bottles of beer into each pocket of his rented tuxedo and gathered up four glasses of champagne.

Having worked as a bartender back in Seattle, he was skilled at carrying several drinks at once, so Matthew managed to arrive back at his table without spilling a drop of champagne.

"I thought you had to be Italian to be in the Mafia," Matthew heard Rachel saying to Buzzy, who sat across from her.

"Not in South Boston," Buzzy replied.

Matthew wasn't paying close attention to the conversation until Rachel looked up at him and said, "So, Matt, is it true that your brother Francis is in the Mafia?" Rachel was Anne's maid-of-honor and best friend from Alaska. She had the look of someone who loved being outdoors. Rachel used a napkin to wipe water that had condensed on her beer bottle, then placed the cool, wet cloth on her forehead. Buzzy looked at her, puzzled.

"The world's cheapest air conditioner," she laughed.

Matthew laughed too, but Rachel's question caught him by surprise. He lowered the champagne glasses onto the table, retrieved the beer from his pockets, then sat down. "Who told you about my brother?"

"Buzzy was giving me the rundown on your family," Rachel said.

Matthew turned to Buzzy Driscoll, his best man and best friend growing up in South Boston, and gave him a look that said—thanks for opening your big fucking mouth.

It was something that everyone in South Boston knew, but it was also something you didn't talk about. Being asked point blank caught Matthew off guard.

He would have reacted worse if somebody else was doing the asking. He didn't mind it from Rachel though. She never apologized for her bluntness, and Matthew respected that. It was something that people had after living in Alaska for a while, he learned, and Rachel had lived there all 26 years of her life. Matthew's wife, Anne, got hers after moving to Alaska as a kid. It was one of the things Matthew found irresistible about his wife. Most of the time.

Matthew glanced at Buzzy, whose attention was turned to the crowd of guests beneath the blue tent. Since leaving South Boston at the age of fifteen, Matthew had hardly spent any time with Buzzy, but he knew what his old friend was thinking as he sized up the various guests. Had any of them left anything valuable in the cars parked along Plum Point Road? And were any of those cars unlocked?

Matthew took the toothpick that had held a shrimp appetizer moments before and flicked it at Buzzy's face. It went high and landed in Buzzy's hair, where it lodged. He had a thick mop of reddish-brown hair cut in a shaggy style. It was 1987, and the style hadn't been popular in ten years. In South Boston, the standard was now short on top, shorter on the sides.

"So, where is your brother Francis?" Rachel asked, looking around the tent for a face that looked like Matthew's, only older. "I'd love to see what a real-life gangster looks like."

"He's miles away. My other brother Jimmy is here, so Francis knows not to show up," Matthew said, stretching back and draping his jacket around his chair to cool off. At twenty-eight years old, he weighed thirty pounds more than when he left Massachusetts and moved to Seattle. In those days, he was playing a lot of hockey and getting into a lot of fights.

He had never liked the idea of tattoos, but his face showed a distinct badge from those days, a scar that curled across his chin like a corkscrew. It would have healed in a way that was less noticeable if he had gotten stitches at the time. It was a decision Matthew Mahoney regretted every time he shaved, when he had to carefully drag a sharp razor across the bumpy landscape.

"Too bad your brothers don't get along," Rachel said.

"They get along fine," Matthew said. "It's for Jimmy's sake. They can't be seen together in public. At least not close enough for a photographer to catch them in the same picture."

Rachel didn't look like she understood, so Buzzy added, "His brother Jimmy is a state senator and it doesn't help his image to be seen with a member of a certain profession, especially if it's his brother."

"That makes sense." Rachel paused to take a swig of beer. "So does Francis have a nickname like gangsters in the movies?"

Matthew was getting a little tired of the talk about his brother. "Gangster" sounded so stupid. Then again, so did all the other names that described his brother's line of work. Matthew thought of him only as his brother, or Francis.

"Some of the older people still call him Frankie," Buzzy said. "Everyone else calls him Francis. I heard that when he was a kid, some other kid called him Spankie Frankie and Francis beat him so bad they had to take him to the Massachusetts Eye and Ear Hospital because one of the kid's eyes was all screwed up."

"Speaking of nicknames," Matthew said, "Why don't you tell Rachel how you got yours, Buzzy?" The truth, as Matthew knew, was that by the time Buzzy was twelve he had made his start in the world of drug dealing and was high more often than he was straight. The question was payback for telling Rachel about Francis.

Buzzy looked toward the distant shore to summon the inspiration and imagination necessary to generate the appropriate drama.

"Well, Rachel, the truth is that I had always wanted to be a beekeeper since I can't remember when," he began.

Matthew let out a little chuckle as he tried to sip some champagne. Buzzy heard it and got annoyed.

"You asked me a question. Do you mind not interrupting my answer, for Christ's sake?"

Buzzy swept a dismissive hand in Matthew's direction, then turned to Rachel. "Anyway, Matt doesn't like bees, but I do. They're industrious and trusting, and they're the reason why cockroaches don't take over the world. When they're not making honey, bees are usually out stinging cockroaches to death. And lots of other important things. I kept some bees when I was a kid, but when I got stung they found out I was allergic."

"That sounds ridiculous," Rachel said, picking up on Matthew's chuckle.

"Not if you're the one who's allergic. It can be deadly," Buzzy responded, not realizing that Rachel was referring to the idea of bees saving the world from a scourge of roaches.

Matthew was chuckling so hard that he had to put down his champagne. After wiping his eyes and taking a deep breath, he reached for his champagne again. But another hand got there first. It was Anne reaching from behind. His hand pursued the captured glass in vain.

"Champagne is for sharing, Mahoney. Didn't anyone ever teach you that?"

Anne stood behind Matthew, one hand on his shoulder. She wore an alabaster silk wedding dress that her mother was married in thirty years earlier. The first to wear it was Anne's grandmother, who grew up in Paris and had the dress tailored in a fashionable salon. Anne was taller than her mother and grandmother, normally requiring a simple alteration to the hem, but her father's genes had given her a leaner build, making more complicated alterations necessary.

She was paler than her friend Rachel and might have been considered plain looking except for her eyes. Their color fell somewhere between bright blue and aqua-green, depending on the light. The color alone caught attention, but it was more the way Anne had of looking at people. Her gaze often came across as a little too intense, whether she intended it or not.

It had to do with the fact that she never wore sunglasses. They made her feel claustrophobic, and she would only wear them when absolutely necessary—if she were fishing with a low sun directly across the water, or on the highway driving straight into a sunset. She compensated by squinting. Over the years, her general expression took on a slight squint. It also became her way of focusing on a person or a thought. As a result, when she looked at someone who didn't know her, or even someone who did, she would sometimes make them feel like they were being judged, or at the very least, being scrutinized.

It's exactly how Buzzy felt when he noticed Anne staring at him. He returned the squint. "What?" he asked.

Anne took a drink of champagne, then rested the glass on Matthew's head. With her free hand, she pointed at Buzzy's head. "There's something in your hair."

Buzzy looked up, then ran a hand through his hair, causing the toothpick to fall behind him. "There's nothing in my hair. My hair is in my hair."

Anne took her seat beside Matthew, who said, "Anne missed hearing how you got your nickname, Buzzy. You don't mind telling the story again, do you?"

"I have a better idea, Matt," Buzzy said. "Why don't you tell her how you got your nickname. Anne knows about it, right?"

Matthew slowly sat back in his chair. "She's heard them all. There's Matt, Matty, Matty Mo. Stuff like that."

Buzzy leaned forward and raised his eyebrows, as if raising a bet.

Matthew shook his head in a very subtle way that was imperceptible to anyone but Buzzy.

"And?" Buzzy asked.

"And nothing, you asshole," Matthew said, knowing he couldn't stop Buzzy.

"Goldfinger!" Buzzy said, then began humming the James Bond theme song.

"Goldfinger?" Anne gave a curious look.

"We were thirteen when Matt gets this idea…"

Matthew interrupted. "It was your idea."

"Hey, I'm sorry if this hurts, Matt, but the longer you drag it out, the more painful it's gonna be."

Matthew ignored the comment and reached to the center of the table for a couple of prawns and a fresh beer.

"Matt hears that the dome of the Massachusetts State House in downtown Boston is made of gold. The golden dome, they call it. So Matt tells me that if we sneak up there and get some of it, we'd be rich. Like the Klondike gold rush. So one night I get the spare key from his garage, and I sneak into his house and wake him up.

"It's two o'clock in the morning when we get to the State House and Matt shimmies up a drainpipe in the back. He's got a hammer and chisel and a big bag to put the gold in. I'm standing below watching for cops. He's not up there two minutes before somebody spots him and we're busted. He got the name because he was the one on the roof. Goldfinger, like in the James Bond movie."

"Did you get arrested?" Rachel asked.

Buzzy shook his head. "They gave us a ride downtown in the back of a cruiser, but Matt's dad knows all the politicians and cops. He got us out, then Matt got a beating when he got home."

As Buzzy was finishing his story, Kathleen Sutliff approached the table and gave Matthew a hug. She had grown up in the Old Colony housing project where Buzzy still lived, and was the on-again, off-again girlfriend of Matthew's brother Francis.

"I'm so happy for you, Matty. Both of you."

Anne had met Kathleen once briefly, so Matthew introduced her to Rachel. Kathleen had always been an honorary Mahoney and like an older sister to Matthew. Being half Portuguese gave Kathleen deep olive skin, which made her extremely exotic to the pale Irish kids growing up in the project. Matthew was one of many boys who had a crush on her as a teenager.

The death of Kathleen's daughter a few years earlier had not diminished her spirit, but it had cut into the charm. Matthew had never met Kathleen's daughter, but in pictures of her he could instantly see how much she looked like her mother. The way she died was one of many sad stories to come out of the Old Colony housing project in the last few years. It was even more of a shame, Matthew thought, because unlike some of the other women in the project, Kathleen was an exceptional mother.

11

"Matty, when you get a chance, go talk to your father. He was looking for you earlier. It's important."

"OK," Matthew said, but he had no intention of talking to his father, who had spent much of his life trying to become mayor of Boston. When Matthew was a kid, "See your father. It's important" usually led to Matthew holding a campaign sign at a South Boston intersection in the pouring rain.

Kathleen looked at Buzzy, then at the empty chair beside him. Buzzy had arrived with a woman named Christina, a drop-dead-gorgeous Puerto Rican. "1985 Miss Puerto Rico first runner-up," according to Buzzy. Most of the women at the reception had opted for the practical breezy dress, but Buzzy's date had shown up in a close-fitting red evening gown designed to reveal as much of her amazing figure as possible. A spiral of sequins further pushed the glamour boundaries.

Christina, or Miss Runner-Up as Matthew referred to her in her absence, had gone in search of a bathroom twenty minutes ago.

"I noticed your date earlier, Buzzy. She's very pretty," Kathleen said.

"I'd have to agree with you, Kathleen."

"So how much did she cost?"

Matthew's laughter sent the tail of a prawn into the air.

"Fuck you," Buzzy said, giving her the finger as well.

Kathleen leaned across the table. "Buzzy, what's the matter with you? You used to date girls from South Boston, but what, they're not good enough for you now?"

"They used to be, but now they're all talking about getting married and having kids on the second date. That's all they care about."

"Buzzy, wake up and look at the clock. You're twenty-eight. That's the same age as Matty and you see what he's doing today. Smarten up, that's what I'm saying." Turning to Matthew, she said, "I've got to go back and keep an eye on your cousins. I saw Bobby sneak two bottles of scotch from the bar. By the way, Anne, I love that necklace."

Anne's necklace held a series of sapphires, which picked up the subtle blue sheen of her silk dress.

"Thanks. A birthday gift from Matt."

"Are you paying attention to this, Buzzy?" Kathleen asked. "Anyway, you looked beautiful up there today, Anne. Both of you did."

Buzzy's date, Christina, returned from the bathroom. Of the few women who had made the mistake of wearing high heels to a backyard reception, Christina was the only one who managed to maintain a degree of elegance in her walk as she returned to the table.

Matthew took another good look at Christina as she sat down. He decided that there was something unspoken about her and Buzzy being together. His guess was drugs. That was usually the case when he and Buzzy were growing up. Whenever some hot girl was hanging onto him, it was always because she had free access to Buzzy's stash. He assumed that was the case with Christina. She was way too good looking to be with Buzzy otherwise. Not that Matthew would ever suggest it to his old friend.

"That was some bathroom break," Buzzy said to Christina. "I thought maybe you fell in or something."

The table was cluttered with glasses that held varying amounts of champagne. Christina searched for one with her shade of lipstick on its rim. "I had to call my brother in Jamaica Plain. He's starting a new business, and he can't find enough containers for all the batteries and ovens."

Kathleen had lingered at the table out of curiosity, and now she looked across at Matthew to see if he was just as confused by Christina's comment.

As an afterthought, Christina looked at Matthew and said, "By the way, I met your brother while I was in the house."

Matthew stood up and looked across the tent. His brother Jimmy was sitting at a table with his wife and kids. "My brother Jimmy's over there," Matthew pointed. "He's not in the house."

Christina gave up on finding her own champagne glass and selected the one that looked cleanest. "I just saw him in the house. He's in that room over there. He said he wants to talk to Kathleen," Christina said, pointing more deliberately than Matthew.

His confusion vanished. When he looked at Kathleen, she seemed to know exactly what was going on, too. "Matthew's brother said he wants to talk to Kathleen?" she asked.

"Yes."

Buzzy caught on as well. "Oh wow, Matty. Sounds like it's all in the family."

Matthew felt mixed emotions at the news. The arrangement Francis had with Jimmy made perfect sense, but Matthew couldn't deny he was disappointed at not getting to see Francis on his wedding day. Growing up, he had been much closer to Francis than Jimmy, although he hadn't been close to either one for many years.

"I'll go in and see him," Matthew said.

Christina shook her head. "He said he didn't want to talk to you. Just Kathleen."

Matthew didn't know all the details about Kathleen's relationship with Francis. They had dated as teenagers, then gotten serious before Francis went off to Vietnam. When he ended up in prison, Kathleen had married and moved to Texas for several years. That didn't work out, and she came back to South Boston with her daughter. At some point, she and Francis became a couple again, until sometime in the last year when they broke up once more. Whether they were a couple or not, their interactions usually included a fair amount of combustion.

Christina continued, "He said it's an emergency and he wouldn't be here if it wasn't. He only wants to talk to Kathleen for five minutes. Then he's leaving."

Kathleen said. "What a selfish bastard to come here today! No way am I talking to him."

Heads began to turn, so Matthew walked over to Kathleen and spoke softly to her. "Maybe it's better if you do, Kathleen. If you don't go in there, he might just come out here. That's probably not a good thing."

Kathleen considered her options, but she really had only one. She stood up. "OK, five minutes. That's it. Start the fucking clock."

* * * * *

The Boushay home was a farmhouse built in the 1890s. It had two doors leading onto the back lawn, one from the kitchen in the original section, another from the living room in the addition, which was built in the 1940s. It included a dining room, large living room and small study on the ground floor.

In the study was a fireplace made of fieldstone gathered from the Boushay orchards. Next to the fireplace sat a small mahogany table with a built-in chessboard and ornate chess pieces carved from dense exotic wood. Purpleheart for the black, zebrawood for the white. The set was purchased years before by Anne's father on a trip to North Africa.

Francis Mahoney held a zebrawood knight in his hand. It had a stone-like weight. He studied the fine stripes that wrapped around the horse's head.

"Don't even think about stealing it," Kathleen said as she entered the room. Despite her direct, sometimes gruff, manner, Kathleen had maintained over the years an air of grace in her gestures and attitude. That evening it was complemented by an emerald dress that flattered her slender figure. Her small diamond stud earrings captured enough light in the dim study to cast a modest brilliance.

Francis looked up from the chessboard and showed Kathleen a warm smile. "I wouldn't dare. This chess set is too beautiful." Francis Mahoney stood six feet tall and weighed a trim one hundred and eighty pounds. His reddish-blond hair was cut short and had receded more than his brothers'. A running suit, or jeans and sweatshirt, functioned as his standard wardrobe, but Francis now wore a tailored blue suit that was so dark it was almost black, and a crisp white shirt with an open collar.

Kathleen approached him but kept what she felt was a comfortable distance. "OK, what do you want?" she said, getting to the point.

Francis put down the knight and stepped toward Kathleen, who threw out a hand like a traffic cop at a dangerous intersection. "Don't, don't, don't. Just tell me what you want. I'll say no. Then you can leave."

There was a couch next to Francis. He leaned against it, half sitting, and drew a hand across his unshaven face. "Tonight I'm doing something you've been asking me to do for a long time. I'm leaving the business. For good."

"Tonight," Kathleen said with more than a hint of skepticism.

Francis nodded and crossed his arms. "It's what you said I needed to do, and now I'm doing it."

A silence ensued while Francis waited for an acknowledgement and Kathleen waited for a catch.

Francis looked down at his watch. "It took me six months to do it, but now it's done. And I've kept my distance like you asked, even when you moved into my father's house, and you know that doesn't sit right with me. I haven't interfered with you at all."

"Except for threatening to burn down my hair salon."

Francis smiled. It was half amusement, half embarrassment. "C'mon, you knew I was bullshitting."

Kathleen sensed a side of the story that was being kept well hidden. "You're not telling me something, Francis. Why did you drive all the way up here tonight? Why not talk to me tomorrow?"

"You remember when we used to make plans, and we'd talk about traveling overseas. Italy, Ireland, France, Portugal. Well, let's start off on the right foot with a trip through Europe. All first class."

"Tonight?"

"Why wait?"

Kathleen stared at Francis with her mouth slightly open. When he tried to speak, she raised a finger to silence him. The jazz band was beginning its second set, and the first notes of a spirited tune seeped into the book-lined study. Kathleen searched for the one piece of information Francis was withholding that would make sense of this whole strange situation.

When she found it, she tilted her head to the side, "OK, now I get it. You've been indicted, haven't you?"

Francis nodded.

"You're not getting out of the business tonight because you want to. You're getting out because you have to."

"Disco called me today. He says it'll happen in the next 72 hours, but it could be anytime after midnight tonight."

"So you're leaving the country tonight. And you think I'll go with you."

"It's what you always asked for. Me to leave the business and us to travel the world together. We can thank the federal government for bumping up the schedule."

"You're dreaming, Francis," Kathleen said in a tone that mocked the proposal and disguised the fact that flying off to Europe at a moment's notice was actually appealing to her. Had her daughter still been alive, it wouldn't have appealed to her at all.

Francis looked at his watch again and walked over to the window. He peeked through the blinds at the reception. "They make a good couple, don't you think? I can tell by the way they move around each other. She looks like a smart girl. Matt can get bullheaded sometimes, but I bet she's good at handling that."

Francis turned to Kathleen and held up an imaginary champagne glass. "Here's to marriage and finding that one true love."

He smiled. Kathleen didn't. Francis' nose curled up slightly to the tip in an Irish sort of way, which gave his smiling face a mischievous look. He continued in a more serious tone, "You don't think that's funny? Maybe it's not if you consider how many people go through life desperate to find the one person who fits them like a glove. People all over the world die a little every day because it hasn't happened for them.

"It's sad, but that's how it goes for most people. They compromise. They surrender. They pick someone because they both went to the same college, or they like the same TV show or the same ice cream, or they both hate their mothers. They get married and fool everyone else into believing that what they have is the real thing. Sometimes people can see through it, so they need to run to a place where nobody knows them and nobody can see through the lie. Some place like Texas."

"You were in prison," Kathleen said, surprising herself with the emotion in her voice. "And you broke a promise that you'd stay out of trouble. How many times do I have to go over that with you?"

Francis held up his ringless left hand. "I've never been married," he said and turned back to the window. "It's one of the nicer sacraments, I suppose. I won't marry for a lie though. I won't compromise. If I don't marry you, then I'll never get married." He turned back to Kathleen. "That's what I was thinking on the way over here tonight. Then I thought, wait. I am married. You and I have been married since the day we met in 1965.

"We don't have the rings and the documents and the blood tests, but let's face it. In all the ways that matter, you and I are married. We think of each other all the time, we read each other's minds and each other's hearts. Right now, you're thinking that I might be correct, but you're worried that people might say you're making the same mistake again. Your mother, Debbie at the salon, my father. You're wondering how to make them understand that I'm finally giving you what you've been asking for."

"Yes, I do worry about what I'd say to them, and I worry about making another big mistake with you." Kathleen's rich black hair fell straight to her shoulders. She pulled strands of it together and wrapped them around her finger. "This doesn't feel right, Francis. It feels like a fire drill. It shouldn't be that way."

"Look, I know what you're saying, Kathleen, and I wish it wasn't this way, but it is what it is."

Francis paused, then began speaking more slowly. "Everything's arranged. We've got two first-class tickets for later tonight. We'll be in Paris for breakfast."

Kathleen was feeling a clash of emotions and it showed on her face. "We don't speak French."

Francis sensed her yielding, and he knew he just had to keep turning over cards. "It doesn't matter what you speak. When you live first class like we can afford to do, the world will talk to you in whatever language you want. And we don't have to stay in France. We'll go anywhere and everywhere. You've got family in Portugal and you said you wanted to meet them, find out what they're like, learn the language. We'll go there. You want to open a hair salon? We'll buy one. Your friends want to visit? We'll pay for it. The beaches in Portugal are beautiful. We'll buy a house on the ocean. You know I've saved enough so we'll never worry about money. Ever."

It was hitting Kathleen like a series of waves that soon could knock her over. She was reaching for some reason to say why it wouldn't work. It was what she had asked him to do for the longest time, and now he was doing it. He was being forced to do it, but that didn't seem to matter really. The idea of them living some kind of a normal life together without Francis being involved with the underworld was a dream Kathleen hadn't turned to in such a long time. She almost didn't know how to tear it free from the layers of cynicism that had accumulated around it.

She might have said yes, finally, but Francis would never know because the door to the study opened and his father, Salty, appeared. He looked at Francis the same way he did when Francis was fourteen years old and had been caught stealing his first car.

Francis knew that he was very close to getting a yes from Kathleen, and the last thing he needed was his father whispering in her other ear. He pointed at Salty, "Hey, hey. We're in the middle of something here. Do you mind?"

Salty ignored Francis. "Come outside, Kathleen," he said.

Kathleen hesitated and Francis yelled to his father, "Hey, what did I just tell you? Leave us alone."

Salty continued to ignore him. He extended a hand and spoke softly to Kathleen, "It would be nice if things changed with him, but they won't. You know that."

Kathleen took Salty's hand and headed for the door. When Francis called to her, his voice betrayed a touch of desperation. "It has to be tonight, Kathleen. Do you understand? I can't come back and see you tomorrow. I don't have any more tomorrows here."

Salty closed the door. In a matter of seconds, Francis had shot from relatively calm to incredibly tense. His first impulse was to dash after Kathleen, even if it meant fighting his way past his father. In fact, he felt like giving his father a beating whether he was in the way or not.

He suppressed the urge and walked to the window, where he saw the two of them crossing the lawn. The son of a bitch stepped right in the middle of it, he thought, right as I had her. The way she changed her mind so fast at the first words out of his mouth. She was living under his roof, and that was obviously giving him a lot of influence over her.

As improbable as it seemed, the thought occurred to Francis that they might be sleeping together. It was a thought he was forced to dismiss several times a day.

Francis paced back and forth between the window and the fireplace. He checked his watch. Maybe he could be patient and wait until Kathleen left the reception, but there was very little cushion in the amount of time he had left to close out his affairs before boarding the flight. And going out to the back lawn after Kathleen could create problems for all the Mahoneys.

* * * * *

The sun that had been so oppressive that afternoon was quickly vanquished by the arrival of low grey clouds that brought a sudden chill to the air. Lightning-like flashes from the photographer's camera illuminated faces beneath the tent.

Guests returned to their tables as a half-dozen caterers brought trays of salads to stations around the tent. From a glittering purse, Christina pulled out a vial with an assortment of vitamin pills. She arranged them in a row by her water glass and said to Buzzy, "If the salads are small, you give me yours because I'm only having salad tonight. You don't like salads."

Buzzy was staring at the house and lost in thought, so he hadn't heard Christina.

Matthew had been worried when he saw his father follow Kathleen into the house, then felt relief when the two re-emerged.

"Well," Matthew said to Anne. "I guess we dodged that bullet."

Matthew's back was to the house, but he noticed Buzzy suddenly sit up straight in his chair.

Christina looked toward the house as well and said, "Oh, that man looks angry."

Matthew spun around. Walking from the house was his brother, Francis, moving with purpose toward the bar, where Salty and Kathleen were talking.

"Holy fuck," Matthew said as he stood up.

"What's the matter?" Anne asked.

"It's Francis. This is a problem."

Matthew turned to the Mahoney tables, where his cousins sat. When Matthew was fifteen, he left South Boston and moved in with the Mahoneys in Quincy, on the south side of Boston. He had a special kinship with his cousin Richard, who was as large as a bear and had bushy red sideburns. Richard worked as a fisherman and owned Mahoney Seafood with his brother, Bobby.

Matthew called over to their table. When Richard stood up, Matthew pointed to the bar. He gave a wave in that direction and began running there himself, but it was clear he was not going to reach it before Francis.

Matthew's other brother Jimmy had a four-year-old daughter, who had been playing outside the tent. She now began wandering toward her grandfather. Jimmy Mahoney came rushing to remove his daughter from the scene.

Francis reached the bar, where he and his father got into a shouting match that stopped conversations back at the tables. Matthew arrived at one side of the bar as Richard and his brother arrived at the other. It was too late.

Kathleen yelled as Francis charged, but Salty stood his ground. Francis lifted, then plowed his father toward the ice boat. Salty managed to throw a punch to the side of Francis' head before their two bodies smashed into the beam of the boat. The stern sawhorse gave way, and the two Mahoneys spilled onto the grass in a cascade of ice and raw oysters.

Richard and Bobby moved in on Salty. That left Matthew to handle Francis, who had gotten to his feet and was about to pounce on his father.

Matthew came at Francis from behind and tackled him. The two tumbled onto the ground. Francis jumped back to his feet. The best Matthew could do was reach out and grab hold of his brother's ankle. Francis jerked his foot in every direction, but Matthew wouldn't let go.

Glancing down, Francis gave a look as if to say, help me. Join me. When that didn't happen, Francis drew up his foot and shot it back hard. His shoe slammed onto the top of Matthew's head.

The sound of voices in Matthew's ears was replaced by silence, followed by a faint buzzing. Then the oddest of sounds. A long-lost voice calling to him. Matthew couldn't hear words, just the singsong rhythm of an Irish lilt and a slight accent. It sounded like his mother.

Matthew looked around. The voice seemed to be coming from the far end of the lawn where it sloped down to the salt marsh. He tried to stand but collapsed backwards onto a patch of shaved ice.

Richard and Bobby managed to pull Francis clear of his father. The fight was over, but Francis wasn't finished. As he was being dragged away, Francis screamed across at Salty. "I could kill you anytime I want! Remember that."

At the edge of the tent, Francis' swinging arm grabbed hold of a pole and managed to uproot it from the ground, causing a corner of the tent to collapse across the bar.

Guests of the Boushay family were shocked into silence, anxious about what might happen next. Still on his knees, Matthew drew a hand through the ice, then ran it across his face.

The salads were served.

* * * * *

Anne's mother, Joan Boushay, had been practically invisible during the reception, managing the entire affair from behind the scenes. Everything down to last-minute changes in the band's playlist, the replacement of asparagus with green beans when the asparagus failed to pass the firmness test, and an emergency trip to the Ipswich Liquor Mart when what seemed to have been a more-than-adequate supply of beer, wine and spirits had been nearly drained in just over an hour.

Everything about the wedding had been planned for several months, even years. Some aspects of it, including the marriage ceremony at Ipswich Presbyterian Church and Anne's wedding dress, mirrored Joan's own wedding.

As meticulous as her planning and adjustments had been, the backyard brawl was completely off Joan Boushay's radar. She left the caterers to serve salads to the rest of the guests and instructed the band to play some upbeat tunes while she set up an impromptu first-aid station in her kitchen.

Since divorcing fourteen years earlier, Joan had earned two graduate degrees and worked as a professor in the mathematics department at Salem State College. Anne's father, Dylan, had remarried barely a year after the divorce, but Joan had remained single. However, she did have what Anne called a "man friend," who happened to practice medicine.

Brian Livingston was an eye doctor on the staff at Beverly Hospital and also ran a small optometrist shop in downtown Ipswich, but his credentials in general medicine gave Joan confidence that all the Mahoneys would be sent home in one piece.

Salty emerged unscathed except for a few scratches. He refused treatment and set himself to righting the corner of the tent that had collapsed. That put the bar back in business. Matthew's cousin Richard sat at the kitchen table, where Brian Livingston swabbed a deep cut on Richard's knee with gauze soaked in hydrogen peroxide.

"No serious damage, Dr. Livingston, I presume."

Matthew sat on the other side with a bloody towel stanching the cut on his head. He smiled at Richard's lame joke.

Livingston smiled as well. "Would you believe me, Richard, if I told you that you're not the first to use that line on me?"

Richard's left pinky finger was broken, so Livingston rigged up a splint and taped the pinky and ring finger together. Bobby was treated next. He had a bloody nose that he thought was broken, but after a quick examination, Livingston announced that it wasn't. Both the injured nose and a split lip had come from getting too close to Salty's elbows.

Anne stood beside Matthew, and parted his short black hair to dab a gauze at the cut, which seemed to have stopped bleeding. "Let me see the peroxide," she said.

"This is medical peroxide, Anne. I assume you don't want to bleach your husband's hair?" Dr. Livingston asked. He handed her an alcohol wipe instead.

Joan returned to the kitchen and saw Anne cleaning Matthew's cut. "Honey," she called. "Be careful not to get any blood on that dress."

When Livingston was done, he and the Mahoneys returned to their tables, where dinner was about to be served. Richard looked the worst with his bandaged fingers and a white gauzed knee showing through a large hole in his pants. They had been ripped by a broken oarlock on the appetizer boat.

Anne stayed with her mother in the kitchen, where Joan was wiping down the table and the counters, even though Livingston had already done so. Overcleaning. It was something that her mother was fond of. Overcleaning the house, overcleaning her car, and even Anne's apartment when she visited her daughter in Seattle.

Anne stepped out of the way as two caterers carrying stacks of blue china stepped carefully through the kitchen. Most of their work was carried on outside where the catering service had a prep station and vans, one having recently arrived with the hot dinners.

"Mom, I'm really sorry about what happened out there."

Joan swept her hands down the front of her dress. "Anne, it's the Mahoneys who should be apologizing, not you. I can't tell you how upset I was when I saw them fighting. Anyway, there are too many other things to focus on at the moment, so I've pushed it out of my mind. I've decided this is going to be the most wonderful wedding day that the town of Ipswich has ever seen." She smiled.

Despite her fastidiousness, Joan had the ability to rise above difficult situations. If the weather turned stormy on a day when she wanted to paint in the garden, she would set up her easel in the study and decide she would create the most amazing still life. If a cooking experiment took a disastrous turn, she would start again and decide to make it the most spectacular culinary comeback ever.

Anne would sometimes tease her about it. When her mother would ask Anne to pick up a blueberry pie at the Ipswich bakery, Anne might say, "I've decided that what you really want me to pick up is the most delicious chocolate cake ever."

Despite the teasing, Anne admired her mother for having the will and determination to never let a difficulty rise higher than her ability to make something good of it. That was not always the case. When Anne was growing up, her mother struggled and lost many such battles. The change came as a result of the painful divorce, but it did not come before Anne's relationship with her mother suffered from it.

Over the past ten years, the relationship had been rebuilt somewhat, although not restored. Each year, Anne made one or two short visits back to Ipswich, and her mother made one or two short visits to Seattle. There was a fragile quality to it all, with neither one wanting to bring up details of the terrible time before and immediately after the divorce. Neither wanted to say or do anything to threaten what they'd rebuilt together.

"You've done an amazing job today, Mom. I'm very grateful," Anne said as she hugged her mother, who was shorter and had a fuller figure than Anne. The only noticeable physical feature that mother and daughter shared was a cleft chin.

"I've enjoyed it, honey. I really have. I only have one daughter, so I only get one chance to do it right. You should go outside and enjoy dinner with Matthew. I'll be joining Brian in a moment. I'm all right here. The caterers don't really need my help. I was just hovering about and making them nervous anyway."

"I told you earlier, Mom," Anne said, "but I'll tell you again. You look wonderful."

Joan wore a silk lavender dress that had been made along with Anne's wedding dress sixty years earlier for Anne's grandmother and had been worn to a number of important family events. Nana B, as Anne's grandmother was called, wore it to Joan's wedding in 1957.

"You'll get to wear it someday to your daughter's wedding, but today you wear the best dress of all." Joan's pride showed in her smile. "I'm so happy for you, Anne. You must be too, aren't you?"

"Of course," Anne said. "Very."

Her mother took one last admiring look. "My goodness, Nana B would be so thrilled to see you wearing the same wedding dress she and I both wore."

Joan's thoughts drifted toward memories of Nana B, but she remembered something and was quick to add, "Your father would be happy for you too, of course. So proud. I'm sure you're a little sad that he's not here. That's natural. Emotions can go all over the place on a wedding day. Just look at the Mahoneys."

They both laughed. Then Anne said, "Yes, I am a little sad about that."

Joan turned her attention to a blue-checkered dish towel waiting to be returned to the towel rack above the sink. "Well, it's too bad he couldn't have been more careful," she said as she picked up the towel and shook it out.

Her mother's comment took Anne completely by surprise. The words cut right through her, and she felt her face flush. This was an old sore spot, one that had became sorer, still, fifteen months earlier when her father had been killed in a rock climbing accident. His climbing party of five had encountered a rockfall, and her father went to the aid of an injured climber. He managed to pull the climber and himself out of the fall zone by swinging them both to the other side of the rock face. Her father was carefully lowering his friend to the ground when a separate rockfall occurred directly above them.

One climber was killed on the scene that day. Two were injured, including her father, who was the more seriously hurt and taken unconscious to the hospital. Anne had just gotten her first job as an environmental engineer and was working in the field when news of the accident reached her. She flew directly to Anchorage and spent the next thirty-six hours at her father's bedside. He died of intracranial bleeding that could not be stopped, and Anne felt helpless as she watched him slip away.

The rockfalls occurred in an area considered by all local climbers to be safe in that regard. Her father had made the wisest move by swinging the injured climber out of the first fall zone. The odds of landing in another fall zone were remote.

It was accepted as fact in the Anchorage climbing community that the accident was unpredictable and due in no part to the decisions of her father, who was not only a climbing expert but an extremely careful one. In spite of that, Anne's mother had made a number of comments since the accident suggesting that it had occurred as a result of carelessness.

The comments led to measured disagreements between Anne and her mother about her father, his lifestyle, his climbing, Anne's climbing and how she was perhaps tempting fate to deliver the same ill fortune on herself. The disagreements sometimes threatened to escalate into suggestions of how perhaps Anne loved her father more than her mother, or of how Anne had made her mother's life so difficult after the divorce that Joan finally relented and allowed her only child to move to Alaska to be with the man she considered unfit as a husband and reckless as a father. When any of their disagreements approached those dangerous cliffs, Anne would back away and change the subject.

"I'll see you outside," Anne finally said and left the kitchen before her mother could see how upset she was.

* * * * *

Anne joined Matthew at their table for dinner. Generous portions of grilled lamb with herbs, scalloped potatoes and crisp green beans were served on blue china. The tent was lit with discreet electric torches and the conversations that ceased with the fight had returned with added energy. It had been scary in the moment, but now that things had settled down, the fight took on an almost mythical quality, and people felt privileged to have witnessed firsthand what would no doubt assume a prominent place in family lore for generations to come.

Dinner was followed by toasts. Buzzy's was short. He started with a story of how he and Matthew had grown up together in a crazy special place called South Boston, and how Matthew had always been there to protect Buzzy when he got himself into trouble, which was often. The toast ended with a quote from the band U2.

"'Oh, don't sorrow. No, don't weep. For tonight, at last, I am coming home.' We're brothers in this world, Matt, and I was full of sorrow when you left South Boston. But I thank you for coming home to share this special day with us. May you and Anne always find happiness wherever you go. And whenever possible, may you also find your way back to your people and to the place that will forever be your home."

With dessert came the last Boushay tradition of the evening. Six trays were carried out in dramatic fashion with flames rising from large bowls of gateau flambé. The recipe had been carried from France with Nana B. As with the dresses, this very special Boushay dessert had been served at the weddings of Anne's mother and grandmother.

The desserts made their safe landing on trays set up ten feet away from the tent to avoid the risk of fire. Joan Boushay became noticeably relaxed as the last of her hurdles had been cleared. The dessert was a cherry and chocolate cake with a consistency closer to pudding or custard, surrounded by whole cherries in cognac. It was enjoyed by everyone who ate it, except for Richard, who on a dare from Bobby, attempted to eat a piece of gateau flambé while it was still flambé, causing one of his sideburns to catch fire momentarily.

The band returned from a break and brought many people to the dance floor, while others relaxed with coffee or more drinks from the restocked and repaired bar. In the sky above, the clouds had broken and stars were visible.

Buzzy didn't care for dancing, but Christina made him get on the floor for one song. After that, he was left to watch her from his table as Richard, Bobby and several other men insisted on at least one dance with her. Christina's red gown, which had looked so out of place earlier, seemed made for the romantic evening.

After playing an especially long set, the band took a final break. The reception had reached the unannounced point where the first to leave began exchanging farewells.

Anne moved among tables of Boushay guests, recognizing many and thanking all for joining her family on her wedding day. She spent time with her friends who had traveled all the way from Seattle.

Matthew did the same at the tables of Mahoneys and Flynns, the two sides of his family that both lived in the same community but seldom socialized. Three of his good friends from Seattle had traveled east for the wedding, and they were having a great time with the Mahoney cousins. Richard handed Matthew a beer, and they all kidded him about living in a place as far away as Seattle.

After a while, Buzzy found Matthew and led him out to his 1978 Grand Prix, which was parked in a line of cars that flowed out of the driveway and down Plum Point Road. As Matthew climbed into the passenger seat, he saw that the floor of Buzzy's car was awash in crushed paper coffee cups and hamburger wrappers.

"That was the most fucked-up thing I've ever seen Francis do," Buzzy said. He reflexively checked his rearview mirrors as he packed the bowl of a pipe. "Francis really lost control of himself tonight. He never does that. Believe me, I work with the man and I've never seen it happen," Buzzy said.

The idea of Buzzy being connected to Francis seemed strange to Matthew. Francis had always hated drugs and anybody associated with them. When Matthew was growing up, he had gotten more than one beating when his older brother caught him stoned. On top of that, Buzzy had long been known as one of South Boston's premier potheads. Francis had to be aware of that.

Buzzy put the pipe to his lips and teased a flame into the bowl.

"Thanks for the nice toast, by the way. And the bachelor party," Matthew said. A nightclub on Fort Point Channel in South Boston had been rented for the event two nights before. It included a punk band that played several songs by the Pogues, an open bar, a spread of food, and a back room with a large buffet of drugs.

Matthew's friends from Seattle enjoyed it, along with a bunch of guys from South Boston, most of whom Matthew didn't know or couldn't remember knowing. "Maybe it's because it was mine, but I think that was the best bachelor party I've ever been to. I hope it didn't set you back too much."

Buzzy laughed. "Here, take this." Buzzy handed the pipe to Matthew. "You think I could afford that? Francis paid for it. The whole thing."

Matthew hardly ever got stoned anymore. It was more a ritual he felt the need to reenact for the sake of their friendship. He drew a light hit before handing the pipe back. "Well, I'm gonna have to thank Francis then."

"That's gonna be tough, Matt. I talked to Kathleen. She says Francis is gonna be indicted. That's why he was here tonight, to convince her to leave the country with him. He has to be long gone before the indictments come down."

Matthew considered this. It put the evening's battle in a different light. "I thought he just hated Dad."

"We all do," Buzzy said. "I hope you don't mind me saying it, but Salty's been an asshole to all of us."

Matthew took the pipe again. "He said he wanted to have a talk with me tonight."

Buzzy laughed. "Salty have an actual conversation? Matt, that would be the first conversation he's ever had with any of his kids. I mean, an actual conversation where both people have to listen to the other person. He probably wants you to become his Amway rep for the West Coast or something."

"I'll call him when I'm back in Seattle. If I was sticking around longer, I might swing by the house to see Kathleen since she's living there now."

"You'd be wasting your time. She and her friend are going up the coast from here tonight. She won't be back until Tuesday."

"That's too bad. She's still a really attractive woman, don't you think?"

"Sure, when she's not being a bitch," Buzzy said, and relit the pipe to draw out the last of the bud.

"Speaking of attractive," Matthew said, "Where did you find Miss Runner-Up? She's giving everybody a hard-on," Matthew said. Then he noticed people walking toward them.

"Uh-oh," Matthew said.

"It's alright," Buzzy said as they watched the people unlock their car and get inside. "I don't get this. We're in the middle of nowhere out here in Ipswichland, and all these bastards lock their cars."

Matthew laughed. "And how would you know that?"

The car drove past, and Matthew saw that more people were leaving the reception.

"I better get back," Matthew said. "Thanks again, Buzzy. I don't care who paid for what. You've done a lot for me this week. I appreciate it."

Anne was saying goodbye to some of her mom's friends near the driveway when they rejoined her. The three of them walked back to the house to say farewell to Joan Boushay.

Anne could guess where Matthew and Buzzy had been. She could smell the pot on them. She was OK with Matthew getting high with his friends occasionally, even though she never did, but she was aware of Buzzy's reputation and wasn't comfortable with it.

In the kitchen, they thanked Anne's mother for making the reception such a success. Matthew began a heartfelt apology for the behavior of his family, but Joan cut him short.

"Anne and I were joking a little while ago, Matthew. If you can endure all of the Boushay family traditions on your wedding day, I can certainly endure the more difficult members of the Mahoney family. Now you should both get going to the hotel in Boston if you're going to get the rest you need before your flight tomorrow."

Buzzy thanked her as well. "You have the most incredible view of the ocean I've ever seen. You should have boats down on your beach or something. I would definitely be putting boats down there."

Joan hadn't really listened to what Buzzy said. She was looking at the similarity between Buzzy's face and Matthew's. "By the way," she said looking at Buzzy, then back at Matthew. "I just noticed this, Matthew, but you and your friend look remarkably similar in some ways. Your nose and your mouth. You could be brothers."

Matthew chuckled. Buzzy was silent before saying, "I don't think that's possible, Mrs. Boushay. Matthew is ugly, and I'm not."

When they stepped outside, they ran into Kathleen.

"You're not going anywhere until you say goodbye to me, Matty." She gave him a hug, and said to Anne, "He's been like a little brother to me and I'll never forgive him for moving so far away. Make him visit home more often."

"I will," Anne said.

"You handled it well tonight, Kathleen," Matthew said.

Kathleen sighed. "Not really, but Francis left without me. That's all that counts. Matt, I think your father's going to sing a song. Why don't you stick around long enough to hear it?"

Under the tent, the band fumbled the first few bars of an Irish tune. Salty was trying to get them to play a song called "Carrickfergus." He was famous for singing at social gatherings of every kind. He had a deep, booming voice that was made for a good Irish ballad.

The band made one more false start, then seemed to get it. Salty's voice rumbled slowly through the melancholy tune. It seemed odd to Matthew, even disrespectful, that his father would sing about love for a departed wife when he had neglected his own wife so badly when she was alive, particularly while she was dying.

"Anyone else you want to say goodbye to?" Anne asked.

"We're all done here. Let's go," Matthew said.

The final lyrics traveled with them into the night.

> But the sea is wide and I can't swim over
> and neither have I wings to fly.
> I wish I could find me a handy boatman
> to ferry me over to my love and die.

* * * * *

From the reception, Brian Livingston drove Matthew and Anne to the Rowes Wharf Hotel on the Boston waterfront. Anne's mother had paid for a spacious two-room suite as well as their ten-day honeymoon in Ireland, which would begin with a morning flight from Logan Airport.

One question that many people at the reception had was why Matthew and Anne were a couple at all, never mind a married couple at this point. Brian was among them. During the forty-five-minute drive into Boston, he tried to tease out an answer. Anne and Matthew were both tired though, from the wedding and from hearing the same old question that friends had pestered them with for the past four years.

When Matthew and Anne first started dating, their friends considered the relationship doomed and counted the days until they broke up. Anne's friends saw Matthew as someone who lacked ambition, an opinion which Anne suspected her mother shared. While Anne had gotten her master's degree and, like her father, was working as an environmental engineer, Matthew had only attended one semester of college at the University of Massachusetts in 1978 before dropping out.

He worked as a bartender with no plans of going back to college or moving up in the world, except to maybe open his own pub someday. He was also considered sarcastic to a fault by many of Anne's friends, particularly the ones who had grown up in Seattle, where the staid, earnest character of the Scandinavian settlers still lingered.

Matthew's friends from the bar, his hockey and rugby teams, had an equally negative assessment of Anne. She took herself too seriously. She could be cold. She was also impatient and quick to judge people. If someone didn't live up to her expectations, she wrote them off and moved on without a second thought. One of Matthew's friends told him flat out that Anne was a bitch.

As a result, the first year they were together played out like a high-wire act with friends on both sides waiting to see who would fall first or whether they'd both bring each other down. They had many disagreements that year, some intense. Through it all, Matthew continued to put up with Anne, and Anne, at the insistence of her father, resisted the urge to dismiss Matthew for his shortcomings.

At the hotel, Matthew took a quick shower and changed into jeans and a T-shirt. Their suite was on the top floor and came with a surprisingly large terrace overlooking the harbor. Through the glass French doors came a cool breeze, so Matthew threw on a sweatshirt before joining Anne outside.

She lay curled up on a chaise lounge. He walked over, and Anne made room for him on the wide cushions. Matthew stretched himself out and put his arm around her. They lay there for a while quietly, both thinking of the same thing.

They had both lost the parent they were closer to, and they knew that a large wedding celebration might only heighten the bittersweet fact that with all of their family members present, the two who mattered most would be painfully absent. They had promised each other that morning that they wouldn't allow the joy of the day to be ruined by dwelling on that fact.

It hadn't worked. They had both done their share of dwelling throughout the ceremony and reception, while putting on an act for one another.

"This is why I didn't want to come back here," Anne said, breaking the silence. "It's why you didn't want to come back here either."

"It hit me at the reception," Matthew admitted. "I heard her after Francis kicked me in the head. I mean, I thought I heard her voice coming from somewhere." Matthew took a deep breath and let it out slowly. "It sounded exactly like her, too. Just like I remember her talking."

"What did she say?"

"It wasn't words really, just the melody of how she talked. It was nothing maybe, or just my Aunt Eileen, my mom's sister. She was at the reception and she's always talking. I don't know, but that's when it really hit me."

Anne's loss was more recent than Matthew's, and he knew she would have the tougher battle that day. She was especially close to her father. When Anne left Ipswich at twelve and joined him in Alaska, the two became partners in adventure, with Dylan teaching Anne everything there was to know about climbing and about spending time in the outdoors, whether it was an afternoon hike or camping deep in the Alaskan backcountry.

"God, I wish it was colder out here now," Anne said. "I wish it was as cold as Anchorage in the fall. I remember when I first moved there, Dad would wake me up for a hike in the morning when it was still dark. He wouldn't tell me where we were going, and he'd hand me a pile of maps and hiking guides. It really pissed me off. He wanted me to figure out everything for myself, and he kept doing it until I learned."

"And you did learn," Matthew said. "You learned good."

Anne turned and looked at Matthew. "Now I feel like I have to learn it all again. This pain…missing him…it feels the same as it did right after he died. It's been over a year and I keep waiting for the pain to not be so sharp, but it still cuts right through me, Matthew. It's so frustrating. I don't have a map for it. I don't know how to get through it or around it. I need to know that it won't always hurt this much."

Matthew kissed her. "It won't, and it won't come as often. But it'll always be able to hit you when you're not expecting it. The pain dies down with time, but it never goes away completely. That's what my map shows me anyway."

It was almost midnight, but there were still plenty of boats crossing Boston Harbor in one direction or another, making themselves visible by their colorful lights. Across the harbor in East Boston, a jet arriving from overseas made a graceful descent onto a runway at Logan Airport.

"I like being outside right now," Anne said. "I can only feel his spirit when I'm outside, looking up at the stars like this."

The suite came with a king-size bed. Matthew wrestled the mattress across the room and onto the terrace, while Anne gathered up pillows and blankets. They fell asleep listening to the sound of waves slapping against boats and the ceaseless, soothing hum of cars on the nearby expressway.

* * * * *

Their flight didn't leave until ten o'clock, but Matthew was up at five thirty. He jogged down Northern Avenue as far as the Coast Guard base. The air was damp and still. After finishing his run, Matthew walked into a convenience store next to the hotel.

He was paying for a small cranberry juice when he saw something familiar on the small TV perched behind the counter. It was tuned to a station broadcasting local news. Matthew couldn't quite hear what was being said, but he saw a house that looked a lot like his father's house on E. Third Street in South Boston.

He strained to hear the TV, but a bell at the store's entrance sounded as another customer entered. On the TV screen, he saw an image of his father displayed beside the news anchor. It was an old photo from Salty's last campaign for mayor years before.

The small Lebanese clerk placed Matthew's change on the counter, but Matthew's eyes were frozen to the TV.

"What is the guy on TV saying?" Matthew asked. "Do you know what that story is about?" Then Matthew saw an equally out-of-date image of his brother Francis. He felt a tightness in his chest, and he realized that he was holding his breath.

The clerk pointed at the TV and spoke in a heavy accent. "He is the son, and the one who you see before, he is the father. He is killed. The son does this. The police look for him."

Matthew leaned over the counter and reached for the volume knob on the TV. The news blared throughout the convenience store. "Salty Mahoney, a well-known and controversial figure in the world of South Boston politics, has been found shot to death in his home on E. Third Street. Francis Mahoney, second oldest son of the victim, is being sought for questioning in the slaying."

Matthew left the change. He left the cranberry juice. Walking down Atlantic Avenue, he wasn't aware of his legs moving or his feet landing on the sidewalk at the end of each step. It was all happening automatically.

Chapter Two
The Zugzwang

After leaving his brother's wedding reception, Francis Mahoney stopped by the Lancaster Street Garage. It was near Boston's North End neighborhood, home to the Romano family that ruled the local Italian Mafia. Francis had chosen the garage as his headquarters because it provided a convenient location for meeting with the Romanos while not encroaching on their sacred ground.

Cars were repaired in the front section of the garage, and bookies and loan sharks paid their tribute in the back room. Tribute was the money they kicked up to Francis for operating their business in those parts of Boston considered under Francis' control.

Francis went through the garage collecting scraps of paper, newspapers with horse races circled, a matchbook cover with a phone number written on it, anything the FBI might find interesting when they raided the place sometime in the next few days. He put it all in the garage's old wood stove and burned it. Then Francis stirred through the ashes with a screwdriver to make sure that not a shred of information remained.

The garage had been the scene of some very amusing attempts by law enforcement to bug conversations among Francis and his associates. The latest had occurred when the state police staked out the garage from an apartment across the street. They spent months documenting the comings and goings of various figures known to have underworld ties.

One night, two state police detectives broke into the garage and planted several bugs. When Francis showed up the next day, the state police had tape recorders ready. The first problem occurred when Joe Zannino, a regular visitor from the Romano family, plopped his 300 pounds onto the couch where a microphone had been planted. One of the detectives almost suffered permanent hearing loss from the deafening noise.

The next problem had to do with bugs as well. Conversations which normally took place in the back room, where bugs were hidden, began taking place inside one of the cars parked in the front of the garage. The detectives broke in again and bugged that car's interior. The following morning, they listened in on a conversation between Francis and a colleague named Larry D'Amico.

"This sure is a nice car," the police heard Francis saying.

"Yes, it's very nice," Larry replied. "The vitality of the dashboard has been sustained with a regular application of that spray that makes tires look good too."

"Using it helps to maintain the resale value of the vehicle," Francis continued. "And being able to resell your vehicle for a high price is important for people who take home shit for pay. Like, say, state police detectives."

"Yes, state police detectives are probably the poorest and laziest motherfuckers in the policing business. I would have to agree with you there."

The next sound heard was the car's door panel being ripped open. By the time the detectives rushed to the garage to retrieve their expensive piece of surveillance equipment, Francis was waiting for them, holding up the bug like a rat by its tail.

The scene was tense until Francis handed over the equipment and smiled. "Hey, relax," he said. "We're all good guys here. You're the good good guys, and we're the bad good guys."

The remark alluded to the fact that Francis and Larry were FBI informants and received sanction for some of their illegal activity because they provided information that helped the FBI fight the Italian Mafia. The state police didn't know this for a fact, but they certainly suspected it after a number of the surveillance attempts ended in complete failure. It was obvious that another law enforcement agency was tipping off Francis.

On top of that, Francis and Larry had people sympathetic to them inside the Drug Enforcement Agency and the Boston Police Department. The state police were the only ones going after Francis, and every time they tried to tap his phones, bug his cars or set up any kind of sting operation, Francis and Larry heard about it and avoided the trap.

The tip on the state police bugs had come from FBI Special Agent Terry Callahan, nicknamed Disco by Francis because his blown-back hair looked just like John Travolta's in the movie *Saturday Night Fever*. Disco and Francis had grown up together in the Old Colony housing project in South Boston, and that bond was more powerful than any oath Disco ever took.

Disco had recruited both Francis and Larry as informants in 1980. Larry was Italian and had once been offered membership in the Italian Mafia but turned it down. It was a risky decision. The Romano family could have taken it as an insult, but they didn't. They respected Larry too much. He carried out a lot of murder contracts for them, and he knew how to do it quietly and cleanly. They weren't about to lose their most reliable contractor.

Francis respected Larry as well. He knew how to keep his cool, and he knew how to keep secrets. And he was probably the most professional independent hit man in all of New England. Like Francis, Larry had served in the Army during the Vietnam War. Unlike Francis, he received an honorable discharge along with four years of training as a sharpshooter, which came in handy. Not only an excellent shot, Larry knew how to set up a hit, get away discreetly and keep his mouth shut when the business was done. The Romanos contracted him for their most sensitive hits, ones that even their own foot soldiers couldn't know about because occasionally one of them was the target.

Larry had good connections to everything that happened on the Italian side of the underworld, and Francis was connected to everything else. They decided to form a loose partnership around their most lucrative business, drugs, while maintaining their own independent side rackets. The unspoken understanding was that the two men would be equal, but that Francis would be more equal.

As official FBI informants, Francis and Larry enjoyed ironclad protection from federal prosecution. Disco had not only helped Francis during his rise to power, he made it possible. It had been two years since the FBI had conducted Operation Beanpot, which succeeded in decimating the Italian Mafia in Boston. It still existed as a branch of La Cosa Nostra in America, but it was a very withered branch. Although Francis would never say this to any members of the Romano family, he was in fact the last underworld chieftain remaining in the city.

Francis had been enjoying his view from the pinnacle, but that all ended with the indictments. He and Larry both got the same bad news early that Saturday. Disco left out a couple of details about the indictments—where they were coming from and what evidence was behind them. He just relayed via code that the indictments were on their way in the next 72 hours and that Francis and Larry needed to flee. The only certainty was that the indictments would not go into effect until after midnight Saturday, a very small window to make a complete escape.

As Francis closed the door to the wood stove and tapped the ash from the screwdriver, he looked across the garage. The old chessboard on his desk showed the position of the pieces from the last game he had played with Zannino, a capo in the Romano family who was now serving twenty-three years in a federal prison. Francis had spent his own time in prison, where he learned to master the game.

Twice a week Zannino would walk over from the North End and visit the Lancaster Street Garage to settle disputes between the Romanos and Francis. Issues with the cops, turf battles among bookies, payment problems with loan sharks.

During those visits, Francis and Zannino would play chess. The last game had been close but ended when Francis forked Zannino's queen and rook with a knight. Zannino had been blind to the threat, and he was forced to pick which of the two valuable pieces he wanted to lose.

In a zugzwang, a player was compelled to choose between two courses of action, both of which produced disadvantageous outcomes. The dilemma crushed Zannino. He couldn't accept either sacrifice. So he resigned the game.

Now Francis knew how Zannino felt. If he stayed in Boston long enough to convince Kathleen to leave with him, he risked being arrested and would have to remain in hiding. If he left at that moment, he'd do so without her. He had almost convinced her at the wedding. In fact, he had convinced her before his father fucked it up.

Francis rubbed the sore spot on his temple where his father's punch had hit home at the reception. It was still hard to believe that Kathleen was living in his father's house on E. Third Street. As friends, she claimed. She had refused to see Francis for the last six months. She wouldn't even return his phone calls.

Dwelling on it all would only distract him, and tonight he needed to be free of distractions. Already a quarter to nine, he had less than two hours to accomplish a number of tasks before catching his midnight flight to Paris. Alone.

Standing under a street light outside the garage, Francis examined the sleeves of his jacket and brushed away blades of grass he had picked up while wrestling with his father. His car was parked nearby, but Francis left it there and walked across City Square Bridge into Charlestown. The stars were bright overhead as he made his way through a maze of cobblestone alleyways that led him to the back door of the Tam-O-Shanter Pub.

It was one of a half-dozen bars across Boston that were popular among IRA sympathizers, although these watering holes weren't popular with Francis. Whenever he was forced to visit one for business, he found them full of barstool sentimentalists who were often moved to sing melancholy tunes about a dear old sod that most of them had never set foot on. Not that he had ever been to Ireland himself, but his connection to the place was strictly business.

Coffee cans for Sinn Fein contributions lined the bar like parking meters. Its owner, Jerry McNulty, was a soldier in the provisional wing of the IRA and operated an underground railroad for IRA refugees fleeing Europe, providing them with new identities, new jobs and new homes. Although he was only a stone's throw from the North End, home of what remained of the Italian Mafia, McNulty never had any problems with the Italians. That's because he fell under the big umbrella of Francis Mahoney.

Francis waded through a small crowd at the bar watching the Red Sox game on an overhead TV. He had arranged a 9:30 meeting with the guys who managed drug dealers in South Boston. From pot and prescription pills to heroin and cocaine, South Boston was swimming in drugs, and nobody sold as much as a joint on its streets without kicking up a percentage to one of Francis' guys. That included wholesalers as well as dealers.

Francis drew his income from a number of sources, including loan sharking, protection money from bookies and legitimate businesses. He got twenty thousand a month from Global Jai Alai. The Connecticut establishment was a fronton, a series of courts for jai alai games.

All those sources were peanuts when Francis discovered how much money he could make providing protection to wholesalers funneling drugs into South Boston.

It began when Francis learned of a tractor trailer loaded with pot sitting in a South Boston warehouse. The owner of the shipment was from Charlestown. Francis knew the guy and liked him. He also knew you never let anybody do anything in your backyard without your permission.

Francis called Disco, who called his brother, who worked in the DEA. An hour later, the DEA raided the warehouse and Disco's brother got a gold star. So did Disco, who was able to tell Boston's FBI field director, "See, Francis Mahoney is playing on our team."

A few days later, the owner of the shipment ran into Francis and cried to him about losing a half-million-dollar investment.

"That's a shame," Francis said. "You should have told me. Next time you want to store anything in South Boston, you just let me know. It'll cost you a hell of a lot less than a half million."

He and Larry began arranging some of the drug shipments themselves, undercutting business from existing wholesalers. They regularly sent men to Florida to negotiate cocaine shipments from South America. For wholesalers still sending drugs into South Boston, Francis provided protection in exchange for a steep fee. If a wholesaler didn't pay the fee, his name would be passed to Disco. The wholesaler would then be set up for a bust.

On the distribution end, Francis created a structure that insulated him. All drug dealers in South Boston fell into one of three geographic circles. Each circle was controlled by one man who would manage the flow of money coming from all the dealers in his circle.

"The three wise men," as Francis liked to call them, would never deal directly with him. Instead they would go through Connor McCain. The wisest of the wise, Connor would manage the three circles and act as a firewall. He was the only one to talk directly to Francis about business. Anything and everything that had to be communicated up or down the chain went through Connor. That way, nobody other than his most trusted man could ever offer direct testimony against Francis.

Connor was also the only one to pass the money coming from the three circles to Francis. None of the dealers or wise men could ever testify that they had given Francis a dime, and none could ever say that they talked business with him.

Connor wasn't at the Tam-O-Shanter Saturday night. He was over in Chelsea meeting with the loan sharks and bookies that Francis controlled, and delivering the same message that Francis was about to give to the three wise men. With the indictments, a firewall was no longer necessary.

They sat in a booth at the back of the bar. There was Tim Hynes, who had served in the Marine Corps with Connor and whose father had run against Salty Mahoney for mayor and won. And "Bottle Face" Bill O'Leary, who had received seventy-three stitches after being attacked in a tavern by a guy wielding a broken bottle, leaving him with a ragged roadmap of scars across his face. Third was Chris Farragut, owner of Farragut's Four, a bar on West Broadway in South Boston.

Francis sat down in the open seat and got right to the point. "You're not gonna see me around town for a while. Maybe a long while. Don't come looking for me in the usual places because I won't be in any of them. Don't talk to anybody about where I am because you won't know. That's the only thing that's changing. Everything else is business as usual. Keep things tight on the street, keep sending your dues to Connor. Any questions, call Connor. Any problems, call Connor. As far as you're all concerned, Connor is me. If I have anything to tell you, you'll hear it from Connor."

Francis looked into their faces and searched for any hint of doubt. "We've talked about this before, so just follow the plan and keep your eyes open for anybody trying to take advantage of the situation. Let Connor know and he'll tell you how to handle it. Play the game smart."

There were a few questions. Francis answered them and sent the three wise men on their way. With that, Francis went to take a piss. When he emerged from the bathroom, the three were gone. Most of the people at the bar had their eyes focused on the TV, where the ballgame was now in its eighth inning. Francis sat on a stool and waited until he saw Larry D'Amico walk through the front door.

Larry was the same height as Francis but spent less time in the gym, so his waist-length leather jacket fit snugly when buttoned. He also had heavy eyebrows that grew close together and a hairline that began low on his forehead, giving him what Zannino called "the Neanderthal look."

"How's it?" Larry asked when Francis met him at the front door. Larry held an unlit cigar in his mouth, which tended to pinch some of his words. It was a recently acquired habit that annoyed Francis, who hated the use of tobacco in any form.

Francis patted him on the back and they walked outside.

"I'm parked up by the monument," Larry said. "Did you meet your boys?"

There was an urgency in their steps as they crossed Warren Street and headed up Monument Avenue. Larry checked his watch, aware of the tight schedule Francis was on.

"All done," Francis said. "How about you? Have you figured out where to hide yourself?" Francis asked because when he had spoken to Larry earlier, Larry sounded like he was dragging his feet. They both knew they were only guaranteed safe passage until midnight. After that, Larry would be rolling the dice, and the stakes would get higher with each passing hour.

"Maybe tomorrow night. I think I'll head down to Florida. I've got a cousin down there who can set me up in a condo in this retirement community. I'll hide out there for a while and see if these indictments are for real."

"Disco says they are, and that's good enough for me. If you fuck around, Larry, you're gonna get caught with your dick hanging out."

* * * * *

They drove south on the elevated expressway in Larry's new sapphire Cadillac DeVille. The lights of downtown Boston seemed especially bright to Francis. Everything seemed more alive, in motion. The elevated road offered an almost uninterrupted view of Boston Harbor, and Francis stared out at the colorful lights across the water. He noticed details on nearby buildings he had never noticed before. The last time he remembered looking at the Rowes Wharf Hotel, it was still under construction. Now the dome at its center was ablaze in orange lights.

"Are we picking Kathleen up in South Boston, or is she meeting us at Logan?" Larry asked as the road before them descended into a tunnel lined with yellow tiles covered in dust and grime.

The question brought Francis back to the unfinished business from the reception. "I talked to her at Matt's wedding, but things got all fucked up. My father was there and he stepped into the middle of it."

Larry chuckled. "Good old Salty. He's your cross to bear, Francis. I told you that you shouldn't let Kathleen move into his house. He's one crafty motherfucker and you know he's been talking shit about you to her."

Driving through the tunnel was a noisy experience, but inside Larry's DeVille it was almost quiet enough to hear the ticking of the dashboard clock. Larry turned to Francis. "If she's going with you, she has to do it tonight. If she leaves after the indictments come out, they'll follow her. They'll use her to find you."

"I know."

"So we're not picking her up then?"

"We're not," Francis said.

"Good. That'll buy us time. We'll be at your condo in fifteen minutes."

Francis looked at his watch. It was 9:50. After visiting his condo, he had another appointment to keep, his last before the airport.

They emerged from the tunnel, and the expressway rose onto a stretch where potholes littered the road. Most of them passed unnoticed because of the car's advanced suspension system, but the DeVille banged loudly into a particularly deep pothole. "Jesus, there goes the alignment," Larry said.

Coming up on the right was the exit to the Broadway bridge into South Boston. Francis made a quick decision. "Pull off here, Larry."

"Right here?"

The exit was coming up fast and Francis was so intent on not missing it that he grabbed the steering wheel. "Right here!"

Larry checked his rearview mirror before swerving sharply across two lanes of traffic to pull onto the exit ramp.

"Cross the bridge. We're going by my father's house," Francis said.

At the end of the off ramp, Larry turned left under the expressway and onto the Broadway bridge. He glanced at Francis a couple of times but didn't say anything.

"I know what I told you," Francis said. "I changed my mind."

Below them sat the stagnant, tea-colored water of the Fort Point Channel, where floating garbage lay tangled among the remnants of rotting piers.

"Just make it fast," Larry finally said. "You know I've got a thing about schedules."

South Boston was a peninsula extending into Boston Harbor. Broadway was its main artery. It began at the far side of the bridge as West Broadway and continued east to the intersection with Dorchester Street. There it jogged slightly north and became East Broadway, ending a mile later at City Point, where Salty lived.

The Cadillac's immaculately polished hood reflected the lights from the tightly packed storefronts where so much of South Boston did its shopping, its dining and its drinking. It all grabbed Francis the way the city lights had, except now it was more intense.

They passed Farragut's Four, one of the places where Francis held court. It had been bought back in 1973 by Ned Farragut and it was named for his four sons, including Chris, who worked for Francis. He recognized some people who were stepping through the door and onto the sidewalk.

Would he ever see the place again? Now it was really hitting him. Every storefront they passed called out to Francis with the memories of his thirty-eight years in The Town, which is what people in South Boston sometimes called their home.

They passed the South Boston Savings Bank. Francis had foolishly considered robbing it when he was seventeen years old. Then Malloy's funeral home, where Francis had gone to many wakes but not the one that mattered most—his mother's back in 1974—when he was left to mourn her alone from prison. It took him two years before he got out and paid his proper respects at her granite tombstone in Forest Hills Cemetery.

Growing up, Francis knew he was a drain on his mother. It hurt her to see him get into trouble, into fights, into prison. She suffered for her husband as well, but that was different because Salty was a grown man and should have treated her better.

Thinking about how selfless she was and how much she felt for all of her children was too much for Francis to consider all at once. It brought on the kind of intense sadness that could plunge him into paralysis. So he put it in a place he allowed himself to visit only on rare occasions and only for a brief time.

After his mother was diagnosed with cancer, she realized she would not be there to see Matthew through his teenage years. Understanding how similar Francis was emotionally to his younger brother, she asked Francis to promise her something.

After she died, she wanted him to watch over Matthew and see that he steered clear of the trouble Francis had so often wandered into. He promised he would and he did his best, even sending Matthew the occasional letter from prison, warning him of the traps that were so easy to fall into in the world, and how many more of them there were in South Boston.

Seeing Matthew at the wedding, noticing how well he and Anne got along, and knowing how happy it would have made their mother, was a consolation to Francis. A confirmation that despite all the ways he had disappointed her, perhaps he had played some small part in seeing that Matthew was now firmly rooted in a life that would have pleased her.

They were coming up on the bakery where Kathleen Sutliff's mother bought donuts every Sunday after mass. The Sutliffs had moved into Old Colony when Kathleen was eleven years old and Francis thirteen. He had been in gangs for a couple of years and had a reputation that troubled Mrs. Sutliff, but it wasn't long before he and Kathleen were spending a lot of time together. Francis let it be known in the project that any other guy seen with Kathleen would have the shit kicked out of him.

They started openly dating two years later when Mrs. Sutliff reluctantly agreed to it, as long as they followed the Catholic rules. Francis had had a few sexual encounters before meeting Kathleen, so he didn't like the idea of conforming to any rules except his own. Kathleen didn't make him wait as long as the Pope would have liked, but she did make him wait a few more years, which seemed like an eternity to Francis.

He and Kathleen had the same sense of humor, which was a little quirky, a little sarcastic, but through the open windows of the project, people could hear them arguing with each other more often than laughing.

Over the years they had spent as much time apart as together. The real trouble started when Francis joined the Army and shipped off to Vietnam at nineteen. They planned to marry when he returned after his tour, but two months later he was headed back in shackles to serve three years in military prison at the Army Regional Confinement Facility at Fort Knox. He had smashed an officer's head with a can of frozen beer, then his boot.

He was in military prison when word came that Kathleen had married some guy who wasn't even from South Boston. He also heard that they moved to Texas, which was like moving to the other side of the world.

Francis returned to a South Boston without her. He tried living the legitimate life and took a job as a courthouse janitor, which his older brother Jimmy had arranged for him. It was boring, demeaning work, and it didn't pay well.

He stayed at it for three weeks before going back to the old business with his old friends. Their bread-and-butter was hijacking trucks carrying liquor, apparel or anything that they could turn around fast. They'd track the routes the trucks took through downtown Boston or the South End and surprise the driver when he stopped to take a piss or park at his warehouse after hours. Sometimes they even got the truck driver to collaborate ahead of time. The first heist took a total of three hours, and Francis earned ten times what he made in one week of pushing a broom.

Three weeks later though, Francis was in front of a judge for his part in a botched robbery, earning him four more years behind bars, this time at Walpole State Prison.

His cellmate was an older Native American from Oklahoma named William Trey, who became the silver lining to Francis' time in prison. William was in Walpole for murdering a man who insulted his wife while the two were vacationing on Cape Cod. Intelligent and insightful, William became a father figure to Francis and taught him the difference between survival and success.

He also taught Francis how to play chess, and during one game William told it to Francis straight. "You have no job skills, no education and you don't want to push a broom for the rest of your life. You're a smart guy, but you're not living smart. That's why you're here. Whatever you do when you get out, you have to do it differently. Let the other guys play checkers. You play chess."

Larry drove his DeVille over a small hill on East Broadway and passed Kathleen's beauty salon. Its name was spelled out across its darkened windows. The Hair & Beyond. That's where she'll be next week, Francis thought, and I'll be in another world.

As much as Francis hated the idea of leaving South Boston forever, he knew he could do it, but suddenly the idea of being separated for the rest of his life from Kathleen was too much. He knew it sounded corny when he told her at the reception, but he believed that they were meant to be together for the rest of their lives.

Larry drove to the end of Broadway at City Point and backed into a parking space across from Carson Beach. From this spot, he could view Francis coming and going, and any cops that might be passing through the neighborhood.

"Ten minutes and we start running late," Larry said.

The Mahoney home was a single-family house on E. Third Street, a few blocks from where Larry had parked. Francis walked down E. Second Street so he could come up from the back of his father's house. He wasn't completely sure what he would do when he got there. He just wanted another chance to talk to Kathleen. If his father was there, and he probably would be, he'd just have to deal with it.

The McDevitts' house on E. Second Street was directly behind the Mahoneys'. When Francis reached it, he snuck down their driveway and into the backyard, which was enclosed by a six-foot-high chain-link fence with a gate at the driveway and another one at the far end of the yard, where it connected with the Mahoney backyard. Francis opened the first gate, closed it behind him and then crept to the other side of the McDevitts' backyard, where he passed through the second gate.

His father's home was newer than most in the neighborhood. A two-story house with three bedrooms upstairs and a small yard in front and back. His father's and Kathleen's bedrooms faced the back. None of the windows in the back of the house were lit. He knew which bedroom was Kathleen's. He may have kept his distance from her over the last six months, but he made sure to find out the details of her living situation.

He moved quietly across the dark lawn. A tall hedge ran from the backyard to the front. Francis moved in its shadow.

The living room windows at the side of the house were also dark. He heard no sound coming from inside. On the other side of the hedge was their one-car garage. Francis peeked into the garage window and saw his father's white LTD parked inside.

So he was home. And asleep. Francis checked his watch. It was five after ten. Kathleen had always been a night owl and usually was up until one or two in the morning, unless his father had changed that about her as well. She drove a red Honda, but Francis didn't spot it anywhere on the street. Kathleen almost certainly wasn't at home.

A door slammed in the direction of the McDevitt house, so Francis crept back into the shadows of the hedge. He waited for a minute, then walked to the other side of the house, checking every window for any sign of Kathleen.

Finally he returned to the hedge and tried to decide what to do. It seemed simple. Kathleen wasn't there and Francis had no time to wait for her. That was it. It was over. He had to leave alone. Something kept him there though, crouched beside the hedge.

Francis looked up at the house. When they moved in, he was fifteen and barely able to stay in school. He never felt at home in the new City Point neighborhood and spent every night back at the Old Colony housing project with his gang. He often came home well after midnight, which really pissed his father off.

With his oldest son Jimmy, Salty's punishment never extended beyond a hard slap, but with Francis he went much further. Once, Francis came home at two in the morning. The house was dark, and his father was waiting for him at the top of the stairway. With one punch he sent Francis tumbling down the steps.

The encounter left Francis with a bloody lip, a loose tooth and twelve stitches to the back of his head. It wasn't the first time his father had beaten him like that, but it would be the last.

Hiding beside the hedge, Francis remembered it quite clearly and how it made him feel about his father. The hatred had been white hot but had cooled since then.

Now it was heating up once again because of the fight at the reception. If Kathleen stayed with his father, and Francis had to admit that's how the game was ending, that left Salty the winner and Francis the loser. He would move alone through the world with only the memories of Kathleen and the knowledge that his father had the privilege, even the joy, of her company at the breakfast table, at a Red Sox game, at the movie theater.

A sudden noise broke the spell Francis had fallen into. From the darkness came a growl, then the barking of a dog. Francis walked slowly toward the McDevitts' chain-link fence, where their Doberman lunged.

The back door of the McDevitt house opened and Mrs. McDevitt called to her dog. The Doberman ignored her at first but finally trotted back to their porch and inside the house. When the porch light went out, Francis crossed the McDevitts' yard and headed toward Larry's car. All the way he felt something pulling him back to his father's house, a faint voice that he had been ignoring since he was fifteen.

"Where the fuck have you been?" Larry asked when Francis got into the seat beside him. "You said ten minutes and it's been fifteen, so we're late." He started the car. "No Kathleen, I guess. Well, you tried."

"Where's my piece?" Francis asked, referring to the gun Larry had brought in case they encountered trouble. Like all smart mobsters, Francis and Larry rarely carried guns. Flashing one in public, or even carrying one concealed, was sloppy. You only carried a piece when you knew you were going to use it. When the need had passed, you got rid of it quickly.

"What?"

"You've got a piece for me, I want it now."

"Why now?"

Larry could see that Francis was worked up. He had that cold grey look about him. Larry could think of only one reason why he would be this way.

"Leave him be, Francis. We haven't got time for this. You're on an international flight and they can be real pricks if you don't show up plenty early."

Francis bent over and began fishing under the seat with his hand. "Where the fuck is it, Larry?"

"Alright, alright. Jesus." Larry reached his fingers down a vent at the top of the dashboard. A moment later a plastic bag tumbled from beneath the dash and onto the car floor. Francis ripped it open, pulled out the 9mm pistol and two clips.

Larry shook his head slowly. "I don't believe you're doing this, Francis. It isn't like you. It's unprofessional. Sure, he's an asshole, but he's your father…"

"I'll be back in ten minutes, and I mean ten."

Francis climbed out of the car, tucked the loaded pistol into the back of his belt and began jogging back to his father's house. The voice that had been calling to him quietly was now screaming so loud that Francis couldn't hear anything else. All he could see was the path that lay between him and his sleeping father.

He took the same route as before, but paused this time at the first gate in the McDevitts' chain link fence. He whistled faintly to be sure the dog had gone back inside. Then he passed through the two gates to his father's backyard.

Francis decided the basement window on the far right side was the best way in unless his father had fixed the lock. Even as he approached it, Francis could see the shiny new hardware. He wouldn't be able to get in that way unless he broke a window, which would make too much noise.

The back door was the next best bet. It was hidden from the street and covered in darkness. It would probably be locked, but there was a spare key hidden in the garage. Francis walked to the door, and pulled his sleeve over his hand to avoid leaving fingerprints on the knob. To his amazement, the door was unlocked. He drew the pistol from his belt, slid in a clip, then loaded the chamber. He waited at the back door for his eyes to adjust to the dim light. If he wasn't sloppy about it, the whole matter should take less than a minute.

* * * * *

Larry D'Amico sat in his DeVille and counted off the minutes. Four. Five. At seven there was no sign of Francis. Larry had rolled down his window, and just after eight minutes had passed, he heard two gunshots. They were followed by two more. Larry slapped a hand down on the steering wheel and shook his head. "This is crazy," he said to himself and looked up and down the avenue for cop cars. He started up the DeVille and swore he would leave at ten minutes no matter what.

At nine, Francis came charging from around the corner with the tail of his jacket whipping behind him. Larry had never seen Francis run so fast. He turned on the lights, put the car in gear and met him halfway.

Francis jumped into the DeVille with a groan as Larry hit the gas and sped toward Day Boulevard. Larry said nothing, focusing on the road and any sign of police. He was driving fast but making sure not to squeal the tires.

Beside him Francis was breathing heavily with his head bent over as he examined his left hand. The left cuff of his shirt was stained crimson. Francis pulled out a handkerchief to clean his hand. When Larry stopped for a red light in front of the L Street bathhouse, he looked over to see what Francis was doing.

"Don't tell me you shot yourself."

"No, the fucker surprised me," Francis said as he patted sweat from his forehead with his clean right cuff.

Larry raised a hand to Francis and said, "Look, I don't want to hear about it, OK? It was fucking stupid. It wasted time, and it put us both at risk." The light turned green and Larry took another look around before continuing along the boulevard as it curved along Carson Beach.

Francis pressed the handkerchief onto his hand and took a deep breath. "You were right. It was stupid."

"It was, but let's put it behind us. We have more stops to make and you've completely fucked with my schedule. I hope it was worth it," Larry said.

Francis slid down in his seat and closed his eyes.

Larry pushed the cigarette lighter and pulled his cigar from the visor pocket where he had stashed it. He cracked his window and lit up. Francis absolutely hated being in the car when Larry smoked, but at the moment he cared so little it took a minute to register that the cigar was lit.

Francis could move his hand and he still had all the feeling throughout it. The bleeding seemed to have stopped as well, so he tried to do as Larry suggested and put this big mistake behind him.

They took the expressway south, and at Neponset they exited and crossed the bridge into Quincy. It was only a quarter mile to Francis' condo complex. Larry stayed with the car in the back parking lot, and Francis walked up to his third floor unit. From the living room bookshelf he pulled out several volumes of an encyclopedia.

Using a razor knife, he cut the backings from the inside front covers and retrieved his blue American passport and a green Irish passport. Both in his own name. Francis qualified for the Irish passport because his mother had been born in Ireland. With it, he could move at will through all countries in Europe.

Both passports were legitimate. It was necessary to hide them though. Without any warrant, his condo had been searched many times by the state police. If they had found the passports, they would almost certainly have taken them. To keep better track of Francis. Or simply to fuck with him.

From the other encyclopedia volumes he pulled out two sets of fake identities in two different names and tucked them into a money belt. He took off his jacket and shirt and strapped the belt around his waist. In the bathroom he quickly cleaned his wound, patted it dry and covered it with Band-Aids. A bandage wrap would have been better but would draw more attention passing through security at the airport.

Francis cut the bloody shirt into small pieces and flushed them down the toilet. He put on a fresh shirt from the dresser, then grabbed a bag from his hallway closet. It was small enough to bring on board the plane as carry-on luggage. Into it he tossed a paperback book on classic chess openings that had been given to him as a going-away gift by his old cellmate, William.

The condo had a sliding glass door that led out to a balcony. When he moved in, Francis had replaced the glass with a one-inch-thick steel plate. If somebody was going to kill him in his home, they'd have to earn it and not snipe him from two hundred yards away.

He unlocked the heavy steel door and moved it slowly on its rollers. From the balcony, he had a clear view across the Neponset River to Dorchester. Next to a car wash stood a small brick bar called The Pony Room. A blue neon sign lit up a second-story window, indicating that it was safe for Francis to pay a visit.

They drove back across the bridge and parked behind The Pony Room. A lonely pay phone stood under a streetlight.

"You should've taken some clothes," Larry said when he noticed that all Francis had in the bag was a book.

"I've got plenty to carry without clothes."

While Larry waited outside, Francis used a key to open the back door to the bar. A creaky stairway brought him to the basement office where Archie Collins sat puffing a cigar as the Red Sox wrap-up show played on a black and white TV. Archie was a short, heavy man who wore a blue wool cap over his bald head. He lived in a large house in Quincy with his wife and eight children, who he seldom spent much time with because of the business hours he kept.

"Well, look who's here," Archie said without removing his cigar. "You're dressed like you're going someplace special."

"It'll be special when I show up there," Francis said. "Especially if I bring Mr. Franklin."

"Sure thing," Archie said. He pulled himself slowly out of his chair and led the way to a back room where he got down on one knee and dialed the combination to an old steel floor safe. Archie stepped out of the way so Francis could remove the entire contents, over $650,000 in bundles of circulated one hundred dollar bills.

Every few months for the past several years, Francis had been taking stashes out of the country. There were safe-deposit boxes in the Caribbean and around Europe. He had several million dollars stashed away, along with more fake identities. He had made additional deposits with his IRA friends in Ireland. Francis was like a squirrel, except that he remembered where every single acorn was buried. And he knew exactly how big they all were.

Archie stood patiently and watched as Francis filled the bag. When he was done, Francis counted out a small pile of cash and placed it back into the safe.

"I already took my cut, Francis," Archie said.

"I know. I'm giving you a bonus."

"That's not necessary, but thank you."

Francis had done it to see whether or not Archie had been satisfied with his two percent for each stash held in his safe. Even though Archie had agreed to the percentage, it was important for Francis to know that Archie still considered it fair.

"I won't need this for a while." Francis handed over his back door key to the bar and zipped up his bulging bag. As he stepped outside, he saw Larry returning from the pay phone.

"I called the airport, Francis. Your flight's leaving on time at midnight. If we're lucky and there's no traffic, we'll make it. Get out your rosary beads."

* * * * *

At eleven twenty-five, the sapphire DeVille pulled up to Logan Airport's international terminal. It was crowded with passengers from two overseas flights that had arrived at the same time. Traffic in the three-lane terminal road was continuously clogging as people double- and triple-parked. A state trooper who was trying to direct traffic seemed at the point of exasperation.

Francis reached behind his back, removed the pistol from his belt and tucked it beneath the front seat. "Get rid of it for me."

Francis grabbed his bag and said, "Wait for me to blow you a kiss from the ticket counter, OK?"

"Adios," Larry said. "Don't forget not to write."

The terminal was slowly clearing out as passengers from the arriving flights collected their luggage and made their way into the Boston night.

At the counter, Francis handed his ticket and his American passport to the attendant, a young woman with a southern accent. She asked if Francis wanted to check his bag.

"No," he said, "this is carry-on. Listen, I'm running a little late. My flight leaves in thirty minutes. Is that gonna be a problem?"

"You're supposed to be here earlier," she said in a sing-song voice, "but we'll forgive you this time...Mr. Mahoney."

Francis noticed a state trooper stepping behind the far end of the ticket counter. He was making his way toward Francis, stopping to speak briefly with each ticket attendant. The trooper was also placing a sheet of paper in front of them.

"I'm sorry," Francis said, "What gate is it leaving from?"

"That's gate number fourteen. Up the escalator, and to your right. You better go straight up there if you don't want them to leave without you."

"Why don't you hand me my passport and boarding pass, and I'll get going." Francis glanced quickly at the trooper who had finished speaking with the neighboring attendant and was now approaching his.

"I'll have your boarding pass printed in just a few seconds, Mr. Mahoney. Then you're free to go."

Francis tried to display only a casual interest as the trooper asked the woman to examine a sheet of paper. It was a security alert from the State Police station at Logan Airport. Francis' eyes scanned down the document. They stopped when he saw his name printed in large type.

That's all he had to see. He immediately knew that he would not be leaving the country on a plane. The trooper didn't seem to realize that Francis Mahoney, the person named on the alert, was standing right in front of him. Francis slowly retrieved his passport from the counter and tucked it into a jacket pocket. As he did, he got a sudden whiff of fear from the ticket attendant. Her hand reached out and touched the trooper's sleeve.

The trooper, who looked no older than twenty-five, picked up on the woman's fear also. He glanced at the computer printer, where the attendant was directing the trooper's eyes to Francis' boarding pass.

The trooper looked directly at Francis. "Mr. Mahoney?"

"Yes?"

"Would you mind stepping to the end of the counter for a moment, please?" The trooper's left hand rested on his belt, his right rested over the pistol that was secured in its holster.

Francis casually glanced one way, then the other. The trooper was the only cop in the terminal as far as Francis could see.

"I'm very close to missing my flight," Francis said, trying to decide which way he should break. His immediate concern was to get somebody else in the trooper's line of fire, so he wouldn't dare shoot. That would buy Francis enough time to mix with some of the other people exiting the terminal. There was no way to know whether the trooper would even draw his pistol, but he might.

Standing at the ticket counter to Francis' left was a middle-aged couple having their baggage checked in.

"It will only take a moment, Mr. Mahoney." The trooper tried to sound calm, but Francis could hear the adrenaline in his voice.

"Sure, I'll just grab my bag," Francis said. As he bent down, Francis heard a snap from the trooper's holster strap. If Francis stood up, he knew the trooper would have his pistol drawn and pointing at him. Francis glanced quickly toward the large windows at the front of the terminal. Larry was standing on the sidewalk, watching.

Remaining in a crouch, Francis grabbed his bag and ran down his side of the counter. When he reached the next attendant's station, he pushed his way between the couple. The state trooper vaulted the ticket counter, and his boots landed with a clap on the polished floor. He yelled for Francis to stop.

The middle-aged couple stood between them, so Francis was safe for the moment. Larry, he saw, was mirroring his movement along the sidewalk outside. A few people were entering the terminal through the revolving door to Francis' left. Halfway to the door he passed a woman and her two tired, cranky kids, who sat on the edge of a baggage carousel. They would now be in the line of fire if Francis decided to break for that door.

Behind him, Francis heard the squeaking of the trooper's rubber-soled boots. He made a dash across the wide terminal and headed for the exit, weaving between the incoming crowd, then pushing his way through the revolving door.

Once outside, Francis tossed the bag to Larry. "Take it to the car!" Francis yelled. "Pick me up here!"

A number of baggage trolleys were scattered along the sidewalk. Francis quickly grabbed one and brought it to the revolving door, which was split into four wedge compartments. He waited for the trooper to begin pushing his way outside.

When the trooper was halfway between the inside and the outside of the terminal, Francis tipped the baggage trolley over and shoved it inside the open compartment in front of him, jamming the door in both directions and trapping the trooper.

Francis hesitated long enough to show a smile to the frustrated trooper, then ran to the curb where Larry was pulling up.

"Here comes the other one!" Larry said as Francis jumped into the DeVille. The trooper that had been working traffic duty noticed the commotion at the door. As he ran to his colleague trapped in the door, Larry pulled into traffic.

All but one of the lanes ahead were jammed with double-parked cars. The DeVille sped down the narrow tunnel of space in the third lane. When a taxi began to pull out, Larry blasted his horn. The DeVille sideswiped the taxi, careened off the cement barrier to the left, then returned to the lane where it sideswiped another car. They were glancing blows that didn't slow them down or cause much damage, but Larry muttered a curse at each one.

Forty yards before they reached the end of the congested terminal road, a small brown van pulled out in front of them. Larry pushed both feet down on the brake and the DeVille skidded to a stop.

Francis rolled down his window and stuck his head outside. "Move it, asshole!" he yelled. Leaning back inside, he asked, "Where's my fucking piece?" and started rummaging under the front seat. Larry leaned on the horn and the small van moved forward a short distance before coming to a stop again.

"It's one of those new minivans!" Larry yelled. "I hate those goddamn minivans!"

"I can't find my piece. Just hit the motherfucker."

Larry bumped the minivan and it jerked forward before stopping. He bumped it again much harder, pushing the minivan forward five yards. Shards from the DeVille's headlights tinkled to the pavement.

"This isn't gonna work, Francis."

"Go around him."

"There's not enough space."

"Make space!"

Larry backed up again and aimed for the small space between the cement barrier and the minivan, then sped toward it. There was a crash as the DeVille slammed into the rear corner of the minivan, which shot like a billiard ball into an open space in the second lane. The DeVille went the opposite way into the cement divider before bouncing back onto the road.

Both front corners of the DeVille were crumpled. As Larry sped off toward the airport exit, a screeching whine developed under the hood.

"I hope that's not the water pump," Francis said, "we're fucked if it's the water pump. We won't even make it to the tunnel."

Both headlights had been knocked out, and bits of plastic and metal spilled from the front end at every bump. The DeVille's speedometer topped seventy miles an hour as Larry wove in and out of traffic along the three-lane exit road.

The road banked to the left and dipped toward the toll booths at the entrance to the Callahan Tunnel, which ran beneath Boston Harbor and surfaced in downtown Boston.

"My Caddy's dying. We need to get another car," Larry said.

"Do you think we can make it through the tunnel?" Francis asked.

"If they radio the Boston cops and they close the tunnel at the other end while we're inside, then we're screwed." Larry said.

As the toll booths approached, Larry turned sharply onto an East Boston side street. "I have an idea," he said.

Francis was still breathing heavily. "I don't know what happened back there. That statee had a sheet on me," he said, using the common nickname for a state trooper. "It's not even midnight yet. Disco said nothing would happen before midnight."

"The shots at your dad's house?"

"How could they know that was me?"

The air conditioner had been broken in the collision, making the air inside the DeVille warm and stale, so Larry opened both front windows. "The electric windows still work," he said.

In the distance they heard the sound of sirens. Larry turned onto a more narrow side street densely packed with triple-decker homes, then turned onto a dark wide boulevard with warehouses on one side and vast car rental lots on the other. The elevated airport exit road beyond the rental lots was lit up with the blue flashes of state police cars rushing toward the tunnel entrance, which was in the opposite direction.

"Where are we going?" Francis asked. "Are we gonna just drive till this thing dies?"

"I know somebody here with a garage."

"Is his garage open at midnight?"

"Our garage on Lancaster Street usually was."

Larry turned left onto Saratoga Street and left again a few houses down. A narrow driveway led them to a garage at the back of a warehouse. Larry shut off the engine and beeped his horn twice. "The horn still works."

The eerie silence was suddenly filled with the sound of barking dogs. "No more fucking dogs tonight, please," Francis said.

"We're gonna get a trade-in, Francis. This is Phil Iannello's place. He lives here most of the time." Francis knew the name; it belonged to an associate of the Romano family who didn't like Francis. In fact, he hated Francis. In 1980 Francis outmaneuvered Phil for the open Somerville rackets.

Somerville belonged to an old gang that was slowly falling apart as one leader after another was hauled in on charges, convicted and sent to prison. The FBI was cleaning up and nobody in the old gang knew who was informing.

Francis told everyone it was the Italians. They believed him. What nobody knew, and what nobody would have believed, was that Francis was responsible. With the FBI's help, Francis was tearing down the old leadership and preparing to replace it with himself.

In the temporary power vacuum, Phil tried to bite off pieces of Somerville, telling bookies and loan sharks to start making payments to him despite threats from Francis. It could have gotten bloody, but the Romanos were smart, at least on this matter. They knew they could never control Somerville. Unlike La Cosa Nostra in some other big American cities, the Italian empire in Boston was limited to the North End, downtown and certain neighborhoods to the north, like Malden and Medford, and to the east, like East Boston.

There was a meeting between Francis and the Romanos. The two mobs would respect each other's turf and even cooperate in certain ventures. For the larger good, Phil Iannello would have to get out of Somerville and stick to East Boston. Phil saw it as a betrayal by the family. In effect, Francis had humiliated him in front of Boston's underworld community.

"Phil hates me, Larry. He's not gonna give me any car."

"Let me worry about the car. You worry about what we're gonna do after we get it."

"Maybe I should get in the fucking trunk, so Phil doesn't see me," Francis joked.

"The dogs would sniff you out," Larry said as a motor drew up the garage door. Phil Iannello, a thin man with a bald head that gave off a glow from the garage lights, stood at the entrance among three large Dobermans.

"More Dobermans," Francis said.

Larry stuck his head out of the window. "Phil, it's me. Larry! I need a favor."

Phil stood aside as Larry drove his battered DeVille to the rear of the garage. Three other cars were parked inside. All looked very drivable to Francis.

Phil closed the garage door. When he saw Francis step out of the DeVille, Phil let out a bark. He was more surprised than angry. At first.

"Hello, Phil. How's it going?" Francis said with a sarcastic smile. The last thing Francis was going to do was kiss Phil Iannello's ass.

Phil directed Larry to a large room built into one corner of the garage. Francis followed. In the room were a bed, a kitchen table and chairs, a sink full of dirty dishes, and a collection of doggie dishes on the floor where the three Dobermans settled down to stare at the strangers.

Francis took a seat. Larry looked back at his DeVille and shook his head as he considered the damage. "I waited two months to get it in sapphire," he said softly. Then turning to Phil, "I need a trade-in, Phil. I had a little accident. I'll pay you full price for whatever you have available, and you can keep the Deville. Chop it up for parts. It can't be seen in public again. There's some money to be made. It's only three weeks old."

Francis fiddled mindlessly with an embroidered pot holder at the center of the table and stared at a chewed-up plastic dog bone lying on the floor beside his chair.

"I don't know if they got my license plate, but I should take a new one of those, too," Larry continued.

Phil shuffled over to the sink and brought back two glasses and a bottle of wine. He poured one glass for himself and one for Larry.

There was a silence as Phil poured. "Is the car for him?" Phil was looking at Francis, but the question was for Larry.

"I'll even toss you two points for taking the DeVille," Larry said. "How's that sound?"

"I don't need his money," Phil said and waved a lazy hand toward Francis.

"He's going on a long trip tonight, Phil, and he's not coming back. Now that should make you happy."

"You think you got a lot of balls, don't you?" Phil said as he continued to stare at Francis, but Francis was looking at Larry.

"Ask him how much more money he wants, Larry," Francis said, reaching down to pick up the plastic dog bone.

"Do you think I need your fucking milk money, Mahoney?"

When they got old, Francis thought, the Italians behave more and more like old women. Pouty, whiny and powerless. "What does he want?" Francis asked Larry.

"You think I'm gonna give you one of my cars?" Phil asked.

"He's leaving tonight, Phil. You're helping get rid of him. Think of it that way."

It began to embarrass Francis, listening to Larry placate the old man. But Francis had always kept out of Larry's way when he dealt with the Italians. They might fear Francis, but they respected Larry. So Francis knew when to keep his mouth shut. Larry did the same in Francis' world. It was one of the things that made their partnership work so well.

"Phil!" Larry said in a tone that drew a growl from one of the dogs. "I have to make sure he leaves tonight," Larry said insistently but respectfully. "It's my job, Phil."

"Ask him what he wants again," Francis said, twirling the dog bone slowly. He looked at the dogs. Their eyes were focused on the bone.

"You know what I want, Mahoney?" Phil asked as he looked at Francis. "I want you to suck my dick! That's what I want. Now get the fuck out of here!"

This isn't working, Francis decided. Phil brought the glass of wine to his lips, and when he tipped back his head to swallow, Francis tossed the plastic bone through the open doorway. The three dogs immediately got up and chased it into the garage.

By the time Phil noticed what was going on and called an order to the dogs, it was too late. Francis had slammed the door shut, then took a dirty chef's knife from the sink. He grabbed Phil from behind in a chokehold and pressed the knife to the side of his neck.

Francis might as well have slit Phil's throat. The old man was being humiliated once again, and the taste of this one would be as bad as the first. But Francis didn't want that. He wanted a car. When Phil finally agreed, Francis let him go. Larry simply watched.

* * * * *

They emptied everything from the DeVille into the trunk of a Toyota Tercel that belonged to Phil's niece. As they drove away, Francis looked over at Larry, who looked uncomfortable driving such a small car.

They took side streets through East Boston, Chelsea and then Medford. They were headed to Gloucester, a small fishing town at the eastern tip of Cape Ann, thirty miles north of Boston.

"Jerry McNulty finished loading the Avalon last night," Francis said, referring to the man who owned the Tam-O-Shanter Pub in Charlestown.

"Are you sure it hasn't left already?" Larry asked.

"It's not supposed to leave until tonight." The Avalon was an eighty-foot fishing trawler purchased by McNulty, funded by Francis. Its destination, as Larry and Francis both knew, was Ireland.

The Avalon's trip was the culmination of three years' work. Francis considered it as a sort of Irish Triangle Trade. The IRA had been pushing him to purchase and smuggle arms to them in Ireland. Francis told them he needed a source of funds.

Since discovering how lucrative the drug business was, Francis knew that it would be the quickest way to produce funds. Marijuana was a safer choice because it wasn't as closely watched as heroin or cocaine. The most efficient way to smuggle pot into Boston was by ship, and the biggest impediment to such a large scale operation was the Coast Guard.

Francis explained this to his friends across the water. The IRA took care of it. The admiral in charge of the U.S. Coast Guard fleet in Boston was an IRA sympathizer, so the IRA contacted him. The admiral agreed to keep all Coast Guard boats out of certain areas of Massachusetts Bay on particular nights.

So it began. Ships loaded with bales of pot unloaded their cargo onto small boats, which delivered the bales to an old pier in Chelsea. From there, tractor trailers hauled them to various distribution points around New England. It went like clockwork for over two years, earning Francis and Larry millions of dollars in profit.

The operation was so lucrative, Francis was hesitant to turn off the spigot. The IRA kept asking whether he had earned enough money to purchase the weapons they wanted. Francis milked it as long as he could, complaining about the logistical problems, the overhead, having to pay off the cops.

Finally, it was time to close down the drug-running operation and begin the gun-running operation. Weapons were bought or stolen from several locations across the country, including a load of machine guns taken from an army base in California. Larry managed that side of things, while Francis managed the drug distribution and relations with the IRA.

With funds provided by Francis, McNulty bought the Avalon at an auction the previous October. He paid three hundred thousand dollars for it and spent another half million overhauling it. Special compartments were welded into the boat's fish pens. The storage areas wouldn't be detected if the Coast Guard inspected the boat.

The Avalon had a faster hull than most fishing boats, and they refitted her with much larger engines. The combination would trim days off the transatlantic travel time.

"We should have just skipped the airport tonight," Larry said.

"Going across the Atlantic in a smelly boat is not how I wanted to leave."

"It's how the Mahoneys and D'Amicos arrived in this country, wasn't it?" Larry said with a smile.

The thought was a depressing one to Francis. Like tearing down a house that had taken generations to build. "I just hope they haven't left yet. McNulty said they'd be leaving around midnight tonight."

"What if they're already gone?" Larry asked.

"The Avalon is Plan B. You don't want to hear Plan C," Francis said.

Just before two o'clock, they reached the end of Route 128, where it dipped down to sea level. A steady breeze carried the smell of brackish seaweed that lay exposed on the rocks in Gloucester Harbor.

They took Rogers Street, which followed the contours of the harbor and brought them past the Old Timer and The Mariner, two of Gloucester's grittiest waterfront bars, where some fishermen made more money selling small catches of heroin than they did with their fish at the Boston Exchange.

Francis directed Larry to a boatyard at the end of Rogers Street where Jerry had told Francis the Avalon was moored. He looked through the chain-link security fence at the tightly huddled collection of fishing boats tied along the pier.

"I don't see it," Francis said, suddenly alarmed at the prospect of a much riskier Plan C.

"How can you tell? They all look alike."

"Jerry said he was putting two big cranes on the back. I don't see any boats with big cranes. Maybe it's just too dark."

Larry flashed his headlights at a guard shack across the boatyard. "Ask the Rent-A-Cop," Larry said.

A uniformed guard eventually stepped out of the shack. Francis met him at the fence.

"Where's the Avalon?" Francis asked.

"Left about an hour ago."

"It's gone?"

"Maybe. Maybe not. They might still be over at GMR icing up."

"Where's that?"

"Up beside the Coast Guard station on Rogers Street."

They drove there quickly. The gate to Gloucester Marine Railway was open and they drove right up to the pier where the Avalon, glossy with a fresh coat of grey paint above the waterline, was taking on ice through a long umbilical shaft connected to a windowless warehouse. The sound of the ice pouring through the metal shaft was almost deafening. On the trawler's rear deck were two bulky outriggers pointed skyward.

Before Francis had taken more than three steps up the gangplank, a man in a heavy overcoat emerged from the wheelhouse. He stood at the top of the gangplank and would have called to Francis, but because of the noise he motioned for Francis to go away.

Unable to find the right gestures, Francis continued until the man picked up a pole with a large gaff hook and once again waved Francis off. He just stood there until the ice conveyor powered down suddenly and the sound of crashing ice diminished to an occasional ping.

"Go away," the man called.

He was one of the crewmembers who had never met Francis. Like everyone else on the Avalon, he was being paid by Francis and Larry. "Get Tim Drago. Tell him Francis is here."

The crewman reappeared a minute later with a curly-haired man who wore a leather apron and had a set of welding goggles dangling from his neck. It was Tim Drago, one of McNulty's boys.

"I don't know who this guy is," the crewman said to Tim as they approached Francis.

When Tim recognized Francis, he said to the crewman, "He's Francis Mahoney, you dumb fuck."

It took a moment to register with the crewman. When it did, his eyes grew big with fear and he began gushing with apologies to Francis, until Tim sent him below.

"Good evening, boss," Tim said as Francis joined him on deck. "Is everything alright?" Tim asked with a hint of concern in his voice. "The trip is still on for tonight, isn't it?"

"Everything's fine. I just need a lift to Ireland."

Tim folded his hands over the top of his head. "You're kidding?"

"I'm gonna be indicted and I have to leave fast. They almost nabbed me at Logan a while ago."

"Does McNulty know?"

"Nobody knows. Are you gonna talk to him tonight?"

"We're supposed to stay off the radio until we reach Nahant. He'll be waiting for a transmission from us, letting him know we're off OK. We won't see him again until we're back in Boston after the return trip. Do you want me to tell McNulty you're coming with us?"

"We'll see." Francis wasn't sure whether he wanted to tell McNulty he was on board. A week at sea was a long time for things to go wrong back home. And if McNulty got in trouble, being able to tell the FBI that Francis Mahoney was stuck on a certain boat would be quite a big bargaining chip.

"Will this create any trouble with the IRA?" Tom asked. "Those boys can be a little tense, and a change in plans might spook them."

"When their boys get themselves in trouble, they send them to us to start a new life. Believe me, they won't mind. When do we leave?" Francis asked.

"Twenty minutes, maybe thirty."

"I'll grab my bag and be right back," Francis said. He walked to the car and opened the trunk so he could count out money to cover the Tercel, the dumping of the DeVille and the purchase of a new one. Francis handed it to Larry, shook his hand and said good-bye.

"Don't eat too much mackerel on the way over," Larry said.

Inside the boat, Tim first introduced Francis to the rest of the Avalon's three-man crew. The one who had stopped Francis on the gangplank apologized again, but Francis told him it was OK. He was doing his job and that's what he was being paid to do.

Tim then led Francis to the galley, where five of Francis' boys from South Boston were playing cards. They were riding along to guarantee security for the operation and they were very happy to hear that their own captain would be joining them for the crossing. In their clean and colorful track suits so common on the streets and in the gyms of South Boston, they were a dramatic contrast to the Avalon's crew, who dressed like seasoned sailors. They eyed the guys from South Boston with more than a little skepticism.

Next, Tim and Francis went in search of Steve Collins, a former Navy SEAL and a weapons expert. They found Steve in the fish pens, finishing the task of hiding crates of weapons. There were seven tons in all, from assault rifles and hand grenades to Redeye surface-to-air antiaircraft missiles. The Avalon was also delivering high-tech electronic devices that would allow the IRA to eavesdrop on British communications.

"Francis, what's up?" Steve asked.

"I'm hitching a ride. How's everything going?"

"We've sealed the compartments at the bottom of the pens. Now we're covering them with ice. It's all smooth so far." Steve returned to his work, and Tim brought Francis to the pilothouse to meet the captain, Haven Stead. He explained to Francis that the trawler had taken on nine thousand gallons of diesel fuel for the trip to Ireland and back. The fish hold was being filled with thirty tons of ice to give the impression that the Avalon was going on an extended fishing trip.

After the brief tour, Francis walked out on deck with Tim. He preferred the cool evening air to the diesel and oil stench of the cabin.

"It's gonna be a little cold when we get out there on the water," Tim said. "I hope you've got a warm sweater in that bag."

"Nope," Francis said, "just money."

Shortly after 2:30, the Avalon was cut free from the ice chute. Francis watched from his seat atop a life raft fastened to the foredeck as Stead started the engines and the crew cast off all lines. When they reached the lighthouse at the mouth of Gloucester Harbor, Stead powered up the twin diesels and steered a course around the breakwater and into the light chop of the Atlantic.

Bright light poured from the pilothouse and illuminated the deck in front of Francis, but ahead was nothing but the black of night. Stead steered while his navigator stowed away the charts of Georges Bank and read the information feeding in from the navigational satellite miles above. The navigator transferred the numbers into their Loran unit, followed by the exact latitude and longitude where they'd meet up with the IRA boats: Porcupine Bank, one hundred miles off the coast of Ireland.

When Tim had finished his welding work, he joined Francis on deck and brought him a heavy sweater. The temperature had already dropped to fifty degrees and Francis welcomed some extra warmth. It was a roomy sweater, and he put it on over his suit coat. "Thanks, Tim."

"We're swinging by the Nahant lighthouse soon. Jerry's there. We'll radio him at 3:30. After that, we'll head toward Ireland. I've got cabin number two just fore of the galley. I'll leave the bottom bunk free for you. The head's three doors down. You'll know it by the stink. Speaking of which, I'm cooking breakfast at seven. Don't stay out here too long. You might catch a rogue wave and get soaked." Tim wished Francis a good night and went below for a few hours of sleep.

The trawler dipped and rose with the swells, and as the wind shifted Francis caught a strong whiff of diesel exhaust. He watched the lights along the shore moving slowly by and he felt uneasy. It wasn't because of the airport incident or dealing with Phil and his dogs or even Kathleen at the wedding. He pictured another man named Francis Mahoney, his great grandfather, who had journeyed across these same waters over a hundred years before.

It was in Boston where his great grandparents had stepped off the boat from Ireland. Francis Mahoney, his wife Kate and their three-year-old son, Tommy, Francis' grandfather, settled into a two-room flat in the crowded Irish tenements strung along the waterfront. Francis Sr. found a job as a longshoreman unloading boats on the waterfront. A strong man, he stood six-foot-three and was well-suited for the rugged work.

On a September afternoon, during his first week unloading barrels of nails from the schooner Valencia, Francis was struck in the back of the head by a thirty-pound tackle that had swung loose across the deck. It hit him with such force that the twenty-six-year-old Irishman was dead when his body hit the Valencia's deck.

It was only his third day on the job, so nobody knew exactly where he lived or even his full name, except that he was Irish and lived somewhere along the waterfront. His body was strapped to a cart and carried through the crowded Irish slums. From street to street, the cart was wheeled as the man pushing it called up to the tenement windows, "Who owns this Irisher? Who owns this Irisher?" The grieving widow Kate and her son, Tommy, were fortunate enough to have relatives in South Boston where they were taken in.

More than his mother's family, the Flynns, Francis had seen those early Mahoneys as the people who laid the foundation for Jimmy and Matthew and himself.

Whenever he doubted himself, Francis would always fall back on this idea as a reason not to fuck up the one life he had been given. The efforts of all his ancestors would not be wasted, but built upon, as one brick after another builds a strong house. Let Jimmy follow in Salty's footsteps, and work within the system. Francis would work outside it. And succeed bigger than his great grandfather could have ever imagined.

The boat's movement created a steady breeze on deck. A bank of clouds had broken, revealing stars that seemed oppressively bright. The engines of the Avalon slowed. Off the starboard bow, the Nahant Lighthouse sent rhythmic pulses of red light across the water. The trawler was less than a mile offshore, close enough for Francis to see streetlights onshore.

The trawler bobbed in the light chop for about five minutes. Then the captain revved up the engines once again, and steered the Avalon in a slow curving arc onto a course dead east. Haven Stead stood alone at the helm, but was suddenly joined in the wheelhouse by Tim Drago. He was supposed to be heading off to sleep but had just received some interesting news from Jerry McNulty back on shore.

Francis stood up and turned to the land disappearing behind him. The lighthouse continued to send red flashes in the Avalon's wake. He was leaving his home, the shore where his great grandparents had landed, and was returning the family's blood to Ireland. His relationship with the old country wasn't just about business anymore.

Chapter Three
South Boston's Favorite Son

The murder of Salty Mahoney could not have come at a worse time for his son Jimmy, who was having the most challenging week of his political career. The forty-year-old state senator currently served as the Senate Majority Leader and was only days away from being named the new Senate president. The position was second only to the governor of Massachusetts, and sometimes trumping the governor, in the state's power structure.

It was not so much the fact that his father had been murdered, but the fact that Francis had been implicated in it. Having a brother who was generally assumed to work in the underworld was a cross Jimmy bore his whole political life, beginning in the state House of Representatives eighteen years earlier.

People had always wondered whether there was any collusion between Jimmy and Francis, whether Jimmy's actions as a politician were serving to promote the interests of his brother. Jimmy had been able to put those questions to rest for the most part over the years, but he could never make them go away completely. There was always a political opponent or a fringe reporter with a grudge who would raise the question when it served their purpose. Francis' connection to the murder resurrected the question.

On top of that, Jimmy had Senate adversaries in his own party who could try to capitalize on the current situation to derail his rise to the Senate presidency by withholding their support in a Democratic caucus vote, which was how the new president would be selected. This was particularly possible among senators representing the suburbs and rural Massachusetts, where the names of Salty and Jimmy Mahoney were inextricably linked to Boston's school desegregation crisis in the seventies.

In those areas, people retained a very negative opinion of both Mahoneys, and a majority of them believed Francis had committed the murder. It wasn't based on proof, because the police had not charged Francis with the murder itself. Nor had the police stated that there was any evidence linking him conclusively to the murder. The matter inhabited a grey area, so people made judgments based on how they felt about South Boston and the Mahoney family.

Belief in Francis' guilt decreased closer to South Boston. It was almost zero in South Boston itself, where people considered their gangster hero incapable of the act. They saw it as another attempt to assassinate the character of the Mahoneys by those outside South Boston. The community considered itself the perennial underdog in political battles against the Protestant Yankee establishment ever since the Irish set foot in Boston.

Jimmy had no idea how much support he may have lost in the Senate. Most of his time on Sunday and Monday had been spent with the Boston Police detectives handling the murder case, and making arrangements for the wake on Tuesday and the funeral on Wednesday.

The detectives told Jimmy what he already knew, that Francis was wanted for questioning in the murder but not for the murder. He asked them to elaborate on the distinction. Jimmy was a lawyer and understood the finer points, but he wanted to hear from the detectives how they saw the distinction, in the hope they might disclose what direction the investigation was heading.

Were they slowly building a case against Francis for the killing, or did they merely want to ask him questions as "wanted for questioning" implied? The detectives' answers were elusive and vague, but Jimmy sensed a tone in their responses that gave him reason to be optimistic.

Members of the press had no trouble drawing conclusions, and some were exploiting the situation to settle old scores with Jimmy. Reports were circulating in newspapers and on TV and radio stations that gave a wink and a nod to the notion of "wanted for questioning," suggesting that as soon as the scales tipped in the discovery and examination of evidence, Francis would be formally charged with murder.

At five-thirty on Tuesday evening Jimmy, his wife Peg, and their three oldest children drove to Malloy's Funeral Home on Dorchester Street for the evening wake. They parked in a lot three blocks away because all the street parking had been taken. A line of people already stretched from the front of the funeral home for a half a block up to Broadway. They were waiting for the wake to open to the public at six o'clock.

At five-feet-nine, Jimmy Mahoney was the shortest of Salty's three boys. Although he wasn't overweight, there was a plumpness to his face. It was the result of medication Jimmy took for a heart condition inherited from the Flynn side of the family. It kept him from joining the military during the Vietnam War, but otherwise had little effect on his health.

He was fond of hair gel and used it daily to create a head of hair that was perfectly parted and ready for any combination of wind and weather. At forty, he still had that quintessential altar boy look. That was the impression Jimmy wanted the world to form of him.

Although he had chosen the same profession as his father, Jimmy was in many ways the political opposite of Salty, whose reputation preceded him in a way that forced Jimmy to compensate for it. Where Salty Mahoney was reactionary and bombastic, Jimmy Mahoney had to prove to the world that he would be reflective and reasoned.

With his look and his demeanor, Jimmy evoked the consummate statesman. The people of South Boston were not fooled, however. They knew he was as much of a fighter as Salty. He just fought with velvet gloves instead of bare fists. And they honored him with the same loyalty they gave his father.

At the wake, three Boston Police officers from South Boston had volunteered their time to direct car and pedestrian traffic in front of the funeral home, an old Victorian renovated when its owner sold it to the Malloys forty years earlier. Hundreds of people were expected to show up for the wake, including current and retired politicians, neighbors, friends and devoted fans of Salty's old radio show, Salty's Box.

His job as radio talk show host began in the late seventies and was Salty's way of cashing in on his popularity. The devoted listeners of Salty's Box became known as Salty's Dogs. Over the airwaves from eight in the morning until noon, Salty did what he had done on the campaign trail. He stirred people up. About politics, the economy, the drug problem, Boston traffic, the price of parking, the controversially painted oil tanks visible from the expressway in Dorchester.

The subject was secondary. What mattered more was that people could tune in Monday through Friday morning and get pissed off about something. It was like an anger high, and the city of Boston was full of addicts anxious for their next fix. The show ended in 1985 when the wounds from school desegregation began to heal, and the owners of the station grew sensitive to Salty's bare-knuckled approach to discourse.

Some of the fans of the radio show were lined up in front of the funeral home. As Jimmy and his family walked past, they recognized him and offered their sympathies. He waved in gratitude. Near the front, someone stepped out of line to speak with Jimmy. It was Edward Mullins, a reporter who held a long-standing grudge against Jimmy.

Only rarely in the eighteen years of his life in politics had Jimmy spoken at length to any reporters. After having his community vilified by the media during school desegregation, Jimmy vowed to never trust the press again.

The case of his father's murder would be no different. It was not a sense of decency, Jimmy knew, that was now permeating the editorial meetings of the local press. The Salty Mahoney killing was headline news. Two stations had already run special programs on the life of the man and another was scheduled for tomorrow night.

"Can I have a word with you, senator?" Mullins asked.

Jimmy turned to Peg, "You take the kids in. I'll be a couple of minutes behind you."

The most striking thing about Mullins was an overgrown beard that hid his mouth. When he talked, it sometimes seemed as if his voice were coming from someone else. He was a serious man committed to the task of uncovering corruption, whatever form it took. Jimmy and Mullins had only one thing in common, their mistrust of Boston's two mainstream newspapers, the *Boston Globe* and the *Boston Herald*. Jimmy considered them equally disdainful in their treatment of himself and his community. He enjoyed remarking that the only difference between the two papers was that the *Globe* used verbs.

Mullins reported for the *Boston Oracle*, a weekly and proudly liberal publication that devoted most of its pages to the city's cultural and social scene. Occasionally it published an attack by Mullins on one of Boston's politicians. Although he loved to claim that he never read any newspapers, Jimmy did, including the *Boston Oracle*, if only to determine whether Mullins had ended his vendetta against the Mahoney family.

When Mullins had joined the *Oracle* two years earlier in 1985, he was determined to make a reputation for himself with his first feature-length story. His subject would be Francis Mahoney, who seemed to be well known all over Boston but never profiled in any local publication. Sure that there must be a hidden connection between the worlds of the famous Mahoney brothers, Mullins wanted to see if he could uncover it.

He began by asking politicians and members of the Boston Police Department whether they knew of any political deals the senator had made that might have aided Francis in rising so quickly to the top of his profession. The politicians offered nothing, and the cops answered by telling Mullins that there really weren't any connections of the kind he was looking for. They also suggested Mullins insert the term "alleged" when connecting Francis Mahoney's name with "Mafia" or "mob." Mullins persisted to the point where the cops grew silent.

Two days later, while Mullins was relaxing at an outdoor café in Quincy Market, he was approached by a stranger who looked like a bouncer at one of the local clubs. The man wore a Red Sox cap and walked up to the table where Mullins sat.

"Is your name Edward Mullins?" the man asked.

"Yes, it is," Mullins said. "Why?"

"My name is Francis Mahoney and I kill people for a living. Do you understand?"

Francis didn't wait for an answer but walked away as casually as he had approached. That same afternoon, Mullins applied for his firearm identification card and a license to carry a handgun, then purchased a thirty-eight caliber pistol illegally because he didn't want to wait for the paperwork to clear. For the next two weeks, he slept with all the lights on in his Brookline apartment. No profile was written. Mullins had been utterly intimidated, and when the story got around, he felt equally humiliated.

Francis Mahoney had done it, but since Mullins couldn't touch him, he decided to go after his senator brother who, Mullins thought it safe to assume, had to stay within the limits of the law. He began regular attacks on Jimmy in the *Oracle*.

Eventually Jimmy heard about Mullins' encounter with Francis. He wasn't amused. The Boston press may have attacked him relentlessly, sometimes mercilessly, over his stand during school desegregation, but on the subject of his brother Francis, at least the two main papers went no further than to associate the two brothers by name in some articles. They had long been convinced that the professional worlds of the two brothers did not intersect, and to suggest that in any way would be unethical. Unless, of course, proof surfaced.

Jimmy intended to dismiss Mullins as quickly as he could before joining his family in the funeral home.

"What can I do for you?" he asked.

"First, my sympathies to you and your family."

"Thank you. Anything else?" Jimmy asked with a hint of impatience.

Mullins pulled a sheet of paper from his coat and began reading from it. "As you know, two of your colleagues in the Senate have pleaded guilty to taking bribes from the New York construction firm of D'Angelo and Sons. It's been reported that Senate President Hurley also received a campaign contribution from the same source…"

Jimmy sensed where the question was heading, and it was the very place Jimmy didn't want to go. Now he regretted stopping for Mullins, who was rambling on.

"…Last night a bill was passed by the Senate and approved by the House this morning. The bill had an outside section attached that would penalize Boston by reducing state aid to the city by fifty million dollars if it proceeded with the construction of a waste disposal facility at South Bay. Considering the possible connections between this and your current role as Senate Majority Leader…"

Jimmy glanced at his watch impatiently and was about to walk away when he heard the sound of an overhead jet. South Boston lay on the southerly approach to nearby Logan Airport, and a jet descending over the funeral home drowned out the end of Mullins' carefully constructed question with the deafening roar of its engines.

Mullins tried in vain to shout the conclusion to his question but finally gave up. The noise of the jet gradually faded and became replaced by the sound of the funeral home's awning flapping in the breeze.

Jimmy dramatically cupped a hand to his ear. "I'm sorry, Mr. Mullins, but I'm afraid I didn't catch the end of your question. I'd ask you to repeat it from the start, but I wouldn't want to burden you with such a Herculean task. Good evening, Mr. Mullins," Jimmy said, then walked away.

If Jimmy was right about where the question was going, Mullins had indeed done his homework. Jimmy was the one who had convinced Senate President Hurley to attach an "outside section" to a funding bill the previous night. The fact that it was attached "in the dead of night," as news reports were now saying, raised suspicions further.

An outside section was a way to add something to a bill that had never been debated by the whole chamber or brought up in committee. It was attached anonymously, so there were no fingerprints, making it a great way to reward someone, perhaps by adding years of service to a state employee's record to make him immediately eligible for a full pension. It was also the perfect means to exact revenge on a political opponent without being caught.

* * * * *

At the end of the front hallway of the funeral home, an open archway led to the main parlor. Although smoking was prohibited inside, the air in the room held a trace of cigar smoke. The parlor was a large space decorated to create an intimate atmosphere. Comfortable couches and chairs lined three walls, and lamps in all four corners were turned down low to cast a subdued light. Above the seldom-used fireplace was a portrait of Cardinal Cushing.

Jimmy had been to many wakes at Malloy's, especially over the last few years when many young people in South Boston had lost their lives to drug overdoses and suicides. His experience at entering the main parlor was more intense this time. Maybe it was because the crowd was sparse. Only immediate family was allowed inside until the wake opened to the public at six o'clock. Joining them was Father Coffey, a priest from St. Brendan's Church.

He was the same age as Jimmy, and the two were good friends. Father Coffey was originally from northern California and had made the considerable effort necessary to adjust to the culture of Boston. He also took time to get to know his parishioners and the history of their community.

On entering the funeral parlor, Jimmy lost his breath momentarily at the sight of his father's casket. It stood at the front of the room surrounded by a crescent of elaborate bouquets. In the ceiling above the casket were three small spotlights fitted with special bulbs designed to cast a pinkish glow. At open-casket wakes, the lights lent the deceased a vital, if artificial, radiance. For his father's wake, the spotlights had been repositioned to highlight the flowers and draw attention away from the fact that the casket was closed.

Father Coffey greeted Jimmy with a pat on the back. The two had spoken several times since Sunday, and Jimmy appreciated having a friend with whom he could share his personal experience of the tragedy.

Matthew and Anne had arrived at Malloy's fifteen minutes earlier. Anne was keeping Jimmy's three children entertained by teaching them how to play Rock, Paper, Scissors. The two girls were enthralled with the game, but Tommy, named after his grandfather Thomas Salty Mahoney, was having difficulty with the concept. He couldn't understand why the rock didn't win every time.

That Sunday, Jimmy and Peg had Anne and Matthew over to their house, where they all helped each other overcome the initial shock of the tragedy. Father Coffey stopped by as well. They shared the traditional Sunday afternoon dinner of roast beef and peeled baked potatoes. Later they went for a walk along Carson Beach and ended up at St. Monica's Church, where Father Coffey led them in praying the rosary.

At the wake, Jimmy noticed that Matthew still carried a bit of the shocked, disconnected look that they all had on Sunday. He was talking with Matthew when Leo Malloy entered the parlor and gathered the family to explain how the wake would proceed. The announced closing time was nine o'clock, but Leo agreed to

Jimmy's request to have the parlor stay open until ten if there remained a line of mourners outside.

Leo Malloy was in his late sixties and had served as the funeral director as long as Jimmy could remember. Every time Jimmy had seen him, Leo was wearing a dark suit, the expected attire for a funeral director. Everything was pressed and clean, but there was always something disheveled about the way Leo looked. Jimmy suspected it was the uncombed white hair and the bad teeth that created the impression. Leo lived alone in the top floor of the funeral home, and Jimmy imagined Leo spending most of his day in his pajamas, then jumping into his suit moments before a wake began.

"We have about five minutes until we invite others inside," Leo said calmly. Turning to Father Coffey, he continued, "Father, if you'd like to say a few words now. If you need more time let me know and we'll wait before opening the door."

Father Coffey gave a warm smile and clasped his hands around his bible. They had all spent time together Sunday and gotten to know each other, so there was a comforting familiarity to the priest's presence. His prayer called for the grace of God to visit the Mahoney family in their time of grief.

"All tragedies test us," he concluded. "There are many ways to deal with them, but in the end we must surrender to the will of God and accept his love. Only in accepting his love can we be healed."

The kneeler before the casket extended its entire length, so Peg brought the children over with her, and they offered up their prayers. Like Jimmy, Peg was Irish American and had grown up in South Boston. She had pale skin that blossomed with reddish-brown freckles when she spent any time in the sun. Jimmy teasingly referred to it as her Irish tan.

Peg was a no-nonsense woman who had a great sense of humor, which was seldom obvious in her stern expression. Although Jimmy could speak with eloquence and charm when the occasion called for it, Peg always said exactly what she thought using as few words as possible. It was not the kind of personality that suited her to be a politician's wife, but in Jimmy's case it was a pretty good match. Neither one had any interest in courting public opinion. Jimmy was devoted to the interest of his community, and Peg's focus was on being a good mother to their five children, plain and simple.

When she and the children were finished at the kneeler, Peg gestured to Matthew. He and Anne had already had their time there, so Jimmy spent a few moments before his father.

He closed his eyes and prayed for the man's soul. He'd said many prayers since receiving news of the murder. His first had been composed at two o'clock Sunday morning after he had been woken by a phone call from the Boston Police.

Jimmy had been in a stunned state as he dressed hastily and drove the half mile from his house to E. Third Street where he had the unenviable task of identifying his father's body. The scene would have been horrific enough had it been a stranger, but to see his father's neck and face disfigured by bullets in such a gruesome fashion left Jimmy reaching for the wall.

Before the police had said anything about Francis' culpability, Jimmy had considered the possibility that his brother had committed the murder. There was the fight at the wedding, the threat heard by all, and Jimmy was aware of so much more in the turbulent relationship between his father and Francis that would yield motive enough for ten murders.

Yet it took Jimmy only seconds of consideration before dismissing the possibility. He had watched his younger brother Francis grow up and get himself into one scrape after another, and Jimmy had watched him develop a code of ethics that would allow many transgressions against the law, even some against family and friends, but taking the life of his own father fell outside of what would ever be permissible.

Jimmy's animosity toward his father was more benign. Growing up, he had been respectful to both his parents, devoted to the Catholic faith and hard-working in his studies. It earned him the best response that Salty had to offer as a father: neglect. This absence of bond continued as Jimmy grew up, and the distance between the two only increased as Jimmy stepped into the political arena as a state representative in 1969.

By the time he had managed to create a public image distinct from that of his father's and achieve a degree of success that threatened to eclipse Salty's modest political accomplishments, Salty began speaking badly of his oldest son in private conversations while serving up, at best, luke-warm compliments when questioned in public.

Despite the lack of love and loyalty from his father, Jimmy was able, although not always, to avoid hating the man. He had the love of his mother Nora, who showed him how to stay on the spiritual path while encountering life's challenges.

The Mahoneys had moved into the Old Colony housing project because Salty was such an inconsistent provider for his family. To make ends meet, Nora finally had to get a job at a wholesale company that assembled weekly shipments of health and beauty aids to drug stores.

She worked in a warehouse where it grew cold enough in the winter that she and the other women working there would often need to wear hats and gloves. The job could be tedious, but she enjoyed the security it provided and the camaraderie she shared with the neighborhood women working with her.

Every Sunday, and on many weekdays as well, she and Jimmy walked the short block from the Old Colony housing project to St. Monica's Church, where he served as an altar boy.

As Jimmy surrendered his transgressions every Saturday afternoon during confession, he would also renew his forgiveness of his father. At first, Jimmy considered it a burden to let pass the neglect, indifference and later the betrayal by his father, but at some point Jimmy realized the act of forgiveness was an unburdening. It was through forgiveness that he freed himself from the temptation to hate and to respond in kind.

Francis would have been lucky to receive the same neglect from his father. Instead, he got the full force of Salty's attention. Many times, Jimmy's act of forgiveness had more to do with how his father physically and psychologically abused Francis. Jimmy would witness the beatings and hear the abuse, and those trespasses against his younger brother were the hardest to forgive. They raised an anger in Jimmy that tested his faith almost as much as the neglect Salty showed to their mother after she began her battle with cancer.

It was Francis who Nora worried about most—to the point where she sometimes seemed to be ignoring Jimmy for weeks on end, even during their time together in church, where she would go on about the most recent trouble Francis had gotten into. Or she would air the frustrations she had with her husband.

One night when Jimmy was up late studying for the exam to get into Boston College High School, his mother knocked on the door of the bedroom Jimmy shared with Francis and three-year-old Matthew. It was one o'clock in the morning and Jimmy had draped a dark towel over the lamp to avoid disturbing the sleep of his brothers.

His mother walked Jimmy out to the couch where she sat him down and told him in her soothing Irish lilt, "I want you to know that I don't love you any less than the other boys. It's just that you've outgrown me worrying, it seems. You take care of yourself like a young man should do. It's the rest of the family that takes my time, and I know I do more worrying than I ought to.

"So know I love you, and know that you're going to do well in life. I've no doubt of that, James. Just keep yourself in school and go as far as you're able to with your education. Keep your mind focused on the place you want to be someday, and look beyond the little world we occupy here. Keep yourself free of life's traps, and love God in everything you do. That's all."

It was a piece of advice Jimmy would later hear echoed in studying St. Augustine, who said, "Faith is to believe what you do not yet see; the reward for this faith is to see what you believe."

The Mahoneys moved out of Old Colony when Jimmy was starting his junior year with the Jesuits at Boston College High School. Salty had suddenly gotten a good-paying job at Massport, the Massachusetts Port Authority. He also came into a sum of money to put a down payment on a house. The job and the money, Jimmy learned years later, were the result of Salty essentially blackmailing executives working for the Merrill Lynch brokerage house in Boston. It was also probably connected to the construction of a housing development in East Boston, but that was as much as Jimmy could discover.

He spent little time in the new house on E. Third Street, doing most of his studying at school, the library and anyplace else that offered free light and a moderately quiet atmosphere. He felt guilty about withdrawing from family life, particularly for failing to be much of an older brother to Matthew, who was much younger and growing up in South Boston during the terrible time of school desegregation.

As a kid, Matthew had always been drawn to Francis, and Jimmy just hoped that his youngest brother was taking all the good Francis had to offer and ignoring the rest.

81

Jimmy relived the memories, the feelings expressed and those kept buried, as he concluded his prayer before his father's casket. There were too many emotions stirred up by the murder to make sense of them anytime soon. Jimmy would sort them out in due time, but there were other tasks needing his focus at the moment, so he tucked away the love and the hate, the anger and the pity, and everything he ever felt and thought about his father into an imaginary box and sealed it tight. It was how he had survived being his father's son all these years, and Jimmy Mahoney had become quite good at it.

* * * * *

Peg brought her three children home to a babysitter who was minding the two youngest, and returned shortly after Mr. Malloy opened the front door of the funeral home at six o'clock. The flow of mourners began. They entered quietly and respectfully, but within a short time the parlor was alive with conversation. The sound of serene music coming from the recessed ceiling-speakers was barely audible.

Jimmy, Peg and Matthew stood in reception. Before offering condolences to the Mahoney family, each mourner spent time on the kneeler, offering up prayers. When finished, they made the sign of the cross. The old saying generally held true, that the bigger the sinner, the more dramatic the crossing. There came a muffled laugh from those nearby when Ned O'Neill, finishing at the kneeler, nearly knocked over a floral bouquet with his exaggerated gesture.

There were members of the extended family, neighbors, friends, those who had received favors of some sort over the years from Salty or Jimmy, and politicians from across the state. Jimmy thanked each and told them how Salty would have appreciated their kind thoughts. He did this respectfully, while keeping it as brief as possible to keep the line moving.

Jimmy was thanking Skippy Ahern, an N Street neighbor, for his patience in line and for his sympathies when he heard a commotion in the hallway. A woman was making an accusation in rather strong language. Other voices joined in to rebuke her for doing so at a time and place that were inappropriate. Mr. Malloy moved rapidly to the scene and succeeded in calming things down.

It had all happened out of Jimmy's view, but he had a pretty good idea who was being addressed. The woman accused someone of selling his own people out for a handful of headlines. She also told him that the people of South Boston would hand him his ass on a platter in the next election.

As the line edged forward, Jimmy saw Mayor Danny Sullivan, confirming the accuracy of his guess. The mayor had begun hosting meetings across South Boston to explain his Fair Housing Initiative, a new policy of making South Boston's public housing units available on a citywide basis rather than the tradition of putting South Boston residents at the top of the list.

The first meeting was held the night before at an auditorium next to St. Monica's Church. The mayor received a reception that was downright hostile, accompanied with the chant, "Lies, lies, Sullivan lies!" because residents felt he was betraying his election promise to protect South Boston. Sullivan's program had quickly been labeled "forced housing" just as school desegregation in the seventies had been known locally as "forced busing."

It demonstrated Sullivan's willingness to break the tradition of putting South Boston first in everything. He was reaching out to all neighborhoods, particularly the black community, in what was still a racially divided city. This reaching out to all gave Sullivan the citywide support necessary to win an election, but it came with a downside. In winning the race for mayor four years earlier, he had barely won the vote in South Boston and would probably lose the district in his reelection bid in November.

It also illustrated a very telling difference between Danny Sullivan and Jimmy Mahoney, two South Boston politicians who were opposites in every respect except one. They both wanted to be the top political dog in South Boston. Chief of all chieftains.

Jimmy had considered a run for the mayor's office in 1984 in the hope of beating Sullivan to the prize, being the first South Boston resident elected mayor of Boston. It had been the holy grail of every South Boston politician for almost a century.

Jimmy had polls conducted to see how much support his candidacy would receive from various sections of the city. The results shocked him. He had far less support than he expected, and far less than Sullivan in every area except one. South Boston.

In part this was due to his reputation from the days of desegregation. And to the reputation of his father Salty, who had spent his career insulting and inflaming virtually every voting demographic outside of South Boston. Jimmy knew that his only way to outdo Danny Sullivan now was at the state level. Not as governor, because he lacked popularity beyond his own community, but as Senate president, where the electorate he had to win over would be limited to his twenty-nine fellow Democratic senators.

Unlike Jimmy, Sullivan had been a famous athlete in college and jogged almost daily along the Charles River with his chief of police, Ricky McGonagall, who was also from South Boston. Sullivan's face had a weather-beaten look, from time outdoors and from years of lifting pints well into the night.

When he reached Jimmy, the taller Sullivan offered a firm handshake. "This is a terrible thing, Jimmy. Just terrible." If Jimmy was the perennial altar boy, Sullivan was more the perennial parish monsignor. His face and voice revealed a mix of concern and authority, which was somewhat diminished by a slight lisp. "I want you to know that Ricky is making sure this gets all the attention it deserves. We'll find whoever did this thing."

"Thank you, Danny. I'm sure you will."

After a short pause, Sullivan switched gears. "So, I hear you boys were busy up on the hill last night," he said, referring to the State House, which sat atop Beacon Hill across from the Boston Common.

"I hear you had an interesting night yourself," Jimmy said, referring to Sullivan's raucous reception at his public housing meeting.

Sullivan ignored the comment and continued in a hushed voice, "I read about that outside section this morning and I sent a message to Hurley that if he doesn't rescind it in the next twenty-four hours, I'm going to make things very uncomfortable for him."

Hurley was the current Senate president, and he supported Jimmy as his replacement. "Well, I appreciate your showing up tonight to comfort the afflicted, and I'll warn president Hurley that you soon intend to afflict the comfortable." Jimmy smiled.

Sullivan turned to leave, but he was just getting worked up. "Whoever attached that outside section last night should know that he's wasting his time, Jimmy. The governor and I have come to a quiet understanding, and when he gets back into town at the end of the week he'll make a public statement in support of the South Bay plan. When that happens, it's a done deal and you'll just have to learn to live with it."

The outside section was a wholly unexpected attack against Sullivan's plan to build an enormous regional waste disposal facility on a seven-acre plot of land called South Bay. The site was located in the southwestern corner of South Boston and Jimmy Mahoney was determined to defeat the plan.

Because of Jimmy's outside section, if Boston went ahead with construction, as Mayor Sullivan wanted, the city would forfeit fifty million dollars in state aid immediately. Boston would also lose fifty million dollars every year the facility remained in place. The penalty essentially crippled the South Bay plan, and Sullivan was hoping the governor's support would be his wild card.

Word of the outside section and its consequences for Sullivan's plan set off an angry response from Sullivan's spokesman at City Hall, who called it "a midnight mugging of the public's interest in Jack the Ripper proportions." Mayor Sullivan was said to have dismembered an office chair in his conference room when news reached him.

Unlike Sullivan, Jimmy didn't need a public opinion survey or a downtown business association to tell him where to stand on a facility that would include a trash incinerator in his community. South Boston already had an Edison oil-burning plant. It wasn't enough that the residents of South Boston had to breathe filthy air in order that the city have electricity, they were now expected to suck up more foul air as it burned the city's trash. And it wasn't just the residents of Boston eating up power and spewing out trash. It was also the many commuters who left their safe, clean suburban neighborhoods and made their living in downtown Boston.

* * * * *

As Jimmy had observed when he arrived at Malloy's, his youngest brother had not fully gotten over the shock from their father's murder. Since learning of it at the convenience store, Matthew felt as if he were living someone else's life. It was the stuff of nightmares, and he had trouble believing it had really happened.

Jimmy reached him by phone at the hotel Sunday morning. They had never been close as brothers, but it helped Matthew to hear that Jimmy was experiencing the event just as he was. That's when Matthew accepted that it truly was happening to him.

At that point, an anger began to grow. He may have hated his father for years, but the hate was gone now. You couldn't hate a person who wasn't alive anymore, he decided.

Someone hadn't just murdered his father. They had murdered a Mahoney. Matthew felt it as a personal attack. Someone attacking and killing a part of him. A piece of a tree he was connected to. That was how he described the feeling to Anne. His first instinct was to strike back, but he had no idea who to strike.

All day Sunday, he listened to news reports on the radio and TV. He was obsessed with hearing any new information available. At Jimmy's house, he questioned his brother about the conversations Jimmy had with the police. At no point on Sunday or Monday did Matthew believe for a second that his brother Francis had done it.

It was only on Tuesday morning when Matthew was taking a shower that he caught himself imagining Francis committing the act. It only lasted a moment, and he felt embarrassed for letting doubt creep into him. He blamed it on the drumbeat of accusations he was hearing in the media.

At the wake, he was uncomfortable. Part of it was the uncertainty surrounding the murder investigation. Part of it had to do with the task of standing in reception with Jimmy and Peg, hearing how much his father had meant to so many. Matthew recognized some of the people, others he didn't although they recognized him, including an old hockey coach.

There were a few people who didn't recognize Matthew at all. They would look up at him and stare blankly until he announced who he was.

Another discomfort was the new black shoes he was wearing. The comfortable ones he wore to the wedding had come with the rented tux. He hardly ever wore dress shoes, so despite Anne's suggestion to buy shoes that were well-made and comfortable, Matthew instead focused solely on price and bought the cheapest. Now he was paying for it. With each step, the shoes pinched his feet.

Finally, there was the memory of his mother's funeral in the very same parlor thirteen years earlier. It was without a doubt the worst time of his life, and Matthew had no desire to relive it. He checked his watch to see how soon the wake would end and he could leave.

His mother's side of the family were the Flynns. Matthew saw some of them making their way down the reception line. The Mahoneys and the Flynns had never mixed well. Since the death of his mother, they hardly ever mixed at all. Matthew's wedding had been one of the rare exceptions.

The two families represented the polar opposites within the Irish American community. All the Flynns lived in the City Point section at the eastern end of South Boston. It was the more upscale, lace-curtain end of town, where even the triple-decker homes were very well-maintained.

The other end of South Boston was home to light industry and South Boston's housing projects: D Street, Old Harbor and Old Colony, where most of the Mahoneys had grown up. Matthew had been born in Old Colony.

When he was growing up, the City Point kids took every opportunity to give shit to kids from the projects. He got a heavy dose of it when he first moved to City Point at the age of five.

Matthew recognized Aunt Eileen Flynn. She was the older sister of Matthew's mother. Like his mother, Aunt Eileen had arrived in America from Roscommon, Ireland, as a child and still had a hint of brogue in her voice. She was a short woman who stood straight as a rod. Unlike her husband Pete, who had an easygoing manner and usually held an unlit pipe between his lips, Aunt Eileen had a consistent habit of saying exactly what she was thinking and doing it in a provocative way.

After she and Uncle Pete spent a brief time at the kneeler, they took Matthew aside to speak with him. They offered their sympathies for the loss of his father and their congratulations again for his marriage. Then Aunt Eileen got down to business.

"By the way, Matthew, did you mind not getting married in the Catholic Church?"

"That's none of your business, Eileen," Uncle Pete said.

She stared up at Matthew intently while he looked down on her black church hat.

"I just wanted to know whether he knew what it meant when you get married outside the church. That's all."

"Plenty of people do it these days," Uncle Pete said.

"I know how many people do it, Pete. I'm not ignorant."

"She's trying to tell you that you can't get into heaven," Uncle Pete said with a light chuckle.

Aunt Eileen continued, "I'm sure Matthew knows that you're either in the Catholic Church or you're not. Jimmy certainly knows it. He practices what he preaches. I don't mind whose church Matthew gets married in as long as Matthew doesn't mind. That's all I'm saying. His mother's gone and nobody else is going to tell him these things, are they? His father certainly can't do that now."

Matthew wasn't about to take the bait from Aunt Eileen. The way he saw it, most of the Flynns swallowed the Catholic Church hook, line and sinker. His mother had been the least preachy of them all, but even she was hurt when Matthew stopped going to mass.

At twelve, he realized leaving the Church was going to happen sooner or later because people who prayed were somehow weak. You didn't have to be weaker than other people, but if they began seeing you as weak, that's how you were treated. And in a small world that's what you became soon enough. At least that's what he learned as a Mahoney in South Boston.

Aunt Eileen remained standing in front of Matthew while directing her comments to her husband. "Thank goodness Salty started going to church again before all this. Francis is the only other one who doesn't go to church. But he's a whole different story. That one's going to come home in a pine box some day. Or worse yet, they won't find him at all. He'll just disappear. I've heard that happens in his line of work."

Matthew was checking his watch again when he saw his cousins Richard and Bobby arrive. They had been doing some drinking at Donnelley's Pub next to the Old Colony project farther down Dorchester Street. Richard walked around the line of people and headed straight for Matthew, who could smell the whiskey on his cousin before he started speaking. Richard's eyes were bloodshot and he looked worked up.

He reached out his large beefy hands, toughened and scarred by years of hauling on salt-soaked rope, and placed them on Matthew's shoulders. "This is bullshit, Matt." He repeated it. Richard was acting like he was still back at the pub, without seeming to notice the casket nearby. Then he did notice it, and grew silent.

He stared at it for several seconds, murmuring something unintelligible. Aunt Eileen caught him by surprise when she poked him in the side.

"What do you want?" Richard said with irritation.

Aunt Eileen said nothing but pointed toward the kneeler, where Richard's brother Bobby prayed, silently instructing Richard to do the same.

Richard waved a hand dismissively at the kneeler. "Oh, fuck that." Then his energy came back and he said to Matthew, "I gotta talk to you, Matt. Come over here for a minute."

Along with Bobby, they walked to the other end of the parlor where two bay windows looked onto Dorchester Street. Kathleen was there as well, talking to Anne. Richard put his hands on the waist of his jeans and swayed slightly. Neither he nor Bobby were dressed for the wake. "I can't tell you how pissed off I am right now, Matt. We gotta do something about this fucking thing, Matt. Me, you and Bobby. We gotta take care of the motherfucker who did this. Me, you and Bobby," he repeated. "Somebody set Francis up, and that guy's gonna pay."

Richard took a deep breath and drew his hand over his face. "Man, I'm royally pissed off right now."

"I know," Matthew said. "But what are we supposed to do? I don't even know if the cops know who did it. Either that or they're not saying anything. Nobody is naming names so far except Francis'."

Matthew knew exactly how his cousin was feeling. He understood that Richard was itching to take action because that's what he wanted to do too. There was nothing to act on though. Not yet. And the worst way to go into action was piss drunk, which was Richard's general state. Matthew didn't want to discourage him; he just wanted to discourage doing anything at the moment.

Richard put his hands on Matthew's shoulders again. "I'm working on the situation, Matt. I know one of the cops who is involved in this. He was one of the first cops at Salty's house when it happened. I'm gonna go see him tomorrow, and I'm gonna make him tell me what he knows. Then the three of us—me, you and Bobby—we're gonna handle it. We'll find the guy, and we'll take him on a boat ride. I don't care who the fuck it is, even if the guy's in the Mafia."

Kathleen was near enough to hear Richard and understand what he was talking about. She walked over to him.

"Richard, don't bring that kind of crazy talk in here," she said.

Richard seemed surprised by Kathleen. "What? Hey, I'm talking to Matt, OK?"

"You're drunk, and this is a wake, not a bar room. Go back to Donnelley's if you want to do your crazy talk. It doesn't belong here."

Richard was upset at being interrupted, but Kathleen had made her point. He took his hands off Matthew's shoulders. "I gotta take a piss anyway. We'll talk at the funeral tomorrow, Matt. I'll go see that cop I told you about. Then you, me and Bobby…we'll talk about this."

"Alright, Richard. We can talk later. Take it easy tonight, OK?" Matthew said and gave his cousin a pat on the back as he turned to leave Malloy's.

Bobby stayed behind when Richard left. He ran the retail side of Mahoney Seafood and supplemented Richard's catch by shopping at the Boston Fish Market, where fishermen auctioned their haul to wholesalers every day. Bobby wasn't as emotional as Richard, nor as drunk. He told Matthew that Donnelley's Pub was hosting a Salty Mahoney tribute.

"They've got free cold cuts and hot chicken wings. Their beer distributor kicked in five kegs of Guinness, and they're only charging a buck a pint. I'm going back in a minute. You should join us."

"We'll see," Matthew said. Anne probably wouldn't want to go. As he thought about it, Matthew wasn't even sure he wanted to go.

"Another thing, I wanted to apologize. I should have helped you out sooner at the wedding," Bobby said, "but to be honest, I was afraid. I know Francis is my cousin, but he's still somebody I never want to cross. You're his brother, so I figured it was better to let you take him on."

Matthew rubbed the bump on his head. "I didn't exactly do a good job of taking him on."

The Flynns were gathered at the parlor's second bay window. Matthew heard them speculating on the whereabouts of Francis.

"They're saying he went to Ireland," Aunt Pat said. "Or maybe Nova Scotia. I've never been to either place, but I hear they're just beautiful."

"I know that's what the papers say about Francis, Pat, but they're all wrong," Uncle Pete said. "He's sitting on some tropical beach right now."

"I even heard somebody on the radio this morning say they saw Francis fishing for flounder at Castle Island," Aunt Pat said.

Uncle Pete laughed. "I heard someone saw him buying a pretzel in the Park Street subway stop, and that he was wearing a fake mustache. Someone else said he was collecting tolls on the Tobin Bridge. It's like he's everywhere and nowhere. A real Houdini. He better stay in hiding until they catch the guy who really killed Salty."

"Oh, please!" Aunt Eileen said in exasperation. "Will you let go of that fantasy? Anyone with half a brain knows that Francis was the one who did it. They've been on a collision course for years. It started with the gangs at Old Colony, where those kids do God-only-knows-what, and it ended at the wedding. You were as much a witness as I was. 'I'll kill you!' That's what he shouted. And that's what he did."

Aunt Eileen's voice rose with such passion that she could be heard by the Mahoneys. None of them appreciated her commentary, especially Matthew. After convicting Francis, Aunt Eileen shifted her focus to Salty.

"Oh, Salty was popular all right. For all the wrong reasons," Aunt Eileen said.

Uncle Pete replied, "Why don't you just admit it? You didn't like the man because he didn't kowtow to every Father Flaherty that crossed his path."

"If you want to be honest, then let's be honest. The man was a lousy husband, a lousy father and a failure as a politician," Aunt Eileen said.

The comment may have been very close to how Matthew judged his father, but he wasn't about to listen to it from Aunt Eileen. Kathleen saw what was about to happen. As Matthew turned to march over to the Flynns, Kathleen grabbed him by the arm and pulled him back. "No, you don't. Let me take care of this."

Kathleen called over in a voice that was loud enough to be heard by the Flynns but not the rest of the room, "Hey, Eileen, would you knock it off with the Spanish Inquisition over there?"

Aunt Eileen responded with a look of shock, which turned into an icy stare. Kathleen didn't care and said to the Mahoneys, "You know, if someone shouted that in her ear every five minutes for the rest of her life, she might turn into a half-decent person."

* * * * *

Another politician paying his respects that evening was Carl Hurley, the president of the state Senate. His district included Marblehead, the historic seaside town where his family lived. Hurley stood six-foot-four, so he was easy to spot across the funeral parlor. When he reached Jimmy, Hurley leaned down. "Jimmy, have you got a minute?"

Jimmy had been expecting this. He excused himself and led Hurley to a small sitting room off the main hallway.

At fifty-two, Hurley was in his political prime. Like Jimmy, he had followed the traditional career path for state politicians, beginning in the House of Representatives before moving over to the Senate and working his way into the leadership team. For the last eight years he had served as president of the Senate and was planning a run for the governorship once the current governor left office in his quest for the White House.

Hurley's chances had been considered good, even excellent, until the recent rash of Senate scandals within his leadership team. First to fall was the chairman of the Ways and Means Committee, who was charged with taking bribes from a New York construction company working on the new University of Massachusetts campus in Boston. It was what the reporter Mullins was referring to when he questioned Jimmy outside the funeral home.

Next came Hurley's Majority Whip, who was charged with taking bribes from the same company. Jimmy had been baffled when he heard of the scandals. He had seen this happen time and again in the House of Representatives. It was simply stupid, a career and reputation thrown away for a small amount of cash. Politics, Jimmy knew, was not about amassing money, but amassing power.

Although Jimmy was certainly disliked by some because of his stance during school desegregation, he was considered one of the more intelligent and careful members of the Senate. He was also a man of sufficient character to steer clear of corruption and scandal. It was for that reason that Hurley had asked Jimmy to move into the vacant position of Majority Whip, where he was responsible for keeping an accurate tally of how senators intended to vote on a piece of legislation. It was considered the first stepping stone to the presidency.

Three months later, Hurley's Majority Leader, his second in command, became the next to be indicted in the construction scandal. Jimmy once again moved up when Hurley asked him to take the job.

That might have been the end of the scandals, but in the process of presenting his defense, the former Majority Leader revealed information implicating Hurley in the scandal as well.

The press discovered that Hurley had received a political contribution from the construction company. A two thousand dollar check had been sent to the president's political campaign, and it had been deposited into his reelection account. Hurley claimed it was an innocent mistake and immediately returned the money.

Although he was able to avoid legal repercussions, Hurley's hope of running for governor vanished. The only way to clear the stench of corruption from the Senate was for Hurley to step down as president and make his exit from the political stage within a reasonable time.

That had been in early June. For the next two months, Hurley did little but tread water politically. Jimmy would occasionally spot the president walking through the shadowy hallways of the State House like a man trapped in a nightmare. Hurley seemed to be waiting for an angel of redemption to appear and restore his political future.

Public pressure for his resignation mounted, and at the end of August, Hurley finally accepted the inevitable. At this point, his only wish was to end his political career with some degree of honor. His final decision would be to anoint his successor.

In his new role as Majority Leader, Jimmy helped President Hurley shape the agenda and decide which pieces of legislation would be brought up for consideration. It was the traditional position of heir apparent to the presidency. Nonetheless, many assumed

93

Hurley would choose someone other than the senator from South Boston. Even the *Boston Globe* dismissed the possibility and didn't bother writing editorials critical of Jimmy as the successor. Had the editors at the *Boston Globe* known of Hurley's intention to name Jimmy, they would have used barrels of ink to thwart it.

The caucus vote to officially place Jimmy into the presidency was scheduled for that Monday. Because of publicity surrounding Salty's murder, Hurley had postponed it.

In the funeral parlor's small sitting room, Jimmy looked at Hurley's face. The man seemed tired. "Thanks for stopping by, Carl."

"Of course, Jimmy. My goodness, I'm still trying to take this all in."

"I think everybody is. I know I certainly am."

Hurley sat on a brown leather couch across from Jimmy. The couch had been so worn over the years that Hurley sank deeply into its collapsed cushions. With some difficulty he leaned forward. "You've got responsibilities here, so I'll get to the point. I'm afraid the situation has changed on the caucus vote."

Jimmy's heart sank at the news. He had not spent enough time at the State House since the previous Friday to get any gauge on the situation. "How so?"

"If all this hadn't happened, it was looking good, as you know, for a Monday caucus. You had it by two or three votes. Now it's flipped and, by my count, you're down by the same margin."

"Who are we talking about?"

"It begins with an old fan of yours. George Corbin. He's taken it up as a personal mission to turn votes against you."

"My dear old friend Corbin," Jimmy said.

George Corbin was the senator from Wellesley, one of the state's wealthiest suburban towns. He and Jimmy's dislike of each other went back to school desegregation. Corbin was in favor of it and highly critical of South Boston's resistance to it. He said that only a bigot would fight against a plan to bring the races together, and he labeled South Boston an enclave of racism.

Jimmy didn't mind the fact that Corbin disagreed with him, but he did mind the vitriol. He was also angered by Corbin's hypocrisy when Corbin voted against a measure that would have included suburbs in an expanded school desegregation program. Still, after joining the Senate, Jimmy maintained a respectful working relationship with the man.

"Corbin has managed to peel away four others who were supporting you. It's not your father's murder making the difference but...and I hope you don't mind me saying...your brother's involvement in it."

"Francis did not kill my father, Carl."

"I know, Jimmy. I mean...look, Corbin's using it. That's all I'm saying. He's digging in the dirt for that, and dredging up all the crap from desegregation too."

"I'm fine with that," Jimmy said. "I can beat him on that field."

Hurley continued, "I've heard them being called the Gang of Five, and Corbin is their informal spokesman. They're in search of a senator to champion as my replacement."

"I think I can guess who their number one choice will be," Jimmy said.

"No, Corbin's not proposing himself."

"Then I bet they don't even have anybody specific in mind, at least not yet. It's all about stopping me first. Finding someone else can come later."

Hurley sat back and rubbed his eyes. "Oh God, I just want to get this thing over with. For the most part, I've enjoyed my job, but this part has been the biggest pain in the ass. I need to wrap it up, Jimmy, and if it's not with you it'll have to be somebody else, I'm afraid."

"I understand that, Carl. If it doesn't go my way, you know I'll support whoever you recommend."

Hurley's physical stature gave him a presence and authority that people assumed a leading statesman should have. His expression could easily shift from serious to affable according to what the situation required, but Jimmy had seen little of the affable in his face for weeks.

Hurley ran his fingers through his thinning hair. "That's the trouble. I don't have anybody to recommend. I considered the possibilities again today. Many of them have been accused at some point of, you know, 'influence handicaps.'" Hurley had never been uncomfortable discussing the subject of corruption and bribe-taking until his own situation surfaced, at which point he began reaching for euphemisms.

"And the Senate's like junior high with all the cliques and hallway gossip and old feuds. Everybody would be bringing baggage to the job. One of them will have to do, though."

Jimmy wasn't sure if he was being told in an indirect way that he was out of contention, but it seemed more likely that Hurley was thinking out loud. He did that a lot and made people think he was leaning one way on an issue when he was really leaning the other way.

"I'd like a chance to fight for the votes first, if that's OK with you, Carl."

"Yes, of course. I'm not saying you can't. You just can't do it for very long."

"How long will you give me?"

"The end of the week. It's all you should need, Jimmy. Trust me, I know how these things go. Voting positions are usually like drying cement. They get pretty well set in a short time. If you can't change the votes by Friday, you'd be wasting your time. It would be a waste of my time as well, and I don't intend to stay in this job one second longer than I absolutely have to."

Jimmy remembered Sullivan's threat and said, "Sullivan stopped by earlier and was worked up about the outside section. He said if it's not rescinded in twenty-four hours, he'll respond. I imagine his man Abbott will cook up a media stunt."

"That's the mayor's strong suit. If your votes aren't there in the caucus by the end of Friday, Jimmy, I will rescind it. That's when the governor's back in town. Until then, Sullivan won't have anybody to cry to, so let him put on his media show."

Hurley struggled to raise himself from the couch. He failed once, then groaned with his second attempt, which was successful. They shook hands and Hurley made his way out. Jimmy rejoined the family in the crowded parlor. As he continued to receive mourners, his mind was also engaged in a shuffling of cards, an assessment of everybody and everything he knew that was in play, not just in the Senate but elsewhere. Then he considered other cards that were not in play but might be drawn into the game by one trick or another.

Finally, he focused on what his mother had instructed him to focus on so many years before—on the place where he wanted to be when all this was over, and not the place where he stood right now.

At ten o'clock Mr. Malloy turned out the bright lights illuminating the sign in front of the funeral home. One by one, other lights were extinguished, and the crowd in the parlor thinned to five. Father Coffey, Jimmy, Peg, Matthew and Anne. Outside, the music coming from Donnelley's could be heard clearly.

The five walked down the front steps to the sidewalk and said goodbye to each other until the morning when they would attend the funeral at St. Monica's Church. Matthew shook hands with the priest and thanked him. Father Coffey was not the kind of priest Matthew had been used to growing up. In those days, the priests were hard-nosed and strict. Anybody who messed around with them was likely to get a hook to the jaw. It happened to Matthew once. Those priests were some pretty tough bastards.

In contrast, Father Coffey was a friendly guy who seemed to meet people as an equal. Matthew heard that he didn't mind a dirty joke or sharing pizza and beer just for the sake of hanging out, not so he could sneak in a sermon.

"You're alright, Father," Matthew told him. "I wish there were priests like you when I was growing up."

Father Coffey smiled, "I'm about to put in a plug for the Catholic Church…just to warn you…but you wouldn't be disappointed, Matt, if you decided to stop by a church again sometime. There have been some changes you might appreciate."

Matthew smiled back and put his hand on the priest's shoulder. "That's nice of you to offer, Father, but I've turned a corner on that one." When the priest tried to say more, Matthew cut him off. "Don't worry now. I remember what a cross looks like, so I can always scan the horizon for a church if I change my mind."

Father Coffey chuckled. "OK, Matt. Fair enough. Sleep well tonight, both of you," he said with a nod to Anne. "We'll see you in the morning."

Matthew and Anne were half a block away when Matthew heard Jimmy calling his name. He walked back and the two stood alone in front of the steps to Malloy's.

"I have a favor to ask, Matt. Peg and I are going to have our hands full tomorrow morning with preparations at the church and getting ready to have everybody back at the house for food and drinks after the burial. I won't have time to stop by the house and pick up Mom's photo albums. They go way back to our time in Old Colony and Mom did such a wonderful job of putting them together. It would be nice to have them at the house later for people to look through and reminisce. Anyway, I'd appreciate it if you could swing by Dad's house before the funeral and pick them up."

"Alright," Matthew said. "Do I need a key?"

"The spare key is still hidden in the garage. I used it a week ago and put it back behind the flower pots. And the photo albums are in the basement in a bright red box. It looks like a big hat box. You may have to poke around to find it."

"OK, I can do that, Jimmy," Matthew said.

"Thanks. We'll see you tomorrow."

The question of Francis' guilt was one that Matthew wanted to talk about. Not with Richard or Bobby but someone who was smart enough and sober enough to give an intelligent opinion.

"Hey, Jimmy," Matthew said as Jimmy had turned to leave.

"Yes?"

"I hate to ask this again, but do you absolutely believe that Francis didn't do it? I mean, I don't think so myself, but nobody knows for sure yet. And I keep hearing the same stupid shit on the radio."

Jimmy patted his brother on the shoulder and smiled. "Even the strongest faith can't exist without a measure of doubt." Matthew looked puzzled, so Jimmy added, "Like I told you before, Francis didn't kill Dad. Believe that."

Chapter Four
I Will Follow

St. Monica's Church was down the street and around the corner from Malloy's funeral home. Across from the church sat the squat brick buildings of the Old Colony housing project where the Mahoney family had lived for a number of years. There were twenty-two buildings in the project, all packed closely together. The three-story structures held up to forty apartments each. It was the kind of place where everybody knew each other's business.

In front of the church Wednesday morning, large bouquets were being delivered as small groups of mourners began gathering for the funeral. The politicians would show up later, like movie stars at a premiere. These early birds were the working people of South Boston. The bus drivers, construction workers, grocery store clerks, people who worked the third shift at the Gillette factory. Neighbors who had volunteered to hold campaign signs for Salty Mahoney on street corners in crummy weather.

Some of them owed their jobs to Salty, or the fact that they now lived in a nice house rather than the projects. They were the people who truly loved him and had shown the same degree of loyalty and devotion over the years that he had shown toward South Boston. They all remembered the day during school desegregation, known in South Boston as "forced busing" or "the busing crisis," when he stood defiantly in front of a phalanx of riot police and declared that he was willing to take a bullet for The Town.

Matthew and Anne left Ipswich at nine o'clock Wednesday morning. Joan Boushay had invited them to stay with her as long as necessary. They had moved into Anne's old bedroom upstairs and rescheduled their honeymoon flight for Thursday, the day after the funeral, leaving them six days in Ireland rather than ten.

Matthew wanted to leave Ipswich early in case the roads going into Boston were crowded. Traffic was light and they arrived at St. Monica's Church at ten, an hour before the funeral mass was to begin.

Kathleen Sutliff stood on the front steps and waved when she saw Matthew and Anne approaching.

"Jimmy told me to remind you to swing by the house, Matt," Kathleen said.

Matthew had forgotten. He was supposed to pick up the old photo albums that were stored in the basement of his dad's house.

"Do you want me to go with you?" Anne asked.

"No, that's alright. It'll only take me twenty minutes," Matthew said. There was no sense in both of them being depressed by visiting the place where his father had been killed.

"C'mon," Kathleen said to Anne. "Let's go over to the deli. We have a little time and they have the best scones. They're from an Irish bakery in Andrew Square."

"I shouldn't be long," Matthew said.

"I'll save you a seat in church," Anne said.

Matthew and Anne were using her mother's car on their extended stay. It was a red Subaru wagon that was very fuel efficient but so small that Matthew felt cramped squeezing his large frame into the driver's seat. Thankfully, the trip to his father's house was less than two miles.

When he got there, Matthew opened the garage door and went to the back, which was cluttered with plastic flower pots and cans of motor oil. He reached above the small window, and felt behind a row of flower pots for the spare backdoor key. Jimmy said he had used it recently and put it back in its old hiding place.

Matthew couldn't feel the key, so he removed all the pots and had another look. Nothing. He checked the other shelves, beneath bags of fertilizer and tomato stakes—the remnants of his mother's gardening hobby years before—but still no key. When he stepped outside the garage, the cuffs of the blue suit jacket he bought on Sunday were filthy.

He brushed them off and checked his watch. Ten-twenty. He considered coming back for the photo albums later, but being at the house made him uneasy and he wanted to get it over with. A quick walk around the place showed that the doors were locked, as were all the windows. Except one. Looking up to his father's second-floor bedroom, Matthew could see that the window was open.

It was the last room of the house he wanted to be in, but Matthew retrieved an extension ladder from the garage and set it against the back of the house. The aluminum ladder clanged loudly as it settled against the clapboards. At the sound, a dog in the neighboring yard began barking and throwing itself with abandon against the chain-link fence separating the yards.

Matthew ignored it and climbed the ladder. At the top he managed to raise the window higher. The ladder barely reached, so he had difficulty hauling himself inside, landing hands first on the floor. He felt a pant leg catch on something and heard a tearing sound as a small hole opened at the knee.

He stood up and picked at the hole. "Fucking great." Then he reminded himself of what Anne had said that morning while they were dressing and he was struggling to fit into the blue suit he had bought on sale. "Don't worry," she said. "Nobody takes pictures at a funeral."

When he took a good look around the room, he was surprised. The bedroom was almost bare except for a dresser and the bed frame. Matthew's eyes were drawn to the base of the headboard. Two holes had been blown through the dark maple, the ragged circles made more pronounced by light unstained wood inside.

Bullets, Matthew thought. His eyes went down to where the mattress and box spring should have been. Where were they? Of course, they had been removed because of the blood. He imagined the event. His father asleep or maybe not, the gun being fired, the bullets hitting him, the blood. He had been hit in the face, a detail that Matthew could have lived without.

It was bad enough to imagine it, but Jimmy would have seen it all because the police had called him over to identify the body that night. He would have witnessed the raw scene, an experience far worse than Matthew imagining it.

This is what he had wanted to avoid. He drew in a quick breath and moved immediately to the bedroom door. In the bathroom, he brushed off his pants and washed his hands. As Matthew descended the stairway to the main floor, the sound of his shoes on the bare wooden steps sent echoes throughout the house.

He noticed the familiar smell of the place suddenly. Not offensive, not perfumed, barely noticeable, just the smell the house had always had. Matthew never noticed it before when he lived there, and he couldn't quite tell what the smell was like. It was just one of those things unique about a place you might never notice until you were gone for a long time and returned.

The smell and other familiar details brought him back suddenly. The last time he lived there was the summer of 1974, which began with his mother dying and ended with Matthew moving in with cousins Richard and Bobby in Quincy.

Whenever Matthew would return to the house after his mother's death, he'd sense her spirit. He had a vivid recollection of the time immediately following her death when she seemed to visit him. He would feel her watching him, listening to his thoughts.

Looking back, it seemed like something that a person would think if they were on the verge of going insane. At the time, Matthew considered that a possibility. Then again, having conversations with his dead mother might have been how Matthew kept from going insane.

He flipped a switch at the top of the basement stairway and a faint light showed the way to the bottom. He carefully descended, step after creaky step. The old wooden handrail was layered with dust and swayed under Matthew's grip. Reaching the bottom, he ran his hand along the wall until he found the switch for the basement lights. When he flipped it, nothing happened.

The light at the top of the stairway cast a dim path through the basement, enough to guide Matthew if he walked carefully. He waited for his eyes to adjust and waded through the clutter of boxes scattered across the floor like a sloppy range of mountains. The basement smelled of moldy newspapers. His mother saved everything. Newspapers, church announcements, anything that mentioned the family. And his father kept it all after she died.

Matthew steered around one stack of boxes after another looking for the red box that held the photo albums. Someone'll have to go through this shit and sort it out, he thought. Probably Jimmy. If it were up to Matthew, he'd throw it all out.

When he was halfway across the basement, Matthew felt a movement of air at the back of his neck. An unnatural breeze in the still basement. The next instant a hand closed around Matthew's throat in a tight grip. A force lifted him backward and off his feet. For a moment, he felt free of gravity, as if he was ten years old again and doing a back dive off the bridge at Castle Island.

The same force that had lifted Matthew slowed his fall. His back landed softly on a small pile of newspapers, but his head banged on the cement. Then the weight of a body came crushing down on his chest.

"Don't move," a voice said.

Matthew's hands reached instinctively for his opponent's neck, but he couldn't find it. He let out a sound somewhere between a yell and a growl, and took a couple of wild swings in the air.

"Shut up!" the voice yelled.

Matthew went still. There was something familiar in the voice, something trusted, so Matthew relaxed. He felt the pressure on his chest release. Searching in the faint light, Matthew first discerned the muzzle of a gun. And behind it, the face of his brother, Francis.

* * * * *

"I wouldn't move back there if you put a gun to my head," Kathleen said to Anne. They stood in front of St. Monica's Church, and Kathleen pointed across the rotary to the Old Colony housing project. Its red brick buildings went on for blocks.

"It's where we all started. Our Garden of Eden. My mom still lives there. She doesn't have to anymore but she does. I couldn't get her out of there with a crowbar. She tells me I can have the place when she dies, like she owns the apartment. It's rent-controlled housing owned by the city."

They walked over to a deli next to the church, and bought coffee and scones. The deli had a window counter with stools, where they could look across at the project.

"Mind if I smoke?" Kathleen asked. Her guilty conscience made her add, "I quit a year ago and a year before that, but if I didn't buy this pack of smokes the other day, I was going to lose my mind."

"No, go ahead."

"You've never smoked, have you, Anne? I can tell by your skin. It still has that clean look. Matty says you hike and climb rocks. All that healthy stuff."

Anne took a bite of her scone and smiled. "I did smoke for a while actually. When I was twelve and my parents divorced. I wanted to live with my dad in Alaska. My mom wouldn't agree to it, so I made her life miserable."

"Twelve can be a very mean year," Kathleen said.

Anne was wearing a black cocktail dress she had bought on Sunday when she and Matthew had gone shopping at Filene's Basement in Boston. She brushed some scone crumbs off her lap. "Mmm, these are good scones," Anne said before taking another bite. "I was mean in a calculated way. I'd leave half-empty packs of cigarettes around the house, so my mom would know I was smoking. And I started hanging out with kids who I knew she wouldn't like. We'd go shoplifting and I'd intentionally get caught. Then my mom would have to come get me. When she tried to punish me, I ignored her.

"There was one night during my last winter in Ipswich when she told me that she would never, ever allow me to move to Alaska. I walked out the sliding glass door to the back deck and laid down in the snow in my pajamas. I think I rolled around or made snow angels or something, but I remember laughing at what she said. Just laying in the snow and laughing. I stayed out there until she dragged me back inside.

"I refused to change out of the wet pajamas and slept in them. That night I decided that I would get to Alaska by the end of spring if I had to walk there. I hated my mom so much back then. I'm embarrassed when I think about it now."

Anne picked up a raisin and pushed it around her plate, gathering up scone crumbs like a snowplow.

"She finally gave up about a month later when she got a call from the Ipswich Police Department. They told her to come to the station and get me. A friend and I broke into the Ipswich Apothecary and were pouring Valiums into a McDonald's bag when the police showed up. Everybody in Ipswich was talking about it. My mom was horrified. About a week later, she told me she'd bought me a one-way ticket to Anchorage and that I needed to start packing.

"She warned my dad that I was going to be a big problem, but I wasn't. I never smoked again. I was a pretty good kid after I moved to Alaska. I didn't like it at first, but I was with my dad, and that's all I cared about. There's still this thing between my mom and I. We're just very different people, but I try to respect her and I try to remember that for a while I was pretty cruel to her."

Kathleen had listened attentively with a cigarette poised for the lighting in her right hand. She liked the story and what it said about Anne. "You can't feel guilty about sticking up for yourself, Anne. Even if it means getting into it with your mom." She lit her cigarette and exhaled a long stream of smoke away from the counter.

"I guess so," Anne said.

"Do you believe in God?" Kathleen asked.

It was an abrupt question, but they were sitting next to a church waiting to attend a funeral, and Anne didn't mind. "Yes," she responded without hesitation. "Do you?"

Kathleen reached around to scratch her back where the zipper from her dark blue dress always itched her. "I used to. Then I didn't. Now I think I believe in the idea of God. Like it's a possibility," Kathleen said in a hushed voice, almost a whisper, as if it was a secret to be shared with care. "If I didn't have it when my daughter died, I'd have gone crazy. Or crazier. People need it, even if they know it's just a gimmick. Can you imagine the chaos if people couldn't believe in the big eyes that watch everything? They wouldn't put up with half the shit they put up with now, I'll tell you that much." Kathleen pointed in the direction of Old Colony. "They especially need it over there."

Anne had seen projects like Old Colony when she was twelve years old and her class went on a field trip to New York City. She remembered looking out the bus window as it rolled through the Bronx and seeing one project after another, places that seemed full of danger and loneliness. When she looked over at Old Colony, she saw life, kids playing, a group of women standing on a corner telling stories in loud, animated voices and smoking cigarettes in the mad way people do when they are about to quit.

"So Matt missed all that?" Anne asked.

"No, he was born in Old Colony."

"He told me he hung out there a lot because it's where Buzzy lived, but I thought he was born in the new house."

"The Mahoneys lived in the same building as me and the Driscolls, Buzzy's family. One block down Patterson Way over there," Kathleen said, gesturing with the cigarette. "We lived at the end of the first block on the right. Number seven. That's where my mom still has her apartment."

Kathleen opened her handbag and dropped her lighter inside. "The Mahoneys moved out of the project when Matty was little, but you're right about him coming back there and hanging out with Buzzy. You'd always see them together. They were a team. Buzzy was never much of a fighter, so Matty was always looking out for him. Matty's still a project rat like the rest of us. Scratch deep enough and you'll find it."

Anne found the idea strange. That Old Colony had a claim on Matthew no matter how far he had come since leaving South Boston. Like a loan that could be called in at any time.

"It doesn't look like such a bad place to live," Anne said.

Kathleen shook her head. "Way back it was OK, like maybe in the fifties and sixties, or at least that's what the older people say. Then it went downhill. Since I moved back six years ago in 1981, it's been hell. Nobody wants to talk about it. That's how things are in South Boston. You see that jar next to the deli register?" Kathleen pointed to a jar, which was half stuffed with dollar bills and coins. Above it was a small sign that read, "Donations for the Mother of Sparks McGuire."

"Sparks was seventeen years old. He used to light fires in the dumpsters when he was a little kid, just to see the fire trucks come and put them out. He couldn't wait to become a fireman. About two weeks ago, they found him on the ground in front of his building. He jumped off the roof. Sparks was stealing his mother blind to buy heroin. Then he was stealing from his neighbors in the building. If he didn't kill himself, someone was going to do it for him. Just a matter of time. That's the shit that's been happening over and over around here. I've been to around thirty funerals since I moved back. I've lost count. Most of them kids. I swear, if Malloy's had a punch card, I'd have a free casket by now. I'm so sick of funerals. You knew I had a daughter, right? Did Matty tell you what happened?"

"He said she died when she was young."

"When Francis went off to Vietnam, he screwed things up and ended up in prison. I felt like we were done because he obviously wasn't capable of being responsible with his life. I wanted to make us done, so I got married to a guy I met downtown. He was in the Air Force. We dated for six months, and when they were going to move him to Texas we got married and I went with him. Francis was stuck in prison at the time. I wanted to show that I didn't need him or South Boston to survive. Everybody wants to prove their independence at some point, right?"

Kathleen paused to take another puff. There was a tap on the window as a friend of hers walked by on the sidewalk. Kathleen smiled and waved back. "Anyway, Texas was like another planet after South Boston. Any place is like another world when you leave here. I hated Texas. I hated the people. The way they talked rubbed me the wrong way. After a couple of years, I was thinking that I made a big mistake. Then I was pregnant even though I didn't want to be and we were using contraceptives.

"Suddenly I didn't care where I was or how people talked because I had my little girl. Her name was Diana. I've always loved that name. I decided when I was young that if I had a daughter I'd name her Diana. She had beautiful straight brown hair, and you could see bits of red in it when she was out in the sun."

Kathleen stopped to look down at her black coffee. "And she got my brown eyes. When she was four, her dad almost killed them both driving drunk and getting into a bad accident. That woke me up. Six months later I was back in South Boston divorced, which isn't exactly a badge of honor in this community. I moved in with my mother, who, even though she never said it, gave me the big 'I told you so.'

"Diana was what you'd call a gentle kid. She wasn't quiet, but when the other kids teased her, she'd usually smile and let it go. Most adults I know still aren't capable of doing that. It's not that she never got into fights. Every kid in the project fights, boys and girls, but it was rare for her. After a little adjustment, she made a lot of friends, and they looked out for her.

"I think Diana would have become a teacher. She liked to line up stuffed animals and read to them. Who knows. Maybe if she got older, she'd end up with the same problems everybody has over there, but we'll never know. That's the thing about dying young … you die perfect. She died just over three years ago."

A jet was flying over Old Colony on its descent to Logan Airport. Kathleen paused to watch it. She had reached the part of the story she learned she should skip. It didn't upset her as much because she had told the story so many times, but it upset other people to hear how her daughter died.

It was on Easter Sunday. Diana had been looking forward to it because Kathleen had taken her shopping for an Easter dress at Filene's Basement. She had picked out a dress that Kathleen hated. It was lime green and had purple and pink butterflies. Diana loved butterflies, and everything had to have butterflies. Her shoes, her hair clips, her shirts, her lunchbox. So Kathleen bought it.

She wore it to Easter mass, and when they got home Kathleen made her take it off for dinner so she wouldn't spill on it. That night, when they were watching TV, Diana pestered Kathleen to let her put the dress back on. Either that or let her wear it to bed, which Kathleen wasn't going to do. So she said OK. Diana went into the bedroom she shared with Kathleen. A minute later, Kathleen and her mother heard gunshots outside, which wasn't unusual to hear in the project.

When Diana didn't return to the living room, Kathleen called to her, but heard nothing. She went to the bedroom, and what she saw gave her an out-of-body experience. She couldn't remember the next few moments, but her mother later told her that she screamed so loud it made her mom pee herself.

Kathleen let her eyes drift across the rooflines of the project as she resumed her story. "She got shot accidentally one night. A kid named Chris Kenneally did it. He was high on angel dust and God knows what, and he brought his father's rifle up to the roof of the building across from ours. He fired three shots into our building. Just random. A little while later, he didn't understand why the cops were kicking down the front door to his family's apartment. He didn't remember anything about going onto the roof with the rifle.

"Diana liked butterflies. I asked her one time why she liked butterflies so much. She said, 'Because they're just like people. They never know where they're going, but they always get somewhere.'"

Kathleen turned to Anne, who looked distressed. "Oh shit, I'm sorry. I shouldn't tell that story at all anymore. Anyway, that was it. Diana was dead. Francis was out of prison, and we started dating again because … he was familiar, I knew him. There's a certain comfort in familiarity, you know."

A line of limousines made its way slowly from the funeral home, turning from Dorchester Street onto Old Colony Avenue. Kathleen and Anne stood up to leave. The black cars drove past the deli and came to a stop in front of St. Monica's Church. A large bearded man holding a set of bagpipes on the steps in front of the church began warming up. A stream of atonal groans and wheezes flowed from his instrument.

"Oh, Christ," Kathleen said as they climbed the steps to the church. "I don't want to hear bagpipes today. I bet it's Jimmy's doing. He's a good man, but he can be so goddamn sentimental."

* * * * *

Terry "Disco" Callahan had a number of reasons to attend Salty Mahoney's funeral. First and foremost, he owed it to the man who had used his connections to give Disco his start in the FBI. Salty had a poor record of winning elections, but he was a master at using blackmail, bribes, threats and occasionally begging to do favors for his friends. If it wasn't for Salty's help, Disco might still be driving a truck for the MDC and picking up garbage along Carson Beach.

Another reason was to show his loyalty to Jimmy Mahoney. It was important to stay connected with people who could help Disco transition out of the FBI, and Jimmy Mahoney had close friends in high places, many more than Salty had. Jimmy didn't employ the same tactics as his father, but Disco knew that he could accomplish the same results and do it quietly. Jimmy met him on the front steps of St. Monica's Church as the funeral was about to begin. He asked Disco to serve as pallbearer in Matthew's absence.

Disco had arrived at the funeral in style, wearing a dark grey Armani suit made of Italian silk and a pair of hand-stitched calfskin loafers by Salvatore Ferragamo. He had become something of a superstar, a status reflected in a wardrobe that had reached new heights of ostentation. His nickname in the Boston field office was Gucci because of his taste for expensive European fashion, unusual in a government office where hundred-dollar suits were the norm. Disco was the exception, and everyone noticed. Twice a month, Disco also got a makeover at the Hair & Beyond, Kathleen Sutliff's salon on Broadway, ensuring his jet-black hair never revealed its prematurely greying roots.

Disco was attending the funeral out of respect for Francis as well. They would not be able to speak to one another if Francis were there. The FBI was strict about where and when a handler could meet an informant, and a large funeral was out of the question. As it was, Francis would definitely be a no-show. The thought made Disco wonder where his old friend might be.

He had recruited Francis and Larry as informants for the FBI as Francis was reestablishing himself after getting out of Walpole State Prison. Disco's connection to Francis went back even further. The two had grown up together in the Old Colony project.

His first memory of Francis was from Christmas Day 1958 when the Callahans went to the Mahoneys' for Christmas dinner. The Callahan family had moved to the project two months earlier when their name finally came up on the vacancy list. As the parents cracked open cans of Schlitz beer, Jack Callahan sent Disco and Francis into the children's bedroom with Disco's Christmas present: two pairs of boxing gloves. "Why don't you boys play a while," Jack said and laced up their gloves. "Work off some energy."

Disco was eight years old, six months older than Francis and taller by a couple of inches, but he had been intimidated by Francis since moving into the project. He noticed a smile in Francis' eyes as Francis approached with boxing gloves held high.

They knocked each other around the room for a good fifteen minutes, until Disco caught Francis clean on the side of the head and sent him flying sideways against a corner of a dresser. Francis hit head first with a loud bang. Disco was afraid he had knocked him out. The collision could be heard above the sound of a football game playing on the living room TV.

"Keep at him, Francis," Salty's voice called through the bedroom door.

Francis tried to get up but was too dazed. Finally he stood, panting heavily with sweat pouring down his face. There was a bright red welt on his temple.

Disco apologized, but Francis just smiled. "This is fun, isn't it?" The two continued banging each other around the bedroom until Salty retrieved them for dinner. They were battered, bruised and exhausted. And they had become friends.

The bond grew stronger with time, and the loyalty between the two was more important to Disco than his allegiance to the FBI. It showed itself a year before in Operation Beanpot, which decimated the ranks of La Cosa Nostra in Boston and brought federal racketeering charges against thirty-three men from the boss down to foot soldiers.

It was a huge publicity coup and gave Disco celebrity status in the federal law enforcement community. Within the bureau, Disco made a point of attributing some of the operation's success to the assistance provided by informants Mahoney and D'Amico. Disco lobbied heavily to have the two designated as official informants in the case, which provided them with a protective shield against any attempt by other law enforcement agencies to bring charges for any illegal acts committed during that period.

Francis and Larry had provided Disco with a comprehensive view of mob activity across the city. It was definitely helpful, although some of the information they provided duplicated what the FBI already knew.

In addition to having Francis and Larry designated official informants, Disco shared with them valuable information the FBI had gained from other sources during the investigation. It gave Francis a big advantage over all his surviving adversaries, from what would be a diminished Italian Mafia to rival gangs across the city.

Operation Beanpot cemented Francis' reputation within the FBI as a valuable informant. From that point on, Disco, along with his brother working for the Drug Enforcement Agency, were religious about informing Francis whenever any law enforcement agency attempted to go after him.

When the State Police bugged the Lancaster Street Garage, Francis learned where and when they had been planted. When they bugged the Morrissey Boulevard pay phones that Francis used, he suddenly stopped using them. When the Quincy Police Department planned to install listening devices in the car at his condo, Francis waited for the two detectives to break in, then went at them with a baseball bat claiming that he was defending his property from what seemed to be car thieves.

If a Boston cop started getting too interested in Francis Mahoney's business, the cop was reassigned or demoted. Disco even told Francis which of his enemies and, more importantly, which of his friends in the underworld had secretly become informants.

For Francis and Disco, Operation Beanpot had been a real blessing. However, that had changed recently for Disco. He now feared that his career was in jeopardy. It wasn't anything specific that had him concerned but more of a gut feeling about the new director for the FBI Boston field office.

Disco had had the complete trust of longtime Director Patrick Shea, who was always quick to defend him from charges that his relationship with informant Francis Mahoney might be a bit too friendly. When Shea left the bureau a few months earlier, with him went the bureau's blind trust in Disco.

The new director, Virgil Bunker from Idaho, had been conducting a detailed examination of the bureau's relationship with informants Mahoney and D'Amico. Where it would lead, Disco didn't know, but he sensed that everything he did was now coming under much greater scrutiny.

Disco joined the other pallbearers at the back of the hearse. There were Jimmy, Richard, Bobby and two long-time friends of Salty Mahoney. Richard had shown up at the last minute, hungover and sloppily dressed.

The polished mahogany casket slid effortlessly from the hearse. A large flag of Ireland was draped across the lid. Ushers from the funeral home stood nearby to provide subtle direction to the team. This was Disco's fifth time serving as pallbearer, so he needed none. At the signal, they grabbed their handle and lifted, while placing their free hand underneath the casket as instructed earlier by the ushers. Just in case the handles failed, although Disco had never heard of that happening.

Stationed at the door to the church, the lone bagpiper began playing "Amazing Grace." With the weight of their hero in hand, the six men pivoted left and proceeded slowly up the granite steps. Local TV stations had camera crews there to record the scene. Newspaper reporters were outside the church as well. The rapid click and whir of cameras could be heard occasionally above the bagpipe.

The pallbearers entered the church, where daylight was filtered by the stained glass windows, spilling rich shafts of emerald and ruby across the crowded pews. The air was pungent with the overly sweet scent of flowers, but was slowly being overtaken by the more acrid smell of burning incense.

The church organ began to fill the space with a rich lament. The weight of the casket put a strain on Disco's shoulder, but he was a strong man and didn't mind the burden. Carrying the weight of Salty Mahoney, knowing the man was gone and would never be coming back, gave Disco a feeling that he was being abandoned. Looking around the church he saw that he was not alone. All of South Boston was feeling the loss.

* * * * *

"You know I didn't kill him," Francis said before releasing his weight from Matthew's chest. He reached above him and tightened a bulb in its socket. It barely lit the basement, but now they could at least see each other.

The air in the basement was damp and cool. The neighbor's dog barked at the sound of a passing jet. Matthew tried to pull himself off the dusty floor by grabbing hold of a box, but it collapsed. The back of his head hurt where it hit the cement. He reached up and touched the small egg of pain.

"You forget how to stand up?" Francis asked and extended a hand to pull his brother off the floor.

Francis wore the same suit he had on at the wedding. It stank of sweat and salt water. When the shock of the moment had passed, Matthew felt relieved to see his brother, almost happy.

"You believe me," Francis said. It was a statement, not a question.

"Of course I do. What are you doing here?" Matthew asked.

As another plane passed overhead on its descent to Logan, the neighbor's dog barked and another neighbor yelled for the dog to shut up. Francis walked to one of the small, high basement windows and parted the stained cotton curtains to let in some light. Then he unraveled a bandage around his hand.

"Look at this," Francis said.

Matthew stepped forward to see the wounds on the back of Francis' hand.

"From that fucking dog. Saturday night."

Matthew looked at the wound. It was dirty and ringed with dried blood. Then Francis' words registered. "You were here Saturday night?"

"The dog got loose and attacked me. I never came in the house."

"What were you doing here?"

"Kathleen. I wanted to see her, but she wasn't even home." Francis was distracted by the barking of the dog outside. "I had a pistol and shot in the air to scare the dog. I should have killed the fucking thing. Then I tried to fly out of Logan, but the troopers were waiting for me, so I went up to Gloucester and jumped on a boat heading for Ireland.

"That's when I found out that he was murdered." Francis pointed at the ceiling and Salty's bedroom beyond. "A friend radioed the news to the boat. Someone made it look like I did it. I'll tell you, Matt, that's the biggest fucking mistake that guy's ever made. That's why I'm back."

Matthew thought about the lingering doubt he had confessed to Jimmy, but with Francis standing right there, Matthew's doubt was completely gone.

After a moment of silence, Francis asked, "So what's Jimmy been saying?"

"He said you absolutely didn't do it."

"Is that what he said?"

"That's what he said."

Francis wanted to hear Jimmy's judgment of him. He had always accepted whatever his older brother said, even as he disregarded the judgment of his father, the cops, the courts and pretty much the rest of the world.

"So who believes I did kill him?"

Matthew had to think about it. "Aunt Eileen is the only one, I think."

"Who gives a shit what she thinks? Anybody else?"

"No," Matthew answered quickly, knowing he shouldn't have mentioned anybody.

"Here's what's going on, Matt. The guy who set me up didn't do a good enough job because I'm only wanted for questioning and not the murder. So the cops are already seeing through the bullshit.

"That doesn't make it any less of a trespass, you understand. That guy is fucking with me. He's also fucking with you and Jimmy, because he's putting the whole family through this thing. Jimmy can't do anything about it, and I can't do anything about it. At least not at the moment."

Matthew rubbed the sore spot on the back of his head again. He now had two lumps thanks to Francis. "So where have you been since Saturday?"

Francis had gotten some dust in his eyes tackling Matthew. He rubbed them. "The last few days I've been hiding up in Lynn. And I mean hiding. I haven't talked to anyone I know because I don't know who's involved in this, and I don't know who I can trust. I've been checking newspapers to see what's going on."

"Who brought you back here?" Matthew asked.

"I did, with the help of a stranger who woke up this morning and found his Volvo missing. I left it on Northern Ave. and walked here early this morning while it was still dark. The only one who heard me breaking into the house was that fucking dog. Like I said, I don't know who's behind this yet, which means there are very few people I can trust absolutely. In fact, there are only three people. Jimmy, you and my friend Connor. Like I said, Jimmy can't help me so I need you to run a few errands to let Connor know that I'm back in town and that I need to meet him."

Matthew looked down at his watch.

Francis noticed. "You gotta be somewhere?"

"The funeral. It doesn't matter though."

"I don't know about you, Matt, but I don't like the fact that the guy who did this is free. He's made all of us look guilty. If I do nothing, he's beaten me. And he's beaten Jimmy, and he's beaten you. I don't like being beaten, Matt. Do you?"

It was a line that Francis had used on Matthew before. The first time was when Matthew was seven and started playing in South Boston Youth Hockey as a Mite. Almost every kid growing up in South Boston played hockey at some point. If you could dominate physically on the ice, it was one way to earn respect on the streets.

When the family moved out of Old Colony, Matthew was at the age when the project would have forced him to really fight for respect the same way that Francis had done. Francis realized this, and it irritated him to see Matthew getting relatively soft treatment in his new City Point neighborhood.

So Francis, who was a teenager at the time, showed up one night at the MDC rink at the end of City Point, just a block from the new house on E. Third Street. Under the corrugated steel roof of the rink, the sounds of whistles, cheers and slapping sticks echoed. There were several other fans who showed up for the game, some of them drunk and wanting to see their son or brother score a goal or slam another kid into the boards.

Matthew's team was playing another South Boston Mite team with kids he went to school with. Throughout the game, Francis saw Matthew getting pushed off the puck by pretty much every kid on the other team, and by one kid in particular. He was Greg Walsh, who was a little older and bigger than Matthew and a better skater.

When the game was over, Francis waited for Matthew outside. It was a chilly night. A small group of kids huddled inside the lobby waiting for their rides to show up. Matthew assumed Francis was there to help him carry his equipment bag home. Instead, Francis walked up to Matthew and began shoving him. Soft at first, then harder until the equipment bag fell from Matthew's shoulder.

"Stay on that spot. Right where you're standing," he told Matthew. Then Francis began pushing him again, knocking him off the imaginary spot.

As far as Matthew could tell, there was nothing he had done to make Francis knock him around the parking lot, and he began to resent the treatment. "Quit it," Matthew said.

Francis continued pushing. "Does that work on the ice? Does Greg let you have the puck when you say 'quit it'?" As he pushed, Francis walked a slow circle around Matthew so that even when one push knocked Matthew off the imaginary spot, another one put him right back on it. The few kids who were left inside had stepped out to see what was going on. One of them was Greg Walsh, and Matthew heard him laughing.

Round and round he went as Francis pushed one shoulder, then the other, and with each one Matthew grew angrier.

Suddenly Francis stopped and stepped up to Matthew.

"You know what you're gonna do now? You're gonna go over there and kick Greg's ass in front of his two friends. He's the boss of you right now," Francis said. "But not for long because you're gonna walk right up to Greg Walsh and punch him in the face as hard as you can. Keep punching him and don't stop for anybody or anything.

I don't care how big he is. Hit him so hard and so fast that he can't fight back. Be a fucking lunatic."

Matthew stared back at Francis. "I can't."

Francis bent down and whispered in Matthew's ear, "If you don't kick Greg's ass right now, I'm gonna beat the shit out of you in front of all those guys. Your mommy isn't here, Matt. I'm the boss, and I swear to God, I'll beat you bloody. That's the fucking deal."

Francis wound up and slapped his brother on the face so hard that Matthew went flying backward over his equipment bag. After rolling to a stop, he got up and felt blood coming from his nose.

He heard Greg Walsh laughing, or he thought he heard him laughing. All that mattered was that Greg was there to see him humiliated. Matthew charged Greg and knocked him to the ground with a punch. He jumped on top of him and threw more punches, even when Greg gave up and rolled himself into a ball. When one of Greg's friends tried to pull him off, Matthew turned on him and administered the same beating. Greg's other friend didn't do anything.

At school the next day Matthew heard different versions of the fight. They were embellished with elaborate choreography, a sense that every punch and every movement had been well planned and executed. The fight could have lasted thirty seconds or five minutes. Matthew remembered little about it except that he was swinging wildly and he didn't stop until Francis picked him up and carried him away from the scene.

Learning how to box and throw his punches in combination would come with later lessons, but this one was the most important of all. It was the foundation.

When the fight was over, Matthew was transformed. He had learned the lesson he had been running from until that moment. Until Francis forced him to learn it.

"That's exactly what you do whenever you fight," Francis told him on the walk home. "Whether you're fighting on the ice or the street. Wherever you are. Don't hold back an ounce. Once you decide you're in, you become an animal. The only way you ever lose is if you run from a fight."

With bloody hands and a bloody face, Matthew horrified his mother when he and Francis stepped into the house. Her mood turned quickly to anger when she saw the two of them smiling.

Matthew heard his mother swear for the first and only time in his life when she called Francis a bastard for teaching Matthew the wrong way to deal with a problem.

"It's the South Boston way," was all Francis said in his defense.

Matthew's reputation at school changed overnight. It was for the better with most kids, although a few distanced themselves, which Matthew interpreted as dislike. But it wasn't that at all, Francis told him. "They respect you now because they're afraid of you. It feels good, doesn't it?"

Matthew agreed. It felt good to be feared.

The neighbor's dog stopped barking suddenly. It had been barking so long that when it stopped, the silence in the basement was unnerving to Matthew. "So," Francis repeated, "do you like being beaten, Matt?"

"What do you want me to do?"

"Go upstairs and get me something to eat. If anyone's watching the house and they see me, I'm fucked. Find some bandages. And some alcohol or peroxide. Something to clean my hand."

Matthew turned and headed for the stairs. "I'll be right back."

"I know you will, little brother. You're doing the right thing."

At the top of the basement stairs, Matthew heard a noise on the front porch. Through the living room windows, he saw a darkly dressed figure move slowly to the far end of the porch, then back near the front door. The figure stopped and peered through a window. It was a cop.

Matthew walked to the window and waved. "It's alright," he called, "I'm Matt Mahoney. This is my father's house." The cop motioned for Matthew to open the front door. As he did, Matthew noticed a police car parked out front with another cop sitting inside. He fished for his driver's license to prove who he was.

The cop almost seemed insulted. "Matt, I know who you are," he said. Matthew looked at the cop's face, which seemed familiar. The nose that came to a sharp point, the blondish hair that was shaved so close it made him look bald.

"I'm Kevin Doyle."

"Starchie?" Matthew reached out and they shook hands.

Matthew sat behind Kevin at St. Monica's Grammar School. White shirts were part of the uniform and Kevin would arrive every morning with a shirt so starched that by lunchtime the stiff collar would rub a red ring around his neck. When Starchie wore a T-shirt after school, the red ring made it look like somebody had been keeping him on a leash.

His friends thought it was Starchie's mother who had been heaping this cruelty on her son, but they found out later that it was Starchie himself who was getting out of bed extra early to slave over a hot iron, draining one can of spray starch after another. He did it because he wanted to be just like his dad, who was also nicknamed Starchie.

The nickname supposedly came from his father insisting that his police uniform always be well ironed and crisp looking. Later Kevin found out the nickname came from the fact that when his father wasn't working, he was usually getting drunk at one bar or another. People saw him stiff so often, they nicknamed him Starchie.

"How's your dad these days?"

"He was made for retirement. Loving every minute of it. By the way, Matt, I'm sorry about what happened to your dad. He did a lot for The Town. He helped out a lot of people, including my dad."

Matthew imagined the help involved keeping the drunk cop in a job until he could reach retirement. "Thanks."

"So," Starchie said, looking over Matthew's shoulder and scanning the living room, "having a little trouble getting into the house today?"

"I couldn't find the spare key. I had to climb through a window out back. Did somebody call?"

"McDevitt. Your backyard neighbor. He's got a lot of balls calling us when his dog keeps the street awake half the night. Someone's gonna feed him a bowl of antifreeze one of these days. The dog, that is. You here alone?"

Matthew nodded. Starchie wrote something on a piece of paper and handed it to Matthew. "That's where you can reach me at police headquarters on Berkeley Street. I picked up this patrol today, but I usually work at headquarters. Call if you need help breaking into the house. Or anything else."

"OK. Thanks, Kevin. Good to see you again," Matthew said.

When Starchie reached the patrol car, he called back, "I heard you got married. Congratulations."

"Thanks."

"Where are you living these days?"

"Seattle."

"Supposed to be nice out there."

"It is."

"Heard it rains a lot. I couldn't stand that."

In the kitchen Matthew found a half gallon of milk and a box of cereal, as well as a bowl and spoon. He looked out the kitchen window and saw the neighbor's dog racing mindlessly back and forth along the chain-link fence separating the two yards. The dog paused only to make quick leaps at the top of the fence. It must have seen Matthew because it stopped and began a series of barks.

In the bathroom Matthew found what Francis asked for, and brought it all back to the basement.

"Fucking Fruit Loops," Francis said when Matthew handed him the box. "This is all he ever eats. Or ate. Sugar shit." He put down the milk and cereal box and poured peroxide over the deep wounds on his hand. "Who was that you were talking to upstairs?" Francis asked.

"A cop. The neighbor out back saw me climbing up the ladder and thought I was breaking in. McDevitt, he said."

"That fucker with the dog."

"I know the cop. It's Kevin Doyle. Starchie. We went to grammar school together."

Francis smiled. "Starchie. He's one of my boys." He wiped the excess peroxide from his hand, then dabbed all the dried blood from the wound before carefully bandaging it.

Turning serious again, Francis said, "Get me a towel, a bar of soap and a razor. And find some clothes. Sweatshirt, jeans, socks, sneakers. Whatever you can find."

In the dim light of the basement, Matthew watched his brother walk to the clothes dryer and wiped its top clean with a sock from a basket of clean laundry. Then Francis inspected the spoon and the bowl for signs of improper washing, and hesitated for a moment, in thought or in prayer, Matthew thought, before filling the bowl with cereal and milk. "Are you gonna watch me eat, or get the stuff?" Francis asked without turning around.

When Matthew returned, Francis had stripped and was standing in front of the large laundry sink. His body was lean and muscular. Matthew looked down at his own stomach and wondered how the two of them could be brothers.

Francis splashed his body and lathered with soap. After toweling dry and dressing, he shaved.

"Here's the next thing, Matt."

Matthew was searching through the many boxes in the basement to find the red box.

"What are you doing?" Francis asked.

"I'm supposed to find Mom's photo albums down here."

"The photo albums aren't here, Matt."

"What?"

"Mom's photo albums are at Jimmy's house. They've been there for years."

"Then why did Jimmy ask me to pick them up here this morning?"

"He didn't send you here for the photo albums. He sent you here because he figured I might be here, and he wants you to help me because he can't."

"He didn't say anything like that to me."

"Look, you can be stupid or you can be my brother, but you can't be both. Jimmy knows you're the only one he can trust to find me. Years ago, the first time the cops ever came to this house looking for me, I hid out down here." Francis pointed to a small storage room in a corner of the basement.

"Dad would have handed me over if he knew I was in the house. Jimmy saw me rushing down here, so he checked on me, then brought me food for a couple of days until the cops stopped coming by. I told Jimmy if I ever had to hide anywhere again, it would be here because I'd know that he'd always remember to come help me.

"In this situation, Jimmy needs to be able to say that he hasn't seen me since the wedding, or heard anything about where I am. That leaves you, Matt. You're the firewall. The only one Jimmy and I can trust. Now you're gonna do me some favors and stop worrying about getting to the funeral or the burial or the party after at Jimmy's house.

"If anybody sees me, I'm fucked. And whether I end up at Charles Street jail or not, Jimmy's fucked too because it'll be all over the newspapers. He could kiss his chances of moving up in the Senate goodbye. I can't use the phone here. I can't leave this basement. I'm blind, deaf and mute right now."

"Just tell me what you want me to do, Francis," Matthew said as he glanced down at his watch again. "I'm wondering though. If I'm not at the funeral or the cemetery, someone might come over here looking for me."

"Go upstairs and call Jimmy's. If nobody's there, leave a message. They've got a machine. Better yet, call Donnelley's Pub. Ask for Tony. Tell him who you are and that you need an important message sent over to Jimmy. Tell him your car broke down. They're towing it to a garage in Dorchester and you have to wait there for an hour or so while it's being fixed. You'll see everybody at Jimmy's place after. A nice little story. After you make the call, I'll tell you exactly what you're gonna do for me."

Matthew had started up the stairs when Francis stopped him.

"One more thing. I apologize for what happened at the wedding. I didn't plan that. It just happened, and I'm sorry it did. That's all. Go."

* * * * *

One of the few blights on the South Boston skyline was the Boston Edison power plant. It marked the point where the residential area along L Street ended and the light industrial zone to the north began. The power plant, a large oil-burning facility with two huge exhaust towers, belched clouds of smoke and soot across the South Boston peninsula when the wind was blowing from the north.

In the third grade Matthew had done a painting of the plant and won an Honorable Mention for it in the school's art fair. "When I'm mayor, I'll have that goddamn thing torn down," was his father's reaction. "I'll have them build a turnpike extension through it if that's what it takes. Don't ever paint that goddamn monstrosity again." Matthew threw the painting away but saved the paper award with its embossed gold seal.

Across from the power plant was the Power Bar, a large tavern by South Boston standards. Matthew had never been inside but remembered it being nicknamed the Powerbarf as a kid. At one o'clock that afternoon, the regulars consisted of two guys playing pool, and two guys at the bar, one in an MBTA uniform, the other wearing a carpenter's tool belt. Along one wall were high-back booths. If it weren't for the few bright lights hanging over the pool tables and the light coming from a bathroom where nobody bothered to close the door, it would have been hard to see much at all in the dimly lit bar.

The bartender was channel surfing on the color TV at the end of the bar where Matthew took a stool. He had folded his tie into a jacket pocket, but his blue suit still looked odd in the setting, odder still because of the torn knee and dust-covered back.

The bartender was nicknamed Gabby Hayes for his habit of speaking in a rapid, animated voice. With his round belly, wide flat face and large protruding ears, he reminded Matthew of one of the seven dwarfs. "What can I get you?" Gabby asked, his eyes lingering on a soap opera.

"How's your coffee?"

"Best in the city," Gabby said, settling on a station showing highlights of the previous night's Red Sox game.

"That's more like it, Gabby," the carpenter said in a thick Irish brogue. The guy in the MBTA uniform looked disappointed.

Gabby put the remote down and brought Matthew coffee in a chipped ceramic mug along with an ancient-looking shaker of powdered cream. Matthew declined the powder and tasted the black coffee. It was terrible and barely warm.

"The coffee might be a little past its prime." Gabby's giddy voice startled Matthew. "We'll only charge you a buck," he said, picking up a pencil and starting the crossword puzzle in the *Boston Herald*.

"It's alright," Matthew said. "Hey, can you tell me if you've seen Connor McCain lately. A friend of his is looking for him."

Gabby stared suspiciously at Matthew.

"I'm Matt Mahoney. I grew up on E. Third Street." Matthew pointed in the direction of his father's house a few blocks away. "Maybe you know my family."

Gabby's expression lightened again as quickly as it had darkened. "You're Matt? The youngest one? Didn't you move to California?"

"Seattle."

"Wait, now I remember. Goldfinger! You climbed onto the State House dome one night."

"Me and Buzzy Driscoll."

"Your dad must have ripped you a new one for that." Gabby's laughter stopped abruptly. "Hey, I almost forgot. I'm sorry to hear about your dad."

"Thanks."

"So you're looking for Connor?" Gabby asked, returning to his crossword puzzle.

Matthew lowered his voice. "Do you expect him anytime today?"

"You know Connor?"

"My family does. I've got a message for him. I'd appreciate it if you could pass it on."

"Sure thing." Gabby sounded as if he understood Matthew's meaning, though he might have understood nothing.

Matthew looked at the napkin in front of him imprinted with a round coffee stain, and he was about to ask Gabby for his pencil. Then he remembered Francis telling him not to write anything down. "Zero, dash, zero. That's two zeros with a dash in the middle." Matthew had no idea what it meant, and he felt foolish saying it. He half expected Gabby to laugh. "That's the message. Do you want me to repeat it."

"Nope," Gabby said without looking up from his crossword.

Matthew stood up to go and pulled out his wallet.

"No charge, Matt. Hey, it was good to see you again. Give your family my best," Gabby said.

"I will."

When Matthew was halfway to the door, Gabby called out, "Hey, isn't your father's funeral today?"

Matthew looked down at his beat-up suit. "Yes, it is."

* * * * *

There were two more bars where Matthew needed to leave Francis' message, as long as the bartender on duty matched the one Francis had described. The last bar was Donnelley's Pub, which Matthew knew well. It was next to Old Colony.

The second bar was one that Matthew had never heard of. It had opened after he had left South Boston. Francis had told him the name, but now Matthew was having trouble remembering it. It was something Irish, like the Shamrock or the Four Leaf Clover. He knew it was several blocks west of the Power Bar. Matthew wasted time wandering all the way down E. First Street to where the industrial zone began. Then he returned on E. Second Street. Nothing.

He went back down E. Third Street and checked all its side streets. Just as he was about to give up and ask directions, Matthew saw a bar one block ahead.

It was named The Rover. Rover, clover. It might be the one, it might not be, but it sounded Irish enough. It was already 2:30. He and Anne needed to pick up their new tickets at the travel agency in Ipswich before it closed at 5:00. He called Jimmy's house at a pay phone across from The Rover, and asked for Anne.

"We got your message, Matt. Is the car fixed yet?" Anne asked.

Matthew wasn't sure how to explain what had happened and what he was now doing. "Yes, the car is OK. It's fine."

"So you'll be over here soon then?"

Matthew looked up and down the street and wondered where he should begin. It was a complicated story and it might be better not to begin it at all right now. "Well, the car is OK, but I don't know if I can make it to Jimmy's soon."

On the other end of the line he heard a crowd of voices at Jimmy's party. He continued, "Something came up today, Anne. It's family stuff and I'm going to have to take care of it. I'll be able to tell you about it later."

"That sounds strange," Anne said.

"Very strange, yes," Matthew said. He rubbed the fresh bump on the back of his head. "I wanted to call because I know we need to pick up our tickets for tomorrow's flight. I don't know if I'll be over at Jimmy's in time to drive us up there. Is there any way you could get a ride to North Station and catch a train to Ipswich?"

"Kathleen already offered to give me a ride all the way home. I guess I can do that if I have to."

When Matthew called, he didn't realize how awkward the conversation would be. "I'm sorry, Anne. Like I said, I'll explain it later."

"Matt, promise me you won't be doing anything stupid."

"Why do you say that?"

"Because you sound the way you do when you're about to do something stupid."

He laughed. Anne didn't.

The Rover had a classic tavern shape, long and narrow like a railroad car. Even darker than the Power Bar, it had a long bar along the right and stand-up counter to the left. It was the kind of place where you didn't want to spend too much time unless you knew the crowd.

Matthew walked to the bar and took a seat. The bartender noticed that he had a new customer but didn't seem to be in a hurry to check on him. He had a wiry build and wore a white Adidas tracksuit with light blue stripes. He looked a good five years younger than Matthew, so he definitely didn't match the description of Neil, the forty-five-year-old bald bartender who Francis said would be working there.

Either this was the wrong bar or Matthew had missed Neil. Or maybe his workday hadn't started yet. When Matthew's eyes adjusted to the dark setting, the bartender's outfit seemed almost too bright. The tracksuit looked brand new and totally out of place in the dingy bar. The bartender faced away from Matthew, and with one foot perched on a beer cooler he quizzed his friends sitting on stools at the other end of the bar.

"So how many beautiful women are having sex around the world right now? At this very moment."

"One million," said Donny, the guy on the left. He had a cigarette burning in his mouth and was tapping another on the bar.

"Not a bad guess," the bartender said. "But this is how you calculate it. There are what…three billion people in the world. Give or take. That makes approximately one point five billion women. Take out the kids and old women, and you have maybe five hundred million. Then deduct for women who are ugly or just average looking or only a little bit attractive…"

"Like somebody's girlfriend I know," said Briggs, the guy to the right. Briggs' remark was followed with a sharp, hyena laugh. Definitely stoned, Matthew decided. The bartender took a quick glance at Matthew to see how he was taking to being ignored.

"Watch your mouth Briggs, and listen up," the bartender said. "Make those deductions, and you have fifty million, being conservative. From that you deduct ten million for beautiful women who are pregnant, sick, etc.

"Of the remaining forty million, ten million are working, ten million are sleeping, ten million are busy shopping and doing other shit. That leaves ten million who are available."

"Available?" Briggs asked.

"Free and clear. Ready for action. Of those, I very conservatively eliminate nine million, which leaves one million not only available but also ready and willing. The last deduction is for those beautiful women who are ready and willing, but can't find a guy. This is the smallest deduction, percentage wise, because let's face it, a beautiful woman doesn't have to look too hard to find a guy to fuck her. So we could say seven hundred and fifty thousand, but very conservatively we can say…," the bartender raised a pointed finger high in the air for emphasis, "that half a million gorgeous women around the world are, as I say these very words … as you light your twentieth cigarette of the day, Donny, half a million women who are beyond beautiful are giving it up."

When Donny finished lighting his cigarette, he said, "But the real question is how many homos are getting fucked around the world right now." He and Briggs laughed. The bartender waved his hand at them in disgust. He lowered his foot from the beer cooler and glanced again at Matthew, then turned back to the other end of the bar where his friends were still laughing. "How many fags are fucking each other right now? Too many, Donny. That's the answer. Way too many."

The bartender adjusted the elastic waist of his pants and held out his arms as if to confirm that the sleeves were still the same length. Finally he turned to Matthew.

"What do you want?" he asked in a matter-of-fact way that told Matthew he wasn't particularly welcome. Matthew had looked around for a coffee pot but hadn't seen one, which was just as good considering the coffee at the Power Bar. He decided to get right to the point. "I'm looking for Neil. Is he working today?"

From the other end of the bar, Donny called, "How many one-legged women are giving blow jobs right now, Scott? Conservatively."

Scott, the bartender, ignored them. "Who are you?" He shot back at Matthew. His neutral tone was gone, and now he sounded pissed off.

"Matt Mahoney."

"Mahoney?"

"I grew up on E. Third Street."

"E. Third. Is that the same Mahoney as Francis Mahoney?" Scott asked.

"He's my brother."

Scott stepped away from Matthew and called to his friends. "Here's another one who says he's Francis Mahoney's brother."

"How many brothers does he have?" Donny called.

"I don't know, but I don't think that cokehead in here yesterday was one of them. Donny, are you paying these guys to come in and fuck with me?"

"That guy used to sell some fine weed. Speaking of which, Scott, you got a zippy for me?" Donny asked, referring to the plastic bags Scott packed his pot in. A zippy was the small size.

"I'll have some tonight."

The talk surprised Matthew. Not because they were talking about drugs. Since he had been ten years old, it had been the subject of many conversations with friends. In the project, at school, at the hockey rink, on street corners and on the bus where they'd sit in back and roll joints with the bus transfer slips. What surprised Matthew was that these guys were talking about it in a bar. He had never heard of it as an open topic of discussion in a South Boston bar. People would never stand for it. Then again, things change, even in South Boston.

Matthew realized that he had made a mistake with The Rover. It was the wrong bar and there definitely was nobody named Neil who worked there. He was getting up from his stool when Scott said something loud enough for Matthew to hear.

"If my brother had just killed my old man, I don't think I'd brag about being a Mahoney."

Matthew walked back to the bar and stood across from Scott, who was facing his friends but noticing Matthew out of the side of his eye.

Matthew had a sudden recollection of a high school hockey game. When he had left South Boston and moved in with his cousins in Quincy, Matthew played on the North Quincy High team. In his freshman year he made the junior varsity team, then played varsity his sophomore year.

He was a good defenseman and scored more goals than someone in that position usually did. The coaches liked him. So did most of the other players, once they had given him enough shit for bullying his way onto the team.

The only problem was that Matthew got into a lot of fights, especially in his sophomore year. He was warned several times that he would get benched and even kicked off the team if he kept it up. It got so bad in his junior year that the coach told him straight out that if he got into one more fight in the final five games, he'd be kicked off the team and would never be allowed to play again for North Quincy.

Matthew managed to avoid fighting for three games and he thought he would make it to five. Until the fourth game against Marshfield High. A left winger for Marshfield, who had gotten a good beating from Matthew the previous season, had heard about the fight ban and took advantage of it, taunting Matthew every time the two were on the ice together.

Halfway through the third period the left winger skated up behind him and asked if it was true that Matthew was afraid to fight anymore, that he was scared. The next time they were both on the ice, the guy had Matthew against the boards and dug the butt of his stick into Matthew's back. The ref called a penalty, and on his way to the penalty box, he skated by Matthew and called him a pussy.

Taking an insult without responding went against everything he had learned from Francis, and Matthew knew what he was about to do would mean he'd be kicked off the team and probably never play school hockey again anywhere.

He skated over to the penalty box. When the left winger said he was blocking his view of the game, Matthew leaned into the penalty box, grabbed him and pulled him onto the ice, where he pummeled him. It took a ref and three teammates to pull Matthew off the guy. He didn't even bother waiting to hear whether he had gotten a penalty or had been ejected. He went right to the locker room, changed and left his uniform behind.

It took a second for Matthew to remember it all. Scott, the bartender, was still talking to Donny. Out of the corner of his eye, Scott sensed motion and stopped talking. He turned to face Matthew just as he lunged across the bar. In one forceful motion, Scott was lifted over the bar and thrown to the floor, with Matthew's knee landing on his chest.

The first punch hit Scott's nose and Matthew felt the bone let go. Scott let out a howl and grabbed his nose, which was bent to the right. Blood poured down both sides of his face. Matthew grabbed Scott's hair and turned his head, aiming for a spot where he could break his jaw with one punch. He suddenly realized his back was open to the other two guys. He grabbed Scott and shifted him sideways like a rag doll, so he would see if the other two were coming at him.

They were. Matthew shot out an arm that caught Donny's swinging foot, but it still knocked him off Scott. Matthew rolled over before standing up. It took an instant to come up with a plan. He would hit Donny once, hard enough to hurt him and discourage Briggs. Then he'd finish business with Scott.

"Take it easy," Donny said to Matthew, who looked on the floor for Scott. He was nowhere to be seen. Then Scott stood up, behind the bar once again. His face was a mess of blood. It continued to run from his nose and down the front of his tracksuit.

Donny kept his distance from Matthew, and Briggs looked even less inclined to get involved. The one to worry about was Scott. Matthew watched him walk around the near end of the bar, then saw a long knife in Scott's hand.

The knife changed things. Matthew took a step back and glanced quickly to spot the front door in case he had to get out fast. He eyed a short wooden foot ladder to his right, which he could use on Donny or Scott but not both.

"Holy shit, Scott!" Donny said when he saw the knife. "Don't be stupid."

Looking at Donny, Matthew pointed toward Scott. "If he comes at me, I'll cripple him. And you won't stop me."

"I think he's a Mahoney," Donny said.

"I don't give a fuck," Scott said. He wiped some of the blood from his face. When he looked down, he was deeply distressed at how badly his tracksuit had been soiled.

"You better give a fuck," Donny said.

It's over, Matthew thought. And it was. He took three steps back and pushed the door open. Halfway across the street, he glanced back to make sure he was alone.

* * * * *

Matthew made his way up to Broadway, where he intended to walk to Dorchester Street and Donnelley's Pub, his last stop. On top of the new bump on his head, Matthew's shoulder was now sore, and his knuckles were scraped. He thought about Jimmy, and the fact that he set Matthew up for a morning surprise. Matthew didn't mind running the errands for Francis, but he suddenly didn't appreciate being tricked into it by his oldest brother.

Jimmy knew that Francis would be at the house if he was in South Boston at all. Matthew understood why Jimmy couldn't go there himself, so sending Matthew made perfect sense. He was family, he could be trusted, but it still pissed Matthew off that Jimmy had deceived him.

Passing a deli on Broadway, Matthew was distracted by hunger. Once his blood came down after a fight, he was usually overcome by a powerful appetite. The deli was clean and inside Matthew could smell corned beef, salami, the cheese melting on an Italian sub, bread cooking in a toaster.

There were several people sitting at tables. Matthew walked up to the counter and glanced at the menu. The woman working there was nice in a South Boston way. No slavish attitude, no smile, and no patience for people who asked whether the ham was Danish or German, whether the olive loaf was low fat or low sodium.

The woman looked to be in her early sixties, the age his mother would be if she were still alive. She fixed him a sandwich thick with chicken salad and two slices of provolone, then loaded the plate with chips and a pickle. As she passed it to Matthew, she did a double take on his suit. Ringing up his sandwich and Coke, she said, "Looks like you've had an interesting day."

"That's putting a shine on it," Matthew said.

"There's a dry cleaners up the block," she said as she pointed behind her with a thumb. As Matthew picked up the change, she added, "I hope the other guy looks worse."

Matthew ate standing up at the window counter. It was the best chicken salad sandwich he had eaten in a long time. Maybe ever. Across the street was Flanagan's Market. Its flat roof was where he, Buzzy and all their friends would go when they were teenagers to get

131

stoned speechless and watch the St. Patrick's Day parade. It was an event he looked forward to every year.

The last parade he had seen was in 1974. At the time, he had no idea it would be his last. Down Broadway came the marching bands, veterans groups and community organizations. For Matthew, the proudest moment occurred when his father and Jimmy passed Flanagan's with all the other politicians from South Boston waving to people and blowing kisses. As much as he hated his father, this was the one moment every year he forgave him, when Salty Mahoney made Matthew feel blessed to share the same last name.

The Mahoneys were a South Boston institution and knowing he mattered, knowing he was an important part of all he could see from Flanagan's rooftop and beyond, gave Matthew a powerful sense of belonging. He'd die for this place, his family, his friends. He would never leave it, and it would never leave him. He'd never betray South Boston, and he knew South Boston would never betray him. That's how his life was going to play out.

Remembering how passionately he had once felt about the place, how he wanted to spend the rest of his life there, surprised Matthew. That was his world, his foundation, something you could never change without tearing a person inside out.

What a dream it had been, Matthew thought as he finished his sandwich. But if you did dream, and you had to, it should be a powerful one. Flanagan's looked the same as it had on that last St. Patrick's Day parade. Stuck in 1974. To the right were new shops Matthew couldn't remember. They had a boutique look to them. A little too colorful and a little too pretty to be taken seriously. Farther up was the dry cleaners the woman had mentioned. It made Matthew think of the laundromat across from Old Colony where he would go with his mother while she did the weekly laundry.

The memory came to him quite clearly. His mother hauling a big bag of laundry with one arm, taking him by the hand with the other as they crossed Old Colony Avenue. After loading up a couple of washers, they walked to the corner deli where his mother would buy him a jelly donut and a grape tonic. Grape was Matthew's favorite flavor of soda, and Buzzy's too as Matthew found out later. With his donut and soda, he'd watch *I Love Lucy* on the laundromat's black and white TV.

He would get yelled at for turning up the volume, but he had to because his mother would be talking with a half dozen of her friends, and they had to shout to hear each other above the racket of so many washers and dryers.

Oh God, how he missed her still after all these years. Matthew took a quick glance around to see if anybody was looking before wiping his eyes with a napkin.

Chapter Five
King Castles Short

Matthew arrived at Donnelley's Pub just after five o'clock. It was already filled with people who had finished work, some who hadn't worked that day and a few who hadn't worked in years.

In one room was the bar along with tables and booths, in the other room sat a large pool table surrounded by small tables with red and white checkered cloths coated with plastic. Two posters decorated the back wall of the main room. One was a black and white photo of Bobby Orr scoring the winning overtime goal against the St. Louis Blues to win the 1969 Stanley Cup.

The yellowed poster showed Orr, who had been tripped only seconds after scoring the goal. The defenseman who tripped him wore a scowl. Orr was in midair—horizontal with his arms outstretched. He was smiling, as if his championship winning goal had given him the power to defy gravity. Matthew remembered the poster and the game.

The other poster was a close-up of Larry Bird of the Boston Celtics and Julius Erving of the Philadelphia 76ers. It was a posed shot of the two icons. Their expressionless faces were only inches apart, and each held the other's neck in a stranglehold.

On the TV behind the bar a baseball game played, but it couldn't be heard above the din of conversations. Every stool was taken, so Matthew found an opening at the bar where he checked to see if either bartender matched the description Francis had given him. The one down at the far end of the bar didn't, but the closer one with his back to Matthew might.

"What are you drinking?" the bartender asked after turning around. Matthew recognized him immediately as the kid whose skin would wrinkle horribly when he went swimming at Carson Beach. It earned him the nickname 'Prune.' His green eyes were looking a little puffy. Especially the left one, which drooped so heavily, it seemed it had been frozen in mid-wink.

"Prune!" Matthew called. He had seen Prune the week before at the party arranged by Buzzy and paid for by Francis.

"Matty Mo. Good to see you again. That was some bachelor party, man. I was completely out of action the next day."

When he saw Prune at the party, Matthew couldn't remember his real name. He still couldn't. Prune was one of the best street hockey players in South Boston when the two were growing up, although he never learned how to skate so all his talents were useless on the ice. He still lived in South Boston and had never moved farther than ten blocks from where he had grown up on G Street. For three years Prune had been married but was now separated.

Matthew ordered a beer, and Prune told him it was on the house. Between serving other customers, he told Matthew how sorry he was to hear of Salty's murder.

"It's crazy they're trying to pin it on your brother."

Even though Prune wasn't the bartender Matthew was supposed to talk to, he knew he could trust him.

"Do you know if a guy named Connor McCain has been around today?"

"Don't know him, Matt."

As Prune spoke, Matthew saw a figure in the mirror behind Prune. A guy racing across the other room and out the back door. Matthew couldn't get a clear picture, just a brown jacket and blue jeans. He waited to see who might be chasing the guy, but nobody was.

"Did you see that guy booking out the back door?" Matthew asked.

"Buzzy," Prune said.

"That was Buzzy?"

"He'll be back in a minute," Prune said, undisturbed by Buzzy's dash through the bar.

"Why was he running?" Matthew asked.

"He's been going out with this Puerto Rican girl from JP," Prune said, referring to the Jamaica Plain section of Boston. "Buzzy says she was Miss Puerto Rico of 1985. Coming from Buzzy, that means she's Puerto Rican and in 1985 she saw the Miss Puerto Rico contest on TV.

"Anyway, she belongs to this guy in a JP gang. The guy finds out Buzzy is screwing her, and he puts out the word that he's gonna get Buzzy. That's the story as Buzzy tells it, so who knows how much of it is bullshit. Buzzy thinks the guy is gonna show up at the bar any minute. I keep telling him there's no way the guy is coming in here and doing anything. It would be suicide."

Matthew remembered how in the old days he'd be the one to protect Buzzy from situations like this. Some of them were a real pain in the ass for Matthew, but that's what he did. Protect Buzzy whether he was a victim or whether he had brought the trouble on himself, like it sounded in this case. For a moment, he considered asking Prune if he knew more about the guy, what his name was, where he lived in JP, but he decided he wasn't going to step back into that role again.

Matthew also knew how Buzzy could pile on the bullshit. Even when the whole world was laughing at him, Buzzy would tell you with a straight face that his story was absolutely true. Matthew could always tell if he was telling the truth or not because of the way Buzzy would tilt his head in a funny way when he started into a lie.

"I don't know, Prune. I saw Miss Runner-Up last Saturday and she definitely looks like the real deal."

Buzzy returned, walking calmly through the front door. "Prune," he called and raised a hand. Matthew turned around.

"Look who it is. Hey, what happened today, Matt? You weren't at the funeral."

"My car broke down while I was running an errand for Jimmy," Matthew said. He was not a good liar, especially if he had to come up with a story on the spot, but he had this particular story down well.

Buzzy was preoccupied searching through the pockets of his worn suede jacket that was at least a size too big for him. He emptied his pockets onto the bar. Among the matchbooks and crushed packs of cigarettes grew a pile of keys, some on plastic chains, some on metal chains, some loose.

"Jesus, look at this. I feel like a fucking valet at Pier Four," Buzzy said, referring to the popular seafood restaurant on Northern Avenue.

"Is this it?" Buzzy asked pulling a pair of silver colored keys from the pile.

"No," Prune said. "It's got like a toy on the end. Like a tiny beach ball."

"Wait a minute," Buzzy said. He patted his chest, then began fishing through some inside pockets. "So how did you get here, Matt?"

"The car's fixed. I waited at the garage while they worked on it."

Buzzy noticed the condition of Matthew's suit. "Wow, it looks like you crawled here."

Matthew hadn't taken a good look when he was at the deli, but he could see that his scuffle in The Rover had damaged the suit even more.

"I went to pick up something from my dad's house, and I had to crawl through an open window because I couldn't find the spare key. You remember, the one in the garage?"

Buzzy had used the key in 1973 to sneak into the house at two-thirty in the morning when the two were thirteen years old. It was their night of infamy when Matthew climbed onto the roof of the State House to chisel gold from the dome. They had planned it for weeks. Buzzy made a last-minute decision to carry out the plan that night because his mother had locked him out of their apartment for coming home after midnight.

Buzzy looked distracted. "The spare key?"

"You know, the spare house key. You used it to wake me up when we did the State House thing."

"That's right," Buzzy said. "Too bad you couldn't find it. You would have saved your suit. The funeral was impressive, Matt. A packed house. Speedy did the honors, so we were out of there in less than forty minutes."

Monsignor Gonzales had arrived at St. Monica's parish in 1969 and quickly earned the nickname Speedy Gonzales because of how quickly he said mass. He would typically have people out the door in less than a half hour, the record being 22 minutes. His was the mass that most kids attended every Sunday.

Buzzy dug deep into a jacket pocket, drew out another set of keys and held them in the air. "Presto," he said and lowered them into Prune's hands. "There you go, Prune. Happy motoring."

He began returning the pile of keys to his pockets.

"Buzzy, Matt's asking about a guy named Connor McCain. You know him?"

Stuffing the last of the keys away, Buzzy stopped suddenly at the mention of Connor's name. He looked at Matthew with a mix of confusion and suspicion. "You're looking for Connor?"

Despite what Francis had told him, Matthew had the urge to tell Buzzy what was going on, but Francis had been strict about it. Even telling Prune had been a mistake, which was now obvious. Matthew needed a good lie, and fast. He drew a blank.

From the street came the sound of screeching tires and car doors slamming. Buzzy's eyes grew wide, and he dashed once again to the back door.

"He's so fucking paranoid," Prune said when it seemed Buzzy might not be returning for a while.

"What's up with all the keys?" Matthew asked.

"Buzzy's deal of the week. His friend has a garage that does vehicle inspections. If you have a shitbox that won't pass the safety inspection or the new emissions test, like mine, you give Buzzy a hundred bucks and you pass the inspection. No questions asked. Half the cars in South Boston are on his list. He has to be making some decent bucks."

* * * * *

From Donnelley's Pub, it was a shorter walk to Jimmy's house than back to E. Third Street where Matthew had left his car, so he went to Jimmy's to catch what was left of the after-funeral gathering. Jimmy and Peg lived at the end of N Street near Carson Beach, which ran along the southern end of the peninsula to City Point. Like most of South Boston, the homes in Jimmy's neighborhood were packed tightly together. The street had a mix of double- and triple-decker houses interspersed with small single family houses. Few of them had yards in front or back, but in Jimmy's stretch of the street the houses had small backyards.

When Matthew arrived it was almost seven o'clock. He wondered how Jimmy and Peg could raise five kids in such a small place. The front hall was crowded, and the air inside was thick with the smells of coffee, whiskey and tobacco. Peg was herding a couple of smokers through the living room and onto the back porch. "You can smoke all you want on the porch, I told you. Otherwise this place'll reek for a month."

The living room was filled with many of the same faces Matthew had seen at the wake. Relatives, neighbors and politicians. In the middle of the room were a sofa and two easy chairs. Folding metal chairs filled every inch of available wall space, and every seat was taken. Almost as many people were standing, and the noise of their conversations gave the feeling of a barroom on a Saturday night.

Wading his way through the crowd, Matthew searched for Jimmy. His anger at being duped by his brother hadn't diminished, and Matthew knew if he didn't tell him off tonight, he would carry it like a stone in his stomach back to Seattle.

Aunt Eileen spotted Matthew and called to him from the couch. "What in God's name happened to you today, Matthew?"

"My car broke down. I got it fixed in Dorchester."

"I'd never get my car fixed in Dorchester. They gyp you over there," Uncle Pete said, lighting his pipe.

"I told you not to light that thing in here," Aunt Eileen said. "Didn't you hear Peg telling you to smoke on the back porch?"

"She always lets me smoke my pipe in here."

"That's why everyone is lighting up inside. They're looking at you and doing the same. You're setting a bad example."

"Do you know where Jimmy is?" Matthew asked.

"Well, he was in the kitchen the last time I got a refill, but that was a while ago," Aunt Eileen said. "You should get yourself some food. Peg's got two trays of cold cuts and buckets of potato salad. My goodness, look at your suit."

Matthew started toward the kitchen.

"Bring me back a chocolate cupcake, will you, Matt?" Uncle Pete asked.

In the large kitchen and dining space, the table had been pushed against a wall. It was covered with food at one end, bottles of hard liquor and mixers at the other. Next to the table was a trash barrel filled with ice and bottles of beer. Everyone seemed to be enjoying themselves, which was the idea behind the ritual. Everyone except Peg, who was muttering under her breath as she cleaned the filter from a huge stainless steel coffee maker she had borrowed from the church.

"Hi, Peg," Matthew called.

Without turning around, Peg returned the greeting from the sink where she was rinsing out the filter before packing it again with fresh Eight O'Clock coffee, one of the cheapest brands in New England and the top seller at Flanagan's Market.

As Matthew looked at all the food, he found he was hungry again, so he made a salami and provolone sandwich with mustard. Kathleen came through the back door carrying three bakery boxes tied with colorfully striped twine.

"It's easier to use the back door instead of coming in the front and fighting the crowd," she said as she plopped the boxes onto the kitchen table with a sigh. "So you finally made it, Matt. I heard you had car trouble." Kathleen took a good look at Matthew's suit. "Jesus, where the hell have you been rolling around?"

"I crawled under the car trying to fix it," Matthew said before realizing that he could tell Kathleen the truth, sort of. That he did it crawling through a window at the house. Matthew was already getting confused about who he had to lie to and what story to tell them.

"These people just keep eating and eating," Peg complained. "The funeral was wonderful, Matthew. I'm sorry you had to miss it. Sad but wonderful. The choir was wonderful, too. Unfortunately the news cameras were there as well, but they didn't spoil it. It was still wonderful."

Kathleen leaned close to Matthew and whispered, "It's a wonderful world after all."

Matthew smiled. "Hey, thanks for giving Anne a lift home."

"I didn't mind. The ride gave me a break from this madness." Kathleen rubbed her forehead and sighed. "God, I just know I'm going to wake up with a migraine tomorrow. By the way, Anne said she'll see you back at Ipswich."

"So where's Jimmy?" Matthew asked.

"You just missed him," Peg said. "He had to run up to the State House. Same thing happened last night. The phone rings, and Jimmy dashes off to the State House."

"When is he coming back?"

"It might be a late night."

"I hope you guys don't mind if I take off," Matthew said. "It's been a long day, and we're flying out tomorrow."

"Send us a postcard from the old country," Peg said. "I hope to see you both back here for a visit soon."

"That's what I told him Peg, so he better do as we say," Kathleen said. Then to Matthew, "I like Anne. She's what you've needed for a long time if you don't mind me saying."

Matthew smiled and gave her a hug. He turned to leave, then remembered the cupcake. "Uncle Pete will lay into me if I forget his cupcake." He brought it to the living room. Uncle Pete's chair was empty. "He's in line for the bathroom. You can leave it on the coffee table," Aunt Eileen said.

That's when Matthew saw them. The photo albums spread out on the coffee table. That son of a bitch, Matthew thought. Out on the sidewalk, he wondered whether he was overreacting. I can just go back and pick up the Subaru on E. Third Street, he thought. I could forget the whole thing and drive back to Ipswich.

A brown and white cab stopped half a block away. When the driver had dropped his fare, the taxi came rolling down N Street toward Matthew.

* * * * *

Connor McCain grew up in the D Street project, the lowest of the low places to live in South Boston. He was called a white nigger by anyone from the Old Colony and Old Harbor projects, and especially by anyone from City Point. Connor had been arrested a number of times as a teenager but managed to avoid prison time.

Growing up, Connor loved to fight. On the streets, in the subway, at school, in the bleachers at Red Sox games, at the underage disco in Kenmore Square, once in Malloy's funeral home and twice in St. Monica's Church, where he had been banned from attending any mass other than the 7:00 mass on Sunday morning.

Built like a fireplug, Connor stood five-eleven and weighed 190 pounds. He had faster hands than anyone who ever fought him, and before the first punch was ever thrown he unnerved many opponents with the stare of his eyes. They were ice blue like a Siberian Husky's.

At eighteen Connor was exactly the kind of man the U.S. Marine Corps was looking for, and when he finished his stint four years later, Connor was exactly the kind of guy Francis Mahoney was looking for. The perfect combination of toughness, street smarts and the discipline the Marines had drilled into him.

One Friday afternoon in 1980, when he had finished teaching the last class of the day at his kickboxing school behind the Broadway Appliance Mart, Connor got a phone call telling him to go to Blarney Liquors. Everyone knew that Francis Mahoney and Larry D'Amico ran the place, which is why all the bars in South Boston agreed to buy their beer and booze from Blarney at a steep markup.

And like everyone in South Boston, Connor knew about Francis. He saw him occasionally at O'Brien's Tavern and Tyler's Gym, where Connor boxed. He and Francis would occasionally exchange a brief critique of a fight, short comments that made them the barest of acquaintances. So Connor had no idea why he was being called to the liquor store.

When he walked in, the front door was locked behind him and Connor was told to go down to the basement. Waiting there for him was Francis, along with Larry, who held an Uzi. Connor was told to stand at the far wall, so that two bright lights and the Uzi were all aimed in his direction. If Connor had been confused before, he was now completely baffled.

"What's this about?" he asked.

Francis said to him, "Do you think you can fuck with me? You owe me twenty thousand dollars, and I want it here by nine o'clock tonight."

Connor spoke into the lights. "What? I don't owe you anything." Connor's confusion turned to anger. He was insulted at the obvious attempt to shake him down and at the way Francis was treating him without any of the respect he showed when they talked at the gym.

Francis pulled out a 9mm pistol and cocked it. "Are you calling me a liar? Did you hear him, Larry? You pay us that money tonight, or we cut you into pieces and take you out of here in garbage bags."

Francis pointed his pistol at Connor's face and Larry drew back the bolt on the Uzi.

Connor didn't flinch. He spoke into the light. "Do what you've gotta do. I'm not giving you anything."

Seconds passed and nothing happened. Francis began laughing, then Larry. Francis stepped up to Connor wearing a broad smile. He put his hand around Connor's shoulder. "You've got balls, Connor. Congratulations, you passed the test."

"Test?" Connor asked. His anger was fading, but the confusion remained.

"You're qualified," Larry said. "Have we got a job for you."

"Fuck, we've got a career for this guy," Francis said.

"Stock options."

"Pension plan."

"Country club membership."

Larry laid down the Uzi and walked upstairs, so Francis could talk to Connor alone. Once he got over his shock, Connor felt a cautious pride. "Look, Francis...," he hesitated in addressing Francis Mahoney by name for the first time, "...I don't gamble, not really, and I don't do drugs..."

"Good," Francis said. "Neither do I. You don't make money using drugs."

Connor became Francis' constant companion as he learned the business. He helped Francis pick the guys who would become the three wise men. Francis was the older brother that Connor never had. He taught him how to think strategically and how important it was to do everything the smart way, as Francis' cellmate William Trey had instructed. How to play chess while the others played checkers.

In the years that followed, Connor turned out to be as good at his job as Francis had hoped. Even when dozens of street-level dealers and two of the wise men were rounded up in 1986, Connor stayed out of the snare and managed the business so that money continued to flow up to Francis. With the money coming from the wholesalers, it was millions of dollars a year.

When word broke about Larry and Francis being indicted, Connor made himself scarce by spending a few days on Cape Cod before returning to the streets of South Boston, where he remained a free man. Francis, he knew, had left town and would not return for quite a while, if ever. They had a long-standing plan on how Francis would communicate with Connor during his time in exile. Relayed through relatives and trusted friends, the messages would be coded using chess terminology.

Connor was surprised when Gabby passed on the "0-0" message that Matthew had left at the Power Bar. Gabby was not part of the contingency network, and the message he delivered when Connor stopped by the bar meant that Francis was still in town. That made no sense because the last Connor had heard was from Larry, who said Francis was on his way to Ireland on the Avalon. Connor suspected a setup, but he had to make the meeting.

Castling was a chess move in which the king goes to a protected corner where the rook is able to guard him closely. 0-0-0 meant "king castles long," which would have meant to meet Francis in the Pony Room at Neponset. 0-0 was "king castles short," which told him to meet Francis inside the old fort on Castle Island.

At the far eastern end of South Boston was the City Point neighborhood, which ended at a beach on Pleasant Bay. Across the bay was Castle Island. A long causeway encircled the bay and connected City Point to the island. It was a favorite route for joggers and people wanting to take in the salt air and a cool breeze.

At eight o'clock Connor was waiting inside the old fort on Castle Island. It was a massive stone structure built by the British before the Revolutionary War, then upgraded and used against them during the War of 1812. The fort had been well-positioned to defend the narrow approach to Boston Harbor.

As Disco informed Francis in 1982, Castle Island was also the perfect landscape to neutralize the ability of high-tech parabolic microphones to pick up conversations from a long distance away, a tactic used by the FBI, the DEA and other law enforcement agencies. As a result, the benches along the causeway became one of Francis' favorite places to hold meetings.

A friend of Connor's conducted public tours of the historic fort. Connor arrived in time for the last tour of the day, and his friend let him stray into the fort's interior as the last tour group returned to the main gate.

A light mist had been falling for an hour. The only one still in the fort was Connor. Wearing a raincoat, he sat on a parapet and scanned both sides of the causeway, which connected behind the fort. On the well-lit causeway, he could see anyone approaching from a long distance off, but in the rain there had been only a few souls braving the foul weather for an evening stroll.

The last light of dusk had faded. Connor watched an old man walking slowly with the aid of a cane and bending down occasionally to pick up a piece of litter and dispose of it in the nearest trash can. After doing so, he would turn to take a quick glance behind him.

As he drew closer to the fort, the old man stopped and lifted his head. He caught Connor's profile and raised his cane in a greeting before continuing his slow shuffle to the backside of the fort, where he wandered up the grassy slope and stood beneath one of the large steel plates that covered the old gun ports facing the harbor.

Connor pulled out one of the steel pins holding the plate. It levered open, and Connor lowered a rope from the gun port, which was twelve feet above the ground. Francis hung the cane from a pocket and climbed the rope. Once he was inside, Connor raised the steel plate back into place.

Francis took off the coat and hat he had pulled from his father's closet and threw them onto the stone floor.

"Well, well, look what the tide washed in," Connor said. They moved into one of the spacious gun rooms, which still held its long cannons and a stack of heavy shot. Connor turned on a small, battery-powered lantern he had brought with him. As they spoke, their words echoed in the vaulted space.

"I got off the Avalon in Lynn. We got word on the radio that someone had killed my father and made it look like I did it," Francis began. "Do you know how hard it's gonna be for me to get out again? It's gonna be a real pain in the ass." Francis slapped the cane against the cannon.

"I have an idea who did it," Connor said.

"The guy made some mistakes." Francis considered the cane for a moment. It had been his mother's, and she had used it in the last six months of her life when she had become increasingly weak and unstable on her feet.

Connor continued, "I talked to Starchie today, and he told me there was an anonymous call to the State Police on Saturday night."

"Ah, that's why they had a sheet on me at Logan Airport," Francis said.

"Whoever it was knew not to call the Boston cops or the FBI. He knew that only the statees would seriously hunt you. He also planted a gun in the car you left in front of the Lancaster Street garage. Starchie said they did a ballistics test and it matches the slugs found at your dad's house. So it's definitely the murder weapon. He also said it had been wiped clean but that there was a silencer on it, and they picked up a couple of prints from it."

"Did he say whose prints they were?"

"No, but he said they're definitely not yours."

"How's everyone behaving the last few days?" Francis asked.

"Everyone's been good. The three wise men have been checking in and kicking up. Everyone else is kicking up and meeting their payments. Except Chelsea, and they've been running late for five weeks." Connor said. There was a bookie joint in Chelsea that Francis took control of after Operation Beanpot, when the Italians no longer had the organization or muscle to take it back.

"Nobody has done anything to draw attention to themselves. Like I said, though, I have a feeling."

Francis looked at Connor, who said, "I hope I'm wrong, Francis, but I think it's Buzzy."

Francis looked away from him and tapped the cane on the stack of metal shot. The old iron cannonballs had been painted a glossy black to keep them from rusting in the salty air. "You're not wrong, Connor. That's who I figured too. I'd like to take care of that Judas tonight, but I've got a handicap." Francis rubbed his wrist nervously. "I can't go out in public. The indictments still haven't come down, which is strange, but I'm wanted for questioning so I can be picked up just for showing my face. I have to stay invisible. It would be easier if we could get Buzzy to come to us."

"By the way, I ran into Larry last night," Connor said.

"Larry?"

"He was coming out of his cousin's restaurant in Quincy Market."

Francis raised his voice in a rush of anger. "He's had four and a half days to get out of town. What a stupid fuck."

"I think his genes kicked in."

"The goombah gene" is how Francis referred to the way Italian mobsters who seemed so intelligent in the way they ran their business would become incredibly stupid when it came time to go into hiding. They were like ostriches.

"I also talked to Disco yesterday," Connor said.

"Did he find out who's behind the indictments? Not that it matters at this point."

"It's our jai alai friends," Connor said, referring to Global Jai Alai, a company that owned jai alai arenas in Florida and Connecticut. The arenas were known as frontons, where gambling on the fast-paced games was legal. Francis had a man on the inside of Global Jai Alai who had been working as an accountant in the Connecticut office. The accountant was the middle man in a deal between Francis and the owner of Global Jai Alai. The accountant funneled twenty thousand dollars a week back to South Boston. In exchange, Francis and Larry provided protection so the company wouldn't be shaken down by any New York mobs.

The arrangement worked fine until the owner of Global Jai Alai decided to sell. The new owner was Randy Hudson. He and his wife lived in Cumberland, Rhode Island, just over an hour's drive from the Connecticut headquarters, where Mrs. Hudson worked as the general manager. She had been looking into the books, and word was that she and her husband were threatening to go to the authorities with what her keen eye for accounting had discovered.

The situation was complicated by the fact that Chris O'Malley was the vice president of security at Global Jai Alai. Chris left his job as a feeb, as FBI agents were called, at the mandatory retirement age of fifty. He had made the leap that all agents hope to make, into the more lucrative private sector at the age of fifty-one. Chris had been the agent whose influence brought Disco from a lousy assignment in the New Jersey FBI field office back to the Boston office, where Chris served as Disco's mentor.

Randy Hudson and his wife were afraid of Chris O'Malley. They reasoned that Chris must have known about the payoffs to Francis and Larry. So the Hudsons weren't about to take their complaints to the Boston FBI office, where Chris still had lots of friends. They did take the steps of firing Francis' inside man in accounting and ending the weekly payments.

Disco had always known everything that was happening in the Boston FBI office, as well as the DEA where his brother worked. He was also kept informed of some of the things the State Police were doing but not everything. On Global Jai Alai, he was in the dark.

"Disco found out where the information came from," Connor said. "It was the Attorney General's office. That's who the Hudsons talked to. The Attorney General's office brought it straight to Disco's new field director, who sounds like he doesn't keep Disco in the loop like old Shea used to do. The first news Disco got of this was when he overheard a conversation about your indictments."

Hearing that the Hudsons had gone not only around his back but around the FBI's back as well brought back a rage similar to what Francis had felt when the payments had stopped.

"Who the fuck do they think they are?" Francis' voice echoed across the pitch dark courtyard of the fort.

"Francis, keep it down."

Francis clenched his jaw and drew the cane into the air. He smashed it down on the stone floor. The wooden cane snapped in two. Francis walked over to the massive cannon. He smashed the stump of the cane across its back until bits of wood flew away and there was nothing left but the curve of the handle. He began stabbing this onto the cannon repeatedly until most of the wood was gone and it became Francis' fist hitting the old iron gun.

Connor knew enough not to interrupt. This was better than Francis yelling and the two of them getting caught inside the fort. When Francis stopped, he was breathing hard. He opened his hand and threw what remained of the handle into the darkness of the courtyard before sitting back down by Connor. He placed his head in his hands, less from fatigue than a desire to concentrate. It's what typically followed his rage, producing the clarity he needed to make a calm, focused decision.

Francis' breathing returned to normal, then went lower and lower until Connor thought that he might be sleeping. But when Francis slowly raised his head, he looked more alert and focused.

He spoke deliberately. "The third thing is I leave. Again. The second thing is we take care of Buzzy. The first thing is we visit the Hudsons. I'm not leaving the country without saying goodbye to them. That would be rude."

* * * * *

Jimmy's closest friend in the Senate was Junior Flaherty. Like Jimmy, Junior had followed his father into the world of Boston politics. He lived in Dorchester, which bordered South Boston, and he had a summer home in Cohasset. It was a town on the South Shore, also called the Irish Riviera because of all the Boston Irish who moved there to enjoy the beaches.

Since Junior and his wife bought the place in the sixties, the value of the home had increased almost five fold. The Flahertys had also recently purchased a vacation home in sunny Florida to escape the harsh New England winters.

Jimmy enjoyed teasing Junior about his Cohasset "estate," even though it was a simple two-bedroom saltbox. Behind his back, other politicians joked about Junior financing his second and third homes with the kickbacks he had received over the years. They also joked about how bitchy Junior had become lately with cops delivering the kickbacks. "Never let a cop be your bagman," Junior was supposed to have said. "They think they're entitled to their own cut, and they don't ask first before taking it."

Junior was twenty years older than Jimmy and knew the workings of the Senate better than anyone, so Jimmy considered himself fortunate to have him as a mentor. It also helped that Junior was not from South Boston and didn't have close ties to Mayor Sullivan.

It was partly Jimmy's nature and partly the nature of politics in South Boston that made it nearly impossible for him to fuse close, long-lasting alliances with fellow South Boston politicians. But in the Senate, where the urban interests of greater Boston were often at odds with those of the suburbs and rural areas of western Massachusetts, it was important not to let local grudges divide the power of the Boston delegation.

Jimmy had gone up to the State House after the burial to get Junior's take on events. When he arrived at Junior's office, the door was closed. He knocked, and the door was opened by Pat Tierney, known since childhood as Flash because he ran so slow. Flash was famous on the baseball diamond as the only player who could be thrown out at first base after hitting a grounder to the outfield.

Flash served in the House of Representatives and was also from Dorchester. With Junior, the two of them worked closely to control the demi-world of Dorchester politics, where the once dominant

Irish-Catholic community now stood alongside, and often culturally at odds with, a large black community. This large section of Boston was also home to an increasing mix of people from Haiti, the Dominican Republic, El Salvador, Vietnam, Laos and other countries.

It was the kind of uncharted political landscape that Mayor Sullivan was expertly navigating, but waters that Jimmy steered clear of. In many situations Junior and Flash were equally uncomfortable with it.

"C'mon in, Jimmy," Flash said with a wave. Despite his nickname being a joke, those who didn't know its origin thought it fit Flash perfectly. He was a short, thin man who spoke rapidly and who channeled his excess energy into an extensive repertoire of quick, exaggerated gestures. "We're just trying to decide how many people still think Curley was guilty of mail fraud. Or, how many people know who James Michael Curley was."

Junior had always been fascinated with James Michael Curley, the legendary Massachusetts politician, and took every opportunity to recount stories about him. Jimmy sat down and they discussed Mayor Sullivan's South Bay waste disposal plan and the effect of Jimmy's outside section, which would penalize Sullivan if he tried to proceed with the plan.

"I saw the Gang of Five having a powwow in Hurley's office this afternoon," Junior said. The five Democratic senators opposed to Jimmy's election as the new Senate president were all from suburban or rural districts, and most harbored a dislike or outright hostility toward Jimmy that went back to the days of desegregation. The leader of the group was Jimmy's most ardent critic: George Corbin, the senator from Wellesley.

Junior sat with his feet on his desk and considered the dark sky outside. He was a stocky man with a ruddy complexion acquired after many summers of sailing and golfing in Cohasset, and many afternoons drinking vodka tonics with friends on his backyard deck. He had a head of wavy white hair that grew thick at the sides and sat firmly planted on top of his head in a heavily lubricated combover.

"You know how some guy duped Curley into buying a mine out in Nevada?" Junior asked not to either man in particular. "On the day before Curley showed up, the owner of the mine packed a shotgun with silver dust, then blasted it all over the walls of the mine. When he gave Curley a tour the next morning, he'd keep scratching the wall and showing his silver-tipped fingers to Curley. The stupid son of a bitch fell for it."

"Serves him right," Flash said. "Wasn't his money to begin with."

The conversation moved from the political past to the current plight of Senate President Hurley. Flash shook his head and gave a helicopter-like whirl of his right arm. "I don't want to be too negative, Jimmy, but I don't think that Hurley can help you gain votes. I think your support in the Senate is like an iceberg off the coast of Florida in July. It's melting fast."

Junior hummed noncommittally and drew his hand slowly across his combover, a gesture displayed whenever he was mulling competing points of view. "Hmmm, icebergs. Well, I walked past his office a little while ago, and he was sitting there with his hands flat on his desk staring into a cup of coffee, just staring into it and sucking in the steam like it was going to give him strength. The man is highly fatigued, Jimmy. He's dying to get out of his job."

"He told me at the wake he'd hold out until the end of the week and that's all," Jimmy said.

"That's only two more days, and I think you'll be lucky to get that out of him," Junior said. "You also have to worry about the press. Particularly the *Globe*. Let's hope the ghouls on Morrissey Boulevard have so much contempt for you and South Boston that they'll refuse to dignify the possibility of your presidency with an editorial."

"Hurley's the poster child for political despair," Flash said.

Junior rose to Hurley's defense. "He's the real loser, Flash. Jimmy keeps his job as senator no matter what happens. He can maneuver, but Hurley's trapped by his aura of corruption. He can't go to the press to help him build support for Jimmy. Anything he says will be turned against our friend here."

Flash joined his thumb and forefinger to make a circle and held it in front of him. "I have zero sympathy for the guy. He walks into his bank in Marblehead and cashes a two thousand dollar check from that construction company. I don't know how guys like that can get a high school diploma, never mind be Senate president. I don't care so much that he was on the take, but I really resent how stupid he was about it."

"All he wants is to leave with a little dignity," Junior said. "Until this week, he saw you as his savior, Jimmy. You're not everybody's first choice, especially in certain suburbs, but there really is no favorite. It's all about being clean, returning respectability to the Senate after all this stuff that happened. All this..." Junior paused and searched for a word that would differentiate Hurley's taking bribes from his taking bribes.

"Stupidity. All this stupidity," Flash said.

"Sure," Junior continued. "Jimmy's the only one in leadership that looks clean and is clean. By the way, Jimmy, now would be a good time to let me know if that's not truly the case."

Jimmy said nothing, so Junior continued. "Everything else falls away. The *Globe* might not like your background on busing, for one, and they'll fight like hell to keep you from becoming president if Hurley announces you as his choice. The question is whether they'll use any ink to criticize you before you're officially offered the job. So that's the first hurdle. The second is your age. You're only forty, but you have the experience and temperament that people are looking for. Then there's the third hurdle. The new one," Junior frowned and folded both hands over his head.

Jimmy waited to hear what the third hurdle was. He looked at Junior. Junior turned to Flash. Flash turned to Jimmy. "Bloody Sunday," Flash said, referring to Salty's murder and Francis' implication in it.

Junior groaned. "That's very tactful, Flash."

"I don't care what people are calling it," Jimmy said. "I just mind where it leaves me. There's not a thing I can do about it, you know. It's the same crap I've had to deal with for years. They always want to tie me to Francis. This is no different."

Junior took his feet from his desk and drew up straight in his chair. "I think it is, Jimmy. The funny thing is that the *Globe* isn't making much of the story at all, and I don't think they will. Unless Francis is charged. And the tabloids are waiting for the body to cool, so to speak, before they trumpet it. Which is only a matter of days.

"The real trouble rests with some of our Democratic friends in the Senate. The ones who have to vote for you in caucus. For the most part they've never believed you have anything to do with Francis' world. But some of them have really gotten skittish with this story. If your brother is mad enough to kill his own father ... not that I believe he did it, mind you … but they wonder what he might do next to put your name on the front page. That's what scares them. Having your brother's reputation damaging the reputation of the Senate."

"I was up by two or three votes last week. Hurley says I'm now down by the same. Does that sound right?" Jimmy asked.

"You seem to have lost five votes, which could grow to seven by my estimate, and you'll need to get them back before we caucus. Hurley knows this. He won't call a caucus until the numbers are there. In the meantime, your support is like a big balloon with a tiny hole, slowly losing its strength. Yes, a balloon. I think I like that better than the iceberg, Flash."

"I can probably guess some of them," Jimmy said. "But if you know any for certain, I'd like to hear, so I know who to lobby."

"I know one for sure," Junior said. "Chesterton."

Flash clapped three times in rapid succession. Junior found this to be the most annoying of Flash's tics because it made him flinch every time.

"That seed sucker from Stockbridge?" Flash asked. "Jimmy, tell him you'll do something for Massachusetts farmers. All ten of them."

"I can't think of a good strategy right now, Jimmy, so I suggest you not make any moves yet. You might do your case more harm than good."

"Yes," Jimmy said. "A Greek who lived centuries ago would agree with you. Know the right moment, he said."

Jimmy liked to quote the classics to his colleagues, who could be amused or annoyed by the habit. Junior liked to make a game of guessing who it might be. "Let me see. Aristotle?"

Jimmy shook his head.

"Sophocles?"

"Pittacus," Jimmy said.

Junior smiled and said, "Hmm. Pittacus. What a … pity cause … I never heard of him."

"He must have been a second stringer," Flash said.

"Anyway," Junior continued, "there are times when inaction is the best action, and until a new dawn spreads its rosy fingers across the golden dome I suggest you do just that. Nothing."

"I won't do anything. Not tonight, of course," Jimmy said. "Do you want to know what's making them hesitant to support me? When you boil it down, it's fear. In the experience of one certain politician, there are only two ways to defeat fear. The first is to dispel it. The second is to introduce an even greater fear."

"Cicero?" Junior asked.

"Mahoney," Jimmy said.

* * * * *

Matthew paid the cab driver, then climbed the wide granite steps to the main entrance of the State House. The building was dark except for a few lit windows in the west annex where legislators had offices. He tried opening the enormous doors, but they were all locked and as he was searching for some kind of door bell, he heard a voice behind him.

"The State House is closed." A member of the Capitol Police Force had arrived seemingly from nowhere and waved Matthew away. It was the Capitol Police who caught Matthew up on the State House dome years before. The cop spoke in a blunt tone followed by an admonishing stare.

Good old Boston charm, Matthew thought. "I need to see Jimmy Mahoney. How do I get inside?"

"You can see him tomorrow if you call for an appointment in the morning."

"I'm his brother, Matt Mahoney. It's important."

The officer stepped around Matthew and scanned the windows of the annex. "Well, it looks like your brother's still here. He never leaves his lights on when he goes home. Go to the entrance out back. Somebody will call him. If he wants to see you, he'll come down."

Matthew turned down Bowdoin Street, which ran along the east side of the State House, and arrived at a tunnel, yellow-tiled and brightly lit, through which he could see Joy Street on the west side of the Capitol. Automobile traffic flowed in and out of the tunnel, stopping at a guard checkpoint before either descending to the interior parking lot or exiting on the other side.

Through the high wrought iron fence to his left, Matthew saw the famous drain pipe in a dark corner of the building. It was where he shimmied up to the dome so long ago. What a crazy thing to have done. Looking at the top of the drain pipe, Matthew saw something new, or at least new to him. A cone of barbed wired encircling the pipe to prevent a repeat of the stunt.

He approached the guard shack and was directed to a small office inside the tunnel entrance. Matthew was familiar with the office. It was where the Capitol Police put him after making him climb down from the dome. He had to wait until the Boston Police picked him and Buzzy up and drove them to their station. Matthew remembered the glare of the fluorescent lights in the office.

The same ugly lights still hung from the ceiling. Below them sat a heavyset officer. Various parts of a disassembled computer printer lay strewn across his desk.

"What can I do for you?" the officer said, neither looking up nor standing up.

"I need to see Jimmy Mahoney. He's in his office."

"Is the senator expecting you?" the officer said, still not looking at Matthew but staring at the maze of parts arranged on his desk as if he were in the middle of divining some meaning from their arrangement.

"No..."

"You'll need to call in the morning, and arrange an appointment. That way the senator can be prepared to adequately address whatever needs you may have."

"Jimmy's my brother, and this is important."

"Your brother?" the officer said, finally glancing at Matthew for the first time and standing up. As he did so, the officer bumped the table and sent several of the printer pieces tumbling to the floor. "Jesus Christ, why didn't they just let us keep our typewriters?" Then turning to Matthew, "You mean you're his other brother. I didn't know he had another brother. Let me call him."

"Can't I just go up?" Matthew asked.

"He has to come down and sign you in."

When Jimmy arrived, he didn't seem surprised to see Matthew. He was dressed in a suit and tie, and his hair looked as neat as when he combed it before the funeral. "Matt, this is wonderful. I got called up here, and I was afraid we wouldn't get a chance to say goodbye. Eddy," Jimmy said turning to the officer, "this is my younger brother, Matt. He and his wife are off to the old country tomorrow on their honeymoon."

"When he said he was your brother, I thought I was hearing things." Jimmy and the officer laughed.

"No, Matt is the wise one in the family. Wise enough to keep his name out of the papers and to live where his family can't bother him," Jimmy said.

Turning to Matthew, he asked, "Are you hungry? I know a couple of places if you want to grab a bite. By the way, did you get the car fixed?"

"The car's fine. I'm not hungry. I thought we could talk for a bit."

"Sure. We can go to my office. Eddy, where do I sign for the package?"

Eddy opened the log book and handed Jimmy a pen. Matthew clipped on a visitor's badge, then followed Jimmy down poorly lit hallways. He gave Matthew an account of the funeral service. "It's not a big deal that you missed it," Jimmy said.

They stepped into the small elevator that took them on an excruciatingly slow ride to the fourth floor, where Jimmy had his office. Halfway down the hall they ran into Junior, who was leaving for the night.

"Junior, this is my younger brother, Matt."

They shook hands and Junior said, "I can tell which Mahoney ate more spinach growing up."

Junior looked at Jimmy and pointed to the ceiling and the gold dome beyond.

"Yes, he's the one."

"Don't stay too late, Jimmy. I'll see you tomorrow. Bright and surly."

Behind the neatly arranged desk in Jimmy's small office were two large bookshelves, filled with government manuals and books ranging from *The Orations of Cicero* and *The Confessions of Saint Augustine* to *The Essays of Ralph Waldo Emerson*. Above the bookshelves ran a row of photographs and illustrated portraits, a who's who of the Boston Irish leaders famous for wresting control of the city from the Yankee Protestant establishment. Patrick Collins, Bishop Fitzpatrick, Martin Lomasney, John "Honey Fitz" Fitzgerald of the North End and beside him Patrick Kennedy from East Boston, John McCormack, James Michael Curley and Patrick McGuire.

Matthew's eyes moved from one face to the next.

"Recognize any?" Jimmy asked.

Matthew shook his head. The office had only one window, and from its height, Matthew could look down on Boston Common and see a pattern to the chaos of pathways and lights.

Jimmy sat down behind his desk and pointed Matthew to one of the comfortable leather chairs facing his desk. He had gotten a quick look at Matthew's battered suit in the office downstairs. Now he noticed that the knuckles on one of Matthew's hands were cut. Suddenly Jimmy realized what a mess he had sent Matthew into and that it had been wrong. More than simply wrong, it had been selfish.

The realization sent Jimmy's spirits tumbling, but he maintained a façade of cheer. "From the look of your suit, I'd say you've had an adventurous day."

"I went over to Dad's house this morning. You want to know what I found there?" He waited to see if he could upset Jimmy, send a ripple across the calmness that surrounded him.

"Well, Matt, only if you think I need to know."

Matthew was expecting Jimmy to resist him, ask him please not to say anything that would get Jimmy in trouble. In his words and his expression, Jimmy was showing nothing. Matthew was frustrated by his inability to read him the way he could read Francis.

"I didn't find the photo albums. They're at your house, Jimmy. They've been there since Mom's funeral."

"Matt, I made a mistake sending you to Dad's house."

"That's right, Jimmy."

"So," Jimmy said and rested his chin on the tip of his folded hands. "I know you'll feel better once you leave this mess behind."

Matthew knew he shouldn't mention anything to Jimmy about seeing Francis, but he found himself tempted, very tempted, to do just that. At the very least, he wanted to fuck with his oldest brother. Get him back somehow.

"Maybe I should tell you who I ran into today."

Jimmy rocked back in his chair. "If you think it would serve a purpose," said Jimmy as he stretched his arms before him and placed both hands flat on his desk.

There followed a silence in which Jimmy seemed to grow more resolved and Matthew less. From somewhere down the fourth floor hall of the State House annex came the faint sound of a reluctant door being forced closed and the jingle of keys as the door was locked.

"I'd never do to you what you did to me today," Matthew finally said. "It's the same old shit you pulled on me when I was a kid. You know, Dad was an arrogant prick. I think you're a lot like him."

Jimmy looked down at the worn edge of his desk and ran a finger over its surface. "Fair enough, Matt. At least on the first part. It was a mistake, and I apologize. You and I live very different lives, and we've never been that close, but I want you to know that I still care very much about you."

"You show it in a funny way," Matthew said. He felt the fatigue of the day catching up with him, and he found nothing else to say to his brother. "I'm going," Matthew said and stood up. Jimmy stood to join him. "Don't bother. I'll find my own way out."

* * * * *

He considered taking a cab back to his car in South Boston, but it was only a few miles, and a walk in the cool evening air would revive Matthew. He had bought a second pair of shoes on the way home from the wake. They cost twice as much as the pair he ended up throwing away, but they were far more comfortable.

A light mist began falling as Matthew went through the deserted financial district. He crossed into South Boston on the Northern Avenue Bridge and walked a dark desolate mile down Northern Avenue.

It was a worn-down district of warehouses, abandoned lots, fishing piers and a few scattered restaurants and bars. Technically part of South Boston but more of an uninhabited space between the residential neighborhoods and downtown Boston. An in-between place, the kind of land Matthew felt he had been inhabiting since leaving South Boston. Half of him still belonged to it, half of him never would.

It was September 1974, when forced busing tore South Boston apart. The odds were that Matthew would be assigned to Roxbury High that fall. It was in the heart of Boston's black community, and everyone knew it would be a place of chaos and violence come September. It would be even worse at South Boston High School, where hundreds of black students would be bused into the heart of an almost all-white neighborhood.

Matthew had only one hope of staying in South Boston without being bused. He took the entrance exam for Boston Latin, a public school that had been made exempt from busing. If you passed the exam, you were home free. Unless you later flunked out like Buzzy did in his freshman year.

In April, Matthew received a letter informing him that he had failed to score high enough on the Latin School exam. It was followed by another letter from the Boston School Committee. In compliance with Judge Rafferty's plan to achieve racial balance in the Boston public school system, Matthew was being assigned to Roxbury High.

That May, Matthew's mother put away the cane that allowed her limited mobility when the chemotherapy and radiation left her too weak to stand. Her next month was spent in a hospital bed in the middle of the living room, an arrangement that seemed just plain wrong to everyone else in the family.

Her reason soon became clear to Matthew. From the living room, she was able to see her family's comings and goings, to hear meals being prepared in the kitchen, to watch the family at the dining room table, whether they ate together or separately, as was becoming the case since there was just Matthew and his father.

Matthew remembered his mother for her laugh. It was a pleasant, light way of laughing that could breathe life into the house the way a fire in the fireplace warms it. Having spent her childhood in Ireland, her sense of humor was free of the sarcasm and bitterness that was more typical of people raised in Boston, and that included Matthew. He never once heard his mother laugh at another's misfortune.

She was devoted to Salty and played the part of a traditional wife. Even when she was the only one working a full-time job, she still did all the laundry, the cleaning and the cooking. It was her cooking that Matthew and his brothers liked to make fun of. Not that she was a bad cook. She just had no imagination in the kitchen. All of her recipes were cut out of the newspaper and followed precisely. She taped the newspaper clippings to index cards and kept them in a small metal box.

The regular dishes included pork chops, spaghetti, meatloaf, hot dogs and what their mother called American Chop Suey, which she would make for special occasions. The name sounded exotic, but it was simply hamburger meat, macaroni and spaghetti sauce.

No matter how many times his mother had cooked a meal, she would still retrieve the recipe card from the box and refer to it as she prepared dinner. Every meal included some form of potato, and vegetables out of a can. When they moved from Old Colony to City Point, they began having the traditional roast beef meal every Sunday afternoon.

With all the fuss about the photo albums that day, Matthew had not had a chance to sit down and browse through the pictures and celebrate his mother's life once again. He wished he had done so. The photos captured her spirit. They showed her quite happy with life. She was a beautiful woman and the photos captured that as well. Matthew got his black hair from his mother. In the pictures, her hair was long and wavy.

That changed with the chemotherapy and radiation, which had barbaric effects in Matthew's opinion. As his mother's appetite faded, he could see her body diminishing as well, her vitality leaving her the way a blazing fire fades to embers and finally ash. Nurses stopped by every day to care for her, clean her and administer doses of medication to address the constant pain.

Father Gonzales, who Nora had become fond of, visited as often as possible. Sometimes it was three times a week, other times only once. He ministered to her, and entertained her with his quirky anecdotes about the odd people he encountered throughout his day. He left Nora with a smile that could linger into the dark night.

Jimmy lived with Peg in their new home on N Street, but he stopped by every chance he got. He would feed his mother and read to her from the Bible and *Reader's Digest*. Aunt Margaret traveled up from Quincy on weekends, and she would leave behind a tray of lasagna or a pot of beef stew. For the boys, as she called Matthew and his father.

Aunt Eileen and Uncle Pete would visit as well, but it was Aunt Eileen who was at her sister's side more often than anyone else. Matthew couldn't stand her then, and still couldn't now, but he respected her tremendously for her devotion to his mother. When Aunt Eileen came to visit, he would find a convenient excuse to leave the house.

Toward the end, his mother's days were filled with people who loved her and cared for her. It was at night when shadows could draw close. Some nights Matthew would sleep on the living room couch, talking to his mother when she could manage conversation, watching TV with her, fetching her a glass of water or the plastic yellow bucket when she was nauseous.

One night, she told him what a wonderful life he was going to have and how proud she was of him. Matthew thought it was the strong pain killers talking because he didn't see anything wonderful waiting down his road. He had done little to make her proud in his fourteen years, especially considering his three trips to the police station, a poor record in school and a tendency to see a fight as the best solution to a problem.

The one person missing most from the scene toward the end of Nora's life was her husband. Salty spent many of his evenings at anti-busing rallies, attending strategy meetings with other leaders who advocated a more defiant approach. Many of the meetings were held at Donnelley's Pub or some other neighborhood bar.

There were nights Salty would arrive home late and walk through the dark living room without acknowledging his wife before going upstairs to sleep in their bed. Matthew had seen this from the couch where he lay sleeping or trying to sleep, and he would follow the figure of his father, hoping he would come back downstairs to say goodnight to Nora or give her a kiss.

On some nights his father would not come home at all, and wouldn't offer any explanation when he arrived home the next morning. Everyone noticed his neglect at the end. Not just family, but friends and even neighbors.

Jimmy said nothing and never confronted his father about it. Although he regretted it for years to come, Matthew followed his brother Jimmy's lead. It came out of a sense of misplaced respect, a sense of loyalty extended to the absurd, and even a fear that Matthew still had of his father, that crossing him in such a fragile time just shouldn't be done.

Francis was in prison at the time, and had been depending on family to keep him up to date on his mother's condition. On the day she died, Matthew volunteered for the task of breaking the news to him. Peg drove him out to the prison in Walpole. Matthew sat stoically waiting for Francis, looking at himself in the glass that divided prisoner from visitor.

As soon as his older brother sat down opposite him, Matthew broke down and began crying. So did Francis, and the two of them sat there saying nothing, not even looking at each other for several minutes as people walked by and conversations took place on either side of them.

"Alright, that's enough of that," Francis finally said.

Matthew tried to pull himself together but had difficulty.

"Matt, look at me," Francis said.

Matthew took a deep breath and pulled his chair close to the glass, where he wiped his eyes and looked at his brother.

Francis slowly extended his arms outward, palms facing up, the way a priest would do during mass when it was time to consecrate the host. "Be thankful for everything she did for us, little brother. She's gone now, and if she's anywhere, she's not where she can feel pain anymore. You're gonna be thinking about her a lot, and when you do you can't think about her the way she was after getting sick. She's not in the place where your memory will want to take you. If you start to feel guilty about all the things you did to piss her off or disappoint her, you have to stop yourself. She's free from it, and you have to be free from it too. Get control of your feelings and keep it that way."

A guard on Francis' side of the glass indicated that the visit was over. Francis pushed back his chair and stood up. Without a trace of emotion in his expression or in his voice, he said to Matthew, "That's it, little brother. Now go."

Matthew sat up straight in his chair and watched through the glass as Francis walked to the other end of the room, where he passed through a security door and disappeared. For a moment, Matthew thought he might come back and sit down with him again. He wanted to hear more from his older brother, but he wasn't going to. What he got was all there was, and he decided that if he needed more, Francis would have given it to him.

He left the visiting area and returned to the parking lot, where he got in the car with Peg. Matthew didn't want to talk to her or anybody else about the visit and what Francis had said. It was for him only.

One week after the burial, Salty announced that Matthew would be going to live with his cousins in Quincy. The city just south of Boston became Matthew's new legal residence, making him eligible to attend North Quincy High and placing him beyond the reach of Boston's desegregation court.

With the realization that busing was indeed going to happen in a matter of weeks, South Boston families scrambled to place their children in private Catholic schools, which quickly filled up. As a result, scores of South Boston youth were shipped away by families unable to bear the cost of a private education and unwilling to send their children to school in the black neighborhood of Roxbury, where the racial tension and likely violence would ruin any hope of getting an education.

Although he knew his father could have afforded to send him to a private school, Matthew didn't question the decision to send him to Quincy. He welcomed it as a chance to escape the grief he felt for his mother and anger toward his father. He shared a room with Richard and got along well with the rest of the Quincy Mahoneys.

For one unholy week, Matthew tried any way he could to vent his anger and grief. In early September, when he was to attend his first day of classes at North Quincy High, Matthew instead took the subway to Andrew Square and walked down Dorchester Street to Old Colony. The sidewalks were crowded with people waiting to see the yellow school buses arrive in South Boston.

It was the first day of school across the city, and events exploded even more violently than expected. It began with lines of police motorcycles, more than anybody in South Boston had ever seen, clearing the way along Dorchester Street, the same route used for the St. Patrick's Day parade. State troopers on horseback were stationed along the road, facing sidewalks full of people.

After the motorcycles came the yellow buses, lots of them. The tension built until somebody threw a brick at a bus. Then all hell broke loose as rocks, bottles and anything that could be picked up went flying through the air, at the buses and the cops. Police in riot gear appeared and charged the crowd with batons swinging, targeting men, women and kids alike. There was no discrimination. It blew into a full riot along the route and later at the high school, where the buses were headed.

Most of South Boston didn't go to school that first day. Matthew moved with one of many teenage mobs across the community. All the old divisions were gone. Old Colony, Old Harbor, D Street, City Point, the Heights. No matter what neighborhood you came from, you were all on the same team now, united against the invaders.

The Boston Police Department responded with the TPF, Tactical Police Force, a unit that had been formed in the sixties to respond aggressively to large-scale riots. Their goal was to intimidate the neighborhood. Dressed in jumpsuits, boots, leather jackets and gloves, and helmets with Plexiglas shields, they roamed the projects in packs. As they approached, they banged their batons rhythmically against light poles, the sides of cars and buildings.

Matthew joined others on rooftops where they showered police with bricks, bottles and anything else they could find. When the parade of buses returned to Dorchester Street at the end of the school day, they harassed the state troopers on horseback and swung hockey sticks at the horses' legs to make them throw their riders. In retaliation, the cops chased kids into the project courtyards, where they beat them with batons in plain view or dragged them off to beat them out of sight.

Instead of relief, the evening brought helicopters hovering overhead and bands of TPF patrolling the projects. They responded with hostility toward anyone caught doing wrong or simply being in the wrong place. In the morning, there were more helicopters. The TPF positioned men on the rooftops of Old Colony, where the residents felt like they were under siege.

The week continued like that. The violence spread everywhere, including the Gavin Pub, a bar across from the project. It was where members of the toughest gang in South Boston hung out. One night, the TPF chased someone into the Gavin and tried to arrest him, but they quickly found themselves outnumbered by an angry mob that didn't give a shit who the TPF were. The cops were forced to make an embarrassing retreat.

The next night, the TPF retaliated by raiding the Gavin and smashing heads indiscriminately. They had their badges covered with black tape, a time-honored tactic to keep victims from positively identifying the offending officers. They beat everybody in the bar, then smashed everything that could be smashed in the place.

Blue lights and sirens filled the night as more police arrived, then ambulances. One by one, people were carried out of the bar, many unrecognizable because of all the blood. Over a dozen had had their skulls cracked.

It was only a matter of moments before word reached the project, sending a stream of angry people to the scene with bats and hockey sticks. Rocks went flying, shattering the windows on police cruisers. A riot broke out with cops beating more people, including mothers and kids.

In the days to follow, the state troopers and TPF grew even more aggressive, beginning and ending their day by marching in formation along the bus route. The sound of boots pounding on pavement could be heard blocks away.

People in Old Colony grew more organized. Whenever news spread through the project of a police attack, it was announced in a loud voice from a window accompanied by the clanging of pots and pans. Large crowds, including mothers, formed in the courtyards to respond with whatever they could grab that could do damage. Defiant music played from speakers placed in apartment windows. Paddy wagons were constantly flying by with sirens blaring, along with big blue buses filled with TPF in riot gear.

Matthew slept on the floor of different Old Colony apartments during that week. Many others were doing the same to defend what they saw as a direct attack on their community. At night, they would watch the news on TV to relive the events of the day and see if any of them had made the highlights.

With every rock he threw at a cop, Matthew took a sadistic pleasure at hitting his target. He especially hated the cops who rode the big Harleys. They seemed to be hiding behind their machines.

One afternoon, he and Buzzy were part of a group taunting a team of six motorcycle cops a block from Patterson Way. A few of the rocks they threw hit home, enough to provoke a charge. The cops rode right into an ambush. Molotov cocktails hit the front two bikes from either side of the street. Both motorcycles spun out as the two riders rolled around and brushed the flames from their arms and legs. The other four motorcycles came to a stop, and rocks began raining down from the roofs above.

The cops were in serious trouble. When the last two tried to flee in the direction they had come, Matthew and two other kids flung a heavy metal bed frame and brought the bikes down. From the other end of the street came the crashing of boots as a group of TPF ran onto the scene, turning the tide in favor of the police. All the kids broke up and fled.

Matthew and Buzzy ran into their courtyard and through an archway leading into the next courtyard. They had done it a number of times that week, dashing through the maze of courtyards before ducking into a building where people would hide them. Matthew was fast and Buzzy was even faster. As Matthew barreled through the third archway, he glanced behind him, wondering why Buzzy hadn't overtaken him.

Buzzy was nowhere in sight. Then Matthew saw him emerging from the second archway with a limp. Behind him was a motorcycle cop wielding a baton. The cop caught up to Buzzy and brought him down with a swing to the ribs. Grabbing Buzzy by the ankle, the cop dragged him back through the archway, taking a few more swings at the back of Buzzy's legs.

As Buzzy's screams echoed in the vaulted space, Matthew ran to help. The scene in the next courtyard was chaotic. People were yelling insults from windows on all sides. Pots and pans were banging. Some kids were being beaten by the cops, while others were being hauled back to the street where a TPF bus had pulled up to take those who had been arrested.

Matthew searched the scene for Buzzy, but the courtyard was too crowded and noisy to spot him easily. Just moments before, the cops had the upper hand. Now the tide had swung once again. Bricks and bottles rained down onto the TPF bus, breaking several windows. People were coming out of the buildings and challenging the cops, pulling back a couple of the kids being hauled away.

The TPF and the motorcycle cops were forced into a tactical retreat, dragging one last suspect into the bus. Finally Matthew spotted Buzzy on the ground. The cop holding him stood with his back to Matthew. Buzzy had scrambled away, but now the cop had him once again and swung his baton into Buzzy's back. With his other hand, the cop held Buzzy's pant leg to keep him from escaping.

With all of the noise, the cop couldn't hear Matthew come up from behind. As the cop lifted the baton to take another swing, Matthew grabbed the weapon with both hands and pulled it from his grip. He then swung it with all his might into the side of the man's knee.

The cop screamed and dropped to the ground clutching his leg. His eyes were squeezed shut in agony. Matthew stared down at his face, ready to smash the cop in the mouth with the baton. He drew back and swung just as the cop rolled to one side. The baton struck the cop's light blue fiberglass helmet with a loud crack and broke the outer layer.

Matthew dropped the baton, then grabbed Buzzy's belt with one hand and the neck of his shirt with the other. He picked him up and carried his friend back through the archway, across the courtyard and through the next archway.

He heard footsteps coming up fast from behind. Matthew was prepared to put Buzzy down and fight. It wasn't another cop though. It was Joey Flynn. He helped Matthew carry Buzzy to a car. They drove him to the emergency room at Boston City Hospital, where Buzzy was treated for a broken ankle, a broken nose, two broken ribs and a concussion. He had also lost a tooth.

Matthew's name ended up on a list that was sent to the Quincy Police Department. Quincy cops showed up at his cousins' house to announce that if Matthew was seen again in South Boston anytime soon, even to attend mass at St. Monica's Church, he'd be hauled off to jail.

The battle was not over for South Boston, but for Matthew it was. It had lasted a week, enough time to discover that in the right circumstances he was capable of almost anything. There was no way of extinguishing his anger or his grief, and no matter how much he wanted to stay a part of South Boston, he knew he never could.

Matthew's first trip back to South Boston after the busing madness was for Thanksgiving at his father's place, where Salty announced that Buzzy was forbidden from ever again visiting the house on E. Third Street. Salty said it at his dining room table, where Matthew and Jimmy's family were in the middle of the holiday meal. It had been a strange thing to say, but stranger still since Matthew no longer lived there himself, so Buzzy would have no reason to visit. Matthew was baffled and asked why.

"He's in the wrong business," Salty said.

"What?" Matthew asked.

"Drugs. Your friend's a drug dealer. But you already know that, don't you, Matt?"

The term seemed too glamorous to describe what Buzzy did, which was sell drugs, or mainly a drug—pot—and share it with Matthew. They had first gotten high when they were nine years old. Walking home after hockey practice, they saw a fastback Mustang get into an accident on Broadway. Matthew and Buzzy watched the driver dash behind a convenience store, then return to the scene as a police car arrived. While the driver was being questioned, the boys went behind the store to see what he had hidden. It was a bag of pot.

Carrying the stash, they laughed as they walked past the driver, who knew what they had done, but in the presence of the cop was helpless to reclaim his goods. Sitting on a bench overlooking Pleasant Bay, they smoked two joints, then stared in amazement at the planes flying low and directly overhead on their approach to Logan.

Buzzy bought more that week and was dealing within the month. The whole time he lived in South Boston, Matthew would never have to pay for pot again. He made it understood in the project, where he was spending more and more time, that if anybody messed with Buzzy, Matthew would bust their head. Buzzy did business everywhere. On the street, in the subway, outside the hockey rink, and before, during and after concerts at Boston Garden.

That Thanksgiving when his father announced the ban, it felt to Matthew as if his father was accusing him as much as Buzzy of selling drugs. Buzzy's name was never mentioned again by his father except to say, "Drugs have no place in South Boston and neither does Buzzy. And I never, ever want to see you with Buzzy or hear that you've been hanging around with that loser."

That fall Matthew made a spot on the North Quincy High hockey team. He made new friends. He had his first real girlfriend. As his old life receded, his new one grew. On the odd weekend night when Matthew had no plans, the longing for the old life would send him north to Old Colony, where he'd look for Buzzy and find him partying on the streets with a crowd. Matthew knew some of the people, but there were many he didn't know. They hung out on Patterson Way, blasted music from car stereos, danced on the sidewalk and got into fights.

It was when a lot of pot was being laced with angel dust, and kids would be acting out of their minds. Matthew saw one girl on a project rooftop, screaming hysterically at anyone who approached her. Then, to stop the snakes that were squirming around inside her head, she jumped to the pavement three stories below.

It was different than before. The kids were different. Whenever Matthew got the urge to return, he resisted it. The only relationships he maintained were with his family and with Buzzy. He survived his four years of high school and began college the next fall at the Boston campus of the University of Massachusetts, a stone's throw away from South Boston. It was an odd feeling to sit in a classroom with a view of Carson Beach, to gaze at his hometown and know that he was no longer connected to it and probably never would be again.

Matthew thought of his grandparents, who had left their home behind to start a new life in a new place. If it worked for them, it could work for him.

When he had been very young, Matthew remembered watching a corny show on a black and white TV. Playing Monday nights, it was a story about three brothers making a life in a new frontier town called Seattle. He would curl up next to his mother on the couch and the two would watch it faithfully every week.

The memory of that show and the peace he felt remembering it were all that Matthew really considered when choosing Seattle as his new home. He quit school near the end of his first semester. On his last weekend in Boston, he called Buzzy and they went to a show at the Paradise Club behind Fenway Park. They got there early so Buzzy could set up shop, and after selling most of his goods, they went inside.

The place hadn't quite filled up when the opening band started playing. They had a sound that Matthew had never heard before and a name he couldn't remember hearing either, but they were good. So good that they were called back for two encores, a rarity for an opening act at the Paradise. By comparison, the main band sucked. Many people left during their first set, including Matthew and Buzzy, who made well over a thousand dollars that night.

That was December 18, 1980. In two days Matthew would be on the road, but not before buying the one officially released cassette and a concert bootleg of that band from the Paradise. It was the first time U2 had ever played in Boston, and the spirit of their music, how it spoke to anger and displacement in a uniquely Irish way, comforted Matthew on his lonely drive through the desolate heartland of America and into the rainy streets of Seattle.

Asking Buzzy to be his best man at the wedding was Matthew's way of acknowledging that the two had once been as close as brothers. It was also a way for Matthew to stage a small and long overdue rebellion against his father's rejection of Buzzy. He might not have been able to do it for the way his father neglected his mother, but doing it for his old friend was the next best thing.

* * * * *

As Matthew was approaching the Edison plant across from the Power Bar, the drizzle turned to a steady rain that was being blown about by a sea breeze. His father's house, where he left his car, was still several blocks away so Matthew broke into a jog.

He stopped suddenly when someone shouted his name. He couldn't see anyone. When he resumed jogging, Matthew heard it again. In front of the bar sat a dark blue cargo van. Its headlights flashed to life for a moment. Matthew could think of only one person who would recognize him in the dark and the rain and who would call to him from the window of a van.

"Buzzy?" Matthew yelled across the street. The headlights flashed again.

Matthew walked over to the van. It had tinted glass, which kept the occupants anonymous. The driver's window opened a crack.

"Hey, Buzzy," Matthew said.

Matthew heard a laugh inside as the window rolled down further. It was Francis.

"That's right," Francis said. "It's Buzzy."

"I'm headed back to the house to get my car," Matthew said.

"Jump in," Francis said. "I'll give you a lift."

Matthew took off his wet suit jacket and draped it over the back of the passenger seat, then climbed in. Except for the pale glow from the dashboard, the van was dark, but Matthew could make out boxes and bags of clothing in the back.

"I just dropped off Connor here. By the way, did you go by Jimmy's?" Francis asked as he headed up E. First Street.

"Yeah, then I went to see him at the State House, which is where I'm coming from."

"Everything worked out fine today," Francis said. "You did a good job, little brother." Then, as if addressing a great audience sitting just on the other side of the windshield, Francis said, "I'm so glad I'm alive today. I feel like a cop at Christmas who just collected his holiday kickbacks."

"I only left your message with one bartender. Gabby," Matthew said.

"Sometimes one is all it takes. Connor told Gabby to keep his ears open and Gabby's got the biggest fucking ears in South Boston." They laughed.

It occurred to Matthew that with Francis now mobile, he would be going after the guy who killed their father. He wondered who it was, but he hesitated to ask directly. "Francis, do you have any idea who might have done it?"

"I do," Francis answered. There was a silence in which Francis sensed the question his brother was about to ask. "Don't ask who it is, Matt. I'll tell you one thing, though. I'm absolutely positive about the guy. If you hear anything, and it makes you wonder whether I was sure, remember that I am. Don't ever doubt it."

That pretty much closed the subject. Matthew shifted in his seat so he could massage the shoulder he had bruised in his tumble at The Rover. Remembering the fight, he thought of telling Francis, but he didn't because it was the wrong bar and he shouldn't have been there in the first place. "When I was at Donnelley's today, I ran into Buzzy. He was working some inspection sticker scam."

Francis pulled the van over suddenly. When it came to a stop, he turned in his seat and gave Matthew a serious look. Matthew wondered if Buzzy was doing something he wasn't supposed to do.

"Did I just spill the beans on Buzzy?" Matthew asked.

"What time was he at Donnelley's?"

"I don't know, maybe five thirty. He took off fast because he thinks someone's after him. The boyfriend of that girl he brought to the wedding. You remember, Miss Runner-Up? Then again, maybe you don't."

Francis asked who Buzzy was with, what time he left, and Matthew told him.

"OK, Matt."

They were still a few blocks from where Matthew's car was parked. The rain was falling steadily and Matthew was tired and sore. "Can you drop me off now?"

"You'll have to hoof it from here. I'm not taking the chance of driving down E. Third Street," Francis said, turning to Matthew with a face more friendly this time. "Thanks again, Matt. Someday you'll know how much you helped me. And when you do, don't be surprised."

"No problem," Matthew said, although it certainly had been. He reached for his jacket and stepped into the rainy night.

"Remember," Francis said. "Trust me on this."

* * * * *

Anne had gotten back to Ipswich in time to get the plane tickets and be at the house to join her mother for an evening walk through the orchards and out to the beach. She changed into sneakers and comfortable clothes as her mother called up the stairs to hurry if they were going to beat the storm coming in.

The Boushay farm had originally consisted of 95 acres of orchards, gardens and fields when it was purchased by Anne's grandparents back in 1919. They had arrived from France with the ambitious plan of starting a working farm.

An interesting bit of family lore came from an incident when Nana B and Grandpa B were clearing immigration in Boston. According to Nana B's account, an immigration officer misplaced their documents, although Joan suspected her mother may have lost them on the passage from France. In any case, Nana B was asked for her family name.

"Boucher," she said and the immigration officer wrote "Boushay" on the forms. Grandpa B noticed this and was about to protest, but Nana B shushed him. There were members of the Boucher family notorious in America at the time for running liquor into the States from Canada. Having a different last name on public documents, she realized quickly, would be a convenient way to distance themselves from that criminal branch of the family tree.

The Boushays were fortunate in having first pick of the best land along Plum Point Road. A competing farm started up one year later next door to them. The Boushay orchards had eight varieties of apples, along with peaches, apricots, cherries, pears and plums. In the gardens grew vegetables, herbs, strawberries, raspberries, currants and blackberries. The woods were home to maple trees, which were tapped to make syrup in early spring. Most of what the farm grew was sent by train to Boston for sale in neighborhood markets. The rest was sold at a stand the Boushays set up at the end of Plum Point Road where it intersected with old Route One.

Joan Boushay was just a girl when she began working the stand. During the peak of the season when her parents and their hired help were busy harvesting, she'd manage the stand by herself. Her mother would stop by with lunch and they'd spend an hour sharing duties. Workers would come by with fresh fruits and vegetables to replenish the wooden bins, which were kept well shaded under a large canopy.

Joan didn't grow up with the green thumb her parents were gifted with, but she did have a better sense for business. When her father died and her mother was later forced to sell the greater part of the property to the farm next door, Joan knew how to reorganize what remained to keep the family business alive. She had talked for years with the local people who stopped at the family stand. She knew what produce they cared to buy, and she knew how to set prices that were both fair and profitable.

Anne grew up without the history of the farm that her mother had. To her, the orchards were a playground, a jungle of trees to climb. She and her friends would spend hours pulling themselves up and over the branches of the plum trees and the higher cherry trees. In the summer, they would lose themselves in their leafy castles until Anne's mother called them to the house for dinner.

In the year after her parents divorced, Anne read a book about a boy who was so upset with the world that he chose to leave it behind for a life in the trees. He spent years jumping from tree to tree, and traveled from one country to another without ever setting foot on the ground again.

Anne thought that would be the greatest thing anybody could ever do, and she wanted to live that adventure. Then she moved to Alaska and her father took her rock climbing. It was different from climbing trees, but it was just as fun and even more challenging. And where trees were limited to thirty or forty feet, a multi-pitch climb could offer hundreds of feet of challenge.

Anne was remembering how much she loved to climb in the orchard as she and her mother strolled between rows of plum trees. The air had cooled and they could feel the humidity building. Anne told her mother about the funeral earlier that day.

Joan tried to listen. She wanted to be sympathetic regarding the Mahoneys' tragedy, and she certainly felt bad for Matthew. The fact was that she didn't really care much for his extended family. She had little or nothing in common with them and she couldn't imagine ever getting together with them socially. They had brought trouble to the wedding reception, and they were more interested in drinking among themselves than getting to know any of Joan's friends who were there.

Joan noticed that some of the trees held fruit that had been overlooked by the men harvesting a week earlier. They were small oval plums that were delicious to eat just as they were. They also made fragrant, sweet freezer jam and chutney. She reached up and picked a couple, rubbed off the dust on her canvas jacket and handed one to Anne.

"You'll be leaving tomorrow, so I wanted to mention something that really doesn't need mentioning. I don't mean to be morbid, especially this week, but you know, Anne, that the farm will be yours when I'm gone. I don't believe I've ever actually said it to you. It's always been my intention, and Nana B's as well.

"As long as these acres bring in enough income to pay operating costs and taxes. They should be able to do that for quite some time as long as they're maintained. I'm doing that now, but they will always need somebody here to care for them."

Joan paused to look at her daughter to see if Anne understood what was being implied. That at some point, either when Joan had died or become incapable of caring for the farm herself, Anne would need to move back to Ipswich permanently. With the death of Anne's father, Joan assumed her daughter's attachment to Alaska and the West Coast would diminish. She imagined Anne's eventual return would be the completion of a long yet inevitable circle.

Joan continued, "I promised Nana B that we would never sell the farm unless we absolutely had to. Between us, I'm sure that can be avoided."

Anne had finished the plum and was sucking on its pit. They had left the orchards and were on a path that led down a slope, then through tall grass to the beach. Anne was catching her first glimpse of the ocean when she began to realize what her mother was suggesting.

They had never talked this directly about her inheriting the farm. Now that it was being spoken of openly, Anne was understanding for the first time that it came with an obligation. She would have to resettle in Ipswich at some point. Her mother had always dropped hints that it would be nice if Anne could come home more often and stay longer, but now Anne was seeing the formal plan that was in place to make that happen. It was definitely not part of the plan that Anne had for her future, but she could see the tentacles of the Boushay family reaching out for her.

It was breezy near the water. Anne pulled back her hair into a ponytail. She turned to her mother. "Matthew and I like living in Seattle, Mom. We're comfortable there."

"Well, that's good. You should be comfortable when you start a family. You mentioned you're planning on having children fairly soon. Is that right?"

Anne wondered where her mother was steering the discussion now. "That's the plan. Find a house first. Then we'd like to have kids."

"Well, I think it would be good to start a new family tradition of having the children spend time here in the summer. We have all these beautiful beaches with the big waves that kids love. They could play in the orchards the way you did. I was thinking you could bring the kids in June, and they could stay on for the summer."

Anne now understood her mother's plan. "Mom, it's probably too early to…"

"It doesn't have to be the whole summer, really. It could be a month. Or even two weeks to start with when they're young. Then as they get older, they can stay longer. The point is that just as the farm will be passed to you, Anne, it will also be passed to your children when their time comes. Our family is tied to this land. That's something your father never understood."

After a walk along the beach, they returned to the house. Joan had borrowed Brian Livingston's car for the day. They used it to drive to the Choate Bridge Bistro, named for the stone bridge that had been built in 1764. It overlooked the Ipswich River and had a warm, rustic feel. Joan and Anne ordered wine and scanned the menu.

It was already eight o'clock. Anne tended to get up early in the morning, and go for a five-mile run before breakfast. She also liked eating dinner by five or five thirty, so she wasn't in the mood to eat a big meal this late. She was on her mother's schedule though, and Joan was a night owl. The earliest class she taught at Salem State didn't begin until eleven thirty, so she typically rose at nine or even ten o'clock, and often wouldn't eat dinner until eight or nine o'clock at night.

It was raining when they left the restaurant an hour later. As they rounded the last turn on Plum Point Road, they saw the red Subaru wagon parked in Joan's driveway.

* * * * *

Anne was about to follow her mother in the front door when she caught a whiff of cigarette smoke. She told her mother she was going to go around back because Matthew might be out there relaxing. She walked quickly in the light rain and saw the glowing tip of a cigarette as she approached. He was sitting in one of the Adirondack chairs on the covered back deck.

Matthew had quit smoking a few months earlier. Not that he smoked every day. Generally when he'd go out for drinks with his friends from work after a long shift at the bar. He wouldn't smoke when he went out with his teammates after a hockey game or rugby game though. That's because his friends on the teams didn't smoke. It all depended on the crowd he was with.

Anne had wanted Matthew to quit his job at the bar and find another way to make a living, a healthier way, but she decided it would be good for him to take a smaller step in the right direction before they got married. And that was to quit smoking. Part of her didn't care what kind of week he was having. There was no reason to fall back on a promise to quit, and Matthew had promised her. She didn't listen to that part of her however, and greeted him with a kiss. She tasted tobacco and liquor.

A glass with bourbon and ice sat beside Matthew's chair. He bought it on the way home because he knew there were no hard spirits kept in the Boushay home after the divorce, except for very special occasions.

"You could use a shower, Mahoney," Anne said as she sat down in the chair beside him. It was dark on the deck. An awning protected them from the rain, but they were still exposed to a clammy breeze blowing across the salt marsh. In the light coming from Joan's bedroom upstairs, the back lawn showed signs of an ongoing recovery from the reception. Flattened patches of grass shedding their memory of tents, tables and chairs. Flower petals from the many bouquets still strewn here and there.

"I can't wait to take a shower," Matthew said and smiled. "Did you guys go out for dinner?"

Anne told him about her day. She included some of what she and her mother discussed but left out the part about Anne returning some day to live on the property in Ipswich.

A light came on in the living room downstairs and cast enough glow onto the porch for Anne to get a better look at Matthew. His suit was dirty and torn. "What happened to your new suit, Matthew?"

Matthew took a drink of bourbon, then sat back in his chair. He went through it all, every detail, except for the part about the fight at The Rover. He was almost finished when Anne noticed his bruised knuckles.

"You promised you wouldn't do anything stupid, Matthew. Did you get into a fight?"

"Anne, believe me, it couldn't be avoided."

"You always say that."

"That's at the bar. If people make trouble, I have to throw them out. It's my job. This was different. It was personal."

Anne changed the subject. "I know you did what you thought was best for Francis today. He's your brother. It sounds like he doesn't know what he's going to do next. I think that makes it dangerous to be around him."

"Actually, Francis knows exactly what he's going to do next. He's sure now about the guy who set him up." Matthew told her about the conversation he had as Francis dropped him off near E. Third Street.

"Thank God we'll be far away tomorrow," Anne said. "I think it's better that we don't stay here much longer."

"At your mom's house?"

"No, I mean generally back here. With the stuff we both have. The complications."

Matthew laughed. They had had this discussion before. One of the big differences between Matthew and his two brothers had to do with their worlds being centered around the place they grew up. "I agree. My brother Jimmy loves it here. He'll never leave South Boston. He spends his whole summer vacation at Carson Beach. It's just down the street from his house."

"Jimmy seems nice. I'm surprised he sent you over to the house if he knew you'd miss the funeral."

"It's strange, but I feel OK about that. I didn't earlier, but I do now. When I was younger, I never called Jimmy on that kind of shit, but I did today. Besides, going to my mom's funeral was horrible. I'm fine not having another one of those memories to drag around for the rest of my life. If you're Irish, the wake is more important." Matthew reached for his pack of cigarettes. They were gone.

He looked over at Anne. "One more," he said.

"You're cut off. By the way, I fixed everything with the travel agent. Our flight takes off tomorrow afternoon at one o'clock. It's a good thing the funeral was today because there isn't another flight with two open seats until Saturday. Mom will drive us down to the airport at ten. C'mon, let's go upstairs. I'm tired, and you must be, too," Anne said.

Matthew leaned forward in his chair and stood up with unexpected difficulty. His shoulders and back were stiff and sore. They went upstairs and he took a hot shower, which helped.

As they lay in bed, Matthew began drifting off to the rhythmic splash of surf on the distant beach. Anne was wide awake, thinking about Francis. In the boat to Ireland, in his father's basement, now on the loose. She turned to Matthew and whispered, "Why wouldn't he tell you?"

Matthew was pulled from his descent into sleep. "Hmm?"

"Why won't Francis tell you who it is? Who he thinks did it?"

"I don't know. He just said that I shouldn't be surprised when I find out."

Anne considered this for a while, then whispered. "It must be somebody you know, Matt. Otherwise, he probably wouldn't say that."

Matthew was lost to sleep, his snores sounding a lot like crashing waves.

Chapter Six
The Mahoney Gambits

Anne's sapphire necklace dangled from a lamp on the dresser where she had draped it the night before. It spun slowly in the morning breeze, and the many facets of its stones caught the sunlight and sent glints of color around the bedroom. Revolving flashes of blue, like the lights of a police car so distant you couldn't yet hear its siren.

Anne had gotten up at six to go for a run on the beach. Matthew rolled out of bed a half hour later. He grabbed his shaving kit and moved quietly down the hallway to the bathroom. He was in the shower when it hit him out of the blue. Buzzy. Matthew opened his eyes and felt the sting of shampoo. He let out a curse.

There was a knock on the bathroom door. "I'm back," Anne called.

Matthew toweled himself dry, and as he shaved he became certain. Yes, Francis believed Buzzy murdered their father. That's why he reacted by pulling the van over when Matthew mentioned Buzzy's name.

It had nothing to do with the inspection sticker scam. Francis wanted to know when Matthew had seen Buzzy and how he was dressed. The kind of information you want if you're hunting someone down. And it was why Francis said that if Matthew heard anything later, not to be surprised. It had to be someone Matthew knew. Otherwise, why say something like that?

The greater shock came when Matthew realized what this meant. When Francis found Buzzy, he would kill him. There was no question about it.

Yet the idea was ridiculous. Buzzy couldn't possibly have committed the murder. It made no more sense than Matthew doing it. Maybe Francis was looking for a scapegoat. Reacting out of anger or exhaustion.

Anne was in their bedroom when Matthew returned. He explained his theory.

"I told you it had to be somebody you knew," Anne said.

"You know what Francis is gonna do when he finds Buzzy?" Matthew lowered his voice. "He's gonna kill him."

Anne hadn't changed out of her running clothes. She sat on the edge of the bed and began unlacing her shoes. She stopped and stared at Matthew. "How could he do that? Buzzy's like family."

Matthew dressed in a T-shirt and jeans and sat beside her on the bed to lace his sneakers.

"Is there any chance Francis could be right?" Anne asked.

"No way," Matthew said. "Buzzy couldn't do it. And he has no reason to. No reason in the world. You know what I hope? I hope I'm wrong about this. I really do."

"Matt, you should call Francis. Ask him."

"I don't know where he is. Even if I did, he wouldn't talk on a phone. He took a lot of precautions yesterday. He was almost paranoid. He's not going to risk exposure by talking on a phone."

"What do you want to do then?"

"I have to find Francis. That means going back to South Boston."

Anne finished unlacing her shoes just as Matthew finished lacing his. "You know that we're supposed to leave for the airport in three hours," Anne said.

"If I go looking for Francis, it's probably gonna take more than three hours."

"We'll have to postpone the trip again, Matt. There aren't enough open seats on a flight until Saturday."

"I know. I'm sorry."

"And we have to be back in Seattle next Wednesday. With a day to fly each way, that's three days in Ireland. It's almost not worth going." Anne tossed her running shoes in the general direction of her suitcase in the corner of the room. "Who's gonna tell my mom?"

Joan had been understanding about the circumstances of the week and how they required a shortening of the trip to Ireland, which had been her wedding present. She was a little less understanding with Anne's reason for having to shorten the trip further. Matthew's friend was in trouble and it involved the Mahoney family.

That was the extent of the explanation she got when Anne woke her from a sound sleep. Anne didn't dare tell her mother more. It was probably better that she was still sleepy. Otherwise, she would have pressed Anne for details.

Anne took a quick shower and got dressed as Matthew finished his coffee on the back deck. Joan had not come downstairs to the kitchen yet, but Matthew didn't want to risk an encounter with her. He knew she wouldn't be reacting well to the new situation.

Anne opened the door to the deck. "Let's go, Matt, before my mom comes down. Have you got your wallet?"

Matthew patted the pockets of his jeans. "I'll go upstairs and get it."

"And your jacket. It's supposed to rain later this afternoon," Anne said.

"We'll be back before then."

Matthew found his wallet in his tattered dress pants. It had grown fat with receipts since leaving Seattle. All he needed was his driver's license, so he put it in his pants pocket and left the wallet on the dresser.

They hadn't even reached the end of Plum Point Road when Matthew asked Anne if she wouldn't mind driving. He hadn't been able to fit into the driver's seat very well the day before, and now he was feeling just as cramped. They pulled over and switched. He was able to push the passenger seat back far enough to be comfortable.

The drive, however, was not comfortable. It was long and aggravating. From Route 128 to the jam-packed Southeast Expressway, they were surrounded by classic Boston drivers who turned without signaling, cut them off indiscriminately, tailgated and blew their horns when traffic was barely moving.

It was nothing new. They had both grown up with it and re-experienced it whenever visiting home, but Anne was not reacting to it very well that morning. Her back stiffened. Her hands gripped the wheel tightly. Matthew noticed.

"I can drive if you want, Anne."

"No, I'm fine. We're almost there."

They crept along the elevated highway that followed Boston's waterfront before it dipped into a tunnel for a short stretch.

"I am so glad I don't live in Massachusetts anymore. Look at this tunnel," Anne said, pointing at the filthy walls, which they could see in great detail because traffic was moving painfully slow. The yellow tiles were covered in a thick layer of dirt and grime. "Nobody cleans anything here. And the smell is disgusting. Everyone just accepts it. I could never live here again."

Once they reached South Boston, Matthew drove, which gave Anne a chance to calm herself down. It was not so much the Boston drivers or the state of the tunnel that was bothering her. She didn't like how she had left things with her mom that morning. This visit was longer than most, and it was far more complicated. It was Matthew's situation complicating things, but Anne didn't want to blame him for something that was beyond his control.

They went first to his father's house. Matthew looked through the basement windows, rapped on them all loudly until he was satisfied Francis had not returned there. They stopped at the Power Bar and Donnelley's, asking where to find Connor McCain. Nobody knew, or they just weren't willing to tell Matthew.

It was almost lunchtime and he was getting hungry, so they drove to City Point and walked along the causeway out to Castle Island. Dark clouds were rolling in, but the sun still broke through occasionally.

Matthew put his arm on Anne's shoulder as they walked. "If you think it'll be better, we can move out of your mom's place and stay in a hotel."

Anne shook her head. "We can't. She's my mom. That would make things worse."

"Are you sure?"

"If you can survive being back here, then I will too."

As he had hoped, Matthew saw the shutters on his favorite hot dog stand opening for lunch. It had been over ten years since he had been there, but as they got closer he remembered that instead of boiling their hot dogs they would grill them. They also grilled the buns so they were crisp and buttery outside and soft and warm inside.

"Want to have a hot dog? This place is opening up and they used to make really good ones."

"Yes, I'm starving."

"They close up in winter, but every fall when they close and every spring when they open, they drop their prices really low for a while. One time I was able to buy a dozen hot dogs for about two bucks," Matthew said.

"You didn't eat all twelve yourself," Anne said with a critical stare.

"Of course I did," Matthew said.

"That's disgusting."

"No, that's delicious," Matthew said, and they both had a good laugh.

* * * * *

The only thing Jimmy Mahoney ever asked of the media was a decent weather report. On Thursday morning WEEI, the news and weather radio station, told him that another storm front would be blowing in with rain and much cooler temperatures, but that he could expect a rain-free commute to the State House. Typically he was on his way to work by seven o'clock, but this morning he left the house at 9:30 and walked the long way in, a route that brought him along Northern Avenue, where the pavement was so worn that the occasional patch of ancient cobblestones showed through.

The view to his left showed warehouses and empty lots. To the right was the waterfront with its piers serving the cruise industry and the fishing fleet. Along the wharves, fishing boats sat almost motionless in the still harbor. Garbage trucks filled the air with the sound of their diesel engines and the smell of rotting refuse from seafood restaurants along the waterfront. Gulls shrieked as they circled overhead in search of scraps left behind by the sloppy work of the garbage haulers.

Jimmy's morning stroll along Northern Avenue was his living walk through history. This was the exact place where many of the Irish arriving in Boston in the 1800s joined their countrymen in crowded waterfront tenements. It was where those who had ruled Boston since its founding, the blueblood Yankee Protestants, wanted to keep the Irish, who they considered a mob of heathens.

Uneducated, unmannered, superstitious. They gambled, fought and got drunk in public, a big taboo for Protestants.

Most of the Irish were Catholic, and it was assumed their allegiance was to Rome rather than their new country. Catholic neighborhoods were occasionally terrorized by mobs of Protestants vandalizing property, damaging homes and assaulting the immigrants. In 1834 they even burned down the Ursuline Convent in Charlestown after being incited by the Reverend Lyman Beecher with tales of scandalous activities occurring inside, including the imprisonment of young girls.

In public schools, Catholic children were forced to sing Protestant hymns, read from the Protestant Bible and study history texts that had a strong anti-Catholic and anti-Irish bias.

Many businesses posted signs saying "No Irish Need Apply" or "No Catholics." Those able to get a job discovered that the cruelest treatment the Boston Irish had to suffer was in the workplace. Laborers making fifty cents for working a fifteen-hour day in jobs that were very hazardous. Many families ended up fatherless because of workplace accidents, forcing the oldest children to leave school to support the family.

Boston's greatest Irish leaders began their lives that way. James Michael Curley, Martin Lomasney, Patrick Collins, John McCormack, Patrick Kennedy, John F. Fitzgerald. They all had fathers who died well before their time, and they all had to leave school to keep their families in food and shelter.

Jimmy had been accused more than once of having too sentimental a view of his people's history, and he pleaded no contest because it was all so personal for him. The South Boston Irish who had come before him were more than mere names in a church registry.

They came to life for Jimmy as he walked along the waterfront. People leaving for work in the dim light of early morning with little or no breakfast and returning in the dark of evening. Crowded homes where a light was kept burning long into the night when word might come that there had been an accident, a misstep, a machine that malfunctioned or a rope poorly tied on a cargo ship, as was the case with Jimmy's great grandfather.

It was around the time of Francis Mahoney Sr.'s death when the Protestant establishment began driving the Irish onto the peninsula of South Boston. There were pockets of Irish throughout the city, but Protestants were eager to compel as many as they could onto the unappealing piece of land stretching into the harbor. To isolate them there.

Fine, the Irish replied. Keep us out of the downtown neighborhoods, and we'll create our own Boston within South Boston. Erect barriers to political power, and we'll build a machine to tear them down.

It was the Catholic Church that held the community's spirit together, but it was by the political machine that the Boston Irish were saved here on earth. They had a number of political bosses like Martin Lomasney, affectionately dubbed "The Mahatma" by his devoted constituents. He ran the West End while John Fitzgerald ruled the crowded North End.

They were among the chieftains of their respective neighborhoods and they looked after their constituents' every need, from a ride to work every morning to a new pair of glasses for their child, and maybe a basket of food when times were really tough. The chieftains knew what mattered most: food, clothing and shelter. Guarantee your people those essentials, and in return they'll give you what costs them nothing. Their vote.

For Protestant Yankees, the future eventually became clear. It was not a question of if they would have to share or perhaps lose the reins of political power to the Irish, but when.

It was an interesting coincidence that the sound of garbage trucks dominated the morning scene along Northern Avenue. Hot on Jimmy's agenda this morning was the struggle over the waste disposal site. He calculated that his political fate hinged on that very issue.

* * * * *

The Massachusetts State House was built in 1798. Its Bulfinch front remained, but there had been various wings added as the Commonwealth grew. The famous gold dome had originally been made of copper and was installed in 1802 by Paul Revere & Sons. It received its gilded treatment a few generations later.

Tours of the State House were conducted by volunteer guides. Many of them were older women who were Boston Brahmin, the class of people descended from the English Protestants who first settled Boston. They lived in the stately brick and brownstone townhouses on Beacon Hill and nearby Back Bay.

The standard tour led visitors through a series of spaces, including The Hall of Flags and The Great Hall. Artifacts of Massachusetts' history and portraits of imposing statesmen tended to inspire awe among those seeing them for the first time.

The tour guides and tourists had not yet arrived Thursday morning, but prowling the byzantine halls were a few members of the press in search of a story. Jimmy had entered through the eastern annex, and spotted a couple of reporters interviewing a senator.

As Jimmy climbed the staircase to the second floor, he took another look down at the two reporters and recognized one as Arthur Atkins from the *Boston Globe*. By Jimmy's estimate, Arthur held the record for using the words "insular" and "enclave" more often than any other reporter when speaking about his community. Those were two words reserved for South Boston and never used when referring to any other community in the state. Though it did have a nice sound to Jimmy's ears. Insular Andover. The Anglo-Saxon enclave of Wellesley.

The State House had its own small police force, the Capitol Police. Officer Walter Cook stood at his station outside the door to the Senate's public gallery and smiled as Senator Mahoney passed. "Good morning, Jimmy."

"An excellent proposal, Walter, but still open for debate," Jimmy said returning the smile.

No sooner had Jimmy closed the door to his office and laid his bag on the desk when the door quickly opened again. It was fellow Senator George Corbin, the leader of the Gang of Five opposed to Jimmy's election as Senate president. Corbin was a Democrat representing the district that included Wellesley, one of the wealthiest towns in Massachusetts. It was located just west of Route 128, the highway that formed an arc around the greater Boston area.

Jimmy's relationship with Corbin went back to the early seventies when they were both serving in the state House of Representatives. Although both Democrats, they found themselves on opposite sides of the busing issue. When it became clear that the legislature was going to support the idea of imposing desegregation on the city and have buses roll between the white community of

South Boston and the black community of Roxbury, Jimmy proposed an alternative that could achieve the stated goal of school desegregation.

Allow the parents to choose the school where they preferred to send their children. Give them the same right as the wealthy, who choose which private school their children attend. If parents in Roxbury wanted to send their children to school in South Boston, they would be very welcomed there. The fact that busing was being forced was at the heart of Jimmy's resentment.

Nobody was interested in Jimmy's alternative or even discussing it. So Jimmy proposed that if desegregation and busing were going to be mandated, then every town and city in Massachusetts should participate and they all should be subject to the same rules. Only a small minority of his fellow politicians agreed with this idea.

Corbin sided with the majority, which favored a plan that would make desegregation mandatory for Boston only. The suburbs, including Corbin's district, were excluded from any obligation to participate.

That infuriated Jimmy. He considered it supremely hypocritical of his colleagues to favor desegregation, then say it only had to be fixed in his city. The *Boston Globe* agreed with the majority and did so in a holier-than-thou editorial, in Jimmy's opinion.

It galled him so much, he made a rare trip to the *Globe's* offices on Morrissey Boulevard and spoke with Isabel Tompkins, director of the editorial page. He was surprised to hear a rather candid reply from her.

"You have to see this in a larger social context, Jimmy. Mandatory busing to achieve racial balance in a school system is a social experiment, one step on the road to achieving a racially integrated society. There's a lot at stake, and the experiment can't be allowed to fail. If the suburbs were included in the mandatory plan and had their children assigned to schools in Roxbury, virtually every family with children in a public school system would place them in private schools. They'd build them overnight if they had to and hire a teaching staff in the morning. It would cost a lot, but believe me, the money would be found. And with that, the experiment would fail."

Jimmy did his best to control his frustration. "Most of my constituents don't have that luxury. They can't afford to pull their children out of the public school system and send them to private schools. They're forced to participate in this experiment."

"Who knows, Jimmy? If it works, maybe some of the suburban towns will lose their reluctance and get on board."

"I doubt that very much."

With that, the meeting ended and Jimmy left. At least Ms. Tompkins was good enough to be honest with him. Desegregation adversely affected many relationships on Beacon Hill. With Jimmy and Corbin, the line had been indelibly drawn between the two men. Because Jimmy opposed forced busing, Corbin labeled him a bigot. Because Corbin wanted to keep suburban participation voluntary, Jimmy labeled him a hypocrite.

Since those early clashes, the two had moved to the Senate, where they maintained a cool distance. Jimmy's remarks to Corbin were kept cordial and as brief as possible. Corbin had done the same, but recently his manner of relating to Jimmy had assumed a certain Jekyll and Hyde quality.

On one occasion he praised Jimmy for supporting a measure that made improvements to the state's system of higher education. On another, when Jimmy politely refused to support a transportation bill, Corbin ripped into him with sudden rage, "Very well. Go fuck yourself, you bigot!"

As far as Jimmy could tell, no other senators were the target of Corbin's vitriol. Corbin's occasional diatribes on the Senate floor were generally considered the appropriate theatrics to stir emotion and sway opinion.

Jimmy also noticed a deterioration in Corbin's appearance. His curly hair, once neatly trimmed, was now allowed to rise and meander for dramatic effect. He used to dress sharply, albeit conservatively, but he had gained weight and his wardrobe had grown increasingly sloppy.

Jimmy began avoiding him. As he saw it, Corbin was becoming something of a loose cannon during formal debate in the chamber. Just one month before, when he announced he was setting his sights on organized crime, Corbin made a disturbing comment during discussion on the incinerator issue, a topic that had been alluded to in just about every newspaper article that mentioned Jimmy Mahoney. Corbin suggested the senator's brother was the de facto leader of the Irish mob in Boston, equal in strength to the Italian

Mafia. It became clear to Jimmy that Corbin saw Francis as a co-conspirator in everything Jimmy might do.

According to Senate rules, Corbin could not directly impugn the character of a fellow senator, but he came dangerously close to stating that Jimmy, in his role as a senator, had inserted measures into legislation that would aid his brother. Only after being called into President Hurley's office and admonished did Corbin tone down the rhetoric.

Standing in Jimmy's doorway, Corbin said, "The word is out on you, Mahoney. You don't have the votes for Hurley to call a caucus, and every day those who support you will continue to fall away one by one. You're not the man for the job. You've got too much baggage. Too many rocks thrown at too many school buses in South Boston."

"George, your bedrock support has always been a great comfort to me."

Corbin took a step into the office, and Jimmy immediately gestured him back toward the hallway. Getting into a long and maybe heated discussion was the last thing Jimmy needed. Corbin blocked the doorway, and as Jimmy approached he refused to budge.

"George, I've got work to do."

"Your attempted coup is failing, Mahoney." Corbin braced himself firmly in the doorway.

Jimmy was no longer amused. Now he was annoyed. Stepping forward so that their faces were only inches apart, Jimmy barked up to the taller Corbin, "What do you mean by a coup, George? A coup d'état or a coup de main? They're quite different and I'd like to hear you clarify the charge."

Corbin was puzzled by the question, enough so that when Jimmy gently nudged him toward the hall, Corbin relinquished his hold on the doorway and stepped back. Jimmy quickly closed and locked the door to his office before walking away.

* * * * *

Francis Mahoney had only one item on his agenda Thursday morning. A visit to the Hudsons, the couple who owned Global Jai Alai. They had gone to the Attorney General with accusations of extortion by Francis. The Hudsons lived in a sprawling farmhouse they had renovated after purchasing it in the seventies, when it had been surrounded by lots of woods and farmland. By 1987 suburbia had encroached so rapidly on the town of Cumberland, Rhode Island, that the Hudson farmhouse was surrounded on three sides by new developments. The only remaining patch of woods was a large grove of trees directly across the street.

The Hudsons were usually dressed and on their way to work by eight. Today they were taking it easy because they had a two o'clock appointment with Judge Winthrop at the federal courthouse in downtown Boston. At eleven o'clock Ron Hudson sat on the back deck enjoying his second cup of coffee. He was perusing the *New York Times* and *Boston Globe*, which were spread open across the wrought iron table.

Ron had grown up in Florida and went into the jai alai business as the co-owner of a Miami fronton. His expertise lay in the jai alai culture, recruiting the right players and managing the schedule. His wife Lydia's expertise was in numbers. Making sure the company remained profitable and charting the best course for short- and long-term growth. She had been raised in a working-class neighborhood in nearby Providence, and had worked full time while getting her business degree from the state university.

Lydia was good at what she did despite a management style so direct it was sometimes considered abrasive. It was no surprise that Ron was, by far, the more liked of the Hudsons among the hundred or so employees at Global Jai Alai.

While Ron was cinching his robe against the cool breeze now blowing across the back deck, Lydia stood in her spacious wardrobe closet cleaning a black Anne Klein suit with a lint brush. It was a suit that made a reluctant nod toward fashion but was more about the business of communicating authority and exactitude.

Ron heard a vehicle pulling into the long gravel driveway that wound around back to the barn. He assumed it was the roofer they had called to fix a leak near the chimney. Lydia had made the arrangements, but he thought the roofers were scheduled for Friday, not today. He and Lydia would be leaving soon and he hoped the roofer was not blocking their cars.

He walked to the end of the deck for a look. Yes, rather than pulling into one of the parking spots, the blue van had pulled up so close to the bumper of Ron's Audi that it appeared to be touching it.

The doorbell rang. Lydia had finished dressing and was brushing her short red hair.

The bell rang again. Opening the front door, Lydia saw two men wearing oil-stained jumpsuits and gloves. One of them was Francis Mahoney. He held a coil of rope over one shoulder. Next to him was Connor McCain, who carried a large toolbox and folded plastic bags.

"Are you here for the leak in the roof?" she asked.

"It's kind of a leak," Francis said with a quick smile. "We're the security team for the Barnum and Bailey Circus. We have a show at the Providence Civic Center this weekend. You may have seen the posters."

"Yes, I have seen them," Lydia Hudson responded quickly. "I don't want to buy any tickets. Is that what you're doing, selling tickets?" She spoke as a woman who was most at home managing a crisis, even if it required her to create one for that purpose.

"No, we're with the Barnum and Bailey security team. I'm afraid there was a bad accident a short while ago on Route 295. One of our trucks overturned and two lions escaped. We've just located them by their radio collars. They're right in those trees over there." Francis turned to point across the street. "It's critical that we contact the team with the tranquilizer guns before the lions move on and hurt themselves or, God forbid, someone in your neighborhood. May we use your phone to call the tranquilizer team?"

Mrs. Hudson believed the story but was stunned by its bizarre nature, so she simply stared at them with her mouth open.

"Time is of the essence," Connor said.

"Yes, of course. My heavens," Lydia replied, kicking quickly into crisis mode. "Come in, please, come in. The phone is right over there in the kitchen."

"Thank you," Francis said as they stepped inside. "Is your husband at home?"

"Yes, yes. He's on the back deck." Mrs. Hudson called to her husband, "Ron!"

He turned immediately at the sound of his wife's voice. "Yes?"

"Get in here now. There are lions on the loose!"

Ron jumped out of his chair and gave Lydia a puzzled look, which grew even more puzzled when she added, "These men are from the circus. They're calling the tranquilizer team."

Francis was walking through the kitchen trying various switches on the wall. Some turned on lights and fans. When he found the switch that turned on the garbage disposal, he returned to the living room.

Ron stepped inside and closed the sliding glass door. Connor motioned him onto the couch in the living room. Ron looked very skeptical but deferred to his wife. Francis draped the coil of rope across the top of the couch and told Mrs. Hudson to join her husband. Connor walked through the living room and kitchen closing all the drapes. None of the houses on the street were directly adjacent to or across from the Hudsons' house, but someone driving past might be able to see inside.

"Is that the thing to do? Close the drapes?" Mrs. Hudson asked.

"What exactly is the problem here?" Ron asked.

"There was an accident on 295," Lydia explained. "A Barnum and Bailey truck. Lions escaped. Two lions. They're in the woods across the street. These men are calling the tranquilizer people." She turned to Francis. "Have you called them yet? I didn't see you on the phone."

Francis stood facing the Hudsons while Connor took up a position behind them. "Listen up. We're not from the circus. My name is Francis Mahoney."

Mrs. Hudson's eyes were the first to light up with recognition. She had been hearing the name since the first day she stepped into the Attorney General's office to file her complaint. It was usually followed by an admonition not to involve herself in any legal entanglements with Francis Mahoney. Mrs. Hudson chose to ignore that advice because it was her job to manage entanglements.

"You're the extortionist. My God, I know who you are."

"Wait a minute," Ron said trying to catch up. "If you're not with the circus, are there lions across the street?"

"Wake up, Ron!" Mrs. Hudson said in a tone of exasperation. "It's the man who was stealing money from us. He's going to be indicted. He's going to prison for the rest of his life." She turned to Francis and repeated this, "You're going to prison for the rest of your life."

Finally Ron got it. His jaw slowly dropped.

Francis let out a short laugh. "Ah, dawn breaks on Marblehead."

Ron turned to his wife. "You let them in the house. Why did you let them in the house?"

Mrs. Hudson ignored him. "This is ridiculous. I'm calling the police." As she rose, a loop of rope dropped over her head. Connor tightened the noose. Mrs. Hudson fell back on the couch with her hands grasping at the coarse rope that held her neck tightly. Connor tossed the other end of the rope to Francis. When Ron stood, Connor grabbed him by the neck and forced him back onto the couch.

The kitchen was directly off the living room, so Ron was able to watch his wife being half pulled, half dragged to the kitchen sink. From the moment he sized her up at the front door, Francis knew Mrs. Hudson would put up a struggle. As she tried to gain her balance on three-inch heels, Francis enjoyed yanking her one way, then the next, knocking her down, then picking her up. He waited for Mrs. Hudson to charge him, but she didn't. If she had known what was to come, she would have charged him with all her strength. Not that it would have mattered.

Already her neck was showing abrasions from the rope and her face was turning red. The most her voice could manage was a faint croak. Ron let out a yell. Connor cuffed him. He had taken a roll of duct tape out of the toolbox and wrapped it around Ron's head, covering his mouth.

"Bring him over for a front-row seat," Francis called.

When Connor pulled Ron into the kitchen, Francis fed the other end of the rope down the sink and turned on the garbage disposal. Ron's eyes met those of his wife and he began to sob. This only made her angry, and she tried to shout some resolve into him but all that came out was a throaty growl. It took a moment before the rope became firmly entangled in the device. When it did, the rope grew taut. Mrs. Hudson lurched back violently and lost her footing.

Francis turned off the disposal, leaving Mrs. Hudson bent over backward with her neck pressed against the edge of the sink and her feet struggling to find a grip on the slippery tile floor. One hand clutched her neck and the other went behind her head in search of the tight rope.

Francis turned to Ron and put a hand on his shoulder. "Here's the deal, Ron. You need to tell me everything you told the Attorney General about the skim. Everything. Understand?"

Ron struggled in vain to escape Connor's grasp and didn't seem to be listening. Francis slapped him hard across the face, which brought about a focus. Ron stopped struggling and looked at Francis. He was breathing heavily through his nose and blinking rapidly.

"If you don't tell me everything, she dies. Understand, Ron?"

Ron nodded his head.

"I'm gonna take off the tape, Ron. You're gonna talk, OK?"

For a moment the only sound in the kitchen was the clicking and sliding of Mrs. Hudson's shoes. Francis was about to pull the tape from one side of Ron's mouth when Mrs. Hudson managed to roar out a command, "Don't tell!"

"Shut the fuck up," Francis said. He reached for the disposal switch. When the Hudsons had renovated the farmhouse, they spared no expense, particularly in the kitchen, and had chosen a high-quality German unit. The Kaiser was advertised as "the disposal that refuses to take no for an answer."

Francis turned the Kaiser on. Mrs. Hudson's head whipped back, disappearing into the sink, and her legs lifted completely off the floor. With her upper back pressed against the rim of the sink, her legs swung in the air wildly.

Francis turned off the Kaiser. He walked to Ron and pulled away the tape. "Talk fast," he said.

Ron took in a deep breath and began sobbing as he tried to talk. He had one eye on Francis and the other on his wife. "It's all written down...we wrote it down. She typed it. It's in my office..."

"In Connecticut?" Francis pressed him.

"Here. In my office downstairs...let her go, goddamnit...she can't breathe."

"Your wife's still breathing, Ron. She's OK for now. Connor's gonna take you downstairs. You show him where the papers are, all of them. And don't fuck around or I turn it on again."

Ron led Connor through the living room and down the cellar steps. Francis leaned over the sink and checked on Mrs. Hudson. The rope pulled tightly on her neck, which was bent at an odd angle and bleeding where the rope had cut through the skin. Her face was a deep red, and her bulging eyes locked onto Francis. He listened to her make a thin, hissing sound as she breathed.

He turned his head to the side so it lined up with hers. "What's the matter, honey? All choked up? I know how you feel. It happens to me sometimes. Like when someone gets me indicted. That was really fucking cute of you. So cute that I've gone out of my way to pay you a house call."

Francis stared down at her for a long while. He was silent. She stared back. Each breath was a struggle. Her arms, which were gripping the edge of the sink in an attempt to ease the weight on her back, grew tired. The arms gradually slackened, and Mrs. Hudson squeezed her eyes shut from the pain. Her eyes began tearing, and her breathing lost its rhythm.

She was surrendering. This is what Francis wanted. It's what he had come all this way for. He stared down at her. The rim of the drain formed an arc above her head, like a small tiara, with KAISER spelled out in block letters.

Connor returned with Ron. Francis met them in the living room, where Ron handed him a portfolio.

"I found this in his office, too," Connor said, holding up a thirty-eight caliber pistol.

"It's all in there, Mr. Mahoney. Everything we found about the money being…taken."

"Tape him shut," Francis said without looking at Ron. He was focused on the twenty or so pages in the report. Francis sat down on the couch and read quickly but carefully. From where Ron sat, he couldn't see his wife, but Connor could see her legs dancing lightly in the air, one of them occasionally shooting up as if hit by an electric shock. There was a loud bang when her heel came down hard against a cabinet door.

"She's a kicker," Connor said.

When Francis finished reading, he closed the portfolio and looked at Ron. "You gave them all this? All these details?" he asked angrily. "These exact pages?"

Ron mumbled through the tape.

"Yes or no?" Francis yelled. "Nod your fucking head or shake it!"

Ron nodded.

"You fucker," Francis said. "You and that cunt did this to me." Francis smashed Ron's face with the portfolio, then went into the kitchen. He leaned over the sink and held the report above Mrs. Hudson's face. "This is your death warrant. You've been a cunt your whole life, Lydia Hudson. Well, guess what? Today life is paying you back."

Francis straightened up and reached for the disposal switch. He called for Connor to bring in Ron. He wanted him to watch. When they were all in the kitchen, Francis turned on the switch. The Kaiser came to life and Mrs. Hudson's body twitched as her neck was pulled down. The motor slipped like a clutch as it chewed through some rope, then strained as it regained its grip. A faint gurgle came from Mrs. Hudson as her neck began to yield.

As it did, her legs pitched up. It appeared that her whole body might somehow disappear down the disposal. The rope tore deeper into the flesh of Mrs. Hudson's neck and slowly collapsed her windpipe until her air supply was completely cut. A small spurt of blood shot from the sink and formed a messy question mark across the kitchen tiles.

Francis flipped the switch. The Kaiser motor stopped but the disposal maintained its death grip on the rope. Francis held up a hand to fend off Mrs. Hudson's arms as they swung wildly in the air. He stared down at her face and watched the light fading from her glassy eyes. The arms surrendered and fell limp. The legs went on a little longer with involuntary twitching.

Ron Hudson had watched the gruesome end of his wife with wide, unblinking eyes. As her body fell limp, Ron collapsed. He fell off the chair and lay unconscious on the kitchen tiles.

"Are we taking him with us?" Connor asked. "I say we leave him here. Everything you want to know is in the report. There's nothing more he can tell us."

Francis walked to the window and peeked between the drapes. Everything was clear outside. "I agree. He stays here. But let's create some confusion."

Francis walked over to Ron and pressed his shoe down on Ron's hand until the pain woke him. Ron tried to stand, but Connor had taped his hands behind his back, so he just wiggled around on the floor and moaned.

"Let's get him downstairs," Francis said. Connor pulled Ron to his feet and led him through the living room and down the cellar stairs. There was no resistance in Ron. He moved in a weak stupor until he reached the last step, where he lunged forward suddenly.

Connor yanked him back easily. Ron spun around and drove his head into Connor's stomach. His eyes were wet with tears.

Connor thought the whole thing was funny. He watched as Ron spun around and charged into the dark basement. There was a loud bang as Ron tumbled over a stack of boxes.

Connor laughed.

"Don't fuck around," Francis said.

Connor flipped the light switch and retrieved Ron.

"In here," Francis said when he noticed the Hudsons' wine cellar. With the door closed, the sealed room offered no way for the sound of gunfire to escape. "Just make sure that door won't lock behind us. I don't want to get trapped in here."

Ron continued to struggle until Connor reached down to his hand and twisted it. "If you piss me off, I'll break some bones, Ron."

They sat Ron down on the floor at the far end of the cellar so he was facing the door.

Francis spoke quietly to Connor so Ron wouldn't hear, "You go up and bag the leftovers. I'll finish up here."

When Connor left, Francis knelt down beside Ron and spoke to him calmly and slowly. "She's gone and she's never coming back. You know that, don't you, Ron? And you know that you have to go too, right?" Ron's eyes grew large. They darted back and forth between Francis and the door.

Francis continued in an intimate tone, "Ron, you still have one decision to make. It'll be the last time you have to decide anything. It's my gift to you. I'm going to let you decide whether to have things be easy or difficult. The outcome will be the same no matter what you decide. Do you understand? One decision. Easy or difficult."

Ron continued to consider the door with his eyes. Francis knew Ron's mind wasn't where he wanted it to be. "Look at me." Francis turned Ron's head toward him. "Listen. This is your life. Until today it was like most people's lives. It was a mixture of pain and joy. Mostly joy. Am I right?"

Ron nodded slowly.

"Even on painful days, Ron, you knew that the next day or the day after that or the week after that, the joy would return. Right?"

Ron nodded.

"That's all over now, Ron. Your life at this moment and for all your remaining moments is pure pain. Emotional hell. I know you understand what I'm saying, Ron. After what happened upstairs, the joy has gone and it's never coming back. Not while you're alive. That's your life now. All pain. No joy.

"That brings us to the good news. You're going to go soon. And when you go, so does the pain. Free from life, free from pain. Instead of staying here and reliving what your wife just went through, you'll leave it behind and be with her. Together again. Forever. That's the best outcome you can hope for, Ron. You can understand what I'm saying, can't you? It's the only way out, and the sooner you take it, the better."

Connor returned, but Ron didn't look away. He was staring at Francis. His breathing had relaxed and he was resting his eyes in long blinks.

"Take the tape off his hands," Francis said as he pulled Ron forward. Connor reached behind Ron and pulled the tape from his hands. Francis eased him back against the cool cement wall and removed the tape from his mouth. Ron took in a deep breath and licked his lips. He started sobbing and was soon weeping loudly.

Francis let him go for a couple of minutes before lifting Ron's chin. "OK, enough of that, Ron. Let's face the decision now. You know I'm right about this."

Francis turned to Connor, who handed Francis the pistol he had discovered in Ron's office. Francis put it in Ron's hand and helped him raise it. Ron took a deep breath and summoned his resolve. He suddenly swung the pistol toward Francis, who was ready for this. Francis grabbed the pistol, along with Ron's hand and turned the pistol gently back in the direction of Ron's head.

"Now, Ron, what did I tell you about your decision? Easy or difficult. Why would you choose difficult? Don't be stupid. You're not going to change the outcome. It's going to happen, Ron. You just have to decide, right now, whether you want to experience the worst physical agony you've ever known, or whether you're going to cheat agony on your way out the door. Now is the time, Ron. I know you understand what I'm saying. If you don't, I'll do it for you, and I promise it won't be free of agony."

Ron's eyes welled up and he raised the pistol to the side of his head. Francis gently brought it down to Ron's mouth. "The mouth is better, Ron. Trust me. It guarantees results."

When Ron placed the muzzle of the pistol into his mouth, Francis unlocked the safety. Ron looked down cross-eyed at the pistol and awkwardly worked his thumb onto the trigger, moaning in frustration as he fumbled unsuccessfully to fire the weapon.

A bright flash of light burst from Ron's mouth as the wine cellar filled with a deafening blast that left a ringing in Francis' and Connor's ears. Ron's head snapped back with violent speed and spilled against the wall.

"Fuck, that was loud," Connor said, rubbing his ears.

Francis rubbed his ears as well. He stood up and turned to Connor. "Leave the gun. Take the tape. Take the tool box. Pick up anything else that you see of ours. Watch out for the blood. Don't step in it. Don't take your gloves off until we're inside the van."

Francis took one look back at Ron's face. It was relaxed. He was at peace, that was for sure. Francis wondered if Ron really was together with his wife now. Maybe, but if they were together, he hoped they were together in hell.

In the kitchen they gathered up the rope and cleaned the sink thoroughly of blood and rope fragments. Francis turned on the Kaiser and ran water to wash away whatever rope might remain inside the disposal. Connor cleaned up the floor with a soapy towel, wiped it dry and cleaned up the scuff marks from Mrs. Hudson's heels. He threw all of the cleaning towels into the body bag containing Lydia Hudson.

While Connor finished the cleaning, Francis tried to create a little more confusion. He went upstairs to the couple's bedroom and pulled a suitcase from Lydia's closet. He threw several outfits into it, added a few pairs of shoes, some underwear and everything in the bathroom that looked like it belonged to her. From her dresser he gathered all the jewelry.

Before leaving, Francis and Connor opened the blinds, straightened up the living room, then carried the suitcase and body bag out the back door. As they were loading the van, Francis heard a high-pitched barking behind him.

In the Hudsons' back yard was a chain-link pen containing a doghouse and a small grey schnauzer that seemed intent on getting Francis' and Connor's attention.

"They've got all this property and look where they stick the poor dog," Connor said.

Francis opened the pen and the dog went into a barking retreat. He crouched down and held out a hand before the dog approached him cautiously. The dog had thick scruffy fur. Francis reached out to pet it. "Nobody's gonna hurt you, girl," he said. Turning to Connor, he said, "Grab a couple of those toys, Connor, so she feels comfortable."

Francis carefully picked her up and petted her reassuringly. "We wouldn't leave you all alone in this place."

Connor backed the van into the street. It was clear in both directions, and he drove slowly toward the highway. In the back of the van, the schnauzer sniffed at the body bag before issuing a bark.

Turning to the schnauzer, Francis said, "That's right, Toto, the wicked witch is dead."

* * * * *

"We should talk to Kathleen," Anne said when they finished their hot dog lunch at Castle Island. "She'd know where to look for Francis, and she's the only one in your family you can trust."

Matthew had to admit it was true, but he still felt a need to protect Francis. "We'd have to tell her that Francis is here. I'd rather not do that. Besides, she'd want to know why we're still here and not on our way to Ireland."

"I'll tell her that our flight today was cancelled and that we're leaving tomorrow instead. It'll work."

Matthew used a napkin to wipe the grease left on his fingers from the hot dog buns. His upper lip held a glob of mustard, which Anne wiped off.

"I have another idea. Let's go to Buzzy's first. If we can't find him at his place in the project, maybe we'll risk it with Kathleen. How's that?"

As they drove toward Old Colony, the sky darkened. They parked several blocks away at Carson Beach. Anne put on a sweater she brought. Matthew was wearing just a T-shirt and jeans. Along with the bank of low clouds rolling off the ocean came a cool breeze that made Matthew shiver. He rubbed his bare arms.

"I told you to bring a jacket," Anne said.

As they turned down Patterson Way, Matthew told Anne about his history there. He remembered a little bit of his first five years before moving to E. Third Street, like the memory of going to the laundromat with his mother. After that, his first good memory was of entering the Driscoll apartment when he was seven years old. The place was decorated nicely by Buzzy's mom and it always felt full of life, with neighbors stopping by for meals and people playing cards in the living room.

Mrs. Driscoll was one of the friendlier moms in the project. Very tolerant, especially of her son. The story was that Buzzy's father had left the family when Buzzy was one year old. That's all Matthew knew about it because that's as much as Buzzy would tell. Mrs. Driscoll had died in 1981 when Matthew was in Seattle, and he didn't hear about it for almost a year. Buzzy was twenty-two at the time and he kept living in the same apartment.

After Matthew moved to City Point as a kid, visiting Buzzy meant making the long trek from the new house on E. Third Street and crossing through Dorchester Heights. Matthew enjoyed the mile and a half hike, even though it brought the possibility of a fight with kids whose territory he was passing through.

He usually traveled alone because most of his City Point friends didn't want to hang around with "project rats" or "OC niggers" as they called the people of Old Colony, ninety-nine percent of whom were white.

Surviving the walk to Old Colony didn't mean Matthew was home free. Most people in the project remembered the Mahoneys and knew Matthew, but occasionally he'd be challenged and have to settle things with a fight. By the time of busing, Matthew had become an accepted face in the project, playing bodyguard and dealer's assistant to Buzzy. Toward the end he was stopping by the Driscoll apartment almost every day.

Old Colony didn't look all that different since the last time Matthew had seen it ten years earlier. The red brick exterior of the buildings was painted grey on the ground floor. The places where grass was supposed to be growing were almost all hard-packed dirt.

The sounds of little kids laughing and crying echoed from courtyard to courtyard.

They walked to the end of the first block. In the center of the courtyard, next to the archway, stood a few women talking. One of them held a small child.

"Which building does Buzzy live in?" Anne asked.

"That one," Matthew said pointing to number seven.

"Which one was yours?"

"The same one. We were on the third floor facing the back. Kathleen was below us on the second floor, and Buzzy was across from Kathleen and down the hall."

The wind stirred up again, and Matthew felt a chill. "Let's go inside."

As they crossed the courtyard, Matthew saw two guys in their late teens standing in front of building number five. They were tense and fidgety. Their wide eyes darted up to the clouded sky and along the apartment windows in search of something or someone worth focusing on. One of them chewed intently on his lower lip. They turned their attention to Matthew and Anne, and stared at the two until Matthew stared back.

He had seen this a lot at Old Colony. Kids who were all coked up with nowhere to go. Nothing to do with their high. Calculating how much time they should let pass before doing their next set of lines. As soon as one suggested it, they'd rush off as if they had waited way too long and might have to do an extra line just to make up for it.

As they approached the door to number seven, Matthew looked at the women again and recognized one as the mother of Pinky McKenzie, a girl that Matthew had dated for a while before moving to Quincy in 1974. He forgot exactly how Pinky got her nickname, but he remembered that the other kids sometimes called her Lefty because her left breast was noticeably larger than her right.

Pinky was embarrassed by it, although Matthew assured her, whether she wanted to hear it or not, that guys like having two sizes available. Even back then, Pinky had talked about becoming a nurse, and the last Matthew heard, she was going to school to become just that.

He steered Anne toward the women. Pinky's mom recognized him right away, which made Matthew feel good. He gave her a big hug.

"Look at you, Matty. I was afraid I'd never see you again. Who's this pretty girl you're with?"

Matthew introduced Anne and said hello to the other women. Then he asked how Pinky was doing.

"Pinky's gone. Almost two years now."

Matthew had a bad feeling about this and hoped "gone" meant that she had moved away.

Pinky's mom explained, "She got stabbed right over there," pointing across the inner courtyard to the next archway. "She was working the late shift at City Hospital, which I told her would be trouble, but it paid better and she was saving up to move out. Her ex-boyfriend did it, and he's doing eighteen years in Walpole State Prison. I hope he's getting it up the ass every day."

Without skipping a beat, Pinky's mom shouted into an open window on the first floor. "Maureen!" A woman appeared in the window. "Maureen, look who's here. Matty Mahoney. The one who moved to Canada."

"Matty Mo, how you been?"

"Good, Maureen. Thanks."

They chatted for a few minutes, then Matthew and Anne said goodbye to Pinky's mom and the other women. The heavy steel door leading into the building had one small window with a wire-mesh reinforcement. It squeaked loudly. Some of the lights in the stairway had burned out, and the air was thick with the smell of cooking meat.

Matthew headed off the inevitable question. "Pinky and I went together when I was fourteen, but let's not talk about her right now."

Anne's mind was still focused on Pinky's mom pointing to the exact location of her daughter's murder. She wondered how any mother could survive that. "How about that woman Maureen?" she asked.

Matthew shrugged his shoulders. "I have no idea who she is."

Matthew knocked on the door at apartment 212. They heard the sound of footsteps inside, followed by locks turning and bolts sliding. A guy Matthew didn't recognize opened the door. He was in his twenties and wore a black and yellow baseball shirt that said

Blackhawks. His hair was cut so short on the sides that Matthew could make out a shamrock tattoo above his ear.

The guy studied Matthew's face, then Anne's. "Yeah?" he said in a neutral tone.

"Is Buzzy here?" Matthew asked.

"He's out."

"When's he coming back?"

The guy shook his head slowly and shrugged. He's gonna be an asshole every step of the way, Matthew thought. Hearing the news about Pinky had not only depressed Matthew, it also put him in a foul mood and he had an urge to smash this guy's face. He was about to turn to Anne and say they should leave when she extended her hand and smiled. "I'm Anne and this is my husband, Matthew."

The guy gave Anne a cautious look before shaking her hand.

"And you're…" Anne prompted.

"I'm Mikey. Mikey Rousseau."

"Buzzy was the best man at our wedding last Saturday. We wanted to say goodbye to him before we leave town."

With that, Mikey relaxed and assumed a look that was friendly, slightly embarrassed. "Oh right. Buzzy told me about you guys."

"Do you mind if we wait for him?" Anne asked.

Mikey took another look at Matthew. "Sure."

"Inside," Matthew said and stepped toward Mikey, who quickly retreated into the apartment after holding the door open. "I didn't know who you were. You gotta be careful, you know what I'm saying?" Mikey replied.

The apartment had the same general look as Matthew remembered, especially the institutional green that all project apartments were painted, but now the place had a lifeless look. There were no pictures on the wall and no curtains covering the living room window. A color TV sat on a white plastic chair. Opposite was a sofa with no legs and another white plastic chair serving as an end table. It held a half-eaten bowl of cereal and an ashtray full of butts.

Wheel of Fortune played on the TV, and like most of the televisions Matthew could remember in the project, it was playing way too loud.

"Have a seat," Mikey said pointing to the low couch. "I'm just watching a little TV." Unsure in his role as host, Mikey walked to the kitchen and turned on the light, which caused a number of cockroaches to dash for the shadows.

That was another thing about project apartments. Cockroaches. Big ones. Whenever Matthew stayed over at Buzzy's place, they left the lights burning all night long to keep the cockroaches away. The second you turned the lights off, you'd hear them scratching their way out of the shadows.

"If you're hungry, there's food," Mikey said. "Some chips and stuff in the cabinet. Beer and grape soda in the fridge."

Buzzy still liked the grape soda, Matthew thought as he walked around the room. He ended at one of the bedroom doorways and looked inside. This seemed to make Mikey uneasy. The bedroom was darkened by a blanket hanging over the only window. On a dresser, Matthew could make out a dimly shining object but couldn't tell what it was.

"So Francis is your brother, right?" Mikey asked.

Matthew turned his attention back to the living room, which he knew was where Mikey wanted it. Anne had taken off her sweater and was sitting on the sofa. From a stack of magazines on the floor beside her, Anne pulled out an issue of *Soldier of Fortune* and began reading an article on high-altitude survival strategies.

Matthew ignored Mikey's question and asked one of his own. "If you had to guess, Mikey, when's Buzzy back?"

"It could be an hour or so. Maybe tonight. He didn't say."

They could wait, and maybe that was the smart thing to do. Be patient. But they might be wasting precious time. Matthew walked to the other bedroom. The door was shut and when he tried to open it, he found it was locked. "Where do you think he is right now, Mikey?"

"Driving a cab maybe."

"Can we call him on the cab radio?" Matthew asked.

"It's not a radio cab. He splits a weekly rental with another guy, and they just play the airport and the busy cab stands. Downtown, the waterfront."

"So he could be anywhere around the city," Matthew said.

"If he's driving a fare. If he isn't, he's probably sitting at the cab stand at Quincy Market. That's his regular stand, where he goes after dropping a fare. He drives a light blue cab, number 1350."

"Maybe we should wait here a while, Matt," Anne said.

Matthew reluctantly joined her on the couch and watched *Wheel of Fortune*. Mikey sat down on the couch as well. Then he stunned Matthew by walking over to the TV and turning up the sound even higher.

"I hope you don't mind," Mikey said. "I had a tire explode right next to my head a couple of years ago."

Matthew turned to Anne to see if the sound annoyed her, too. She was completely absorbed in the article she was reading. The obnoxious sound of a game show playing at a piercing volume had zero effect on her. This was Anne when she focused on something. It perplexed Matthew, who could be reading a magazine and be distracted by the sound of a dog barking two blocks away.

He considered what they should do. Hanging around waiting for Buzzy to return would drive Matthew crazy. If he was right about Francis going after Buzzy, how soon might it happen? He turned to the window and saw rain starting to fall. Large drops splashed against the window.

Matthew figured Mikey must be connected with Buzzy's drug business. Otherwise why risk living with a dealer? But he wondered where Mikey fit into Francis' business or if he fit in at all. He decided to test him.

"Mikey, do you know a guy named Connor McCain?" Matthew had to shout to compete with the TV and compensate for Mikey's bad ear, whichever one it was.

"You mean Connor. Sure."

"What does he do?"

The question made Mikey turn his attention back to the TV. "Ask your brother," he finally said.

"If I was looking for Connor, where would I find him?"

"I've been seeing him at O'Brien's this week. You know O'Brien's?"

Matthew nodded. O'Brien's Tavern had a reputation as being one of the roughest bars in South Boston. It was between Old Colony Avenue and Dorchester Avenue in an area that was home to light industry. Off the beaten path and not a place people would consider a neighborhood bar.

Matthew remembered hearing about a number of stabbings and even a few shootings, either in the bar's parking lot or on the sidewalk out front. The craziest O'Brien's story he ever heard was about a biker who was six and a half feet tall and weighed over three hundred pounds. The guy danced drunk and naked across the bar while firing a pair of .357 Magnums into the ceiling.

After a few more minutes of the game show, Matthew had had enough. When Mikey made a run to the kitchen, he turned to Anne. "Let's get out of here."

"And look for him where?"

"Quincy Market. He's bound to show up there. If Mikey's telling the truth."

"Maybe you should go and I can stay here. Cover more options."

"You here alone? No fucking way."

Mikey returned from the kitchen with a beer. Anne was putting on her sweater. "You guys taking off?"

"If Buzzy comes back, or if he calls," Matthew said, "tell him I need to talk to him. It's important." He got paper and pen from Mikey and wrote down the phone number for Ipswich.

Anne said, "If he gets back in the next few hours, tell him to call Kathleen. At her salon." Turning to Matthew, she said, "I'll drop you downtown, then I'll go to Kathleen's salon on Broadway. I know where it is."

Matthew preferred the simpler plan. Go downtown together, wait together. He didn't argue it though. "Fine. Let's go," he said impatiently and opened the door to leave.

"Wait," Anne said. "Mikey, do you have a raincoat or something that Matthew could borrow. He only wore a T-shirt this morning."

"I'm fine." Matthew was already halfway to the stairs, and his voice echoed back to the apartment.

Anne lowered her voice. "He'll freeze in the rain."

Mikey pulled an old suede jacket from the dark bedroom and handed it to Anne. "This is Buzzy's."

"It'll get ruined in the rain," Anne said.

Mikey laughed. "Don't worry, nothing can ruin this piece of shit."

Matthew put on the jacket as they crossed the wet courtyard. It was the same one he had seen Buzzy wearing the day before. He couldn't get the front zipper to work and had to dig his hands deep into the pockets and wrap them across each other. When they got into the car, Matthew smelled a stale blend of odors rising from the jacket. Cigarettes, pot, sweat and God knows what else. It also had stains, burn holes and rips sewn shut, providing a testimony to its owner's odd activities.

* * * * *

Jimmy had arranged to meet President Hurley at three o'clock. When he arrived at the president's office, Junior was leaning against a windowsill, sharing a joke with Hurley, who seemed more relaxed than Jimmy had seen him all week.

"Jimmy, come in. Junior was just telling me about how James Michael Curley would piss off Cardinal O'Connell. For Sunday mass at his church in the South End, Curley would wait until O'Connell had made his solemn march from the sacristy to the altar to officially begin the mass. Everyone in the crowded church would remain standing until O'Connell gestured for them all to be seated. Then Curley would stride up the center aisle with this guy in front of him…what was his name, Junior?"

"Up Up."

"Yes, Up Up would walk in front of Curley calling out 'Up Up! Up Up!' and raise his arms in a lifting motion that told everyone in the whole damn church to stand up for the arrival of His Honor Mayor Curley. Everyone would stand and stay on their feet until Curley took his own seat at his reserved pew in the front of the church. He loved doing it when the Cardinal was saying mass. Sticking it right in his face."

Jimmy knew the story well and liked it, for what it said about Curley, and what it said about Cardinal O'Connell, who was a bit too absorbed in the trappings of his office and would go about town with majestic robes flowing. It also was a reminder to those high in the Catholic Church that their rule of the people was shared with leaders in the political world.

"The Gang of Five wants to meet with me tomorrow," Hurley said. "They say they'll have an alternative candidate to propose."

Jimmy was about to sit down when Junior, who had turned to a window overlooking the front steps of the State House, said, "Do my eyes deceive me? I can't believe what's happening out front right now."

"The ghost of James Michael Curley is picking pockets?" Hurley asked jokingly.

"Even crazier. There's a swarm of media out there. And the Sultan's boys are setting up a podium on the front steps. Holy Christ, I believe the Sultan's going to hold a press conference," Junior said, referring to Mayor Sullivan by a new nickname that was becoming popular. The Sultan of Sling, because Sullivan had become so adept at selling his point of view to the media.

"On the front steps of the State House?" Jimmy asked. For the mayor to stage a press conference on the steps of the State House was a violation of unwritten turf rules.

Jimmy and Hurley joined Junior at the window, and all three studied the unfolding scene, which was taking place beneath a sky growing ominous. The mayor and two of his aides stood off to the side as the podium was fitted with an assortment of microphones from radio and TV stations. One of the aides was Frank Abbott, an outsider brought into the Sullivan team recently to add polish and sophistication to the mayor's image.

There were plenty of politicians who entered into marriages with the media, but there were very few, Jimmy considered, who did it as openly and shamelessly as Danny Sullivan.

Jimmy said as much the previous St. Patrick's Day during the annual political roast at a South Boston restaurant where the banquet room was crammed tight with politicians and reporters. It was his first year serving as host of the event, and Jimmy got to take shots at all the local politicians. His comment on Sullivan drew an especially large burst of laughter from the crowd.

"I found a watch the other day as I took my morning walk out to Castle Island," Jimmy said during the roast. "It couldn't tell time worth beans, but it turned out to be the most amazing instrument. The hour, minute and second hands would suddenly all point in the same direction with such energy that the watch seemed to be humming. I found that by walking in the direction that all the hands pointed, I would inevitably run smack into a television news crew. As soon as I got home, I phoned the mayor to tell him I would return his watch immediately. The poor man wept with joy."

"Do you believe this crap?" Hurley began. "He's setting up a stage. The unmitigated gall. Look at that sky out there. I hope he gets drenched in a downpour."

"He's desperate, that's what it tells me," Jimmy said. "I'll take care of this if you don't mind."

"You shouldn't get in the middle of it, Jimmy," Hurley said. "Sullivan will make a spectacle of you if you go out there. Who knows what he means by doing this?"

Jimmy understood exactly what Sullivan meant. This was the kid at Old Colony who stood outside your building and shouted insults up to you and your family for all the world to hear. Stay in your apartment and pretend you don't hear it, and you would never live it down.

Of all the fights Jimmy had gotten into as a kid, he started only one. He was almost always the loser, but he never ran away from a fight and he always tried to do enough damage to make the other kid think twice before fighting him again.

"Sorry, Carl, but Sullivan doesn't get to shit in our front yard." Jimmy was gone before Hurley could think of a way to stop him. Hurley certainly wouldn't go out there himself. He knew this was as much about who had the biggest dick in South Boston as it was about anything else, but it could be an interesting show. It was a shame he wouldn't be able to hear what they were saying.

Outside, Frank Abbott was speaking into Sullivan's ear. The mayor turned and looked up to President Hurley's window. Hurley pointed a finger to his temple and spun it around dramatically, showing Sullivan that he thought the ploy was crazy.

By the time Jimmy made his way to the front door of the State House, Sullivan had begun his prepared statement. Jimmy listened for a moment to judge the tenor of the speech.

"The city of Boston is being financially crippled by the skyrocketing cost of hauling our trash long distances to landfills in other states. The cost is conservatively estimated to be a quarter of a billion dollars over the next twenty years. The plan that we have been proposing for four years, the South Bay plan, would prevent this city from going bankrupt. It's a plan that has been endorsed by the governor and has been studied extensively by a number of health agencies and found to be safe for the community. But this plan has been jeopardized by an impulsive and irresponsible act by the state Senate. In the dead of night and by voice vote alone ... "

Jimmy had heard enough. He paused to catch his reflection in the glass of the front door before stepping onto the scene. He was checking his smile. Not too weak or he'd look angry. Not too strong or he'd look, well, crazy. Oh God, what a pain in the ass the press were. If they were going to screw him on this, fine, but he was going to maul the mayor in front of them, and fuck them if they couldn't take the joke.

Jimmy buttoned up his suit jacket against the cold wind. With his carefully calibrated expression, he strode energetically down the front steps of the State House. He approached the taller mayor from behind. Waving to the assembled press with one hand and patting the mayor on the back with the other, Jimmy declared, "Hello, everybody. Welcome to my press conference. I'm glad you could all make it."

There was a smattering of laughter from the reporters, but the atmosphere at the podium was tense. Sullivan had been interrupted mid-sentence by the back slap, and his surprise turned to an anger that he struggled to contain. "Good afternoon, Senator Mahoney. I'm surprised you're here."

"The State House is where I do the people's work, sir. What's surprising is that you're here."

"I was just discussing the people's work, Senator. There are some important questions that need to be answered. First of all, maybe you'd like to explain why the Senate chose to pass a bill with an amendment that would penalize the people of Boston hundreds of millions of dollars for proceeding with the South Bay incinerator project. Then perhaps you could explain why this idea was approved in a midnight session of the Senate through an outside section, so that nobody could trace who was behind the effort. For your part, Senator, you have not voiced any objection to the South Bay plan during its four-year planning process."

"With all due respect, Mr. Mayor, I believe it was four years ago when you were serving on the city council, when you opposed the very same plan that you're now so crazy about. I think you had it right back then."

Sullivan hesitated before responding. "That plan hadn't undergone the necessary studies. But they've been carefully conducted since, and the studies prove that South Bay is not only the best economical choice for the city but also the safest one as well."

"Mr. Mayor, I have heard from the experts and they tell me that from an environmental standpoint and a health standpoint, South Bay is one of the worst possible places to put this incinerator site. Right near dense residential areas and a stone's throw from Boston

City Hospital. Truly absurd. I will not expose the people of my community to such a health risk. I live in that neighborhood, Mayor Sullivan."

The first heavy drops of rain began arriving on the brisk wind, just one here and there, but enough to blotch a notepad or sting a nose. The mayor shifted restlessly in his stance and took a small step toward Jimmy. "That's my neighborhood too, Senator, and I resent the suggestion that I would expose my own family to any kind of health risk. That's pure nonsense. The Massachusetts Clean Air Advisory Committee has signed off on the design. And so has the privately funded Alliance Health Foundation."

"I think, Mr. Mayor, that the only privately funded institution you wanted approval from on this Titanic of a trash plan is the editorial board of the *Boston Globe*. Once you got the green light from Morrissey Boulevard, you thought nobody would dare oppose you."

The verbal sparring continued for almost fifteen minutes. The raindrops increased so that those in light-colored jackets took on a leopard-like spottiness. The press observed and recorded quietly without interrupting the epic duel. They savored every moment as if they had been granted ringside seats to the fight of the century.

That it was. The veneer of formal politeness was far too thin to hide the animosity that the two men felt toward one another. Their debate shifted back and forth between a substantive discussion of the incinerator issue and attacks on each other's personalities. On every point they debated toe to toe, neither yielding an inch of ground nor conceding a point.

On substance, Mayor Sullivan held an advantage. He had been working with the governor and various agencies to move the project ahead at a deliberate speed and with the consensus of all. Protesting the Senate's last-minute intervention was politically wise.

Challenging Jimmy on his own turf, however, was looking more and more like a mistake. As the debate moved steadily from a discussion of policy into one of style, the mayor was lured from the high ground by a grudge the city had against the state over money.

"Excuse me, Senator Mahoney, but this fifty-million dollar punishment to the city of Boston comes on top of a continued decline in state attention to us. Boston is struggling with a host of problems, from correctional housing to healthcare for our senior citizens, and the State House is cutting its aid to the city, putting the most vulnerable at risk."

"Forgive me, Mayor Sullivan, but it's rather insincere to show up on the steps of the State House with your hat in hand. A hat that grows exponentially bigger with every visit. Have you ever paused to consider that you are only one of many mayors from across this state who utter the same simple mantra—more? We don't print money in the State House, Mayor Sullivan," Jimmy turned and pointed to the golden dome for effect. "We manage it responsibly for everyone in this state. Fiduciary prudence is something your City Hall might wish to experiment with."

There was a pause, perhaps the first since the half-hour debate had begun. Sullivan realized he had been drawn away from the topic. He was defending the city as a recipient of state funds, and Jimmy would pummel away at all the ways in which City Hall mismanaged its budget. He had to get himself out of this corner or the day would be lost.

The reporters sensed a shift. They moved from their passive silence and began shouting questions at both men. Sullivan waved them off with a raised hand and then slowly brought down his hand and pointed it at Jimmy, who smirked slightly at the dramatic touch. "Senator Mahoney, you've failed to provide an answer to the question at hand. Boston needs a solution to its trash problem, and the Senate has killed a plan that everyone has agreed is the best option. It's irresponsible to defeat that plan without proposing an alternative, and you don't have one."

The rain was no longer sporadic; it began falling lightly but steadily. The increasing drops were whipped around by the wind.

"I do," Jimmy said.

Sullivan interrupted, "We cannot continue to truck our waste to landfills outside the city. It will cost us far more than if we built the incinerator site at South Bay."

"You may have failed to hear me, Mr. Mayor, but I do have an alternative site, and it's better than the South Bay plan."

Sullivan looked at him quizzically. "There are no other sites. Every one that's been considered has been dropped. Except for South Bay. Where have you been for the last four years, Senator?"

"Solving your problems for you, Mr. Mayor. I've had a team researching the subject for quite a while now, and I'm certain the site we've selected is better than South Bay in providing a regional solution to the trash problem."

The mayor let out a quick laugh and shook his head. "If this is a joke, it's not funny, Senator. Nobody is aware of any other viable sites."

"They will be aware tomorrow morning." Jimmy turned to face the cameras and reporters. Those wearing rain jackets had pulled on their hoods. Others had opened umbrellas, less to keep themselves dry than to shield the camera lenses.

Regardless of how much longer Sullivan wanted to keep slugging, Jimmy was not going to be seen on the six o'clock news debating sopping wet in a rainstorm. He stepped closer to the microphones to make a dramatic exit. The image of Sullivan standing alone at the podium in the rain would do nicely.

"The alternative site will be announced first thing tomorrow morning," Jimmy said. "Then we can end this nonsense about South Bay. Thank you, all." Jimmy extended a hand to the mayor, who hesitated for a moment, as if Jimmy's hand held a piece of stinking trash. Reporters shouted possible sites that had been considered in the past.

"Senator Mahoney, is it Leominster?"

"The Quincy shipyards?"

"It's a far better site," Jimmy said. "In fact, it's nearly perfect. You'll all see exactly what I mean when I announce my alternative site tomorrow morning." With that, he waved to the press, flashed a smile that lasted long enough to be captured by the cameras, then turned and strode up the State House steps.

Sullivan watched Jimmy for a moment before turning back to the podium and the press. He felt his moment slipping away. "Well, there you have it. I came here for answers, and Senator Mahoney provides only riddles."

"Are you willing to consider another site outside Boston?" one reporter asked.

"Will the alternative site cost the city of Boston less than the South Bay proposal?" another shouted.

It went on like this. Sullivan was forced to answer questions about Jimmy's mysterious alternative site. A ghost site that might not even exist and about which Sullivan could provide no answers. He wiped the rain from his face and noticed Abbott gesturing. He wanted to go and Sullivan agreed. The day was not completely lost, but it soon could be. Sullivan politely thanked the reporters for their attendance and moved quickly on the short, wet walk back to City Hall.

Junior had wandered out to the press conference soon after it had begun and had blended into the small crowd of reporters and people passing along Beacon Street who thought there might be some important announcement being made. When it had ended, Junior went looking for Jimmy. He found him in his office. "OK, Mahoney, don't keep me in suspense. Where is this mysterious nearly perfect site? Inquiring minds want to know."

Jimmy was standing at his window, watching the camera crews going through their well-practiced drill of disconnecting and coiling cables and stowing their heavy equipment in padded containers. He waved Junior over.

"Don't tell me it's that off-shore platform idea," Junior said.

"No, but that plan is pretty intriguing, don't you think? If the incinerator is out in the ocean, nobody can claim it's in their backyard, and with prevailing winds, the pollution goes straight to Europe. Who couldn't love that?"

Junior was impatient. "But the real site. The one you promised out there."

"Junior, I have no idea," Jimmy said with a laugh. "It seemed like a good line at the moment."

"That's going to make a nice headline."

"Well, I admit it may have been a mistake, but at this stage of the game it might help to introduce an element of confusion. The way the cards have been arranged won't leave me with a winning hand at the end of this week. Let's see what this does to the mix."

Junior wasn't convinced. "I don't know, Jimmy. You may have just turned over a joker. What you need is a real, live alternative site."

"I'll come up with one. I've got a pile of studies on different sites. Leominster, the Quincy shipyards, the off-shore platform. You name it." Jimmy pointed to a two-foot stack of binders sitting on the floor in a corner of his office. "I think they conducted a study on virtually every municipality in the state. What a waste of time and paper."

"Whichever one you pick, it better be good because you really built it up out there," Junior warned.

"I just wanted to shove it to Sullivan. The balls. Trying to slam us on the State House steps. I just wish I could have said what I really thought of him."

"Well, you both came pretty close."

Jimmy wandered over to his desk and sat down.

"I don't think there are any good sites, Jimmy. Every town is going to fight against it. Places like Saugus and Lynn, they've already got their share and they won't take anymore."

"Yes, in a serious light, there is no good answer," Jimmy said. "Not by tomorrow morning. Not in our lifetime maybe. But somehow it has to be handled. Honestly, I'd be fine with South Bay handling the garbage and recycling. I just refuse to let them put a goddamn incinerator there. If I can buy enough time to get a favorable caucus vote, I'd be willing to cut a deal with the governor. Just no incinerator."

"I suppose Hurley is partly to blame for this mess," Junior said. "He let Sullivan do an end run around the Senate. We should put the incinerator in Hurley's hometown. Marblehead. Can you imagine that?" Junior laughed and Jimmy joined in. The idea of the wealthy seaside peninsula, with its lauded Yankee heritage, ostentatious yachts and multimillion-dollar waterfront homes, accommodating a massive incinerator belching clouds of acrid exhaust across the idyllic landscape. Loud, smelly trucks rumbling through the narrow streets of quaint downtown Marblehead. It was too much.

"Oh my God, what a sight that would be," Junior said. "The best part wouldn't be the plant but the announcement. The breaking news. Can you imagine the reactions, the shock when Marbleheadians—is that what you call them?—find out that such a monstrosity was headed down the pike in their direction. It would be the biggest scare to hit the North Shore since the Salem witch trials."

"Yes, I can see it," Jimmy said through an impish grin. "Nobody in Marblehead would get a good night's sleep for a very long time."

"They'd be so incredibly pissed off. I think it would drive some people crazy. Really, I think it would push some people right over the edge just to read the headline in the *Globe*."

Jimmy lost his smile suddenly and scanned the ceiling slowly as a far-fetched scenario played out rapidly in his mind. "Oh, Junior.

You truly are the devil. You've given me the most mischievous idea."

"Jimmy, I was kidding. Please don't go out there and say you want to put a waste incinerator in Marblehead. Seriously, it would be suicide."

"Not Marblehead, Junior. Someplace even better." Jimmy stood up and began walking around the small room in deliberate steps. "Infinitely better. Not just a near-perfect site. A better-than-perfect site. You've heard about killing two birds with one stone? How about five birds." Jimmy walked over to the pile of research binders that sat in the corner of his office and found the binder that described potential sites in the suburbs west of Boston.

When he found what he was looking for, Jimmy broke into a wide, relaxed smile. "Junior, could you call your friend Stanley Higgins at the *Boston Herald?*"

"Stanley's not your biggest fan, Jimmy."

"Stanley slams me sometimes, but he does it strictly with the facts. I can respect that. Stanley also has a lot of pull at the *Herald*. He could get my story onto the front page of the first-edition tomorrow. I don't want to give this one to the *Globe*. I want to catch them flat-footed."

"What's the story?"

"Tell Stanley I'll give him an exclusive on my alternative site. I'm going to have to do some photocopying before I see him to make it look like I'm serious about this. How late can he turn in a piece for the first edition?"

"I don't know. Eight o'clock. Maybe nine. It depends how much work he has to do on it. And who needs to approve it before it goes to press. The deadline could be even earlier."

Jimmy checked his watch. It was quarter to four. "I'll need a couple of hours. Tell him six o'clock."

"That's supper time."

"I'll take him to Locke-Ober if he wants," Jimmy said, referring to the downtown restaurant that reeked of tradition and exclusivity as much as the Ritz-Carlton at the other end of the Boston Common and the Public Gardens.

Moments after Junior left to track down the *Herald* reporter, there was a knock at Jimmy's door. He feared it might be Corbin again. This was no time to be distracted by anyone, particularly the senator from Wellesley. Jimmy considered keeping quiet as if he wasn't there, but President Hurley opened the door and walked inside. "I'm in the middle of something, Jimmy, but I have to tell you that I just heard the news that you're going to make an announcement? I've already answered questions from two reporters, and I'm going to tell you exactly what I've told them: This is not the Senate's alternative site. This is Senator Mahoney's alternative site."

Jimmy was bent over reports sorted into various piles on his desk. "That's fine by me, Carl," he said.

"I hope you didn't paint yourself into a corner, Jimmy. You're going to have to give them something tomorrow. They'll be kicking down my goddamn door if you don't. And I'm not covering for you. Do we understand each other?"

"Absolutely," Jimmy said. "And Carl, it's much more than an alternative site. It's your ticket to a happy retirement."

Jimmy gave Hurley a rundown of his scheme. Hurley listened with a fair amount of skepticism. When Jimmy finished, Hurley said, "How can you control all of those events?"

"The Greek playwright Aeschylus once said … " Jimmy began. Hurley rolled his eyes. He was not amused by Jimmy's tendency to quote the classics.

" … When a man is willing and eager, the gods join in."

Chapter Seven
Poison Rain

It was four o'clock when Anne dropped Matthew at Quincy Market in downtown Boston. She'd return at six, and they'd decide where to look next, and whether to look for Francis again. In the meantime, she would see Kathleen.

Despite a cold breeze and a steady rain, the market was busy with tourists streaming like colorful ants in and out of Faneuil Hall, the famous brick building that dated back to colonial times. Behind it were three long granite buildings that had once been the unloading point for ships delivering goods from all over the world. Now they housed an endless assortment of souvenir shops, bars, restaurants, snack stands, kiosks selling licorice lobsters and maple sugar candy from Vermont, designer clothing shops and plenty of ATMs.

A long line of cabs wrapped around the western and northern sides of the marketplace, dropping people at one end and eventually picking up new fares after snaking their way slowly to the front of the line. Anne dropped Matthew off behind the last cab.

Mikey had said that Buzzy would be driving a light blue cab with the number 1350, so Matthew walked from the back of the cab line to the front, checking the number painted on each vehicle, looking inside at the drivers. No Buzzy. At the front of the line, three drivers were speaking Russian and discussing a fresh dent in a taxi's door.

Matthew crossed North Street and ducked into the upscale Bostonian Hotel to use their bathroom. Returning outside, he settled himself under an awning in front of the Purple Shamrock, a large bar that booked rowdy Irish bands. From where he stood, Matthew had a good view of the cab stand and all traffic moving past the market. When Buzzy's cab showed up, Matthew would spot it.

The wind blew in strong gusts carrying splatters of rain beneath the awning, giving Matthew a chill. He still hadn't been able to work the zipper on Buzzy's jacket, so Matthew dug his hands deeper into the pockets and wrapped one over the other to close the front.

It had been an odd enough day already, but now Matthew found himself growing more restless and he wasn't sure why. It was partly because of Pinky, hearing that she had been stabbed to death beneath an archway that Matthew knew all too well. It was one of the places he and Buzzy would hang out when it rained in the project.

She had been working as a nurse and saving to tear herself free of Old Colony, which was hard for people to do if they spent enough time there. Because of the money you needed to move away, but also because it lured you back and held you closer after you strayed. It made you feel weak whenever you left and it whispered "welcome home" when you returned.

It was as if the project had killed Pinky because she was betraying it by planning to leave. He couldn't get rid of the image of Pinky bleeding to death in the dark.

As water rolled in thin streams off the awning, Matthew pushed his hands deeper into the jacket. There was a hole at the bottom of the left pocket. Through it, Matthew felt something metallic lodged deep in the lining. He picked absentmindedly at its jagged edge. He pressed it from side to side. He twisted it in one direction and then the other. Finally he freed it from the grip of the jacket and pulled it out.

It was an object that Matthew recognized instantly by the hourglass-shaped dapple of dark green paint that had clung to it for so many years. It was what Matthew had been looking for in his father's garage the morning of the funeral. The missing key.

* * * * *

The Hair & Beyond was the salon owned by Kathleen Sutliff on East Broadway. Purchased a year before with a loan from Salty, the small shop provided her with a modest income, part-time work for her friends and, most important to Kathleen, a sense of independence.

Francis had offered to front her the money and wanted to pay to have the place remodeled. Kathleen refused. They had just broken up, and she wanted him out of her bed and out of her business. He threatened to burn the salon down but never did.

Instead of greeting her first customer at ten o'clock Thursday morning, Kathleen lay stretched out on a sofa in the back room with a migraine. She had moved out of Salty's house after the murder and was staying at her friend Debbie's apartment, but the salon offered a more peaceful place to endure the crippling headaches.

The migraines never arrived during times of stress but immediately after. The murder, the wake, the funeral. Each was more than enough to trigger one on its own, so after enduring all three it was no surprise she had woken to a mean, massive attack. The pain behind her eyes was in full rage and every smell she encountered was horribly magnified.

Kathleen had phoned all her appointments for the day and cancelled them before closing all the blinds in the salon and withdrawing into the quiet darkness of the back room. She had not been able to reach her eleven o'clock appointment by phone, Meg Donovan, but Meg would know not to bang on the front door when she saw the sign Kathleen used for such occasions. The sign declared CLOSED below a drawing of a head with a giant hammer crashing down upon it.

She took her prescription medication, which turned her into a sleepy zombie within minutes. Kathleen drifted in and out of consciousness until sometime in the afternoon when she woke to the sound of young girls passing by outside. They shouted over one another with the boundless energy and excitement that kids had. Kathleen thought of Diana. She would be almost ten now, old enough to be with those girls.

She imagined Diana walking to school with friends in the morning and coming home when school was let out. The well-worn scenario had Diana coming by the salon to tell Kathleen about some outrageous event that had happened in school that day, to show her mother something she had drawn or written.

The customers would all know her. They would insist Diana greet each of them in turn, and when she left, all the chatter would be about how fast Diana was growing, how much she was learning, how she was becoming more and more like her mother every day.

Migraines made Kathleen susceptible to that kind of painfully indulgent fantasy. They magnified everything, especially loss. Of her daughter, Salty, and so many others. However, the migraine medication also kept her drowsy, so it wasn't too long before she drifted back to sleep. She might have slept into the evening but instead was woken a little after four o'clock by insistent knocking at the front door of the salon. It was Anne.

"What are you still doing in town?" Kathleen asked after letting Anne inside. She took Anne's coat and hung it on the rack. With the blinds closed, the salon was dimly lit. Kathleen opened them, letting in the light of the fading day.

Anne considered answering Kathleen's question with a lie. She hesitated. "We can't leave yet."

Kathleen didn't seem to hear what Anne said. She was rubbing her temples in a circular motion and stretching her jaw. "I woke up with a migraine this morning. It turns me into a vampire. Do you mind if I run next door for a minute? I haven't eaten a goddamn thing all day. I need a snack and a Diet Coke. Do you want something?"

"I'll take a Diet Coke," Anne said.

Kathleen shuffled out the front door, leaving Anne alone in the salon, silent and gloomy in the pale grey light. It smelled of shampoo, hair gel and the potions used to invoke youth and beauty. She turned on two small lamps in the waiting area and sat down in one of the chairs.

Kathleen returned with a soda for Anne and a large coffee for herself. "This may be a mistake, but I'm going to try some coffee. I need to wake up so I can sleep tonight, if that makes any sense. Do you want one of these?" Kathleen showed Anne a package of miniature donuts wrapped in plastic. "Mini Donut Delights. My weakness. They were out of the ones with jelly filling so I got the powdered." Kathleen offered Anne a donut, adding, "So what gives?"

Anne opened the can of soda and took a mini donut. She knew that Matthew didn't want to tell Kathleen that Francis was back in town. Anne trusted her, and her instinct told her that Kathleen would be a help in this situation. "Remember yesterday when Matthew missed the funeral?"

"His car broke down."

"No. When he went over to E. Third Street, Francis was there. He was hiding in the basement."

Kathleen had taken one of the small donuts from its package and her hand dipped slightly at the news, causing a small clump of powdered sugar to tumble to the floor in a dusty cloud. "Oh, Jesus."

"He had Matthew running around South Boston yesterday for him."

"What an idiot!" Kathleen sat up straight in her chair. "Francis, I mean. If they see him, he'll get arrested. Not all of the cops in town are on his side. If they hold him for questioning and the indictments come out, he'll be screwed. Not that I give a shit."

"He told Matthew that he was leaving the country, but he turned around when he heard that Salty was murdered. He said he didn't do it, but he knows who did."

Kathleen slumped back in her chair and held the donut up for examination before eating it. "I was beginning to like the idea of South Boston without Francis Mahoney. I really don't want to see him again. Getting arrested might be the best thing for him actually. That's not going to happen though. Francis would rather get killed than arrested, even if he has to kill himself. He said that to me more than once."

"He told Matthew that when he heard about the murder, he was on a boat going to Ireland."

Kathleen turned to Anne. "He told me Paris. That's why he showed up at your wedding. He thought I'd leave the country with him. He almost had me. Then my friend Debbie was telling me that he'd have to live in hiding and have a fake name. So if I left with him, we'd be hiding in some filthy French basement crawling with rats and spiders.

"Francis is smart in some ways, but he's so stupid with other things. He doesn't consider that I have friends here. Family. South Boston is where I belong. I already found that out the hard way."

Kathleen paused to pull the plastic lid from the Styrofoam cup and sip some coffee. "He knows how to get to me though. At the wedding, he knew exactly what to say. We really are right for each other, but it will always be wrong to be with him because of what he does. It's all he knows, and he's good at it unfortunately."

Kathleen's coffee was very hot, so she used a mini donut to stir it up, then popped the wet donut into her mouth before it crumbled.

"Matty shouldn't have done anything for Francis," Kathleen continued. "He'll only get himself into trouble. And you too, Anne."

"I dropped Matthew downtown. He's looking for Buzzy. That's why we're still here. Matthew thinks Francis is going to go after Buzzy for the murder."

Kathleen shot Anne a skeptical look. "That's crazy."

"Matthew's pretty worried."

"That Francis will kill Buzzy?" Kathleen shook her head and took a drink of coffee. "Francis can't, even if Buzzy did it, which is ridiculous because he's such a fuckup. Not a mean fuckup, just stupid. Anyway, Francis can't kill his own brother."

Anne was confused by the remark, then she was suddenly concerned at having left Matthew alone downtown. "Why would Francis want to kill Matthew?"

"No, not Matty. Francis would never do that. Ever. I'm talking about Buzzy."

"But they're not brothers."

"Well, not completely," Kathleen said. She paused before telling Anne more, but the secret she had kept, the promise she had made, was to a man who was now dead.

Kathleen began by telling Anne about the rumors she had heard many years ago, about all the things Salty had confessed to her in the last year, and how he had intended to tell Matthew at the wedding, and would have if the fight and the commotion afterwards hadn't messed that plan up.

As Kathleen was adjusting to life without Francis a year before, Salty was going through his own soul searching. The two found themselves together one rainy June afternoon in the Broadway Bakery.

They ordered coffee and scones, and sat at a table by the window, where they shared the strange turns their lives had taken. The conversation went on longer than either had expected and took on a confessional tone. They shared stories they'd never been able to share before with anyone.

It was surprising because Kathleen and Salty had never much cared for each other's company when she was dating Francis. It was the absence of Francis that seemed to make her friendship with Salty possible. They both had friends, but they knew better than to share details about Francis with any of them. They began meeting regularly at the Broadway Bakery.

Kathleen had been sharing a cramped apartment with Debbie, but a month later, she moved into the house on E. Third Street. She and Salty were good for each other. They did crossword puzzles on the large dining room table, played cards, watched reruns on TV. Salty was retired and had plenty of free time, so he prepared suppers and they ate when Kathleen arrived home from work.

They went to movies together, to plays, to Red Sox games, to local museums Kathleen had heard about all her life but had never visited, like the Isabella Stewart Gardner Museum, which looked like an old Venetian palace and had a courtyard filled with gorgeous flowers.

To all the world, especially his sons, Salty appeared to be the same unreflective, unrepentant and unapologetic man he had been his whole life, but to Kathleen he confided how poor a father he knew he'd been and how reckless a husband, particularly for his neglect of Nora toward the end when her suffering was greatest.

He confessed to cheating on Nora. Kathleen had heard the rumor, but had always dismissed it. Nora had heard it as well, but she never confronted her husband. For many years, Salty believed the rumor was the seed of Nora's cancer.

The rumor was that his cheating had resulted in a child. Salty didn't know for sure he was the father, but he was almost certain. The mother was Carrie Siraguso. She lived in Old Colony one floor below the Mahoneys. For a while, she had been good friends with Nora.

The child was born the same year as Matthew, and was named Bradley Michael Siraguso. Carrie shared the project apartment with her cousin and moved out before she was showing. She stayed away almost five years before returning to the same apartment in 1964 with a new husband and a new last name. Driscoll.

That was Salty's big secret, and he confessed it to Kathleen first. She knew what he was looking for. Someone to relieve him of the weight of the sin. Deep down, Salty was still a Catholic, so it would only be in the confessional with a priest that the burden could be lifted.

Kathleen was no priest though. She didn't believe in the sanctity of the mass or of any sacraments, and even believed that most priests were either too ignorant or too fearful to wade into the pools of doubt and hopelessness that life was full of. For her, the best church was a silent, priestless one where she could question God or curse him, and occasionally understand him.

Outside of a funeral or marriage, attending mass was out of the question for Kathleen, but she convinced Salty to begin attending himself, and after an absence of almost twenty years, to step inside the confessional and seek forgiveness from a God who, if he existed, maybe could heal his soul.

"Go to confession on Saturday. Talk to Monsignor Gonzales," she told him.

Salty was offended by the notion of sharing his most intimate sins with someone he deemed not part of their culture. "I'm not getting into the box with a wetback wearing a Tijuana cross."

"Then see Father Coffey. He's a good priest and he's also a good man. Do it."

It took him three weeks to summon the courage, but he did. And he felt better for it. Kathleen could see a long-dead part of Salty coming back to life. Next she urged him to tell the boys. He balked at this as well, but in August, just a month before the wedding, he said he would tell Matthew.

It would not be easy because he had come between Matthew and Buzzy years before, but he hoped Matthew would take the news well. Jimmy and Francis lived in South Boston. If Salty told them, it could stir up troubles all over town.

With the disruption at the wedding, Salty and Matthew hadn't talked. Kathleen thought it was a shame he wasn't able to clear at least one part of his conscience before he died. She decided at the wake that she would write Matthew a letter when he was back in Seattle. After things had settled down. It would be a final favor to Salty. Maybe he would have wanted her to do it. If Kathleen was wrong, well then too bad. It was the right thing to do, and Salty wasn't there to stop her.

"Matthew didn't mention talking with his dad at the wedding," Anne said. "I'm sure he doesn't know about Buzzy."

"Salty treated them both like sons when they were younger, then Buzzy found drugs. One day he was like a son, the next day Salty wouldn't let him in the house." Kathleen squeezed the white plastic lid onto the empty Styrofoam cup. "His solution was to kick Buzzy out of the family and kick Matty out of South Boston. You know the rest of the story with Matty. And Buzzy, well, he became the Buzzy who was at your wedding. Half of his mind is always someplace else, and he's secret about everything. It's like he's locked himself in a box within a box."

"Buzzy doesn't know either, does he?" Anne asked.

"Buzzy told me that he heard the rumors growing up. At some point, I don't know when, he asked his mom and she told him. He said to me once that he wished his mom had lied. Salty tried to talk to him about two months ago. He called Buzzy at home and Buzzy hung up on him. I told Salty to write a letter, and he did. But nothing happened. Buzzy never responded. Who knows if he ever read the letter. Or even got it.

"Salty got pissed off and said it was like trying to reach someone in outer space, and I said 'Yeah, he's in outer space alright, and guess who put him there?' So he wrote another letter a couple of weeks ago. He really wanted to settle things before the wedding or at least get something started. When that didn't happen, Salty was hoping that the wedding would be the thing to bring him and Buzzy together because Matty would be there to help. I didn't say anything, but I really didn't think it was gonna happen. I mean, you don't just turn all that shit around on a dime."

Kathleen tossed the coffee cup into a basket. Rain drummed against the window, and outside cars sped past the salon, their tires splashing through puddles. Kathleen raised the blinds and looked up to the evening sky, which was growing dark. "Francis has wanted his father dead for a long time. Now that it's done, he's just looking for a scapegoat," Kathleen said.

Anne checked her watch. "I better get going and pick up Matt."

"Of course," Kathleen said pulling herself away from the window. "Me too. I need to get out of this place. It gets creepy in here at night. Give your husband a big hug for me. And tell him that he needs to get the two of you out of town before you get stuck here forever. You're already having the most fucked-up honeymoon I've ever heard of."

* * * * *

Francis drove the blue van down N Street past Jimmy's house and pulled into a driveway two doors down. He parked in the garage out back, not only to escape the rain, but also to hide himself from nosy neighbors. Connor swung open the cargo door and dragged the body bag containing Lydia Hudson from the back. He and Francis folded the stiffening body so it would fit into a large plastic bin.

The bin, similar to a large trash container, had two wheels so they could move it easily from the garage and along a cement path to the basement door in the back of the house. "Ducky's Plumbing" and a phone number were printed on the side of the bin above an illustration of a duck in plumber's clothes. The duck wore a broad smile on his oversized face and was tipping his hat to potential customers.

Francis pulled a baseball cap down over his face before he and Connor wheeled the container across the yard to the basement door, where Connor unlocked it. They moved it onto the dirt floor of the basement and locked the door behind them.

The house belonged to Larry's parents, Sabatino and Maria D'Amico. Previously, they had lived in the Mattapan section of Dorchester after getting married in 1945. It was a very safe place to live until the seventies, when increasing crime made a walk to the corner store a risky proposition.

Larry spent years trying to convince them to move, and in 1980 they finally agreed to buy a place on N Street in South Boston just two houses down from Jimmy and Peg Mahoney. It worked out well all around. Sabatino and Maria felt much safer, and Francis and Larry had a secure place nearby for dinners and late-night meetings with Disco and Special Agent Anderson, who worked at the FBI and was almost as tangled up in Francis' business as Disco.

The house on N Street also became a handy storage spot. Unbeknownst to his parents, Larry had tucked away several footlockers beneath the back sunporch. The lockers contained a small arsenal of weapons. Finally, the D'Amicos' new home became the final resting place for bodies. Of the seven victims buried in the unfinished dirt basement, four of the murders had been committed right there while Larry's parents were spending time on Cape Cod or vacationing in Florida.

Two of the resident corpses were a mother and her daughter. The mother had been Larry's live-in girlfriend. She had a daughter, who Larry began sleeping with when she was a teenager. This went on for a few years until the girl accused Larry of messing up her life by having sex with her when she was fifteen. Larry denied it, but he knew she was bound to become a problem. The fact that she made the accusation in front of her mother meant that the mother became suspicious, which meant that she was also a potential problem because of all the knowledge she had about Larry's business.

On successive nights in 1981, each was brought to the D'Amicos' house and shown to the basement where Francis strangled them with his bare hands.

The other two basement murders were strictly business. One was Louis Nave, a bookmaker who worked in Somerville. Nave decided to become an FBI informant and rat out a couple of Somerville gang members Francis did business with. Disco told Francis that Nave was snitching. Before killing Nave, Francis and Larry, who never gambled, placed large bets every day with the bookie.

When they won their bets, Nave paid off. As they started to lose, Francis and Larry doubled down so none of their winnings flowed back to Nave. This went on for a couple of months until they were so heavily in debt to Nave they knew it would take a long time to win anything back from him. When Larry's parents were on a cruise to Cozumel, Nave was invited over to the basement to receive his payment. Instead he received the business end of a mallet that Larry's mother used to tenderize veal, then was buried four feet down.

Another victim was Bobby "The Beach Frog" Beaumont, a French loan shark who worked nights and spent days roasting himself dark brown on the roof of an East Boston car wash next to his apartment. Beach Frog had been part of a crew that robbed a bank in Medford. The robbery had been well planned and executed in every aspect except one. Some of the safety deposit boxes ransacked contained securities, cash and jewelry belonging to a number of mobsters, including the North End's Romano family.

Larry invited Beach Frog over to the basement where he was forced at gunpoint to call all of the other crew members and tell them he needed to borrow cash and that a man fitting Larry's description would stop by shortly to pick it up. Larry drove around and collected over eighty thousand dollars before returning to witness Beach Frog's execution.

Larry did his share of killing over the years, but Francis took care of those four. Larry's task was identity concealment, which began with pulling out the victim's teeth with pliers. Next came removal of the toes and fingers so prints couldn't be used to identify the bodies, should they ever be discovered.

Three additional bodies were buried there. A man who had gotten the better of Francis in a barroom fight several years before. He was shot behind the very same bar, then transported to the basement for burial. Another was a guy whose father had been killed by Francis and had sworn revenge. The day he got out of prison, he was hit by a sharpshooter from a project rooftop in Charlestown and delivered to the basement.

The last was a grossly overweight bookie who was fixing horse races for Francis but showed signs of unreliability. His name was Christopher Flanagan, but when it became known on the street that he was last seen eating pancakes with Francis and Larry at Bickford's House of Pancakes, he was posthumously dubbed Flapjacks Flanagan.

As Connor retrieved a pair of shovels from the garage, Francis studied the expanse of dirt to determine where to dig without hitting another body. He had calculated long ago that the basement contained eight plots. Two rows with four plots each. Any more than that, and they risked digging up buried bodies. Connor handed a shovel to Francis, who walked to the close left corner where he thrust the tip into the rocky soil.

"Whoa. Not there," Connor said.

"What?"

"It's taken. Beach Frog," Connor said.

Francis moved one spot back. This time he looked to Connor before plunging the shovel down. Connor shook his head. "Nave."

"Shit," Francis said. He moved to the third spot.

Connor shook his head. "Nope. The girls, in that one and the next."

"I know we've got an open plot somewhere."

"I'm sketchy on the other four," Connor said.

Francis dropped his shovel and walked over to a shelving unit that held cases of fertilizer and wooden stakes for Maria D'Amico's tomato garden, which had recently yielded one of its richest crops. The top shelf held a number of books and games from Larry's childhood.

Francis rummaged around and found a chess set with a warped board and plastic pieces. On the inside cover of the box were a set of printed chess rules and a diagram showing the proper layout of the board. Long ago, Francis had drawn a rectangle around eight of the squares. Across seven of the squares were black Xs. The only open square was on the back right.

He returned the chess set to its shelf and walked to the corner. "I remember now. I left this spot for last because it's where the sewage pipe gets in the way. No matter, we'll put her close to the third spot so she can get all cozy with Flapjacks."

* * * * *

The rain had increased and the wind slapped loudly onto the awning that protected Matthew outside the Purple Shamrock at Quincy Market. Water cascaded from the awning and puddled at his feet, but he was entranced by a key he slowly twirled between his fingers.

How had it ended up in Buzzy's pocket? Matthew's thoughts raced around and around with possibilities. Didn't Jimmy say he had put the key back in the garage a week ago? Maybe Buzzy had gone over to E. Third Street in the last week, used the key and forgot to return it. Maybe this wasn't the same key, only one that looked similar. Matthew stared at the dapple of paint that years ago had dropped onto the head of the key, leaving a distorted hourglass shape.

Matthew's first impulse was denial of the obvious. Finding the key in Buzzy's jacket didn't necessarily mean anything.

But there had to be an explanation. And not the one that Matthew's mind kept lunging toward, that Francis was right. It was ridiculous. The only reason it had just popped into Matthew's mind was because Francis had planted the suggestion.

A gust of wind blew rain beneath the awning and splashed Matthew. He looked across the street at the line of cabs moving slowly and rhythmically to the front of the stand. There was one way to confirm if this was the key to his father's house, and that was to test it in the lock. Matthew tucked the key in his jeans pocket and ran across the street. He jumped into the first cab on the stand.

"City Point," Matthew called through the opaque bulletproof Lexan glass that separated the back of the cab from the front.

The driver started to pull away. He hadn't heard what Matthew said. "Where are we going?"

"City Point," Matthew repeated.

The driver turned around. He was black. "That's in South Boston. I don't go to South Boston."

Since the days of busing, when blacks could be beaten in South Boston for simply being black, most black cab drivers didn't go there. White drivers would refuse to go to certain parts of Roxbury for the same reason. Who wanted to risk getting his brains bashed in for a ten-dollar fare?

The driver slammed on the brakes and looked back at the stand where another cab was pulling into the front space where he had been. He had lost his spot and would have to go back to the end of the long line. "Shit, why didn't you say South Boston?"

"Sorry, I'll give you a good tip."

The driver had a choice. Lose twenty minutes or take a risky fare. He reluctantly agreed and sped into the rain toward the Northern Avenue bridge and South Boston. Matthew's thoughts were jumping all over the place and he struggled to keep his imagination from traveling too far. Stick to the facts. Jimmy had returned the key a week ago. If this was the key, it meant that Buzzy had taken it at some point in the last week. And that he had forgotten to return it.

Matthew put the key back inside the lining where he had found it and tried to detect it by feeling along the hem of the jacket. He couldn't. The suede was too thick. Buzzy might have thought he lost the key when it was really buried in the jacket lining.

Matthew saw E. First Street coming up. He told the cab driver to turn left, then right onto O Street and then onto E. Third. They parked in front of the house. As Matthew grabbed the door handle, he felt sweat on his palm. "I'll be back in ten seconds," he said. The driver voiced some protest. Matthew ignored him and walked toward the back of the house with the key in his hand.

He hesitated when he reached the back door. The same way he had hesitated at the threshold to his mother's hospital room when he was thirteen years old. It was when she was first diagnosed with cancer and she had stayed overnight at the Beth Israel Hospital so the doctor could run tests. Matthew believed he could keep the catastrophe at bay as long as he didn't see his mother lying flat on a hospital bed wearing one of those gowns that could make you look sick even if you weren't.

Standing in the wet grass of his father's backyard, Matthew suddenly wished that he had turned away at the threshold fifteen years before. If only to maintain for one more day the illusion that all was well.

However, he wasn't thirteen anymore and he couldn't survive on illusions, so he slid the key into the lock. He turned it and the door opened. The key fit. Of course it fit.

Matthew drew in a deep breath before relocking the door and removing the key. He ran back to the cab and jumped in the back seat. "Drive up to Broadway and turn right." He was going back to Old Colony, something he didn't want the driver to know until they were almost there.

With the windows closed because of the rain, the inside of the cab grew warm and the suede jacket began to stink. It suddenly occurred to Matthew that when he saw Buzzy at Donnelley's Pub the day before, he had mentioned the missing key to him. Hadn't he? Yes, they talked about it, where it was hidden, what it looked like. Buzzy even commiserated about Matthew having to use the ladder to get into the house.

Buzzy was lying the whole time. Right to Matthew's face. Didn't that say it all? Matthew opened the window to give himself some cool air, to keep his thoughts from scattering. He would go to the project, find Buzzy and they'd talk about this. Talk. Matthew drew in a deep cool breath and watched people trudging up Broadway with umbrellas angled into the wind.

At the intersection with Dorchester Street, Matthew had the driver turn left, along the same route taken by the St. Patrick's Day parade and the anti-busing marches in 1974. They passed the funeral home, then Donnelley's Pub.

"Bang a left here," Matthew said.

The driver turned onto Old Colony Avenue. "Where are we going? I don't like mystery rides."

Matthew told the driver to make another quick left onto Patterson Way and to pull into a spot in front of number seven. When they parked, the driver stopped the meter and turned to Matthew. "Sixteen fifty."

Matthew reached into his back pocket for a twenty. There was no money. He checked his other pockets. They were all empty. He had left his money and his wallet back in Ipswich. "Oh, fuck me," he muttered, then said to the driver. "Look, I'm gonna run inside and get some money."

"No, no," the driver shot back. "You're not pulling that shit on me. Those are famous last words, and I've heard them before."

Matthew yelled back at the driver, "Hey, what do you want? I don't have any money on me. I'm gonna go inside and get some. That's the deal. I'll be in that building right there. Number seven. Second floor, the last apartment facing the street." Matthew pointed.

"Like I can go looking for you in there if you don't come out? No, you're not going anywhere if you don't leave me some collateral."

Matthew was already on edge and the driver was just pissing him off more. The man was middle aged and wouldn't follow Matthew one step into Old Colony. He knew it. Walking away on this cab fare would be as easy as it had been so many times when Matthew was a teenager. "What do you want me to leave with you?"

The driver looked down. "Leave your sneakers here with me."

"I'm not giving you my fucking sneakers. It's raining out there."

"You got a watch?"

Matthew rolled up the sleeve of the jacket. He had left his watch in Ipswich too. "I'll give you this jacket. OK? It's suede," Matthew said, pulling off the jacket.

The driver took a quick glance at the stained suede and said, "I don't want that piece of shit."

Matthew held up his hands and was about to tell the driver to go fuck himself. Then he noticed his wedding band, still seeming like an unnatural addition to his left hand. The ring had belonged to Anne's father and she had slid it onto Matthew's finger five days before. He hesitated before pulling it off and placing it into the small payment tray.

"This is my wedding ring. It's gold. I'll be back in less than five minutes. You better not go anywhere. I want that ring back."

"OK," the driver said as he inspected the shiny band. "I'll be here. But if I don't get paid, I'm selling this on the street today."

Matthew charged across the wet courtyard. He wasn't sure what he'd do if Buzzy was in the apartment. Or what he'd do if he wasn't there. He took two steps at a time up the stairwell and almost knocked over Kelly McDermitt, who was hauling two large trash bags down to the dumpster. "Hey, watch where the fuck you're going, asshole!"

"Sorry," Matthew called back to her without slowing down. When he reached the apartment, he pounded on the heavy steel door. Inside he heard a crash and someone stumbling for the door. Matthew pounded again.

"Who is it?" A man's voice called from the other side of the door.

"It's Matt Mahoney. Open up!"

Latches turned and bolts slid. The door opened a few inches, stopped by a security chain. Mikey's face appeared in the space. "You scared the shit out of me."

"C'mon, Mikey. Open up."

"What's the matter?"

"There'll be something the matter if you don't open this door."

"OK, OK." Mikey closed the door, undid the chain, then opened it. Matthew pushed past him and strode into the empty living room. "Is he here?"

"You mean Buzzy?"

A car horn blasted outside. Matthew walked into the bedroom to the right, still darkened by a blanket covering the window. He yanked it down. Outside, a few people stood beside Matthew's cab, talking to the driver. Matthew watched for a moment before turning his attention back to the bedroom.

A single mattress lay on the floor with a bong and an alarm clock sitting nearby. He walked over to the dresser. On top sat a shiny metal scale and some *Soldier of Fortune* magazines. Matthew poked through the clothing in the drawers. He didn't even know what he was looking for.

"Buzzy's not here, Matt." Mikey followed Matthew as he walked over to the closet, which was empty. "He hasn't come back." He followed Matthew to the hallway closet. Nothing. Matthew slammed the door shut and walked to the second bedroom. He tried the door, but it was locked. He turned to Mikey and pointed a finger at the door. "Is he in there?"

"No, Matt."

"If you're lying to me, I swear to God, Mikey, I'll kill the both of you." The words came from Matthew as naturally as breathing.

"He's not here at all! That's the truth."

Outside a car horn blasted again several times. Mikey ran to the kitchen, where he frantically pulled open drawers. Silverware spilled onto the floor. Matthew rushed into the kitchen, just as Mikey spun around with something in his hand.

"Take it easy," Mikey said. "He keeps the spare key in the kitchen. Here," he said, handing Matthew the key.

The bedroom was a mess of dirty clothes and two bare mattresses. The air was heavy with a stench that matched the suede jacket. A blend of sweat, tobacco and pot. Matthew inspected the closet. It held only a scale, larger than the one in the first bedroom and so well polished that when Matthew tilted it toward him he could see his own face reflected on a balance.

He continued to scan the closet, then the bedroom again. Buzzy wasn't in the apartment, so what was he looking for anyway? A clue, maybe. A reason why Buzzy would kill his father. It made no sense at all to Matthew. What had happened between the two? His father didn't like Buzzy. That Matthew knew, but what reason would Buzzy have to kill him?

"I think I know where you can find him," Mikey said.

Matthew had been lost in thought, and Mikey's voice surprised him.

"I didn't remember until after you left before. Buzzy's supposed to get his cab fixed this week. Something's wrong with the meter. If he's getting it fixed, he's at a shop in the South End."

"Whereabouts?"

"There's a big parking garage next to City Hospital, and the repair shop is across the street from the garage." Mikey found a pen in the kitchen and wrote down the address for Matthew on the back of a bus transfer. "Like I said before, it's a light blue cab, number 1350."

Matthew heard an insistent car horn and remembered his own cab. He dashed over to the window and saw a crowd gathered around the taxi. One guy was yelling at the driver and giving him the finger. Another slammed a bat down on the trunk of the cab.

"Shit!" Matthew looked down at his bare ring finger. "Mikey, I need some cash. Fast!" He followed Mikey to the first bedroom and waited as Mikey retrieved a pile of bills from beneath the mattress.

"How about twenty?" Mikey extended a bill.

Instead of taking it, Matthew grabbed a half dozen twenties from Mikey's other hand. "Something like that. Don't worry. I'll pay you back."

Matthew walked quickly to the front door where he stopped and called back, "If Buzzy calls from the garage, tell him to stay there."

"Should I tell him you're on your way over?" Mikey asked.

Matthew hesitated. He stared out the living room window and realized he had to make a decision. Why was he doing this? The day had started with trying to save Buzzy. Trying to prevent Francis from reaching him. Everything had changed with the key though. Hadn't it? Matthew still wanted to find Buzzy, but it was no longer about saving him.

Matthew called to Mikey, "No. Don't tell him I'm on my way. Don't tell him I was here."

The cab was long gone when Matthew stepped outside, and the crowd had dispersed. He walked up to a boy leaning against a blue van that was parked where the cab had been.

"What happened? Where's my cab?" Matthew asked the boy.

"That asshole was parked in Joey's spot." The boy slapped a hand against the van and laughed.

* * * * *

The location Stanley Higgins chose to meet Jimmy Mahoney was far less elegant than Locke-Ober restaurant, a favorite place for the Kennedy family to wine and dine city leaders for their political support.

Stanley lived in the Davis Square section of Somerville, which was adjacent to Cambridge. Stanley proudly referred to his hometown as "the poor man's Cambridge." He was equally proud to be working at the *Boston Herald*, which he saw as the workingman's paper with an honest connection to the neighborhoods in and around Boston, as opposed to the *Boston Globe*, which he viewed as an elitist institution. He would never confess it to his colleagues, but Stanley regularly read the *Globe* at home.

He would have been happy to take Jimmy up on a free meal at a fancy restaurant, but on this particular evening Stanley's wife was out of town and he was busy taking care of his two young daughters, one of them sick with stomach flu, another reason why gourmet dining was the last thing on his mind. Stanley had to scramble to find a babysitter in time to meet Jimmy at Olympian Pizza in Davis Square, just across from an old theater that was hosting an animated film festival.

Jimmy arrived just before six at the pizza parlor. It was crowded with theatergoers grabbing a quick bite before the evening's first show. He found Stanley sitting at a window table sipping an orange soda and wearing a dark baggy sweat suit, which on first glance looked like a pair of flannel pajamas.

Jimmy draped his jacket across the back of a chair. "Stanley, you're a champion to meet me on short notice." He extended his hand. Stanley didn't.

"Nothing personal, Jimmy. One of the girls is sick with the flu, and I'm sure I'm covered with germs." Stanley was middle aged, somewhat overweight, and his round face had a pinched look that made him seem in a constant state of uncertainty about everything. The weather, the stock market, his emotional commitment to the Red Sox now that a losing season was all but certain.

Many politicians had learned the hard way that when Stanley seemed most distracted, he was at his most alert, cataloging and assessing every comment and gesture, already writing the column in his head. Jimmy had few friends, if any, in the press, and Stanley was at best neutral on Senator Mahoney. However, there was an element to Jimmy's alternative waste disposal site that Jimmy believed would appeal to Stanley. A David versus Goliath angle. And if Jimmy was right, that would make Stanley the perfect reporter to carry off the task.

"Can I get you some pizza?" Jimmy asked.

"No thanks. The appetite's pretty much gone for the night. Help yourself, though."

Jimmy took a look at the long line waiting to order, then noticed Stanley rolling up his sleeve to check his watch. "I'm fine." Jimmy sat down.

"So what have we got, Jimmy?"

"I heard you can get this in the first edition. Is that doable?"

"I think so. Yes. It might not be very comprehensive, but I can flesh it out for later editions or for Saturday." Stanley took a small sip of his orange soda, then rested a hand on his stomach.

From some reporters, that could sound like hedging, but Jimmy knew that from Stanley it was a pretty firm yes. "OK, here we go," Jimmy said as he pulled a pile of papers from his bag and laid them in separate stacks, then added maps and illustrations. Jimmy described each stack. "Here are the environmental impact statements, health and safety assessments, the applicable zoning requirements for the site, neighborhood impact statements, trucking routes that would minimize residential impact, cost assessments, estimated capacities of the site in general and the waste-to-energy facility specifically."

Jimmy went on to enumerate the many ways in which this site was superior to South Bay in location, cost and capacity. "This is also the kind of site the governor was referring to when he mentioned his desire to find a regional solution for waste disposal, not just a local fix. On this map, you can see how the site presents a hub that reaches out to all surrounding cities and towns, including Boston…"

Stanley was listening as he scanned the piles of documents. His eyes locked onto the map Jimmy pointed to. Then his eyes grew wide. He let out a quick laugh, which sounded like a bark. He looked up and met Jimmy's eyes.

"Wellesley?" Stanley asked.

Jimmy nodded. He knew this was the moment Stanley would be testing his credibility.

"Wellesley," Stanley repeated. "For real?"

"For real, Stanley. The numbers make it too good to pass up. And the obvious concerns have all been addressed."

Stanley stared at Jimmy for a few seconds. "It's the wealthiest town in the state." Stanley considered other towns that might be wealthier but couldn't land on any. "Or close to it."

"The site is a soon-to-be abandoned quarry on the border of Wellesley and Weston," Jimmy said. "Ninety-five acres large as opposed to seven acres small at South Bay. It's right alongside a set of railroad tracks, making it easy to move large amounts of material in and out to other sites for further processing. It has convenient access to all of the major highways, including the turnpike. Because of its capacity, it can handle both residential and commercial waste. A huge plus. And the enormous empty quarry is the perfect place to dispose of ash from the waste-to-energy facility." Jimmy was careful not to use the word 'incinerator.' "The more you study the associated facts, the more it becomes obvious that this site is by far the best. A waste disposal plan that offers a truly regional solution."

Stanley thumbed through the documents, stopping only to sip on his soda and press a hand against his stomach. After ten minutes he looked up at Jimmy. "These impact statements are preliminary."

"Preliminary but conclusive. We already have plans for more complete studies."

"I assume Mayor Sullivan doesn't know about this."

"He will tomorrow morning."

"And the governor?"

"Off the record," Jimmy said, "The governor feels trapped by South Bay. He knows, everybody knows, that a regional solution makes the most sense. But he's busy running for president right now. He'll eventually approve of this site once the pros and cons are debated in public. But he can't afford to propose it himself. I know he'll respond favorably to it. At the right time. I give you my word on that."

"So he knows about this site."

"I didn't say that. I'm saying this site fits the description of what he has asked for. A sensible, affordable, regional solution."

"A sensible, regional solution," Stanley repeated.

"And affordable," Jimmy said.

"I know, but I'm thinking of a sub-headline that will fit under the big headline that I don't get to write. The story can discuss the cost aspect. These are mine?" Stanley pointed to the piles of documents.

"All yours," Jimmy said. "First edition?"

"Yes. I gave my boss a heads-up that this might be coming in late and hot." Stanley stood up and tossed his soda into a trash can. "Jimmy, if you can swing by the office in about an hour, I'd like to get a picture of you beside this map of the site. I can have somebody blow it up." Before picking up the documents, Stanley did a deep back bend and let out a groan.

As Jimmy turned to leave, Stanley stopped him momentarily. "You know what's going to happen tomorrow morning when this comes out, don't you? There's gonna be a big shit storm. I mean, Wellesley. When the president of Harvard University rolls out of bed and hears that his hometown is pegged for a waste-to-energy facility the size of Rhode Island..."

"Let's not exaggerate, Stanley."

"I'm just saying, get yourself a pair of earplugs because you're gonna hear screaming like you've never heard screaming before. Who represents Wellesley in the Senate?"

"George Corbin," Jimmy answered with his best poker face.

"Corbin. That's right. He's gonna go off the deep end when he hears about this."

That's the whole idea, Jimmy thought, but he said nothing.

* * * * *

It was a short cab ride from Old Colony to Boston City Hospital, located on the boundary of the fashionable South End with its brick townhouses and the poorer neighborhoods of Roxbury. Matthew's cab driver was a Russian immigrant who had a wallet-size photo of his two children on display next to his hackney license behind the Lexan shield. It was a department-store kind of portrait in which the two girls had been forced to interact with an odd prop, a short plaster column. Matthew was struck by the girls' mischievous smiles, which seemed to be mocking the ridiculous setup.

As the cab sped down Martin Luther King Boulevard toward City Hospital, Matthew found himself growing too agitated to sit still much longer. He had been angry at his father his whole life, angrier than he had been with any other person, but this thing with Buzzy, this betrayal, was beyond anything.

Domino's Bar sat behind City Hospital parking garage in a no-man's land of empty parking lots and decaying buildings. Above the bar were two floors of apartments with dirty bare windows that gave the building an abandoned look. Next to the bar was an auto repair shop and a liquor store the size of a suburban supermarket. Its vast parking lot was littered with trash.

Matthew stepped out of the cab and walked toward the covered service bays where two cars were suspended on lifts. One was a new white Cadillac, the other a green pickup truck. No light blue cab. Maybe he was too late or maybe Mikey was full of shit and covering for Buzzy.

A mechanic working beneath the Cadillac looked over at him suspiciously. "What do you want?"

"I'm looking for a cab. I thought it would be here. A light blue cab. A guy named Buzzy Driscoll is driving it."

The mechanic gestured to the back door of the garage where it opened onto an alley. "I put a new meter in. It's out back. I think Buzzy's still in Domino's."

"Thanks a lot," Matthew said and walked through the back door and into the alley. There it sat, a light blue Chevrolet Caprice. Number 1350. Matthew felt a surge of anxiety.

Domino's had a back door onto the alley. Matthew opened it and walked inside the narrow, dingy bar, which was surprisingly crowded. He moved quickly between a line of stools on his right and small booths on his left, checking every face he passed.

When he had almost reached the front end of the bar, Matthew spotted the back of Buzzy's head. He was talking on a pay phone. Matthew overheard Buzzy asking, "When did he leave?"

Matthew reached out and placed a hand on his shoulder, and Buzzy spun around. He stared at Matthew without moving. His face had no expression, but it looked tired, very tired. From the earpiece of the phone came an incomprehensible garble. Buzzy sniffled and rested the phone on his shoulder, with the mouth piece facing up. "Matt," he said in a tone that was relaxed. Buzzy tilted his head to one side and smiled. A click came from the phone as the other party hung up.

"So what's up, man? How come you're still in town?" Buzzy asked. His eyes wandered briefly over Matthew's left shoulder, then his right. Matthew was far too familiar with Buzzy's ability to hide his guilt from the cops, from teachers, from the whole world, to be fooled by him now.

He knew what Buzzy was doing. He was sizing up the situation. Checking to see if Matthew had come for him alone. Whatever shred of doubt Matthew might have still had about Buzzy's guilt now vanished. He hated to admit it, but Francis was right.

He grabbed Buzzy's arm in a tight grip. "C'mon," he said as he pulled Buzzy to the back door and into the alley. "I need a lift downtown. What do you say we take your cab? You're not too busy, are you?"

When they reached the cab, Buzzy pulled himself free and spread his arms wide. "Don't fuck with me, Matt. I'm not having a good day."

"You and me both, brother. Get inside, and I'll tell you about mine." He pointed Buzzy to the driver's side. Matthew opened the passenger door, but the front seat was crowded with two large plastic garbage bags, so Matthew climbed into the backseat.

"I have to get back to Ipswich."

Buzzy started the cab and drove onto Mass Avenue. "I can't take you to Ipswich, Matt."

"I don't need a ride to Ipswich. Just take me to North Station. I'll catch a train."

They rode in silence except for the sound of car tires splashing on the busy avenue. Matthew considered how to do this. The problem was that he didn't know exactly what to do, or even what to say. 'Why did you kill my father?' was what he wanted to ask, but it sounded bizarre and if Buzzy laughed or answered in a way that Matthew didn't like, he knew he was just going to explode, and he was afraid how things would end up if he lost control of himself.

The rain made the usual rush-hour traffic even worse. Buzzy left the main roads to weave a course through a maze of side streets and alleys.

As they approached Copley Square, Matthew leaned forward and pulled back the payment tray in the middle of the Lexan shield. He placed the key in the tray and pushed it back to the driver's side.

"What's that?" Buzzy asked.

Matthew sat back and watched Buzzy's expression in the rearview mirror. "You tell me."

Without taking his eyes off the road, Buzzy scooped the key from the tray. He held it in front of him, turning it slowly before placing it back in the tray. "Sorry. Not mine," Buzzy said.

"First of all…" Matthew stopped because he could feel his voice shaking. "Pull over," he said.

They were driving down Boylston Street and the Lenox Hotel was a block away. Buzzy changed lanes and pulled onto the back of the Lenox cab stand. He turned in his seat to face Matthew. "I thought you wanted to go to North Station." He was calm. In the way he looked, in the way he spoke.

Matthew picked the key from the tray. "You know what this is, Buzzy. It's the key to my dad's house. The spare key from the garage. When I saw you yesterday, I told you I couldn't find it. Remember? At Donnelley's?"

Buzzy looked down at the key and tilted his head. He looked at Matthew with lazy eyes. "I was so high yesterday."

"Are you high now?"

"I'm tired, Matt. I'm so fucking tired you wouldn't believe it."

Matthew held the key up to the scratched Lexan shield. "I couldn't find this when I went to the house, Buzzy. It was gone. But I found it today. Right here." Matthew pointed at the pocket. "In your jacket."

"Matt, that's not my jacket."

"You were wearing it yesterday."

Buzzy turned away slowly and stretched his hands across the steering wheel. "Everybody wears it. It's like herpes, Matt. It's been all around town. It has a new owner every day."

Matthew felt a bolt of doubt, which passed quickly. It was certainly a good story, but Matthew didn't believe it because he knew Buzzy. When he was accused wrongly, Buzzy would get loud and pissy. When he was accused rightly, he would turn clever, then shut down.

It was a tactic that had gotten the two of them out of a lot of jams, and it was a thing of beauty to see in action. It's exactly what Buzzy was doing now, Matthew realized as Buzzy bowed his head and let out a yawn. "I need to go home and sleep, Matt. Do you want a lift to North Station or not?"

Matthew had wanted to know why Buzzy had committed the murder, but he was too mad to care about that now. He slammed his fist against the shield behind Buzzy. He did it so hard that it hit Buzzy's head, which shot forward.

Buzzy turned around and gave Matthew an angry look. "What the fuck!"

"You were wearing this jacket Saturday night. You wore it to E. Third Street. You took the key out of the garage and you went into the house … "

Buzzy held a hand to the back of his head. He laughed, "Oh, and who's high now?"

The comment sent Matthew into a rage. He began slamming the bulletproof shield so hard that the screws securing it to the roof of the cab were popping out with each successive blow. Buzzy was only inches away and Matthew wanted desperately to get his hands around his neck.

Matthew kept slamming his clenched fists against the shield. It began to tilt farther forward. It was only a matter of time before it collapsed. The shield showed streaks of blood from Matthew's fists. All of the top screws were out and when he had knocked it forward far enough, Matthew reached his hands over the top and yanked the shield back toward him. A number of screws holding it to the sides of the cab went flying.

Buzzy made no effort to escape. Instead he sat there resigned, tensing a little with every blow against the wall that protected him. A good yank would have knocked the wall completely away, but Matthew stopped. His hands hurt. That wasn't his reason for stopping though. He didn't know why.

The shield hung down like a tray table on an airplane. Matthew's face was covered in sweat and he was breathing heavily. He stared through the empty space at his prey.

"Yeah, OK," Matthew said. "You go home and sleep, Buzzy. Just don't forget to say your prayers. You're gonna need all the help you can get." Matthew reached for the handle to the back door and left Buzzy alone in his mess of a cab.

The Copley Square subway stop was a block down Boylston Street. Matthew headed for it, passing the public library on the way. When he was less than fifty feet from the subway entrance, the light blue cab pulled alongside him and Buzzy called from the open passenger window. "You're wrong, Matt. I don't like the idea that Francis did it either."

Matthew didn't respond. He focused on reaching the subway without reacting.

"What are you gonna do, Matt?" Buzzy called from the cab as it rolled slowly along the curb. "Are you gonna go to the cops? Don't say anything to the cops. Don't be stupid, Matt."

When Matthew reached the stairs, he turned to Buzzy, who was wagging a finger at him. "I'm serious, Matt. Don't tell the cops."

Matthew walked over to the cab and leaned inside. "I don't have to tell the cops, Buzzy. I'm gonna tell Francis."

Buzzy laughed. "He's not in the country, Matt. I don't think he's even on the fucking planet anymore."

Matthew showed an angry smile, "Oh, yes he is, Buzzy. He was waiting for me at E. Third Street yesterday morning. That's why I needed the key to get in the house. That's why I missed the funeral. Francis came back because he heard about the murder, and he knows who did it." Matthew paused to watch the news register with Buzzy, and when it did Matthew watched the fear take over Buzzy's expression.

Satisfied, Matthew turned and headed down the stairs. He bought a token at the window where the attendant sat behind bulletproof glass. Matthew's hands were shaking, and he dropped the token on the ground twice before managing to slip it into the slot of the turnstile.

The platform was filled with people and the noise of their mingled conversations seemed incredibly loud. It mixed with the sound of wheels screeching as a trolley entered the station. From behind him, Matthew heard his name shouted. He turned to see Buzzy pressed against the bars of a barrier.

He was completely in the grip of fear now. Matthew could see it in his face and hear it in his voice. "You don't know everything, Matt. He betrayed me first. He betrayed all of us. I did it for you and me and Francis and Jimmy."

It was all gibberish to Matthew, an emotional eruption that was drowned out by the sound of the trolley screeching to a stop.

Before getting on the trolley, he called back to Buzzy, "I hope he makes you suffer."

The doors closed and the trolley disappeared into the anonymous tunnel.

* * * * *

247

Joan's schedule on Thursday included teaching undergraduate classes in calculus and linear algebra, followed by office hours from 2:30 to 4:30 when students could stop by with questions or concerns. The deadline to add or drop classes for the fall semester was that Friday, so she was busy all afternoon sorting out enrollment in her classes.

It was not until she was driving home at five o'clock that she had time to really consider what happened earlier that morning. It seemed to boil down to Anne not having made the wisest choice by marrying Matthew. Not that Anne consulted her mother much in the matter. She had relied on her father for that kind of advice, Joan knew. Dylan not only approved of Matthew, he approved of him without the least reservation.

Joan had met Matthew a number of times over the last few years when she visited Seattle, and she was more or less neutral about him. No, she didn't like the fact that he was a bartender and had not finished his undergraduate studies. In fact, he hadn't even completed his first semester of classes before dropping out. He was still young, and with the right motivation—becoming a father, for instance—he could get back on the right track.

Matthew liked to drink. It was obvious from seeing the other Mahoneys at the wedding reception that it was a family tendency. As a bartender, he spent forty hours a week in an environment based on the consumption of alcohol. Finding another line of work might help with that. Then again, it might not.

Finally, there was Matthew's brother Francis. It was common knowledge to her and everyone else in Massachusetts that he was involved in illegal activities and had been for many years. His name was all over the news that week, and Joan dreaded the question her friends and colleagues were asking with increasing frequency. "Is your daughter's husband any relation to 'that' Mahoney?" Depending on who was asking, the answers ranged from, "Yes, unfortunately" to "Mahoney is such a common name in Boston, so possibly, in a distant way."

Francis Mahoney had actually been in her house, which was enough to make Joan feel uneasy every time she heard a strange noise while reading alone in the study. Anne had assured her, as her friends had assured her, that being related to Francis didn't mean that Matthew was like him. Just look at the other brother Jimmy. He was a respected state senator. To all appearances, he was also a stable husband and responsible father to his many children.

Anne's father had spent more time with Matthew, and from all she heard, the two got along well. Dylan was the kind of father figure that Matthew needed, and for a while that gave Joan hope. Of course, it ended with Dylan's death. Joan knew it was a terrible loss for Anne, but she wondered how it might have also affected Anne's relationship with Matthew. Had the decision to marry simply been the result of inertia, based more on the way all three of them got along than on the new reality of a world without Dylan?

Those concerns had always been in the background of Joan's thoughts about her daughter's well-being. She had always felt it was beyond her realm to counsel Anne on her marriage decision because she was turning more to, and had always turned more to, her father for advice on all matters.

In the absence of Dylan and with the disturbing situation that morning—again postponing the honeymoon in order to attend to a family emergency that could only be described in mysterious, vague terms—Joan wondered as she drove through downtown Salem if it was indeed time to become more active in offering Anne some candid advice.

Yes, it seemed time for that. Just what kind of advice should she give though? Tell Anne she should go in search of another husband? It wouldn't break Joan's heart if Anne decided to do so, although it was probably too late to hope for that.

Joan thought about it all the way home, but she couldn't land on any specific advice that would be of help to her daughter. She decided that she should at least voice her general concern, let Anne know that she was worried about the way Matthew or Matthew's family or his friends were … well, screwing up their honeymoon and their lives in general.

She was drinking tea and reading her mail on the couch in the study when Anne arrived home at seven o'clock.

"Well, how did everything go today?" Joan called to the kitchen, where Anne was looking through the fridge for something to snack on. She added, "I made a pot of tea. Help yourself."

Anne closed the fridge and poured herself a mug of tea, made from the chocolate mint Joan grew in the herb garden. Anne walked to the study cradling the mug to warm her hands. Outside, the rain continued with occasional gusts buffeting the windows.

Anne settled into an easy chair and kicked her sneakers to the floor. "Has Matthew called?"

"Has he called me? I assumed he was with you," Joan said.

Anne drew a deep breath of the mint vapor coming off her tea, took a drink, then laid the mug on the long teak table between herself and her mom. The table had been purchased by Dylan in Thailand and depicted a pageant of warriors, chariots and dragons beneath a glass top that protected the elaborately carved wood.

"I was supposed to pick him up at Quincy Market at six o'clock, but he wasn't there. Maybe one of us got the time wrong. Anyway, I thought he might have called. He can always take the train back."

Joan tried to fit this detail into what Anne had told her about the trip to Boston that day. She took off her glasses and laid them on top of the letters on her lap. "Anne, honey, none of this is making sense to me. You didn't tell me exactly what it was that you and Matthew had to do that was so important today. And now you're asking me if Matthew has called, which means the two of you went off in different directions for some reason."

Anne stretched her arms above her head, which felt good after sitting in the car for so long. It also helped her relax before launching a difficult explanation. She reached for the mug before beginning, "Here's what happened today, Mom ... "

Joan interrupted, but Anne interrupted her right back.

"Listen, Mom. I am going to tell you because I don't want to keep any secrets from you. I never did that with Dad, and I'm not comfortable doing that with you either," Anne said as she began a description of events that took her mother from the day after the wedding to Anne visiting Kathleen's salon that afternoon, ending with, "so like I said, Matthew wanted to find Buzzy today because he's pretty sure Francis wants to kill him."

Joan absentmindedly opened and closed the temples of her reading glasses. She had been doing it throughout Anne's explanation. When it seemed to be finished—and Joan had heard more than enough explanation for her liking—she blinked a few times and took her first deep breath in five minutes. "Good heavens." She repeated it.

Anne replied. "I know, it's a really strange situation. We're just glad it's almost over." She felt unburdened having told her mom everything and assumed her mom would be understanding once everything had sunk in.

Joan had understood everything, but she was far from understanding. "It's not a strange situation, Anne. It's insane. And it sounds more than mildly criminal. I hope you've contacted the police."

Anne was caught off guard for a moment. "Well, no. Matthew didn't think that would be … "

"I don't care what Matthew thinks, Anne. I'm concerned for you. I can't believe you would allow yourself to be drawn into this. Putting aside the danger you might be in, the physical danger, what you're doing is potentially illegal. In fact, I have little doubt that you're breaking the law right now."

Anne considered her visit to Buzzy's apartment and her discussion with Kathleen, and wondered what could possibly be illegal about any of it. "Mom, I've done nothing except talk to Buzzy's roommate and Kathleen. Please don't let your imagination get going."

"There's nothing imaginary going on. Matthew's brother is wanted by the police. Matthew's had contact with him, and Matthew has aided him in some way. There are laws against that, Anne. Aiding and abetting, I believe it's called. It also sounds like Matthew's brother is plotting a murder. Those are crimes."

"No, they're not. Francis didn't kill their dad. He was framed, so whatever Matthew is doing is not against the law."

"You can split legal hairs all you want, Anne. It's not what an intelligent person would do."

"It's what Dad would do," Anne responded immediately, more out of a well-established habit when disagreeing with her mother.

"You can say that, but your father was not so reckless as to aid a fugitive."

Anne sighed in exasperation. "Mother, he would stand up for his friends if they were wrongly accused."

Joan shook her head.

"Yes," Anne said emphatically. "That's what he did for his brother when the restaurant in Anchorage burned down and he was accused of doing it. Dad knew it was bullshit, and he helped him hide from the police."

Joan waved a hand in front of her. "That's a poor example, Anne. I knew Desmond well. He was as reckless as your father."

There was something in what Joan was saying, or had been saying, that Anne had to admit was true. About the legal risk that she and Matthew were running by their activities over the last couple of days. And she might have acknowledged the point, but the words her mother had just spoken pulled her in a different direction.

Anne leaned forward in her chair. "Why do you always have to describe Dad that way?"

"I knew your father well enough, Anne. Let's leave it at that. And don't give me that stare as if I'm the one who's done something wrong here."

"I grew up with him, Mother, and he was not a reckless man. Or a reckless father. He did a good job of raising me, and we had a great life together until he died."

Joan folded her hands over her reading glasses. "Forgive me if I'd rather not hear how interesting life can be in Alaska. How exciting, how different."

"Will you please stop doing that? You're obsessed with criticizing Dad. You've always tried to tear him down."

"And you've always tried to turn him into some larger-than-life hero. You throw it in my face every chance you get, Anne. You've been doing it ever since you left this home. Maybe some day you'll understand how a mother feels when her only child can't stand the idea of living with her. That she prefers to be with her father, that she loves him more."

Over the years, Joan and Anne had beaten a well-worn path to this contentious point. There were meandering trails down which the conversation might travel, but it often ended up at the place where Joan issued the indictment that Anne had failed in a child's obligation to love her parents equally, or at least to make it appear so.

For Anne, it was the point beyond which she couldn't argue because to do so would be to admit that her mother was right. That Anne did love, or at least like, her father much more than her mother. It was true. She preferred his company, his sense of humor, his sense of adventure and his willingness to look fear in the face.

It's what made Anne feel so guilty as an adult, and why she was always trying to make up for her imbalance of affection. However, to actually admit it to her mother would be like pushing her off a cliff. And whenever their discussions reached the edge of the cliff, Anne always backed away.

Something had changed that evening, however, and for the first time Anne believed that a good push was exactly what her mother needed. She sat back in her chair and spoke calmly, "You're right, Mom. I couldn't stand living here with you after the divorce. I couldn't wait to get out of this house. And I was much happier living with Dad. I hated Ipswich and I loved Alaska."

Anne waited for a reaction. Joan stared straight back at her daughter without a flinch.

Anne continued, "You've been pushing me for years to admit it. Well, there it is. Are you satisfied?"

Joan opened her reading glasses and put them on carefully. Then she picked up the stack of mail sitting beside her on the couch and began leafing through the letters. Without looking up, she said, "Well, I'm sure you're relieved to get that off your chest, honey."

Anne was afraid her gamble had gone horribly wrong. Maybe a good push was not what her mother needed after all. Despite Joan's stoic reaction, Anne knew that it was tearing her apart inside. It was certainly doing just that to Anne.

She stood up and walked around the coffee table to join her mother on the couch. Anne sat there without speaking, just watching her mother the way she would when she was a child and Joan would read from *Make Way for Ducklings* and *Winnie the Pooh*. The only sound came from the rattling of windows in their frames as strong gusts of wind blew off the ocean.

"Mom?" Anne finally said after a couple of minutes. Joan glanced over momentarily before turning a page and reading on.

Anne continued, "It wasn't always that way, you know. I liked you as much as Dad before the divorce. I think I liked you even more. You used to be really fun. And I never wanted to leave Ipswich. I wanted to grow up here with you and Nana B. Just like you did. But you changed that year. I didn't change, Mom, you did. You made me feel like you didn't want me around anymore. It was horrible.

"That's why I wanted to be with Dad. He didn't change really. He was still fun to be with. And he still functioned, as a parent. I don't say this to be mean, but you were kind of a mess. You couldn't have handled me here even if I was the perfect child. So you can't blame me because you went through a really bad time. I needed someone to take care of me, and it wasn't happening here."

A minute passed with Joan reading on. Then she reached to her face and removed her glasses. When she spoke, her voice sounded distant and small. "I can't change the past, Anne. It was not a good time for any of us. So if I was a failure as a mother…"

"No. You were not a failure, Mom."

"That seems to be the point you were making."

"You had a very hard time with the divorce, and it affected you as a parent. You got over that. But by that time I was in Alaska, and to be honest, I was afraid of you."

"Afraid of me? Don't be silly."

"I'm serious. I still loved you very much, but you scared me with the way you criticized everything I did. It was a very confusing time for me being without the both of you. I still feel guilty for the way I treated you. I know I made your life miserable, and I'm very sorry about that."

Joan tilted her head to one side. "Well, you were kind of a … brat, I suppose. I know some people in the Ipswich Police department that might agree with that," Joan said with a faint smile. "You weren't that bad though."

Anne stroked her mother's arm lightly. "I remember when you came to pick me up at the police station. The next day everybody in Ipswich knew what the Boushay girl had done."

Joan looked out a nearby window. The event came back to life for her. The shock at receiving the call from the police, the anger she felt toward Anne, the embarrassment of knowing the whole town was gossiping about her daughter breaking into the Ipswich Apothecary and trying to steal drugs.

Anne was still a child when it happened. Joan looked at the daughter now sitting beside her on the couch. She was all grown up. Responsible, educated and yes, married, for better or worse. The years had gone by so quickly.

"There were some repercussions, I suppose," Joan said. "I can tell you this, I never stopped into that drug store again. I drove down to Hamilton or up to Newbury to have my prescriptions filled. To tell you the truth, I never liked the pharmacist at Ipswich Apothecary. I can't remember his name."

"Mr. Holland," Anne said. "My friends and I joked about him wearing wooden shoes when he worked behind the counter."

"Yes, Holland. Wendell Holland, or something like that. Do you know what he said to me one time when I went in to fill a prescription for you? I think you were about nine years old and had strep throat. I had a prescription from Dr. Livingston Sr., Brian's father, for penicillin. This Mr. Holland tells me that I should double-check that you were sick because he had heard some schoolgirls in the greeting card aisle earlier that day plotting to fake illness so they could stay out of school. I looked at him and said, 'You're neither a doctor nor a police detective. You're a pharmacist, so stop insinuating and fill that damn prescription.'"

Anne smiled, "You didn't really say that to him."

"I absolutely did," Joan declared, her voice once again full of life and energy. "Well, I might be embellishing a tad. But I gave him a piece of my mind. And it was a relief to be free of his meddling. No, you weren't as bad as you think you were, Anne. Not much more than the average teenage daughter. You just had a difficult year. That's all. I think it's fair to say that we both had a very difficult year."

* * * * *

When Matthew arrived at North Station, he had just missed the 7:20 train to Ipswich. Matthew made his way across the spacious lobby to the ticket window, where he paid for a seat on the 9:00 train. Signs around the lobby announced that U2 would be playing in Boston Garden, which was directly above the station.

They were playing Friday and Saturday night, and the place would be a zoo. Matthew had seen them seven years before with Buzzy, and it would be exactly what he'd want to do again if the circumstances were different.

At a bank of pay phones he called Anne's house. Her mother answered.

"Hi, Joan. It's Matthew. I'm at North Station right now, and I'll be taking the next train up."

"Well, I'm glad we found you. Anne went to pick you up downtown. Either you weren't where you were supposed to be, or maybe Anne had the wrong time."

"No, she had the right time. I left early."

"Did you find your friend?"

Matthew pinned the phone between his ear and shoulder as he inspected his hands under the bright fluorescent lights of the station. He had scraped them up pretty good, but there were no deep cuts and nothing was broken. "Yes, I found my friend. Everything's finished here."

"Anne went upstairs to shower. We've just finished a very long talk, and are thinking about having a late dinner at my favorite bistro. You can join us, if you like. Should we wait for you to get back?"

"I'm at a pay phone, and my time's about to expire. Don't bother waiting for me. Tell Anne I'm taking the 9:00 train. It gets into Ipswich around 9:45. If she could pick me up at the station, that would be great."

A tone sounded over the phone and the connection went dead for a moment, indicating Matthew's three minutes were almost up.

"I better say goodbye before we're cut off."

"Are you alright, Matthew? You sound funny."

It was the shaking in his voice, he knew. "I'm fine. Everything's fine. I was just running to make the 7:20 train, and I'm still catching my breath. I'll see you tonight."

Matthew hung up. The intercoms high above announced the arrival of a train, but it was inaudible with the horrible acoustics of the place. Off the brightly lit lobby were a newsstand, a Bruins and Celtics souvenir store, a music store, and a restaurant with a bar. Matthew went into the bar, making a stop in the men's room to clean the blood from his knuckles before settling on a barstool and buying a double shot of twelve-year-old single-malt Macallan scotch, paying almost twice what he'd pay at his own bar.

He sipped it slowly and stared out at the traffic weaving its way beneath the elevated subway line in front of North Station. The scotch was mellow and smooth, almost sublime, but it didn't make Matthew mellow. When he finished it, he ordered another double and paid out twenty-eight more dollars of Mikey's money.

With each sip, Matthew expected to be calming down. It wasn't working, and it wasn't the fault of the scotch. He told Joan that everything was finished, but it didn't feel finished. Matthew was still upset, and he still didn't know why he walked away from Buzzy without laying a hand on him. He could have.

One thing he did know. If he had gotten his hands on Buzzy, he would not have let go until Buzzy stopped breathing.

To think that they had been so close when they were young and that Matthew had put himself on the line so many times to protect him. The betrayal had been living inside Buzzy that whole time. It was as if Matthew now had to review all their years together growing up and recast them in an opposite light.

He felt a sense of shame seeping in. Maybe walking away had been an act of cowardice. The longer he sat at the bar, the more it nagged at him. He still wanted so badly to give Buzzy a beating, one that would not kill him but leave him someplace short of death.

From the bar, he heard the intercom announcing the arrival or departure of another train. He should get the hell back to Ipswich before he did something stupid.

The clock behind the bar showed 7:45. That left him an hour and fifteen minutes. Matthew finished his drink and walked outside to the cabstand. He jumped in the front cab and told the driver to take him to Quincy Market. It was not that far away. That's where he'd start his search. However, he had to be back at North Station by 9:00 or he'd miss his train.

As the cab waited at a red light, Matthew listened to the loud crackle of the dispatch radio. The driver reached over to turn it down. When the light turned green, the driver returned his hands to the wheel and Matthew saw that he was wearing a wedding ring. He looked down at his own bare left hand. Suddenly he changed his mind and said, "You know what? Let's skip the market. Take me to South Boston. Do you know where O'Brien's Tavern is?"

"I do, unfortunately," the driver said as he made a course correction. Matthew took a deep breath. Maybe this would be enough. Mikey had lied earlier when he said he wouldn't say Matthew had stopped by the apartment, but maybe he was telling the truth about where to find Connor. Wherever Connor was, Francis probably wasn't too far away.

When they pulled in front of O'Brien's, Matthew paid the fare plus tip and told the driver to wait five minutes with the meter running and he could take Matthew back to North Station.

"Be quick," the driver said. "I don't want to be in front of this place any longer than I have to."

A stocky bouncer named Jackie stood at the front door. He said nothing, but his eyes followed Matthew as he stepped inside. The bar had a light crowd of truck drivers and men who worked in the nearby warehouses. There were three windows facing the street, and two of them were boarded up. From a corner came the familiar pinging of a pinball machine.

As Matthew walked up to the bar, he remembered the story about the guy firing a pair of pistols in the air. He looked up and saw several small craters in the ceiling above the bar.

"What are you having?" the bartender asked. He was a big guy and looked strong. His nickname was Red, and he had a nose that looked like it had been broken several times. Matthew made the quick assessment he made when meeting someone who might be a potential adversary. He decided this one could be a problem.

"I'm Matt Mahoney. I need to talk to my brother. Is he here?"

Red stared at Matthew for a moment, then looked over at Jackie the bouncer who was preoccupied with a scratch ticket. "I don't know," Red said and walked off in Jackie's direction.

"He's either here or he isn't," Matthew called after the bartender, who ignored him.

Matthew looked to the back of the bar where a dim light shone down from a narrow staircase. "I'll see if he's upstairs," Matthew said. He knew this might create a problem, but he didn't have time to fuck around. He was halfway to the stairway when he heard Red's voice, "Hey, where do you think you're going?" Then came the sound of steps coming up fast behind Matthew.

He stopped at the foot of the stairway to face the rushing bartender. Behind him came Jackie carrying a section of pipe. "I'm Francis' brother. Do you understand? I'm doing his business right now. I've got information that he needs."

The door at the top of the stairway opened wide, spilling a shaft of blinding light down to the three men. Matthew looked up. He couldn't distinguish the figure who stood there. The man walked back into the upstairs office. Then Connor appeared and descended to the foot of the stairs.

Matthew had never met Connor, so he had no idea who he was. Connor recognized Matthew though.

"Where's Francis?" Matthew asked.

Connor said nothing. He wasn't about to acknowledge where Francis was, even to Matthew.

Matthew was taller than Connor. He stepped closer and said, "Are you fucking deaf or what?"

Connor smirked uncomfortably the way he'd do when cops would say things that he knew he couldn't react to. Red looked over at Connor and pointed at Matthew. "He said he's his brother."

Connor decided to play nice. "Look, Matt," he began in a friendly voice, "You don't want to be coming in here and asking questions like that. Now, I have an idea. Why don't you find your way out of this place, then try to stay out of your brother's business? I know that's what he would want you to do."

Matthew was short on time and patience, and he didn't like the way Connor was talking down to him. "I have a better idea," Matthew said, looking down at Connor. "Make that two. First, go fuck yourself. I bet you're pretty good at that. Second, if Francis is upstairs, get your ass up there and tell him I need to talk to him."

He stared at Connor and watched the smile fade. Matthew waited for him to make a move. It was crazy because there were two other guys besides Connor, including one holding a pipe, but in that moment, Matthew didn't care. He was full of an anger that he didn't know how to get rid of, and it was making him take risks he wouldn't take otherwise.

A few seconds passed. Connor stood there looking at Matthew, saying nothing. He wasn't about to take the bait. It was enough time for Matthew to reconsider. He had a train to catch, and he couldn't be sure if Francis was upstairs. He decided to leave, but not before insulting Connor again. He said, "Looks like somebody left their balls at home this morning."

Connor showed nothing in his expression. He raised a hand slowly and pointed with his thumb toward the front door.

On his way past the bar, Matthew saw a pen and a credit card receipt. He grabbed the pen and wrote down a description of the cab Buzzy was driving—the number, the color, the cabstands where it could most likely be found, the name and address of the repair shop in the South End and what Buzzy was wearing.

Matthew handed the slip to Red. "Francis is looking for Buzzy Driscoll. This is how he can find him."

He turned to take one last look at Connor, who hadn't moved from his spot.

"Stay the fuck away from this place," Connor called. "If you come back here, you're gonna have a big problem."

"Not with you I won't," Matthew replied.

His cab was still waiting outside, and he made it back to North Station in time to catch his train, which finally left at 9:05. There weren't many people onboard, and the train made rhythmic sounds as it traveled north through the industrial district of Chelsea and the salt marshes of Revere and Swampscott, through the long tunnel in Salem and across the bridge in Beverly.

Matthew had settled into a seat and stared out the window wondering if it had been enough. He wondered whether the unease had passed completely or if the feeling of restlessness would return.

By the time the train pulled into Ipswich station at 9:55, Matthew was sleeping so soundly that Anne had to search the train to find him, wake him up and lead him across the dark parking lot to the car.

Chapter Eight
Out of Control

Francis was always telling Buzzy that he had to have an emergency escape plan. One that he could use at a moment's notice because that's how long you might have to set it in motion. Buzzy had thought about it, and he thought he did have a plan. But now that he needed it, the plan seemed pretty weak.

The idea was to grab as much of his stash as he could, whatever coke, heroin or pot he could get his hands on, then get on the Massachusetts Turnpike and drive west. That was his plan.

Buzzy had been out of South Boston plenty of times—Cape Cod, New York a few times, and Miami twice. Those were all places where people knew Francis. Buzzy's escape had to take him someplace Francis wouldn't be able to find him. The farthest Buzzy had ever traveled on the turnpike was Worcester, which was 45 miles west of Boston. Beyond that, he knew there were lots of woods and mountains. And towns filled with idiot hicks.

First he had to go back into South Boston. It would be dark soon, and it might be much better to go to Old Colony when it was dark. But if he waited, it would give Matthew time to tell Francis, who might set a trap for Buzzy. Or was Matthew just bluffing? Maybe Francis wasn't even back in town.

Buzzy's mood lifted as he considered the possibility. Matthew might have said it just to fuck with me, he thought as he drove past South Station and crossed into South Boston. Either way, there was no sense being careless.

Buzzy parked his cab three blocks away from Old Colony. He checked his hair in the rearview mirror. He hadn't showered since the wedding, and his hair was all puffed out on the left side, flattened on the right. With his hands, he tried to even out the height. He needed a hat. For his whole fucking life, he'd been looking for a hat that he liked and that people wouldn't make fun of.

His beige corduroy pants were looking pretty dirty, and his favorite green rugby shirt was starting to smell. I need some fresh clothes, he thought as he stepped out of the cab and walked slowly through the rain. His eyes scanned the cars parked along Patterson Way and the cars driving by. He knew the car that Francis and Connor always drove around in. It was a black Chevy Caprice with blackwall tires, the one that Francis had left in front of the Lancaster Street garage.

When he reached the courtyard to his building, Buzzy saw a couple of guys standing there. One wore a Red Sox jacket that was shiny wet. Is that what Francis would do, stand right in front of my building? Buzzy watched them for a couple of minutes before deciding to go ahead. As he got close, one of the guys saw him and called out.

"Hey, Buzzy! We've been looking for you."

Buzzy recognized him as a customer from D Street. He probably wanted coke.

"What's up?" Buzzy asked.

"Can you take care of us?" the guy asked.

Buzzy looked around quickly. "I have to do something that's really important, then I can take care of you. OK? Meet me back here in an hour," Buzzy said, although he had no intention of being anywhere near Old Colony in an hour.

They left and Buzzy walked into his building. All the lights were out in the second floor hallway. Buzzy put a hand to the wall and let it guide him. He could hear the sounds of a baseball game coming from the apartment where the Irishman who chewed raw seaweed lived. It made his breath smell like the muddy banks of the Charles River.

When he reached his own apartment, Buzzy unlocked the door and opened it slowly. There were no lights on, and the space was colored with the dull grey monochrome of dusk.

"Mikey?" he called in a low voice. "Are you here?"

There was no answer, so Buzzy moved cautiously toward his bedroom. He felt the wall for the light switch and turned it on. The room was the same as he had left it. A minimalist mess. He changed into a pair of jeans and a fresh shirt. In the closet he found his duffel bag and carried it to the kitchen. His stash of drugs was hidden behind the refrigerator, so Buzzy slowly maneuvered it away from the wall.

Through a hole in the sheetrock, Buzzy reached down and pulled out a small white brick of uncut South American cocaine. There were eleven one-pound bricks, all wrapped in clear plastic. Buzzy loaded them all into his duffel bag.

He usually didn't have that much coke on hand. One of the three wise men was being watched closely by the state police, so he asked Buzzy to hold onto his supplies for a while.

As he began pushing the fridge back in place, Buzzy heard a voice call his name. He spun around and looked into the living room, where he saw a shape rising.

"Who's that?" he called.

"It's me. Who do you think it is?"

Mikey had been sleeping on the couch when Buzzy came in. He shuffled into the kitchen, yawning and scratching behind an ear. When he saw the bricks of cocaine in Buzzy's duffel bag he asked, "Jesus, what are you doing?"

Mikey wasn't part of Buzzy's escape plan, and anything he told him could end up on the street within five minutes. That was Mikey.

"I've got somebody who wants to buy in bulk."

Buzzy retrieved a few items from the bathroom, an armful of clothes from his closet and piled them on top of the cocaine. He zipped the bag shut and slung it over his shoulder. "See you later," he said to Mikey, who seemed to suddenly waken from his daze.

"Oh, hey. I'm supposed to tell you something."

Buzzy turned around. "Yeah?"

Mikey stared at him.

"What the fuck are you supposed to tell me?"

"Oh, yeah. Francis wants to talk to you."

Buzzy smiled. "Mikey, you're wasted. Francis is gone. Remember?"

"I saw him. Connor made me go to O'Brien's, and Francis was there. He said you should go see him at O'Brien's, and that you shouldn't wait because he didn't want to have to come looking for you."

Buzzy lost his smile and tightened his grip on the door handle.

Mikey continued, "You should probably go see him now before you make your big delivery."

"I will," Buzzy said, with his heart sinking. "I'll go over there right now. If Connor comes by or calls, tell him I'm on my way."

The rain fell in a steady drizzle in the darkening evening as Buzzy fought his way through traffic. He drove his cab to the parking garage by City Hospital, where he transferred the duffel bag to the trunk of his own car, a brown '78 Grand Prix with a cracked windshield.

This was it, he thought as he started the engine. There was no going back now. He'd be dead if he ever showed up in South Boston again. Buzzy smoked a joint on his long drive to the turnpike. He smiled at the woman working the toll booth. "Adios, Massachusetts!" he called out, and the woman laughed.

Ahead of him, the three-lane highway extended due west over slowly rolling hills. In the distance were the Berkshire Mountains, which showed only as grey shadows in the rainy evening. The wipers swished back and forth. An occasional drop of water fell from a leak at the top of the windshield and plopped onto Buzzy's jeans.

He smoked another joint just outside of Worcester. Beyond him somewhere was the New York border. His plan was to cross the border and find a motel, as if the state boundary would protect him from Francis. He pulled his roll of cab-driving money out of his shirt pocket and counted it. Around one hundred and twenty-five dollars.

That's when he remembered that he hadn't grabbed the roll of cash hidden beneath his mattress back at the apartment. Shit! He had no credit cards, so one hundred and twenty-five bucks would be it until he could sell some of his stash.

Buzzy hadn't thought about that detail—how he was going to sell it, who he was going to sell it to. Or where. Now he began thinking about it real hard, and the situation was not looking too rosy. If he tried to sell in Albany or anywhere he didn't know people, he was taking a risk. You didn't sell this kind of bulk on the street, and if he ever got busted with this much coke he'd be completely fucked.

He wouldn't last through the weekend with his cash though. This was a big problem. He needed to sell to someone he knew and trusted. Those people were all in the other direction, back in Boston, where he couldn't go.

The music was starting to irritate him. He tried turning down the volume on the car radio, but it wasn't on. He looked around the front seat of the car for a cassette player or some other radio. There was nothing.

The music was playing in his head. A song by U2. "Eleven O'Clock Tick Tock." He and Matt had heard U2 play that song when they went to a concert at the Paradise right before Matt left for Seattle years before. Now it was playing in Buzzy's head, and he couldn't make it stop.

The song had been sneaking up on him whenever he thought of the murder. He didn't want to remember it, but details of that night kept invading his thoughts. It was like being mugged every five minutes. And with every detail, the song would start playing like nervous background music.

It was an act he had fantasized about for years. He enjoyed imagining all the possible ways he could kill his father. Burning him alive in his house, running him over as he crossed Broadway. Once he had committed the act, however, Buzzy found there was nothing enjoyable about the memory. It only made him anxious. And the song was like a fucking virus he couldn't shake.

He remembered hearing it in his car after leaving the wedding reception. He dropped off Christina in Jamaica Plain, then drove by the Lancaster Street garage to see if Francis had left his black Caprice there. Buzzy had made himself a set of keys while taking Francis' car to get an oil change two weeks before.

It was nine o'clock. Buzzy drove his own car to South Boston and parked where he could see the lights in Salty's house going out one by one, until the place was completely dark. Kathleen had gone up the coast with her friend, so his father was alone.

At nine forty-five, Buzzy went into the garage and retrieved the spare key. He planned on looking into his father's face and saying the things that his father needed to hear. He would be speaking for them all. Francis, Jimmy, Matthew, their mother and Buzzy's mother.

In the end, Buzzy proved unable to articulate anything. Instead, after climbing quietly up the stairs to his father's bedroom, he simply watched him sleep, staring down at a face that was far more peaceful than it had a right to be.

The clock on the bedside table glowed green. Each new second was announced with a loud tick as the second hand jumped forward. In those first minutes, Buzzy thought this might be enough, to stand over his sleeping father with a loaded gun pointed at his face. He considered leaving, but something kept him there.

The steady breathing, the clock ticking. It could have gone on like that until sunrise, or until his father had to get up to take a piss, but a dog began barking in a neighbor's yard. The sound woke Salty, who opened his eyes, quickly but peacefully. Buzzy wondered whether his father was really awake or stuck in a dream.

The gun had a silencer, which made it heavy. The weight caused Buzzy's arm to waver, so the gun drew an imaginary circle around his father's face. It was seven minutes after ten. The clock announced the end of that second's passing without Buzzy acting on his intentions.

"What time is it?" his father asked.

Does he know he's awake? Does he know I'm standing above him, that I have a gun, that I'm here to kill him? What time is it? It's time to die, Buzzy thought. His father reached for the clock.

"Here's the time," Buzzy said and pulled the trigger. The first shot struck his father in the cheek and cut a violent path through his head before exiting at the base of his skull. His father died in that instant, but Buzzy fired four more shots, two of them going wide of their target, which became difficult to see. When it was over, Buzzy was left sweating in the darkness with the sounds of his own breath and the mechanical ticking of the clock. Salty is dead, the clock lives on, Buzzy thought strangely.

He intended to lock the back door behind him and return the key to the garage, but he couldn't find it in any of his pockets. At that same moment, Francis was on his way back to the house with Larry's pistol. Buzzy left the scene moments before he returned. Had he run into Francis there, Buzzy would almost certainly have been killed by him. With his key to Francis' car outside the Lancaster Street garage, Buzzy planted the murder weapon before calling the state police with his tip.

The murder was going to be his gift to everyone, especially Matthew. A secret wedding present. It was at the wedding when Buzzy learned Francis was going to be indicted and would be leaving the country. That's when he decided to act. It couldn't have come together any better. There would be Francis to blame officially, but Francis would never be caught or punished for the murder.

Francis wanted his father dead. Everyone at the wedding heard that. He wanted it even more than Buzzy, but something inside Francis wouldn't allow him to do it. If Buzzy could kill their father, acting for both of them, and accomplish what Francis wanted, shouldn't Francis be OK with sharing the burden?

Buzzy's share was to be guilty; Francis' share was to look guilty. Neither one would get caught, neither one would be punished. It wouldn't be fair for Francis to object to that. And if he did, too bad. Francis was leaving the country forever so he could never come back to object.

Matthew wasn't supposed to find out, and that had ruined everything. It was Buzzy's own fault. He had lost the key. Everything else had worked perfectly. Even so, Matthew's reaction was way out of line. Buzzy knew he hated their father, too. Matthew had told him plenty of times over the years. So why did he get so incredibly pissed off in the cab?

He was ungrateful, Buzzy decided. And he was feeling guilty. Well, that was Matt's problem now. He could spend the rest of his life feeling guilty. Buzzy was the only one of Salty's sons who could do what they all wanted to do. He was done with it, and he was done with all the Mahoneys. The murder had finished everything.

Water falling from the leaky windshield continued dropping onto Buzzy's jeans whether he moved his leg to the left or right, and it was driving him crazy. "Fuck!" He screamed as loud as he could and slammed a hand down on the dashboard in an effort to make the song stop.

Amazingly, it did. Now Buzzy had to think. How far was he going to drive tonight? Where would he stay? He saw a sign for a gas station five miles ahead. His gas gauge hovered just below a quarter tank. When he reached the station, he pulled off the turnpike.

As Buzzy was filling his tank, a state trooper drove through the gas station. As he rolled slowly past, the trooper stared at Buzzy, who tried to look nonchalant. He was too stoned to know whether he was behaving guilty or not. If the trooper only knew what was in the trunk. Holy shit.

Buzzy didn't dare look up until the tank finished filling, and when he did the trooper was gone. Relief washed over him. That's it, Buzzy decided. He had no business being so far away from home without more money. After paying for the gas, he lit another joint. At the next turnpike exit, he reversed direction and headed back to Boston.

He absolutely had to sell the drugs to someone he knew, even if he had to give a big discount. Buzzy considered the people he knew around the city, dealers who would have enough money to buy pounds of coke and who wouldn't contact Francis.

As he got closer to Boston, Buzzy grew more paranoid. Everyone knew his car, and if Francis had put out the word on him, people would be looking for a brown '78 Grand Prix. He considered stealing another car, but he was too stoned to pull it off.

He saw a sign for Roxbury. Buzzy knew a dealer there, a big dealer. His first name was George, but Buzzy couldn't remember his last name. He had met George at the Lancaster Street garage. George was there to negotiate a compensation plan for some coke that had disappeared from a townhouse in the South End thanks to Larry's boys. The coke belonged to George.

When the whole thing had been straightened out, it was Buzzy's job to return the coke to George at a bar in Roxbury. Or most of the coke, since Francis had taken a cut as a finder's fee and Buzzy had taken another small cut on his way to Roxbury.

The bar was called Serendipity, and it sat just outside of Dudley Square. Nobody there would recognize Buzzy. Francis and Larry almost never messed around inside Roxbury.

George would remember Buzzy. It had only been about a year since the two had met. And George would trust Buzzy because he'd assume Buzzy still worked for Francis.

It was one o'clock Friday morning as Buzzy drove down Washington Street in Roxbury. He went past rundown apartments, small businesses occupying decaying buildings and convenience stores with bars on their windows. Many blocks had abandoned lots with waist-high weeds and rusted chain-link fences.

Above him ran the elevated train tracks of the subway's Orange Line. He spotted the stairway leading down from Green Street Station. He remembered getting off there after school when he ran cross country as a freshman at Boston Latin.

He and his buddies, all white kids from South Boston and Dorchester, would walk nervously off the train and through an all-black neighborhood to reach the stadium near Franklin Park. The big joke was that the place was named White Stadium. In one of its old locker rooms they'd change into running gear, then train on a three-mile course that made its way through the woods and around a golf course.

Ten more blocks and he saw Dudley Square ahead. Buzzy found a place to park on a side road beneath a streetlight. If he ended up doing business back at the car, he wanted to see what was going on. And he wanted to know from far away if anybody was waiting for him at the car when he returned.

Serendipity was an L-shaped bar with a poolroom out back. Earlier that night, there were only a handful of locals at the bar, but at one o'clock it was filling with people looking for another venue as clubs began to close. A thick layer of cigarette smoke undulated above the crowd and voices competed with jukebox music from the seventies.

All the faces were strange to Buzzy. All were black. He felt an increasing number of eyes on him as he walked past the cigarette machines and video games. The one time Buzzy had come to Serendipity, George was holding court in a small office off the poolroom, but Buzzy didn't want to walk too far into this place until he got a sense it was OK.

The bartender caught Buzzy's face and did a double take. He gave Buzzy a long stare before asking, "You want something?"

"I'm here to see George. He knows me."

"George isn't here."

"Do you know where he is?"

The bartender laughed. "George is taking a little vacation."

Buzzy felt his fragile hope beginning to fracture. "Well, did he go very far…will he be back soon?"

"Sure, George will be back real soon. Maybe four or five years. He's in Walpole."

Walpole State Prison. Now Buzzy's hope crumbled. The bartender turned and began walking away. Buzzy followed him down the bar. "So who's taking care of his business? Who can I talk to? This is important."

The bartender stopped and gave Buzzy another good stare. "I don't know what you're talking about," he said and walked away.

A group of guys came walking toward Buzzy and bumped into him intentionally. Buzzy had been standing still against the bar, but one guy said, "Hey, watch where you're going." This was it. They would all start taking shots at him if he stayed. He had to leave now or take a risk and see who he could do business with. There was really no choice if he was going to survive.

In the poolroom, three guys were playing a game of cutthroat and a half dozen more stood around smoking and watching the game. They were all in their early twenties. One by one, they became aware of Buzzy standing in the dim light of the doorway.

Buzzy made a quick decision about who to talk to. He picked the guy who seemed to be wearing the most rings and looked oldest. People were calling him Trevor. He was a big guy with a shaved head. On his right arm, he had a tattoo of a serpent swallowing its own tail.

Buzzy waited for the shot at the table to be taken before approaching Trevor. "I was looking for George, but I just found out that he's gone. I've done business with him before, and I was going to bring him some really good business tonight." Buzzy tried to keep the calm in his voice.

His hope came back when Trevor gave him a subtle nod. "Maybe that'll work. What do you want?"

"I'm selling."

"Uh-huh," Trevor said.

"I'm not a cop and I'm not representing anybody else. I've got Bolivian coke. Pure. The bricks haven't even been opened. I've got a lot and I need to turn it into cash tonight. It's a going-out-of-business sale. You know, everything must go. Can anybody here handle that?"

"First of all, if anything you're saying isn't true, you're in for real bad times. You know that, don't you?"

"It's all straight," Buzzy said.

"How much have you got?"

"Eleven pounds." Buzzy knew it was easily worth two hundred thousand dollars wholesale and could be quickly converted to much more than that on the street. In his current situation, he was hoping, praying he'd get a hundred and fifty thousand, but he'd settle for a hundred or even fifty thousand if he had to.

Buzzy continued. "It would normally go for two hundred and twenty-five thousand. Put it on the street and you'll make five hundred percent profit." Buzzy was going to ask for a hundred and fifty, but at the last minute decided to drop it. "I'll sell it to you for a hundred thousand. In cash. Here at the bar."

Trevor considered the offer. Buzzy expected him to counter it, so he was surprised when Trevor said, "OK, a hundred thousand."

"A hundred thousand dollars in cash. And you'll give it to me here at the bar."

"What did I just say?" Trevor said with a hint of annoyance. Trevor scanned the room slowly, then turned back to Buzzy. "Why don't you wait out front?"

"OK, I'll be in the bar."

"No. Out front. On the sidewalk."

"OK." Buzzy caught a wave of stares as he passed through the barroom again. Outside the air was cool and a light mist continued to fall. He waited for five minutes. It seemed like a lot longer, and several times he thought he might be making a big mistake.

He had no idea how reliable Trevor was. He didn't know the guy at all. Selling eleven pounds of coke to someone you didn't know was a huge risk. It's exactly how guys got ripped off. Or worse.

The longer he waited on the sidewalk, the more Buzzy thought he'd be better off taking his chances in the neighborhoods he knew. Some of the dealers in Dorchester were not exactly on friendly terms with Francis and might do business without ratting him out. Although they might make him wait days for his money, or change their mind about paying at all if they found out Francis had a death warrant out on him.

Both choices were shitty. But at least in Dorchester, he'd know who he was dealing with. Buzzy decided to leave. He crossed Washington Street and headed for his car. He thought of all the dealers he knew in Dorchester and decided to start with Paul Keeley, whose apartment was behind the Eire Pub in Adam's Village. The last Buzzy heard, Keeley still lived alone, so it wouldn't be a big deal waking him up at two o'clock in the morning.

Buzzy was half a block away from his car when he began feeling better about his decision. Then he heard someone calling to him. Buzzy turned around and saw Trevor with three other guys. His first reaction was to run for the car, but they were too close for him to make it.

"I thought we were gonna do business," Trevor said. "Are you walking on us?"

Trevor came straight up to Buzzy, while the others circled his car. Buzzy twirled his car keys and said as casually as he could, "Of course we're doing business. I was gonna get my smokes, then come back to the bar."

Trevor wore a shiny green Celtics jacket, and he obviously did the speaking for the group. "Are we gonna stand in the rain all night, or are you gonna show us the goods? You don't get a dime until we see what we're paying for."

"I'll show you. Your friends can meet us back at the bar."

"My friends are the reason this is happening at all. You'll show them what you show me."

This was a situation Buzzy would never, ever let happen normally. Letting any of them walk him to his car to retrieve the coke would have been out of the question. He was used to working on his home turf and setting all the terms.

"It's in the trunk," Buzzy said as he walked toward the car, but Trevor stopped him.

"If you don't mind, my friend Ajax will open it."

"Whatever," Buzzy said. Before he could hand over the keys, Ajax pulled them from his hand.

"It's in the bag. Under the clothes," Buzzy said.

Ajax tossed Buzzy's clothes to the side. He pulled a small knife from his pocket and cut into one of the bricks, then put the knife to his tongue. He looked at Trevor and gave a slight smile. "Oh yeah," he said.

"OK. Deal," Trevor said.

Ajax zipped up the bag and slung the strap over his shoulder.

"Now we'll take you to the cashier and send you on your way. Follow us," Trevor said. They all walked up to Washington Street, then Trevor and his buddies turned right. The bar was in the opposite direction.

"Wait," Buzzy said. "We need to go back to the bar. You need to pay me there."

"The money's at my house up on Gordon Street," Trevor said. "That's only three blocks this way. Why do you want to go back to the bar?"

"That was the deal. I said you pay me at the bar."

"Look, do you want your money or not?" Trevor asked.

"OK," Buzzy said, but it wasn't OK. If he went with these guys, they'd kill him. They had decided this whole scene inside the bar. It was all scripted. If Buzzy had asked for ten million dollars, Trevor would have said sure, fine, ten million. Let's go.

Buzzy joined them but decided that he had to do something real quick. He watched Ajax, who carried the bag. He was big and he had a guy on either side of him. There was no way Buzzy would be able to grab the bag.

Then Buzzy realized he didn't have his keys. He called to Ajax. "Hey, I think you forgot to give me my keys back."

Ajax held up the keys and looked at Trevor. They smiled. "That's right. I didn't give them back." Ajax laughed and jangled the keys in the air. They all laughed.

Buzzy made a quick lunge for the keys. He thought he had them, but Ajax wrapped his other hand around Buzzy's, and the two wrestled each other onto the pavement between two parked cars. The bag fell on the sidewalk, where Trevor picked it up.

"Maybe we'll give the man his payment right here," Trevor said.

Buzzy gave up on getting the keys back and was now struggling to pull himself free of Ajax's grip. He felt a hand tighten around his shirt, and he was dragged closer to Ajax. He drew his knees up and shot them back, hitting Ajax in the nose with the sole of his sneaker.

Ajax recoiled with his hands to his face. Buzzy crawled into the street, where he was almost hit by a passing car. In a second, he was on his feet and running down Washington Street. He heard the steps of Ajax, who was close behind. A steady stream of cars blocked Buzzy from cutting across the road. In an odd flashback to his days of running cross country, Buzzy heard somebody wheezing and he couldn't tell if it was himself or his pursuer.

He was running on adrenaline and he could feel it running out. As he neared the end of the block, he looked over his left shoulder at the approaching traffic and saw an opening after the next car. He shot to his left and dashed across the road.

As he ran by one of the large support columns for the overhead trains, he saw the headlight of a motorcycle coming at him fast. The rider swerved to avoid a collision. Just as he did, Ajax shot from behind the same support column and stepped directly in front of the motorcycle.

There was no time for either one of them to react. The collision sent Ajax sailing through the air and crashing into a steel support column headfirst. The rider bounced several times along the asphalt before rolling beyond Ajax's body. The spinning motorcycle sent out a stream of sparks and came to rest in the middle of the road with its headlight illuminating the tracks above.

Buzzy didn't know exactly what had happened, but when he turned around Ajax was nowhere in sight. He dashed down a side street until he ran out of breath. He couldn't see anyone following him, but he knew they'd be looking for him.

Man, he had fucked up. He had fucked up bad. Things could not be going much worse. His knee hurt, his right hand was sore. He had lost his stash and his car, and he was being chased through the middle of Roxbury by a bunch of guys who wanted to kill him. He had no idea what he was going to do or where he was going to go. He was still alive, but that was about all.

The headlights of a car shone down the dark road from the direction of Washington Street. Buzzy hid between houses until the car passed. He had to keep moving and get out of Roxbury if he was going to survive. He moved through the neighborhood at an angle, turning left on one block, then right at the next. He went on this way for a while, ducking into bushes or behind houses whenever cars approached.

At the end of one street, he saw a path leading into a patch of woods and he ran down it. The dark dirt surface was filled with puddles and slippery mud. The woods opened up, and he found himself in a large clearing. He jogged on, following the sight of distant lights. Something about the surroundings seemed familiar. As dark as it was and as unclear as the details were, Buzzy seemed to know this place.

Yes, he was on the cross-country course where he trained as a freshman. In an instant, he was back at that place, that time when he had discovered who his father was. He had believed then that if he just ran hard enough and long enough, he could escape everything that troubled him.

From where he stood now, Buzzy could see how naïve that fifteen-year-old had been. He hadn't gotten anywhere. He was still in the same place, living in Old Colony with all the pain and disappointment he thought he could get away from. All he had done in the last thirteen years was run in a big circle and now he was back where he had started. Except this time he was running for his life.

* * * * *

At three o'clock on Friday morning, the Hudsons' small dog lay sleeping on a brown wool blanket in the office above O'Brien's Tavern. Francis had taken her for a walk once it was dark enough to move safely down local streets, and Connor had gone to the store for some dog food and dog toys. The office was sparsely furnished with a desk and chair, along with a cot where Francis caught whatever sleep he could. At one end of the office was a small bathroom. At the other was a single window looking onto the back alley.

The bar was closed and empty of people, except for Red, who had restocked the beer coolers and shelves of hard liquor and was finishing his cleanup duties.

Mikey was supposed to call Connor if he saw Buzzy. Even if he didn't see Buzzy, he was supposed to call and check in sometime around midnight. Mikey never got in touch, so at two-thirty Connor had called him and said to get over to O'Brien's fast without talking to anybody on the way.

Francis wasn't surprised that Mikey didn't call back at midnight. He was a fuckup. Just like Buzzy. Between the two of them, it was tough to say who would win a stupid race, but Francis gave Mikey a slight edge.

Francis was sitting behind the desk with the previous day's newspapers spread out in front of him when Connor delivered Mikey to the upstairs office. Francis was in the middle of dinner. A chicken salad sandwich on dark rye, an apple and two bottled waters.

Connor motioned for Mikey to walk over to the desk. There was only one chair in the room, and Francis was sitting on it. After finishing the first half of his sandwich, Francis pulled a clean napkin from a neat stack and wiped his hands. Then he turned his reading lamp so it shone on Mikey.

"Where the fuck have you been?" Francis asked.

Mikey was dressed in tan sweat pants with stripes running down the legs. Dried spaghetti sauce stained one knee. His sweatshirt had a faded picture of Niagara Falls above the line: Where I Fell for You.

Mikey tried to straighten out his hair, which was sprouting at odd angles. "I figured you didn't need me to call, Francis."

"How'd you figure that, Mikey? On a calculator?" Francis asked.

Connor smiled. Mikey saw this and he smiled. "I just told Connor that Buzzy came back to the apartment. I told Buzzy you wanted to see him, and he said he was gonna come over here right away."

"When was this?" Francis asked.

Mikey focused on flattening one particular hair sprout. "Oh, that was about six-thirty maybe."

Francis looked over at Connor and wrapped his knuckles on the wooden desk. "That's over eight hours." He turned back to Mikey and shook his head. "You're the dumbest piece of shit in this whole fucking hemisphere. I tell you to call me if he shows up because I want to see him. Instead you tell Buzzy that I want to see him. Do you understand the difference?"

Mikey nodded his head. "I think so."

Francis stared at Mikey and grew more irritated. He picked up an Anheuser-Busch paper weight on his desk and flung it at Mikey, who ducked. The cast-iron Clydesdale smashed on the wall behind him. "No, I don't think you do, Mikey! That's your fucking problem," Francis screamed.

With the bar closed, the sound of Francis' voice shattered the dead-of-night peacefulness. The dog woke from a sound sleep and jumped to attention. It barked a few times before settling back onto the blanket.

Francis continued in a softer voice. "If you understood what you were told, Mikey, you would have done exactly what I said, not the opposite."

"Buzzy cleaned out the place before he left," Connor said. "Tell him Mikey."

Mikey looked at Francis and waited for permission to speak. Finally he said, "He took everything from the wall behind the fridge. We had about ten pounds of coke."

"What else did he take?" Francis asked.

"Some clothes."

"Did he have any cash?"

"Just whatever he had on him. We usually keep some around, but we didn't have much today. I mean yesterday."

"Anything else?"

Mikey shook his head. "No, I don't think so. That was it."

"Anybody see you coming over here?"

"No."

"Did you talk to anybody?"

"No."

"Because we know how you like to talk," Connor said.

"I swear I didn't talk to anybody. I came straight over here."

Francis looked over at Connor. "Beautiful, isn't it?"

Connor looked over at Mikey. "Mikey, why don't you go downstairs. Wait in the bar."

When Mikey left, Connor said, "Well, it sounds like he's running."

"Yeah, and he's been running for almost nine hours. You know how far you can get in nine hours. He could be in Canada. Assuming he knows where that is. Or he might still be in town. Why don't you call around and see if he tried to sell anything to people we know. And tell everyone there's a prize for information and a bigger prize if they bring him in."

Francis had told Buzzy to make arrangements for this kind of thing, having to leave town at a moment's notice. It happened occasionally to guys who worked for Francis. Disco would call and say that the FBI or the DEA planned to make an arrest. Francis would tell Connor, who would notify whoever it was and send the guy packing for Oklahoma or Louisiana or one of the many places where they had friends who would quietly stash the guy until the heat died down. Sometimes it never did, and the guy would have to assume a new identity and sneak back to South Boston to visit family and friends.

Without Francis' and Connor's help, Buzzy wouldn't know what to do. And he wouldn't have made any great plans for his escape. Francis just hoped that Buzzy wouldn't end up getting busted someplace far away, where being in jail would actually keep him safe.

Buzzy would need to sell his stuff pretty quick for cash to live on. Where would he try to do that? What would he think would be the safest place?

"What are we gonna do with Mikey?" Connor asked.

"He's gotta go," Francis said. "He's too stupid. He'll end up saying something to somebody. You and Red take him to the basement. Tell him you're gonna give him some money from the safe for helping us out. I'll be down in a few minutes for another rope-a-dope. We'll wrap him up down there, then go digging later today when it's dark again. I know the perfect spot if everything else falls into place."

Francis resumed his dinner and scanned the newspapers for what might be going on with his indictments. Connor turned to leave, then hesitated. "Francis. We can take care of Mikey, but I'm wondering if it matters at this point. I mean, for you. Once we take care of Buzzy, you're gone, so anything Mikey might say about you wouldn't matter."

Francis wiped some mayonnaise from the corner of his mouth. "Two reasons. He could talk and make things difficult for you, and people you and I care about. Plus, I've been thinking about these indictments. Disco said seventy-two hours, right? It's been five days, almost six, and we've heard nothing. That's why I had us take Mrs. Hudson and some of her stuff. Just in case."

"In case what?"

"In case there are no indictments. In case somebody changed their mind. In case they need the Hudsons for some reason, which obviously won't be happening."

"Do you think Disco got it wrong?"

Francis brushed some crumbs from the desk, then polished the apple on his sweatshirt. "I think he told us everything he knew. But maybe he doesn't know as much as he used to. Maybe he was given bad information on purpose. It's never happened before, but he's got a new boss these days."

"If he got it wrong, then you could stay."

"That would be nice, but I have to be careful because I don't know what's going on out there. After we take care of Mikey, I want you to call Disco's brother and have him tell Disco that I want to join him for a family meal. Lunch would be great, but dinner would be fine too. Whatever he can manage. Tell him it's to meet you, not me. I'll surprise him."

"You don't want me to call his brother now. It's three o'clock in the morning."

Francis looked to the window and into the dark night. "Yeah, you're right. Wait until nine. Make those other calls first. I want every eye on the street looking for Buzzy."

There was something else Connor wanted to discuss with Francis, but he hesitated because it was about Matthew. Connor was still ticked off about the shit he had to take from Francis' little brother when he stopped by earlier. Nobody ever got away with talking to him like that, and Connor was still in a bad mood about it.

"I gotta tell you, Francis. Your brother Matt is a real prick."

Francis laughed. "What did you expect?"

"He's got a big fucking mouth, and if he shoots it off again at me, I'm not gonna just stand there and take it."

"You won't see him again. Don't worry about it."

"I don't know, Francis. I told him not to come back here again, but I've got a feeling."

"He wanted to deliver his message, and he did. It's useless information, but I'm sure Matt feels like he'd done a good thing. Now that it's done, he's got no reason to come back. Forget it."

Connor didn't agree with Francis' thinking, but he nodded. "Alright."

Francis had to control his growing hope that he could soon be as free as he used to be. He wanted that more than anything. The short time Francis had spent on board the Avalon, not reaching his destination but merely beginning the journey, had depressed him far more than he expected it would.

There wasn't the sense of adventure he enjoyed when visiting Europe or the Caribbean previously. On those trips, he knew he'd be returning. On the Avalon he learned how much it would hurt to leave South Boston forever. The place had shaped him into the man he was. It provided him the friends who would put their loyalty to Francis Mahoney above loyalty to anything and anybody else in the world. That kind of loyalty didn't exist in many places, but South Boston was rich with it.

He didn't want to get back on that boat or any other boat and leave home. The experience would have been different if Kathleen had left with him. That would have been OK. They'd have each other to feel at home in a strange place. He had really misjudged her though. Or he had wanted her to leave with him so badly that it clouded his own thinking. He couldn't let that happen with the indictments. He had to see things clearly and have solid information, which is why he needed to meet with Disco.

That still left Kathleen. What he should do about her, and how best to approach her again, would hinge on the indictments. If they were still on track, he'd again be asking her to flee with him but without his father interfering this time. If the indictments were off, he'd be a free man but have to renege on a promise to Kathleen to leave the business, because he would never do that unless forced to.

After finishing the apple, Francis rolled the core up with the sandwich wrapper and returned it all to a brown paper bag. He poured some water onto a clean napkin and used it to wipe his mouth and fingers.

Francis yawned and closed his eyes for a moment. Sleep. He would have it soon. He'd take care of Mikey, then get four hours on the cot. As Francis searched through the desk drawers for a stretch of rope, he thought about the Hudsons' house. How well built it was. What a nice layout it had. And that disposal. It was an inspiration when Francis considered how many appliances had broken down on him with far less strain. Yes, he concluded, if everything worked as well as the Kaiser, this world wouldn't be so fucked up.

* * * * *

In the hour before dawn, Matthew woke to the sensation of Anne's body pressing against his. She draped an arm across his chest and whispered him awake. Matthew pulled her closer and kissed his way slowly around her neck.

With the craziness of the wedding and all that followed, Matthew and Anne hadn't connected with each other in this intimate way. They made love as quietly as they had when they first met and

Matthew would stay over at Anne's apartment, where the walls were thin and her roommate was a very light sleeper.

The grey light outside gave way to a warmer, brighter shade as the sun appeared. By the time it sat just above the dunes, Matthew and Anne were having breakfast downstairs. They had hardly spoken at all since waking, but the reality of their world and their week could only be suspended for so long.

"I have something to tell you about Buzzy," Matthew said.

"And I have something to tell you about Buzzy," Anne said.

Matthew went first. He told how he had come to the conclusion that Buzzy really had killed his father. The key, the confrontation in the cab, Buzzy's reaction, Matthew's disillusionment and disgust with someone he had trusted since childhood.

"Oh, my God," was all Anne said when Matthew finished.

He got up from the table, refilled his coffee cup and rummaged through Joan's fridge for something to eat. He found two takeout containers from the Choate Bridge Bistro and picked the top one. It contained half a serving of chicken tortellini. Matthew grabbed a fork and was digging in when Anne noticed.

"Matt, no. That's my mom's. You can have mine. It's eggplant something."

Matthew returned to the table with his coffee and cold eggplant parmesan, eating it out of the Styrofoam box. He noticed Anne watching him. "Do you want some?" he asked, but Anne shook her head.

"How can you be sure it was Buzzy?" she asked.

Matthew took two more bites and the eggplant was gone. He closed the container and pushed it aside. "All the lying about the key. He knew I couldn't find it at the house and he was the one who had it the whole time. I wasn't completely sure until I saw him. It was the way he reacted. Believe me, I know Buzzy. Then he was babbling on about why he did it. I can't remember what the hell he was saying, but he was admitting he did it. That I'm sure about."

Matthew took a drink from his cup and made a face. Joan's coffee was worse than the stuff at Jimmy's house after the funeral. "I'll tell you this, Anne, it's a good thing I left him when I did. I felt like I wanted to kill him. I mean, strangle him." Matthew's hands were still sore, and he rubbed them slowly. "I've never felt that way. Not that strong and not about somebody I knew. I've joked about doing that to someone at the bar back in Seattle, but I've never really wanted to grab somebody by the neck and kill them. When I was in the cab, I could see myself doing it. Or about to do it."

"You wouldn't have killed him, Matt. You're not Francis."

Matthew spun his coffee cup slowly on the kitchen table. "I have no fucking clue why Buzzy would do it. My dad didn't like him, and Buzzy didn't like my dad, but you gotta have a really good reason to shoot somebody. That's never been Buzzy's way. He gets people back by stealing shit from them. Or starting rumors. Never violence. It's just not his thing. I can't think of one good reason why he'd do it."

"I can," Anne said.

Matthew let go of the cup and looked at Anne. They heard footsteps upstairs as Joan made her way to the bathroom.

"Let's walk to the beach before my mother comes downstairs," Anne said.

They went out the back door, and made their way through the orchards and down the sandy path to the beach. Low tide yielded a stretch of hard-packed sand where Anne and Matthew walked barefoot. Anne relayed what she had learned from Kathleen, trying to tell it just as Kathleen had told her.

When she finished, they continued to the place where the beach curved gently into the Essex River. Across the wide empty beach were dunes. They climbed one and settled down with a view facing the surf.

"That's just crazy," Matthew finally said.

"I believe her, Matt. I don't think Kathleen would make any of it up."

"I'm not saying that. I mean the whole thing. My dad being Buzzy's dad. I've never heard anything about this before. Ever."

Matthew grew silent for a moment, then added, "And I can't believe Buzzy wouldn't say anything to me. If he knew. Does Buzzy know?"

"Kathleen said he did. Your dad wrote him letters trying to start up a relationship again. Or for the first time, I guess," Anne said.

Just as the night before, when Matthew had to reassess everything he thought about Buzzy, he was now having to recast their years together for a second time. They were brothers, or half brothers, and it had always been that way. How would their lives be different now if they had both known that fact? Or if Matthew had known it, since it sounded like Buzzy had known for some time. "So if Buzzy knew, why did he keep it from me? Why would he do that?"

The sun had risen high enough to warm the breeze that blew in from the water. Anne plucked a piece of saw grass and peeled off a thin strip. It's what she would do as a girl to make a whistle by pinching the strip between her thumbs. "Maybe he was embarrassed by it. Being rejected by his own father."

"Then why didn't Kathleen tell me?" Matthew asked.

"She said that your dad wanted to tell you himself. He meant to do it at the wedding."

Matthew remembered Kathleen telling him to talk to his dad at the reception. "So that's what he wanted to talk to me about. Jesus, what a conversation that would have been."

Matthew stretched back on the sand. "I wonder how many other people know about this." He thought of Francis and Jimmy. Then he considered his mother. "Imagine my mother finding out." Matthew felt the latent anger at his father coming back. It didn't matter that he was dead.

He looked across the water, at the waves being formed far out. "That's why Buzzy killed him. I guarantee you that's the reason."

Anne had reached the same conclusion. "It might be worth talking to the police now. I know you didn't want to before, but this is different. You know that Buzzy did it. If it's a choice between Francis finding him or the police finding him, what do you think is better?"

Matthew remembered the note he had left at the bar with information about Buzzy's cab. It was to help Francis track down Buzzy. At the time, it was what Matthew wanted, for Francis to catch and kill him. Now he wished he hadn't done that. It meant that he wasn't just a spectator. He was a player, and playing on the wrong team.

He also wondered whether Francis knew that Buzzy was his brother.

"I don't think Francis knows about this," Matthew said as they started back up the path to the house.

"Kathleen wasn't sure about that."

283

"If Francis knew, then he wouldn't go after Buzzy. You can't kill your own brother. It doesn't matter what Buzzy's done. You just can't do that."

When they got back to the house, they found Joan sitting on the back deck with a mug of hot tea, a morning edition of the *Boston Globe* and the weekly edition of the *Ipswich Chronicle*.

"There you two are," Joan called. "What a beautiful morning, isn't it?"

As she smiled at Matthew, something about his hands caught her eye. Not something she saw, but something she didn't see. "Matthew, what happened to your wedding ring?"

* * * * *

The Wellesley Athletic Club opened its doors at five o'clock in the morning, when a small crowd of regulars promptly arrived to take their place in a lane of the pool, on their favorite treadmill or exercise bike, or to commence a circuit around the weight room. Some opted for a game of racquetball or squash. A few went directly to the Relaxation & Revitalization Suite, which housed a sauna, steam bath and massage rooms staffed by trained masseuses.

Aerobic and yoga classes began an hour later at six. The Entertainment Suite featured pool and Ping-Pong tables. Next door was the reading room with a fireplace. A small restaurant served lunch, dinner and snacks, as well as alcoholic beverages no earlier than noon in compliance with Massachusetts state liquor laws.

Members worked in a variety of professions, but they all had one thing in common. They could afford to be members. Initiation fees amounted to $5,000 and monthly dues had been recently raised from $200 to $250. Becoming a member also required sponsorship by no less than two current members in good standing with the club.

The Corbins of Wellesley had been among the club's charter members, and Senator George Corbin was religious about arriving with the early birds. He had devised a special workout routine six months earlier and it didn't go unnoticed by his fellow members, many of whom knew George and the Corbin family.

The new routine involved typical stretching and weight lifting. What was unusual was his outfit. Corbin dressed in sneakers and gym shorts, now that it was summer, and a light blue button-down dress shirt from Louis Boston. In his outfit, Corbin looked like an ad for a brokerage house showing how committed it was to going the extra mile for its clients.

To Corbin it was a way to fuse the worlds of athletics and politics, bringing the focus and exertion of the gym to the often confounding tasks of crafting and debating legislation. The same shirt would remain on him throughout the day, wafting its essence throughout the State House. In his own mind, if in no one else's, it made perfect sense.

It was not a routine designed to burn many calories. Corbin had abandoned that goal months before. That's when his wife of eight years announced she was leaving him to live in Hawaii with a geologist who had been in Corbin's graduating class at Dartmouth College.

In his bulging button-down dress shirt, Corbin made a circuit around the weight room, pausing occasionally to catch his breath and glance out at the small pond in the meadow behind the club. It was home to a host of wildlife, including ducks and turtles, and was intended to convey a sense of tranquility and to ameliorate the stress of a workout.

Corbin was taking in the view when he heard his name called by Henry Seward, president of Wellesley Savings & Trust with branches in Wellesley and four surrounding cities and towns. Henry was a few years past the typical retirement age, and Corbin suspected it was an unhappy home life that kept him behind the big desk. The breakup of Corbin's own marriage had definitely been keeping him overly attentive to his own work lately. Friends warned him he was becoming obsessed with his battles in the Senate. To Corbin, it was simply being focused.

"George, have you heard? I was just listening to the news on the television out front." Henry was a little short of breath, having jogged the long distance from the front of the club. His expression fell somewhere between concerned and alarmed, closer to alarmed.

"I don't watch the news, Henry. I read it. That way I can skip the commercials."

"The newspapers are arriving and they mention it as well. Or at least the *Herald* does. They're talking about putting a regional waste facility in Wellesley. That was on channel four, so I tried channel five and they were reporting the same story. It's a plan from your people in the State House," Henry added, making it clear at whose feet he was placing responsibility, and who had perhaps been sleeping on the job.

"Did you hear me, George? Pits filled with waste, incinerators belching foul clouds over Wellesley. Over my house. Over your house. Trucks rumbling up and down our streets filled with half the garbage generated by the Commonwealth. What's going on, George?"

Corbin leaned back and looked at Henry with a skeptical eye. Surely the man wasn't hearing right. "Henry, are you sure the TV wasn't tuned to the science-fiction channel?"

"George, I'm telling you … go up there and see for yourself. It's madness. And if it's true, you need to get on the ball and do something about it."

By the time Corbin arrived in the lobby, the TV newscast had moved to a story about the increasing pollution in Boston Harbor. Beside the front desk was a small stand that held a number of newspapers. Corbin considered the *Globe* to be the only Boston paper worthy of reading. The *Herald* was a tabloid rag that he ignored, even though its headlines could scream at you from ten yards away.

Which is exactly what happened, except this time Corbin paid attention. The huge headline on the early edition of the *Herald* read: 'WELLESLEY GETS TRASHED!'

Corbin walked over and picked up a copy. Beneath the headline was the face of Jimmy Mahoney smiling at him. The photo caption read: "Senator Jimmy Mahoney of South Boston unveils his plan for regional waste disposal. The senator's plan is backed by many studies that point to Wellesley as the 'nearly perfect site.'"

Corbin felt lightheaded. He started reading the story and found his eyes skittering over the lines, crashing into one detail after another: soon-to-be abandoned quarry in Wellesley … ninety-five acres as opposed to seven at South Bay … railroad tracks to move large amounts of material … convenient access to all of the major highways … both residential and commercial waste … plan supported by environmental impact statements …waste-to-energy facility.

That last phrase hit Corbin like a hammer. Waste-to-energy was happy talk for incinerator. Smokestacks belching dark, poisonous clouds across the local landscape. Property values would be decimated.

Corbin had never asked himself what his worst political nightmare might be, but this was both proposing the question and answering it in the same moment. Wellesley the trash hub of the region? It was absurd.

He considered what impact the story would have. Everybody in town would be stirred up. Corbin would be besieged by angry constituents. Wealthy, influential, powerful constituents who were going to demand he do something about it immediately. Corbin tried to take a deep breath and found he could only manage shallow ones.

"You see what I'm talking about? It's madness," Henry said as he came up quietly from behind Corbin and surprised him.

Corbin spun around and gave Henry a menacing look.

Henry continued, "I don't know if this is some kind of a joke, George, but I can tell you it's not going to be taken that way around here."

"I know, Henry. I know. I promise you it will come to nothing. Give me a few moments to take this in."

Corbin brought the newspaper to one of the comfortable couches that lined the lobby. He collapsed into the cushions and tried again to read the article carefully, but he was distracted by the wide grin on Mahoney's face. He had been looking into an anonymous camera when the picture was taken, but Corbin knew that Mahoney meant this smile for him and him alone. This was a personal attack.

Senate President Hurley must have approved this, at least tacitly, Corbin decided. Which meant that he was twisting the arms necessary to get a winning caucus vote. Then he'd crown Mahoney as the new president, and this was the first act of the emerging Mahoney regime. The South Boston senator intended to make Corbin the first fatality, and as the Senate president the bigot would have a whole new arsenal of weapons at his disposal.

The audacity of it. Pure vindictiveness intended to turn Corbin's own constituency against him. His friends and family. This was the manifestation of pure evil. If Mahoney wanted a fight, he was going to get one. You think you can use the press to advance your ends, Mahoney? Let's see how you like a bold, swift reply. Let's see how you handle a personal attack. The gloves are off now, by God.

In a bound, Corbin was off the couch and charging home. It was just after seven o'clock when he called WEEI, a popular AM radio station for news, traffic and weather. Corbin hoped to send his response to a city on its way to work.

He was connected to the news director, Paul Willis. The two had golfed on occasion until Willis improved his game substantially and Corbin had become bored with golf and the people who considered it an athletic activity.

"Paul, have you seen the absurdity on the front page of the *Herald?*"

"Yes, I have, George. It's completely crazy. It's never going to happen."

"No, it won't, but somebody must respond to this nonsense, and do so immediately."

Willis asked if Corbin would like to come into the studio for an interview about the subject, but Corbin interrupted him, "This can't wait, Paul. I have to respond to this as soon as possible. I'd like you to put me live right now. It'll be a phone interview."

Willis was hesitant. "Well, let's see. I don't know just how we're going to work that, George. You know how structured our format is here. I suppose maybe later this morning, perhaps a phone thing or maybe …"

"To hell with your structure! That man has attacked my town and attacked me personally. You work under a public license, Paul, and you have a responsibility to air points of view on issues that are important to the people of this state. Clear out ten minutes for me. Cut out a weather and traffic report. People know the weather by looking out their window, and people know the traffic sucks because it always sucks around here."

As Corbin spoke, he could feel the heat growing in his face. Willis was silent. If he interpreted the remark about the station's public license as a subtle threat, that's exactly how Corbin intended it. "Well, OK," he finally said. "Let me, ah, set this all up. It'll take a couple of minutes. Can I call you back, or would you like to hang on the line?"

"We're not cutting this connection until I've answered the attack."

After a few moments, Willis came back on and said, "OK, George, I think we have it ready. I'm switching you through to Jerry now. You'll be live so…" Willis laughed uncomfortably, "you know, keep an eye on the old language, and, ah, we've got about five minutes for you. Try not to run over."

Corbin's line clicked once and he was hearing the end of a radio ad for a car dealership in Brockton. When the ad ended, he heard the snappy voice of Jerry Schmidt, whose slogan was "Got news? Give Jerry a jingle."

"So, everybody, we've got a special guest this morning. Speaking to us from his home, Senator George Corbin will give his reaction to a story in this morning's *Boston Herald* that his town of Wellesley has been selected as the best possible place to dispose of trash from our region. Welcome, Senator Corbin. Glad you could join us. First, let's start…"

The sound controller had been lowering the volume on Corbin's end because he was breathing through his nose directly onto the mouthpiece of his phone. Corbin jumped in before the show's host could finish his sentence, and his voice came across loud and sharp, causing the sound controller to make another quick adjustment.

"I'll tell you what this is all about, Jerry. It's about the corruption of power. It's about the bigoted tail of South Boston trying to wag the dog of Massachusetts. It's pure vindictiveness on the part of Senator Mahoney. The man is using this plan to attack me personally, but he won't get away with it. The people of this state are too smart to be fooled by this folderol. And the good people of Wellesley absolutely will not stand for it."

As he spoke, Corbin looked out a window onto his backyard and the woods beyond. He held up a hand as if he was standing on the Senate floor and making the speech of his life, and he could feel the heat on his hand, the heat coming from his face and his breath.

"I'm ready to reveal Mahoney for what he is. I'm here to expose him. He is poison to the soul of our Commonwealth. A racist to the core…"

At this point, the host made an attempt to rein in the dialogue, or monologue, back into the realm of the facts as presented in the *Herald* article.

Corbin would have none of it. "You can ask me questions later, but first I must reveal what's going on behind the scenes. I must shed the cleansing light of scrutiny not only on the absurd waste disposal plan, but also on its corrupt creator. And what everyone needs to know is that Senator Mahoney does not make this attack on his own. He has secret coconspirators, and chief among them is his brother Francis Mahoney. It doesn't take a trained eye to see the devil at work with this pair."

Corbin continued with his rant a few minutes longer, attacking Jimmy Mahoney in increasingly ugly terms while suggesting that Jimmy's waste disposal plan might somehow be aiding his brother Francis.

"But there is hope, Jerry. There is hope. We can fight this together, all of us, and we have the agents of the state to provide their support … "

Corbin paused to take a breath, and heard a click in his earpiece. "Hello? Jerry, are you there?" Nothing. He had been cut off. Corbin called the station and was connected again with Willis. "Paul, what happened? I lost the connection."

"Are you mad, George? My heavens, you just made the most outrageous accusations on the air. You were live, George. Live. My heavens, do you know what repercussions this could have for the station? For me?"

"Nonsense, Paul. People respect the truth, however shocking it may sound in the beginning. Now put me back on the air. I have much more to say."

"George, did you hear a single word I said? Our phone lines are already going crazy with reactions. I never should have put you on the air in the first place. Oh, dear Lord. George, please don't call back," Willis said, then hung up.

In the next half hour, Corbin was able to get two other radio stations to broadcast his response live. Giving the same speech, he lasted a full seven minutes on WRKO, but barely managed three minutes on WBZ before being cut off. Word of his on-air behavior spread through the news community like wildfire, so after WBZ no station would allow him on the air live. They all insisted on a taped interview with specific questions and a stipulation that if a response did not address the facts of the issue, it would not be aired.

* * * * *

Boston's old City Hall, where James Michael Curley had once held court, was built in the 1860s and featured the French Second

Empire style of architecture. In the late 1960s, a new City Hall was built a block from the old building. Its architects strove to create a structure that was modern yet respectful of the past, concrete yet creative in design.

The result was a layer cake of brick and concrete surrounded by what one critic called "a vast desert of bricks." As architecturally intriguing as the interior layout of City Hall was to its creators, it often confounded Bostonians with its large central atrium, where glancing up to the floor you needed to visit in no way told you which combination of escalators, elevators and stairways you should take to arrive there.

From his office on the fifth floor of City Hall, Mayor Sullivan had an unobscured view of Quincy Market and the waterfront beyond. More than once he gazed over the pleasant urban landscape while savoring his unequivocal achievement of being the first South Boston resident elected mayor of Boston.

There had been less to savor that week with the state Senate erecting a roadblock to his South Bay plan. Sullivan knew that Senate President Hurley's leadership team had been consumed by corruption scandals and that Hurley had been implicated in the scandal as well. Not in a way that would bring indictments, but it certainly put an end to any hopes he had of running for governor. And every day he stayed on as Senate president was a day the dark cloud of corruption lingered over the State House, making it hard to effectively build and move legislation.

Hurley had to step down soon. The only question was who would replace him. Jimmy Mahoney had been moved into the Senate Majority Leader position, typically the heir apparent to the presidency, but Sullivan had not been alone in assuming that Hurley would bypass Jimmy and back somebody else. Now Sullivan wasn't so sure, and if Jimmy did move up, he would become a far more powerful opponent in the waste disposal battle. Powerful enough to defeat the South Bay plan. Sullivan had put too much political capital in play to let that happen.

That was his idea behind the surprise press conference on the State House steps. To put the full public spotlight on the issue and force the Senate to rescind the amendment penalizing the city of Boston fifty-million dollars a year, should it build the waste disposal facility at South Bay. If he could stir up enough attention, it might

291

make Hurley cave on the amendment and show the governor that there was substantial support for the South Bay site.

There had been barely enough time to assess whether the press conference and debate on the State House steps had been a success because the news about it had been overshadowed by Jimmy's controversial Wellesley proposal.

At ten o'clock Friday morning, Sullivan sat in his conference room with his two top aides, deciding whether to take the Wellesley proposal seriously or not. Sullivan's initial reaction had occurred two hours earlier when he exploded in an angry outburst that brought a security guard charging into his office to see if the mayor was being assaulted. Since then the anger had diminished to mere frustration.

Frank Abbott, who had engineered the mayor's surprise press conference on the State House steps, was the most perplexed.

"I don't believe people will take this for anything but a joke. If you respond to it seriously, it will give the story the kind of weight that Mahoney wants it to have."

The other aide, Bernie Harrington, had played basketball on the same college team as Sullivan. In the off-season the two had regularly hitchhiked down to Harlem to play pickup games for hours, before hitching back to their college in Rhode Island.

The press enjoyed referring to the two aides as Abbott and Costello. There was some physical resemblance to the comedy team, since Frank Abbott was short and stout, and Bernie Harrington was tall and lean. And the two often had very different takes on events.

Bernie had been against the press conference idea, and he now found himself disagreeing once again with Frank's suggestion on a response.

"This is going off like a bombshell right now," Bernie began. "The whole town of Wellesley will go ballistic as soon as they get over the shock. Every suburb between here and there will freak out because if something like this can happen to one of the wealthiest towns in the state, what's going to be headed their way next? It's like the Huns breaching the gates." Looking at Sullivan, he continued. "I think you need to respond fast and get ahead of the reaction. Remember, this is about Boston's trash. It's a Boston problem, and it needs a Boston solution."

Frank shook his head. "Bernie, this is a nonstarter. It's a proposal from the South Boston senator, not the Senate president. There's no indication that the House of Representatives would touch this with a ten-foot pole. And the governor is going to treat it like it's radioactive. Do you know what would happen to the rosy glow of the Massachusetts Miracle if the governor let this happen to the most influential town in the state?

"Wellesley is full of big people who hold high positions in virtually every state institution. Political donations would dry up. The governor would be strangled from within his own party and any thought of becoming president would vanish within the month."

On his first visit to Fenway Park as mayor of Boston, Sullivan had been given a rare bobblehead doll of outfielder Carl Yastrzemski, nicknamed Yaz. It sat on the conference table in front of Sullivan and he had been tapping its head while he listened to his advisers. "OK, you've each got good points, but I don't think we've got a clear picture yet. We have time before we give a public reaction. I think we need to put our finger to the wind." It was a phrase Sullivan often used when the situation did not break down in a black and white way. On more complex issues, his first instinct was to ask for a poll, but there was no time for that.

"Bernie, check on the hill. I agree with Frank about the House not touching the plan, but I want to know where Hurley stands on this. If he voices any reluctance, the proposal goes nowhere. The more time passes, the more pressure he's going to get from the suburbs to shoot this down."

Sullivan stared into space for a moment before tapping again on the Yaz bobblehead. "Why is Mahoney doing it? I know he was the one who pressured Hurley to put that outside section on the bill. Now this. I wonder whether he's been planning this stunt for a long time or if he just cooked it up overnight."

"Spite," Frank said. "The man's incredibly vindictive. But he's digging his own grave. No good will come of this. In the end, it will weaken him, the same way busing did."

"Yes, he's vindictive," Bernie said. "But I don't think he would do this without a very specific goal in mind. If it's not to put the trash site in Wellesley, then his plan is something else. It's some kind of Trojan horse."

"Well," Sullivan said. "I'd like to know what that is, and I'd like to hear back from you both before this evening. It would be good to have something for the five o'clock news. Then the papers will have it in their morning editions. If we don't have a response ready by five, let's shoot for the eleven o'clock news. They'll repeat the story in their morning broadcasts.

"Bernie, after you go to the hill, find out what people are saying around the city and in the suburbs. Note how they're saying it. However we respond, I want people to hear their own opinions coming back at them in the news.

"Frank, you get in touch with the governor. Where is he today?"

"Chicago," Frank said.

"OK. He's already signed off on our South Bay proposal. Now we're going to need him to come out against the Wellesley proposal. I know he didn't want to get into the middle of a local thing between me and Mahoney, but you tell him that it's become a problem that's spilled way beyond Boston. It's in everybody's backyard. Kostakos has to make a public statement," Mayor Sullivan said, referring to Peter Kostakos, the governor of Massachusetts.

"We need to keep Mahoney isolated on this. The man likes to do everything by decree, without building alliances, and if that's how he's handled this, then he's left himself vulnerable. Personally, I think he's going to be surrounded by opposition and this is going to die a quick death in the Senate."

"By the way," Frank said. "Did either of you guys catch Corbin on the radio this morning?"

Bernie laughed. "I caught a little. That was a very funny spoof."

Frank shook his head. "That was no spoof, Bernie."

Sullivan felt an unexpected sympathy for the senator from Wellesley. "Good God, he must be under unbelievable pressure right now."

Whether he was forecasting the score of a Red Sox game or the winner of a local election, Frank Abbott was a man who loved making predictions. And he had an uncanny ability to see outcomes that nobody else could imagine. "I'll tell you what I think. I think the man is going off the deep end. I mean, way off."

* * * * *

Anne's father had left a number of things to her in his will, but there were only a few items that she truly cherished. His wedding ring was one of them, and she had trusted Matthew to care for it. It was more than a band of precious metal to her. It was a connection to her father's past.

Dylan had been born in the Swansea area of South Wales under the name Donald Dylan Barry. When World War II broke out, he was only twelve years old. His father served in the British Merchant Navy on a ship that delivered oil across the Channel and, like so many other English and American merchantmen during the war, he was killed when his ship was torpedoed by a German U-boat.

When Dylan turned eighteen, he followed his father into the Merchant Navy. It was a far safer occupation after the war and allowed a young man to travel the world while learning a useful trade. Like his fellow sailors, Dylan enjoyed a good laugh and a stiff drink, but he never took to gambling and was careful on how he spent his money.

It was in his first year at sea when he began going by his middle name Dylan, in honor of the writer Dylan Thomas, who grew up in Swansea as well. When his shipmates discovered the name switch, he also became jokingly referred to as "The Bard." A tall, thin man with bright green eyes and a head of reddish brown hair, Dylan bore little physical resemblance to the famous poet, but he enjoyed his new nickname.

He loved exploring the various cultures he encountered in his job as a merchant engineer. Although he never finished high school, he taught himself by reading when he was off duty. He'd stock up before a voyage on books about the ports his ship would visit, and on the occasions when he had shore leave, he'd wander the streets of a city, speak to the locals, and visit the churches, museums, bars and restaurants. In whatever time he had, he'd immerse himself in the culture and drink it all in.

At the end of a voyage, he'd arrive home with interesting stories and a curious selection of items he'd purchased. Those that were too large to take on board for the return trip, he'd have shipped back to Swansea. Some of the items he'd keep, like the chess set and coffee table still in Joan's house in Ipswich. Others he'd sell or give away as gifts to those he knew would appreciate them. Over the years, he became popular in Swansea for this, and people would come calling at his flat beside a sail-making loft to see his latest cache of collectibles, make a purchase or inquire about his future trips.

By 1956, Dylan had risen to the Merchant Navy rank of Second Engineer and had seen almost every place he cared to see. The area he enjoyed visiting most was New England in America. In March of that year, Dylan moved to Gloucester, Massachusetts, and rented an apartment in the Rocky Neck neighborhood. He worked on fishing and lobster boats while he waited to become a U.S. citizen and apply for a job in the Merchant Marine.

It was on a train ride into Boston to see the play *Under Milk Wood* on a warm May evening when he met Joan Boushay. The train stopped in Salem to pick up passengers for Boston, but it had to remain in the station because of engine trouble. Dylan took advantage of the opportunity to speak to the woman he had been eyeing since she boarded the train in the town of Beverly.

He never made it to see the play in Boston that evening, but he did have a good chat with Joan, which led to an invitation for lunch the following week in Ipswich. In their first five minutes of conversation on the train, Joan had been struck by Dylan's charm. She admired his easygoing manner, the fact that he was self taught and surprisingly cultured, and the way different languages and the descriptions of exotic lands would roll off his tongue with ease.

Nana B had a more reserved opinion when she met Dylan. Yes, he was all the things, or almost all the things that Joan listed, but Nana B determined that the tall, attractive Welshman was not someone with a firm sense of place. He traveled the world and talked of various cities and towns where he'd like to live some day. The Boushays were a family of place, and their place was Ipswich, Massachusetts.

In the first few years of marriage, Dylan was a happy man. He spent months at sea, then had long stretches of time at home in Ipswich. Nana B's reservations proved warranted, however. After Anne's birth, Dylan felt the itch to live someplace new. Despite his decision to settle in Ipswich, he grew reluctant to commit to a lifetime residence on the Boushay farm.

For Joan, it was a realization that admiring a sense of adventure was not the same as endorsing it for one's own family or engaging in it oneself. One week into their first trip overseas to Morocco, Joan had had her fill of the flies, the heat, the sand, the almost barbaric way some Moroccans dealt with her, and finally the dysentery that left her sense of adventure and desire to experience foreign cultures more than satisfied for several years, if not forever.

After the divorce, Dylan moved to Alaska and used his engineering skills to make a lucrative living on the construction of the Trans Alaska Pipeline. He went to school to study environmental engineering, then settled into a job in Anchorage, where he built a large cabin for himself and Anne.

When she moved to Anchorage at the age of twelve, her legal name was Anne Rhoslyn Barry. Her father asked, then insisted, that she change her last name to Boushay. He knew that Anne was better off living with him in Alaska, but he also understood how wrenching the loss of primary custody would be for Joan. Attachment to place and family names carried little lasting importance to Dylan, but for the Boushays they were paramount to identity.

After spending her first night at her father's cabin, which was more the size of a small lodge, Anne woke to the sight of a moose outside her bedroom window. It was looking at her and its breath blew a cloud of vapor against the glass. The moose's head was so massive it filled the window.

Anne ran into the hallway screaming, "It's coming in! The moose is coming in!"

Dylan had a good laugh once he learned what all the fuss was about. He took Anne to the porch and showed her the family of moose that visited the front lawn every morning.

The moose story was one that Dylan enjoyed telling over the years. As Anne grew, he also joked that her legs were getting as long as a moose's. Anne adapted quickly to her new home and it wasn't too long before she could easily be mistaken for a local. And by the time she traveled to Seattle for college, she had grown as comfortable and skilled in outdoor adventure as her father.

The one skill she had not mastered while living in Alaska, however, was how to choose a boyfriend. She had very specific ideas about what guys she should be interested in, how they should speak and dress and eat, what sort of truck they should drive. They had to be climbers and they had to challenge Anne, but they couldn't beat her publicly in a competition. The list went on.

Dylan joked that Anne went through boyfriends faster than the moose went through flower beds in early summer. It was not until Anne moved to Seattle when she was forced to reconsider who to date. Seattle was a lot bigger than Anchorage and had a lot of what Anne called "delicate city boys." While she was studying environmental engineering at the University of Washington, she was also working as a cook at Donovan's Steak and Oyster House across from the Kingdome in downtown Seattle.

Matthew had been working odd jobs in construction and landscaping for a few years when he decided to apply for a waiter's position at Donovan's. It was a madhouse of a restaurant, and Matthew made lots of mistakes as a waiter, something that Anne, as cook, had to point out to him.

They did not get along well at first, even as coworkers. When Matthew found the job that better suited him in the bar, that removed the friction and they were able to become friends and eventually start dating.

The first real test of their relationship came when Matthew joined Anne and Dylan in Alaska for a week of camping and salmon fishing on the Nushagak River. Dylan took an immediate liking to him. Matthew had been forced to leave the place where he grew up and was struggling to make a place for himself in the world, and he lived without fear. For the most part. Anne and Dylan tried not to make fun of the fact that Matthew lost a couple of nights' sleep worrying about bears attacking their tent when the sun went down. After two nights, though, he was fine.

Matthew liked Dylan as well. He set the sort of example and gave the kind of fatherly advice that Matthew had needed since leaving the East Coast. They had the same sense of humor with the witty wordplay that the Irish and Welsh share. They stayed up late drinking and telling stories of their interesting yet different adventures in life.

One thing that struck Matthew in particular was how close Dylan and Anne were, how much they enjoyed each other's company, how they were so familiar with each other's ways that they often communicated in phrases and subtle gestures.

Matthew was also impressed that their relationship had grown beyond parent and child to where they were good friends. It was something that Matthew envied. His mother's death had denied him the chance of such a relationship with her.

At the end of that first trip, Anne confessed to her father a reluctance to commit to a serious relationship with Matthew. He didn't climb and he had little interest in spending time in the outdoors as she did. That difference in their identities seemed to keep their relationship weak in a fundamental way.

Dylan replied that it was their differences that would make their relationship stronger than most, as long as they trusted and had faith in each other. He encouraged Anne to commit herself to Matthew because he had qualities that she had not yet begun to appreciate. Dylan knew people and knew which ones were worth making part of your life. In his experienced opinion, Matthew was a very good fit for Anne despite what surface appearances might suggest.

It was not until two years later when she was sitting at her father's bedside at the Providence Alaska Medical Center that Anne took her father's advice to heart. He was unconscious so she wasn't able to speak with him, but it was the last time she would see him alive. She held his hand through the short Alaska night and into the long day thinking about the last adventure they shared, which happened to have been the only time they faced serious danger in the outdoors.

They were ice climbing at Sukakpak Peak and standing on a ledge between their second and third pitches when Anne heard the sound of a jet high above. As it grew louder she looked to the sky. They were not in a place where you would normally hear a jet, so it seemed odd.

When she turned to her dad, he was looking up to the sky as well. Then he looked at Anne with wide eyes.

"Avalanche!" he called as the distant roar grew louder. He grabbed Anne and pushed her toward the ice face. "Press as flat as you can!" he yelled above the sound of the first snow crashing past them.

They kept one arm around each other and one against the ice as the roar became deafening and the falling snow blocked the sunlight. Anne felt the snow hitting her backpack and the coils of rope hanging from it. It was happening to Dylan too. The force of the snow striking their packs threatened to drag them off the ledge and pull them into the main avalanche flow.

There was enough light for Anne to look over and see her father's face. In it she saw not fear but an intense focus as he stared back at her. Faster than it had begun, the avalanche ended. Sunlight returned.

On the ground far below was a fresh mountain of snow and beneath it some of the equipment and rope that had been attached to their packs. They rappelled safely down and spent an hour digging out most of their lost gear.

It was a long ride home, and it was almost two hours before either one of them spoke. Dylan, chewing on a plastic straw, told her, "Train yourself well and do whatever you can to prepare for the worst thing that might happen, but when God comes calling you can't say no."

That advice was another one of the valuable things her father had left to Anne. Another was the wedding ring that he wore when marrying Anne's mother. The wide gold band was engraved with images of leaping salmon. Anne had worn it around her neck on a gold chain until her wedding day when she placed it on Matthew's finger.

* * * * *

Standing on the back deck of the Boushay farmhouse on Friday morning, Matthew stared down at his bare left hand. He had completely forgotten about the ring. His confession to Anne was going to be difficult enough, but having to make it in front of Joan would be worse because it would confirm whatever doubts she might have had about Matthew from the beginning.

Fortunately for him, Anne sensed that it wasn't simply a matter of Matthew forgetting to put the ring on that morning. Something had happened to it.

"It's too big, as it turns out," Anne said to her mother. "It's been slipping off. We'll have it fixed when we get back to Seattle."

"That's the wise thing to do," Joan said. "You certainly wouldn't want to lose that ring. It's irreplaceable."

Matthew knew he was in deep shit. If he had only remembered to tell her last night and not have it come out in front of her mother, which only magnified his mistake. Using the ring like a poker chip, betting that the cab driver would still be there when Matthew left Buzzy's apartment, had been a big mistake.

"So, what's on your schedule for today?" Joan asked.

"That's what we're about to discuss." Anne turned to Matthew. "Upstairs."

They went up to their room, and Anne closed the door.

"Anne, I'm sorry. I forgot to tell you about the ring," Matthew began.

Anne scanned the room quickly, checking the dresser, the bed stand, the hardwood floors, even the windowsills before turning to Matthew. "Where is it?"

"I left it with a cab driver when I went back to Old Colony to find Buzzy. I owed the driver twenty bucks and he wouldn't take anything else."

"Why did you give him the ring? Why didn't you just pay with cash?"

"I didn't have any cash on me."

"I thought you took your wallet … "

Matthew interrupted, "I took my driver's license. I didn't bring my wallet."

"So how do we get the ring back?"

This was going to be the hard part, and Matthew plunged right in. "We can't get it back. The cab driver was black and some people in the project were harassing him so he took off. He said he'd sell the ring if I didn't return with cash and I have no idea where he'd sell it or what his cab number was or anything."

Anne did another quick, irrational scan of the room searching for the ring she would never see again. She took a deep breath and held it for a few seconds. As she let it out, her eyes filled. She wiped away the tears quickly.

"I'm sorry, Anne. I don't know why I did it. It was really stupid," Matthew said.

Without looking at him, she said, "We need to leave, Matthew. We need to get out of here. I want to fly back to Seattle as soon as we can. Today."

"Alright."

Anne turned to him, "And we're not going back to South Boston before we leave."

Matthew didn't respond right away. Finally, he said, "I need to see Francis."

"No you don't. You can call the police."

"He's going after Buzzy. He doesn't know that we're all brothers. If I don't let Francis know, he'll kill him. I know he will."

"Listen to me, Matt. Just call the police."

Two of the rules that had stuck with Matthew from his time in South Boston were that you never snitched and you never called the cops.

The neighborhood took care of its own business. If you brought the cops into it, some of them came with their own agenda, including a chance to settle old scores. That had been confirmed during busing when Matthew saw neighbors doing nothing wrong being beaten bloody by the TPF.

"It's not something the police can stop, Anne." Matthew put a hand to his forehead and scratched lightly. "Francis is above the cops in South Boston. He pays some of them to do what he wants them to do. If you want something done or not done in South Boston, you don't go to the cops, you go to my brother. He's the only one who can stop it. I have to step in for Buzzy on this."

Matthew went to the dresser and picked up the keys to Joan's car. He grabbed his wallet as well.

"There's a limit to what you can do out of loyalty, you know," Anne said.

"Not in South Boston there isn't," Matthew said.

"In case you haven't noticed," Anne began sharply, "you don't live in South Boston anymore, Matthew! You haven't lived there for a long time. Stop trying to turn back the clock to when you were fifteen. You said it yourself more than once, that you feel trapped there like it's 1974. That South Boston doesn't exist now. Everybody who was in it has grown up or moved on. And that's what you need to do too, Matthew. You need to move on. Keep what matters, like the memories of your mother. And get rid of the rest, like feeling responsible for Buzzy and being loyal to Francis. Your time there is over. It's done. Move on, goddamnit!"

Matthew listened patiently. When Anne finished, he walked over and kissed her cheek. "I'll be back in two hours."

Anne squinted at him. "Where are you going?"

"It's a bar called O'Brien's."

Anne shook her head. "You didn't hear anything I just said, did you?"

Matthew tucked the wallet into his pocket. "Yes, I did. And maybe you're right, but believe me when I say that I'm not somebody you're gonna want to spend the rest of your life with if I don't at least try to do something about this right now."

"So what's at O'Brien's?"

"If Francis isn't on the move, he's probably there."

"I'll go with you," Anne said.

"Absolutely not."

* * * * *

With the death of her husband Sabatino in 1986, Maria D'Amico lived alone in the house on N Street, but Larry and Francis continued to conduct meetings there. She enjoyed the chance to see her son and his friend, and the meetings gave her an opportunity to cook, which she only enjoyed when she was doing it for other people.

Maria understood in a general way what her son did, and she knew how to keep her mouth shut about it. Francis liked her, and he trusted her completely. She was old fashioned in a good way. If a cop or anyone else with a badge tried to intimidate her into talking, she'd tell them to go fuck themselves, even if it meant spending the rest of her life in prison. Having somebody like Maria host meetings for Francis, Larry and others was priceless.

Twenty minutes after Connor's message reached Disco that morning, a reply came. Disco said he'd be free at one o'clock that afternoon. Connor called Maria at ten o'clock and told her to go shopping right away, which meant that she was going to have visitors for lunch.

Francis took the blue van and parked it in the garage out back. He turned up his collar and wore a baseball hat and big sunglasses in case any of the neighbors saw him walking from the garage to the back door.

The aroma of garlic and the sweet smell of sautéed linguisa wafted from the kitchen to the back porch. Francis called to Maria as he entered through the unlocked screen door. It was supposed to be Connor who was coming by, and when she turned around she put a hand to her mouth when she saw who it was. Francis gave her a big hug.

"Look who's come out of the woodwork," she said in a whisper. Maria was a tall woman who managed to maintain her figure over the years. She had a deep voice, and she spoke in slow melodious tones that you could understand clearly from three rooms away when she was making a point with emotion.

"You don't have to whisper," Francis said. "Just keep this surprise between us, as always."

"Shush," Maria smiled and patted Francis on the shoulder. "Good to see you, Francis."

Francis made a note of Maria's hair, still cropped short and blown back, but instead of blonde it was now a deep chestnut with frost highlights. "Just when I thought you couldn't get any more gorgeous, Maria, you've gone ahead and done it. That hair is really something."

At the obvious flattery, Maria brushed a hand in the air. "It's Kathleen. I can't tell you how happy I am with her work. And I'm not the only one. That girl's become an institution in town. An indispensable institution. Which reminds me, I have to call and make an appointment for a trim tomorrow."

Maria then turned to business. "I wish I could tell you there was eggplant today, but there was no time and the stuff they've been carrying at Flanagan's, I swear to you, is like Styrofoam. I'm going to have another talk with that produce manager, but I don't think it will do any good because the man does not understand the more sophisticated vegetables. All he knows is lettuce. That's it. Useless."

She apologized for what little she was able to come up with, but of course it was a more than an adequate spread. A plate of antipasto, sweet linguisa, pasta, chicken parmesan and red sauce, or gravy as the Italians liked to call it.

"I've got some garlic bread wrapped in foil in the oven above the chicken."

Maria held up a bottle of red wine to Francis and he nodded. Usually Francis would skip the alcohol. When he drank, it was a glass, two on very rare occasions.

After setting the pasta into boiling water, Maria brought two glasses of wine into the dining room where she and Francis took seats across from each other at the old maple table. They talked about his father, and she described the funeral at great length because she knew that Francis had not been able to go to it. She listed who was there, what they were wearing, who they sat with, who wasn't there and who Maria believed should have been.

At the back door came a knock, a formality because it immediately opened and Disco stepped inside. He was wearing a new charcoal suit from the Versace fall collection. It featured a blend of polyester and wool, and what Versace called its "urban fit," which was supposed to elevate any man's look to new heights of dash and sophistication.

Maria greeted him with open arms. "Terry," she said, refusing to call him by "that ridiculous nickname."

"I saw your wife at the store today, your new wife that is. I won't spoil your dinner by telling you what she bought. Sit down and have a glass of wine with your friend while I check the pasta."

Disco thought he'd be meeting Connor and couldn't believe his eyes when he stepped into the dining room and saw Francis, who gave him a sly smile. When Disco got over the shock, he slapped Francis on the back and took a seat. "Well, surprise, surprise, as Gomer Pyle used to say."

Maria brought Disco a glass of wine and placed the bottle between the two men. The table was already set, and Maria returned with a plate of antipasto.

"OK, boys, you help yourselves while I walk down to the card shop and pick out something for my niece Cheryl. She's 43 this month and has to go in for another back operation, poor thing. You got your antipasto, with the hot peppers you like, Terry. Everything else is in the kitchen, covered and warm. Just go in and help yourselves, Army style, like Sabatino used to say. I won't be back for a while, so just lock the back door when you leave."

They thanked Maria and waited until she left.

Disco took off his jacket and draped it over the back of his chair before sitting down. "So, did you leave and come back, or did you never leave at all?" Disco asked as he put slices of salami and cheese onto a small plate. The slices were rolled tight and looked like cigarettes. He added a couple of hot peppers.

"I was on my way when I heard about my dad. And that someone was framing me. I'm looking into it."

"I knew it was a setup the second I heard. Do you know who it is?"

"I have an idea," Francis said.

Disco knew enough not to ask who, even though he was curious. If Francis ended up killing the guy, the less Disco knew about it the better. "I'll bet it was somebody who knew you were leaving. Nobody in their right mind would try that unless they thought you'd have no way of responding."

Francis loaded some antipasto onto a plate and took a bite of cheese. His wine glass sat on the table and he slowly spun it around by the stem as he studied Disco's face. "You look like you're having a bad week."

Disco finished the salami, took a drink of wine and bit into a hot pepper. "I'm breaking in a new boss. He's a real prick. He thinks this is the Wild West and he's the new sheriff." Disco paused to take a deep breath and loosen his silk tie. "We had a meeting yesterday that lasted an hour, and five times I counted him saying, 'How long have we been doing it that way? I think there are better ways to do it, don't you?' He's been turning everything upside down."

Francis laughed. "You never knew how good you had it with Patsy." It was the nickname Francis had given Disco's old boss, Patrick Shea. "I wouldn't worry about him. If he's a reformer, he won't last long. Jimmy tells me that's how it goes in politics. They fuck with everybody's business. They make enemies. Reformers come in with a bang, but they all go out the back door at the end of their first term."

They went into the kitchen and brought back platefuls of Maria's cooking. Francis took a sip of wine and brought the conversation to the subject he cared most about. "I'm curious. How long does it take for these indictments to make their way out? I thought I only had three days of wiggle room. It's been six days now, and I'm seeing nothing about them on the news or in the papers."

"Good grief, does Maria know how to cook or what?" Disco said, taking another bite of the chicken parmesan, which was breaded with Italian spices and covered in a sauce made from tomatoes grown in her backyard that summer.

Disco continued in a more serious tone. "Yeah, the indictments. They looked like a sure thing, which is what I passed on to you and Larry. Then they began sounding like a good bet. This new director hasn't been giving me all the information coming from the grand jury, like Patsy would do. He's kept me in the dark as much as he could. I know it's intentional. He's from Idaho, and he's got an accent that drives me out of my fucking gourd.

"Anyway, this morning I finally found out what's going on. The indictments were never a done deal. One of the biggest hang-ups was the testimony from two major witnesses. Ronald and Lydia Hudson, who run the jai alai joint. Apparently the Hudsons were contradicting themselves. I don't know how many times. Once, twice, ten times. The judge overseeing the grand jury refuses to let things move forward until they submit new sworn depositions.

"They were scheduled to take care of it yesterday at the courthouse in Boston. Their lawyer showed up but not the Hudsons. The lawyer calls them, then goes down to Cumberland where they live in Rhode Island. He finds Ronald Hudson in the wine cellar with his brains blown out. Suicide. The lawyer can't find Mrs. Hudson anywhere. Her car and her husband's car are still there, but her clothes and jewelry are packed up and gone. And the dog's gone. Apparently she was crazy about the dog and would never go anywhere without it. So they think she left with someone, that maybe she's been having an affair and she packed up the dog and ran off after an argument with her husband, which obviously left him rather depressed."

Francis stabbed a piece of linguisa and dunked it in red sauce. His suspicion about the indictments was right. This was the good news he had hoped to hear from Disco, and he tried not to get ahead of himself until he heard everything.

Disco continued, "They won't know what their story is for a while, maybe a long, long while. As far as the indictments go, they're never going to happen unless they find Mrs. Hudson and get her to talk."

Francis felt a sense of lightness washing over him. What a sweet coincidence that he and Connor did their deed yesterday. Even taking the dog backed up the affair story. As for Mrs. Hudson, who was sleeping next to Flapjacks one floor below the dining room table, the likelihood of her ever being found was slim. Even if somebody with a badge was lucky enough to find her some day, she sure as shit wouldn't be doing any talking.

"So I don't have to skip town?" Francis asked.

"That's right."

This news was blessedly sweet, and Francis smiled. He felt like he could have floated up to the ceiling, but he restrained himself. Not that he couldn't look happy in front of Disco, but he didn't want to look too happy.

Disco had been sweeping the last of the gravy from his plate with a slice of cutlet when he stopped suddenly and turned to Francis.

"You didn't hear anything, did you? About the Hudsons, what might have happened?"

Francis shook his head. "If I do, you'll be the first to know, my friend."

He was already thinking ahead about resuming his throne, but as he looked at how distracted Disco was, he grew concerned. Aside from the trouble with the new field director, Disco was having trouble with his longtime partner, Anderson. He and Disco, who had worked as a team for Francis and Larry, had not been getting along for a number of months now. Francis suspected that Anderson had suddenly discovered a conscience and was having severe regrets about his involvement with Francis and Larry.

"How's Anderson these days?"

"I don't even talk to him. I invited a bunch of guys from the office to my wedding, but not Anderson. I don't trust him at all now. It wouldn't surprise me if he's sucking up to the new field director."

"Like I told you before," Francis said. "The guy's probably got a case of the guilts. You should keep an eye on him."

Disco finished his glass of wine and brought his plates into the kitchen where he rinsed and loaded them into the dishwasher. "I've got to get back downtown, but like I said, the bottom line is that you don't have to concern yourself with the indictments. Either you or Larry. Let him know for me if you see him. Apparently he's been ignoring them anyway. He's been seen all over town this week."

"I appreciate the news, Disco."

"Of course I wouldn't go strolling down Broadway just yet. There's your dad's murder. Until they catch the guy who did it, you're still going to be wanted for questioning, and that's as good as being wanted for murder as far as how free you are to move about in public. So wherever you're hiding, I suggest you stay there for a while."

Chapter Nine
"If you are a hammer, strike.
If you are an anvil, endure the beating."
—Anonymous

Buzzy woke in clean white sheets. The only sound he heard was the low smooth hum of a fan as it oscillated in a reassuring rhythm. His body felt rested and his soul quiet. It was such a peaceful feeling, one that he hadn't had for so many years or perhaps ever.

He sat up and looked around. It seemed like he could be in a hospital room, but he wasn't. Buzzy wondered what time it was, so he walked to the window and looked up at the sun. It was high in the sky, so it might be early afternoon.

Three stories below he saw the Southeast Expressway. Beyond it was Andrew Square at the western end of South Boston. Buzzy had checked into the Holiday Inn at four o'clock in the morning, paying fifty-five dollars for a room, adding a ten-dollar bribe so he'd be allowed to stay a few hours after the standard checkout time.

His conscious mind began to pick up where it left off before surrendering to sleep. As it did, the details of the previous day swirled around him and blew away his peace the way a storm rips the blossoms off a tree in spring.

Across the expressway, he saw a man on an apartment balcony staring at him. Buzzy jumped away from the window so he'd be out of view. Was the man looking at him or at something else? He found the cord to the window drapes and pulled them shut.

After taking a shower where the water temperature fluctuated between too hot and too cold, Buzzy put on his jeans and button-front shirt. When he looked at himself in the mirror, he saw the two sides of his shirt misaligned.

As he unbuttoned it, his fingers began shaking and he couldn't seem to work the first button. In frustration he ripped the shirt open, sending a few of the buttons bouncing across the carpet.

"Oh God," Buzzy said and sat down on the edge of the bed. He had to calm down and think. What was he going to do?

He only had thirty dollars left. Probably not enough for a bus ticket to New York City, not that he knew anybody there. His first idea was to get his hands on some money by going back to his Old Colony apartment and taking whatever Mikey had. However, that would be the first place Francis would be waiting for him, so that was suicide.

Instead of trying to find money to get away from Francis, Buzzy realized his best course of action was to seek protection from him right there in Boston. It would be just as good, and it would buy him time to put together a solid plan to leave this place forever.

Buzzy's friends couldn't protect him. Neither could the police. Buzzy knew that lots of Boston cops either looked the other way for Francis or collaborated with him in all kinds of activities from covering up crimes to intimidating people, even other cops.

Matthew couldn't protect him either, that was for sure. Which left only one person that was equal to or greater than Francis. Someone who Francis respected, someone whom he'd never dare to cross. His brother Jimmy. He was Buzzy's only hope, his only sanctuary. He had to get to Jimmy and plead his case.

If Jimmy wouldn't help, then Buzzy would only have one option left. Go to the police and confess. Why the fuck not? It would keep him alive, and maybe he'd get a good public lawyer to defend him.

If it came to that, he'd make sure to surrender to the state police. If he went to the Boston Police or even the FBI, who knows what would happen to him. There was a good chance he'd get murdered before he even got a trial. That kind of shit happened with Boston cops. Buzzy had seen it before.

He walked over to the window and peeked between the drapes. The man across the expressway was still staring. Francis would be paying people to look for him, Buzzy knew, and they could be anywhere and everywhere. Buzzy had to move quickly to avoid them.

The hotel had a complimentary breakfast table in its lobby. The coffee had been brewed at noon, almost two hours earlier, and sat in a large stainless steel container that would continue to cook it until three o'clock when a new batch would be brewed.

Buzzy placed a small Styrofoam cup under the spigot and began to pour. Because his hands were shaking, some of the hot liquid spilled onto his fingers and burned him. He threw the cup to the floor and kicked it under the table.

The front desk was located next to the snack stand, and when the clerk finished handling a phone reservation, he called over to Buzzy in a cheery voice.

"How's your day going?" the clerk asked.

Buzzy heard, "How's your life going?"

He gave the clerk an angry stare. "Fuck you!" he yelled, then grabbed a Danish left over from breakfast and headed out the front door.

The Red Line subway would take him downtown, and the nearest station was Andrew Square, but that was in South Boston. He didn't dare set foot there, so Buzzy walked the extra mile to the Columbia stop in Dorchester.

As cars drove by, Buzzy checked to see if the car or the driver looked familiar. If somebody spotted him, he wouldn't even know it until it was too late. A car would pull up and three or four guys would jump out and grab him. That's how he'd seen it work before.

He took a few bites of the Danish, which was past its prime. It also smelled like it had been dipped in gasoline. So much so that Buzzy couldn't manage another bite and tossed it in the gutter. He soon regretted taking those few bites because his stomach became unsettled.

At the intersection of Dorchester Avenue, Buzzy noticed a man talking on a pay phone. The man was staring at him. After crossing the street, Buzzy turned back and the man was still staring at him. Who was he and who was he talking to?

A steady breeze carried the chill of early fall, but Buzzy found himself sweating, and his heart was beating as fast as if he was in a cross-country race. At the entrance to the Columbia subway station, he knelt down and pressed his head against a dirty iron pole until a wave of nausea passed.

He had to force himself to stand up and step into the station, where he slid a five dollar bill through the mouse hole in the token window. He studied the man making change inside. It seemed as if he was intentionally taking too much time.

On the outdoor train platform, Buzzy felt a tremble return to his arms and spread to his legs. It was subtle, and he wondered if he was imagining it, but when he lifted his left foot slightly, he could see it tapping out a rhythm all on its own. He tried to make it stop but couldn't.

A big sign beside him showed a subway map on one side and a poster for an upcoming movie on the other. Buzzy grabbed hold of the sign, closed his eyes and tried to compose a prayer.

"Jesus and my mother in heaven and God, let me live through this shit that I've caused, and I'll live a life without ever hurting anyone again. I'll live without drugs, I won't sell them, I won't take them, I'll have a regular job, probably as a carpenter, which I've been thinking about for a long time. Now that I'm thinking about it, Jesus was a carpenter, so that might be a sign that I'm on the right road. As you know, Francis wants to kill me and I need you to protect me today and make Jimmy listen to what I have to say and believe me and not hold the murder against me if that's what he believes I did, which we know I did. I'll talk more about that later and explain, although you know about it and I have explained some of it before, but that's for later because I have to deal with this today and it's just not gonna work if you don't help me. If you do, I'll live the kind of life you know I should live, and I'll get rid of all the wrong things and live life right."

There was a rattling in the distance. It grew louder as the six-car train came into the station and stopped with a metallic screech. The doors all opened together, and Buzzy stepped inside a car that held only three other people. He was too anxious to sit, so he stood as the doors closed and the train jerked forward.

Here we go, Buzzy thought, all aboard. As the train sped ahead and plunged deep into a tunnel, Buzzy was already thinking about where in downtown Boston he could buy a couple of joints to take his wicked fucking edge off.

O'Brien's Tavern was on the ground floor of a small two-story brick building with a parking lot on either side. Matthew stopped in front of the first lot, which was covered with great splashes of shattered glass. The other lot was the same. He didn't want to get a flat tire today, so he parked the red Subaru across the street from the bar.

As Matthew knew, O'Brien's was not a good place for a woman to be, which is why he strongly insisted that Anne stay in Ipswich. She had insisted more strongly though. He was worried about leaving Anne alone without something to protect herself, so he told her to take along some kind of knife.

"Did you bring a knife?" he asked.

He had expected her to bring a steak knife or something from Joan's kitchen. Instead, Anne reached for a bag in the back seat and pulled out an enormous curving knife in a sheath covered with an etched silver tip and decorated with numerous silver medallions, including a depiction of a palace.

It was a Gurkha Kukri knife that Dylan had brought back from Nepal. Anne pulled the knife from its sheath and the curving metal blade shone when it caught the sunlight. Matthew could see how sharp the edge was.

"Jesus, I guess that's a knife," Matthew said, reassured that she would have some form of protection. He considered asking Anne if it was even legal to have a knife that long, but in the circumstances he didn't care.

"This won't take long," he said. "I should be out in five minutes, ten tops. If I can't convince Francis to leave Buzzy alone, I guess we can go to the cops. Not that it'll do any good."

As Matthew approached the front of O'Brien's, he removed his watch and tucked it into a pocket of his jeans. It was an expensive Swiss model, a birthday gift from Anne's mother, and he didn't want to lose any more gifts from her family. He opened the front door and stood there for a moment to let his eyes adjust to the dark tavern. Half a dozen guys sat at the bar to the right, and a few more at two of the tables.

Red, the broken-nose bartender was there, and he spotted Matthew right away. Matthew let the door close and calmly walked toward the stairway in the back room.

"Look who's here!" a voice called. "It's the mighty Matty Mo!" Matthew turned to his left and saw Connor standing in a front corner of the barroom, where a pinball machine was lighting up and pinging loudly as the ball rolled down, unplayed. "You were told not to come back here."

Matthew didn't respond.

"It sounds like somebody left their big mouth at home this morning," Connor said, followed with a cold stare.

Matthew remembered what he said to Connor the night before and considered insulting him again, but he wasn't as worked up as he had been.

"I don't see you leaving, Matty. Have you developed a hearing disorder?"

"I have something to tell my brother. Is he upstairs?"

"Well, as it turns out, your brother doesn't want any more messages from you. And he doesn't want you coming back here." Connor made a sweeping motion toward the door with his hand. "So adios, asshole."

Matthew didn't move, and Connor sensed something he didn't like. "You're out of your league here, Matty. Get the fuck out now."

Instead of turning to the door, Matthew headed for the stairway out back. Red had been watching and called out to Jackie, the guy who had been working the door the night before and was now bartending with Red.

Jackie was halfway down the long bar. As Matthew continued walking, Red walked a parallel course behind the bar. Matthew was coming up on Jackie, and recognized him as the guy playing scratch tickets on his first visit.

From beneath the bar Jackie retrieved a two-foot section of pipe. Matthew made as if to walk past him, then turned suddenly and snatched the pipe from Jackie. He swung it backhand at Jackie's head, but he pulled away in time. Matthew saw that Jackie was keeping his balance by holding onto the bar, so Matthew swung the pipe again and smashed it down on his right hand.

Everyone at the bar could hear the snapping of bones, followed by Jackie's scream. Matthew dropped the pipe and walked on. Red had to push Jackie against the bar to squeeze behind him, then hurried to catch Matthew.

Once he entered the back room, Matthew turned and waited for Red to come into view. When he did, Matthew surprised him with a quick left, followed by two more. Then he threw a right. Red blocked it before answering with a hard punch that knocked Matthew against the wall.

Matthew came back with a mix of punches, all of them fast and none of them hard, but they kept Red busy swatting them away. Matthew's goal was to back Red into the narrow space at the end of the bar, and it worked.

With the bar to his left and a wall at his right, Red was limited in the punches he could throw. Matthew pounded away at him while Red kept bumping his arms on the bar and wall. Matthew expected him to attack at some point.

When he finally charged, Matthew guessed he'd lead right. As he did, Matthew stepped up and shifted to his left, which left Red wide open to a left hook. It snapped Red's head to the side, and Matthew could see the light fading from his eyes. He finished with a hard right that dropped the bartender.

Matthew resumed his short journey to the stairway. Blood trickled from his forehead into his eye, and Matthew wiped it away. He flexed his hands open and closed. They were OK. Behind him he heard steps as Connor closed the distance between them. From the sound, Matthew judged that he wouldn't get to the stairway in time so he spun around.

Connor was right there and threw a flurry of fast jabs that Matthew could barely see. He stopped a few, but most of them hit home. One broke the skin on the inside of Matthew's mouth and he tasted blood. Lots of it. More blood flowed from his nose and onto his chin.

Connor was knocking him back easily, and all Matthew could do was play a weak defense. When he felt the wall against his back, Matthew reached for Connor's shirt and shoved him away to create some breathing room. Then he went at him, throwing two punches as hard and fast as he could. Connor easily ducked the first, but he was fighting a little too cocky and didn't pay attention to the second. He stepped right into the punch and it knocked him on his ass.

When he got up, Connor stopped fighting nice. Instead of peppering Matthew with jabs, he came in slowly and picked each punch. They were just as fast but much harder. The first one stung Matthew's cheek and the next slammed into his right ear and knocked him sideways. The third made Matthew see that quick flash of light that meant the fight was not going his way at all.

He decided the only way to beat Connor was to wrestle him to the floor where Matthew could use his weight. As he charged, Matthew saw Connor draw himself up straight. Then his whole body seemed to sink down. He was wondering what the fuck Connor was doing when he caught a dark blur out of the corner of his right eye. Connor's kick caught Matthew square on the side of the head and knocked him out. Matthew dropped straight back, banging his head on the cement floor as he landed.

The guys at the bar had been watching the fight silently from the edge of the room.

"Way to go, Connor," one said.

"You went easy on him," said another.

Connor wiped his brow and looked down at Matthew, who lay unconscious on his back.

"Kenny," Connor called and one of the guys stepped forward. "Come on, let's sit him against the wall."

They each grabbed an arm. "He's a heavy son of a bitch," Kenny groaned as they dragged Matthew across the room and propped him against the back wall. Connor didn't mind teaching someone a lesson when they disobeyed him in his own place, and Francis said it was OK to knock Matthew around. But if he had knocked Matthew's brain back into kindergarten, it could get complicated with Francis.

Outside, Anne had been counting off the minutes. Five passed. Then ten, but no Matthew. The next minute, she saw a man being led from the bar with an ice pack around his hand. He was followed by another holding a bloody rag to his head. Something had gone wrong, she felt, so she got out of the Subaru and walked across the parking lot.

She pulled the front door open and looked around the dim, smoky place for Matthew. She quickly realized there were more eyes looking her way. They were all men. She wondered how long it had been since a woman had been in the place, and if it was even allowed, which was still the case in some Boston bars.

Against the far back wall she noticed a man kneeling beside someone on the floor. When she recognized Matthew's jeans and sneakers, Anne had a sick feeling. She rushed to the back and surprised Connor, who was holding a wet rag to Matthew's head.

"Who are you?" Connor asked.

"I'm his wife."

Anne couldn't take her eyes off Matthew. His face was a mess. Both eyes were swollen, as well as a cheek. Connor had wiped away the blood flowing from Matthew's nose and mouth, but fresh blood took its place.

"He's unconscious," Anne said in a sharp, accusing tone.

Connor stood up. "He's coming around."

She took the rag from Connor's hand and knelt down. Matthew was breathing normally. At the sound of Anne's voice he opened his eyes. They had a glassy look. He was staring straight ahead, and when Anne called to him Matthew blinked and looked up at her but didn't say anything. He drew a finger through the trickle of blood beneath his nose.

Anne felt herself grow weak the same way she had when seeing her father at the hospital in Anchorage. She believed she survived that horrible experience because she had Matthew. Now Anne was looking down at his bloody face and her deepest fear came welling up: that she would lose Matthew, too.

Anne suddenly saw the situation with a clear and upsetting perspective. They had come home to get married, that's all, but they got caught up in problems that had nothing to do with them. It was crazy. She looked around the bar, at the men staring back at her with indifference or contempt, and knew that she'd never be able to forget this ugly place as long as she lived.

Anne stood up and yelled at Connor. "You did this, didn't you?"

Connor waved his hand dismissively. "Hey, I warned him. Twice," he said. "He'll have a headache, and he deserves it. He's becoming a fucking headache to his brother."

Anne was as tall as Connor. She stepped up to him and squinted. "You have no idea what he's done for his brothers. All of them. Especially Francis. Why do you think Matthew is here right now?"

Anne started to turn her attention back to Matthew but swung back for one more shot. She put a finger to Connor's face. "I know you did this to him, and I swear to God if he isn't OK ... "

She left the thought unfinished because she heard Matthew making a sound. She knelt down. "Matt, can you hear me? Do you know where we are? We're in South Boston. We're at O'Brien's."

From above, Connor issued an unrepentant response. "He got exactly what he asked for, coming back. He knew better than that. Now, do you want a hand getting him out of here or not?"

Anne turned Matthew's face toward her. He blinked a few times, then drew a deep breath, releasing it with a slow groan. She cleaned off the fresh blood with the rag, then noticed how filthy it was and how it stank of stale beer.

"Don't you have something clean?" Anne asked.

"If you're gonna get picky … " Connor began, but he stopped to dodge the wet rag that Anne threw at his face.

"I will be picky!" she yelled. "Now get a clean cloth or get some paper towels."

Connor went off muttering something about the female anatomy. When he returned with a stack of brown paper towels, Matthew was able to speak.

His world had a staticky look to it, but he could see the bar in front of him, the stairway to the left. He was at O'Brien's. He saw Anne and he saw Connor, and he remembered coming there that afternoon. He was sitting on the floor and he felt a throbbing pain on the side of his head. He was in a fight with the broken-nose bartender, then he walked into the back room, turned around and Connor was there. Oh shit, he realized, I got knocked out.

Matthew couldn't be sure how much time had passed. "I know where I am," he said slowly. "Let's get out of here."

They helped Matthew stand, and Anne walked him slowly to the front door. As he passed the bar, faces turned to Matthew. There was nervous laughter. One guy pointed at him angrily. Who are these guys, Matthew wondered, and what are they doing with their lives?

Connor stayed at the front door as Anne guided Matthew across the parking lot. Halfway to the car, Connor called out a warning about not coming back to the bar. Without turning around, Matthew replied with his middle finger.

He directed Anne along the confusing route that led them to City Hospital in the South End. Matthew drifted in and out on the ten-minute ride, and Anne had to call his name or give him a poke to bring him back enough to say which way to go.

She spotted the hospital a block away, then the emergency room entrance. They walked into a waiting room as spacious as an airport terminal with a high ceiling and rows and rows of seats, half of them filled with people in varying degrees of pain, which could be judged by the expression on their faces or the sounds they made.

"They've renovated the place," Matthew said looking around. "They did a nice job." He slumped into a seat while Anne went to the admitting station and provided all of the necessary information.

"It might be a little while," she said when she returned. "They're busy."

"This is nothing," Matthew said. "You should see it on a Saturday night."

"You've been here before?" Anne asked.

Before Matthew could answer, the swinging doors to the ambulance bay burst open, and a gurney was rushed in with a paramedic on either side. Its passenger was a squirming, moaning young black man whose blood showed everywhere.

"Gunshot," Matthew said.

"Is there another hospital nearby? I don't like this place."

Anne was getting more and more agitated. Matthew took her hand. "It'll be alright. They're very good here. The line moves fast."

Matthew was feeling tired and just wanted to close his eyes. An hour passed as people were directed to the examination rooms, emerging with bandages, casts, prescriptions. Matthew drifted in and out without really sleeping. With his eyes closed, he heard everything in the emergency room and it all sounded like a dream. He occasionally opened his eyes and watched the people who had been treated and were going home.

He spotted Jackie the bartender, who was sporting a crisp new cast on his right hand. Matthew could tell it was made of the old heavy plaster, the kind you got when you didn't have insurance to pay for the spiffier lightweight ones.

Matthew pointed him out to Anne and told her that Jackie had wanted to use a pipe on him. They watched him struggling to make his signature on some forms with his healthy hand. "He won't be writing any long letters for a while," Matthew said. "Assuming he knows how to write at all."

Jackie was heading for the exit when he spotted Matthew. He came marching toward Matthew, who knew nothing would come of it but words. Every second Jackie spent mouthing off would only make him feel smaller. Matthew learned long ago that when you lose, you keep your mouth shut and chalk it up.

Anne was watching Jackie, too, and as he drew closer she reached into her jacket and drew out the monster knife she had showed Matthew earlier. With Jackie ten feet away, she stood up and pointed the blade at him face-high, looking very much like a fencer. Jackie stopped dead in his tracks, and his eyes grew big. Matthew smiled and gave him a little wave with the tips of his fingers. Jackie considered the situation, then turned around and left.

A security guard appeared from out of nowhere and in a second had snatched the knife from Anne's hand. He was a very big man and his booming Haitian voice gave Anne as much of a shock as his sudden appearance. "You don't bring that in here! What's wrong with you? You want to get arrested?"

Anne pointed to the knife, now in the guard's hand, and protested weakly. "Hey, that's mine."

"You pick it up when you leave. Over there." The guard pointed to the security office at the far end of the waiting area. As he walked away, the guard said, "Crazy bitch."

"He took my knife," Anne said, unable to get over the guard's audacity.

Matthew couldn't hold it back and burst into a laugh that startled everyone nearby.

Anne looked down at him. "Shut up, Mahoney."

* * * * *

Jimmy spent his morning handling the challenges normally faced by Peg, who had volunteered to help in setting up for the annual fall crafts fair at St. Monica's.

His morning duties began with waking all the kids and making sure they were washed and dressed properly. The exception was Kyle, who had woken at four in the morning with an upset stomach. Jimmy suspected he had brought home the virus from his meeting with the *Boston Herald* reporter the evening before. Next, he made pancakes, a popular choice with the kids and the only breakfast Jimmy could produce with any competence.

Before walking the kids to school, Jimmy cleaned the dishes and put a load of laundry in the basement washer. A pile of clean, dry towels sat on top of the dryer. Jimmy folded them.

He had left a radio playing loudly in the kitchen, and as he climbed the basement stairs with the towels, he heard the talk show host welcoming Senator George Corbin from Wellesley. This could be very telling, Jimmy thought.

The radio host said that Senator Corbin would now deliver a response to Senator Mahoney's Wellesley plan. Jimmy stopped and listened to Corbin's agitated voice. His only disappointment was that the radio station apparently had cut Corbin off before the rant could fully blossom. No matter—the first leg of the gambit was coming along well. Corbin's unraveling had begun.

After bringing the kids to school, Jimmy picked up a few groceries for dinner. At home, he checked on Kyle and put the laundry in the dryer. It had been threatening to quit for weeks, and when Jimmy turned the dial it finally did. He called the repairman, and he was left to hang the wash on a jury-rigged clothesline running back and forth across the basement.

Jimmy had warned Senate President Hurley that Beacon Hill would be stormier than the blizzard of '78 on Friday, and that he shouldn't show up at the State House until the afternoon session scheduled for three o'clock. The two men would be the focus of intense questioning from the media as to whether the legislative body was serious about moving forward with Jimmy's plan for a regional waste disposal site in Wellesley.

There also would be a lot of high-pitched squealing from those senators representing districts in and around Wellesley, a hysteria more easily managed within a formal Senate session.

At two o'clock Jimmy arrived at the State House. He noticed that the news crews were back. They were just like sharks, he thought, immediately on the scene at the slightest hint of political blood in the water. The cameras caught a smiling Senator Mahoney, briefcase in hand, striding confidently through the Hall of Flags and up the main staircase. He headed straight for the president's office, where a discussion was taking place that could be heard all the way down the hall.

Despite Jimmy's advice, Hurley had arrived at ten o'clock and had been under nonstop siege first by the media, then by fellow politicians, influential residents of Wellesley and finally by the Gang of Five, who stood in a semicircle around Hurley's desk firing off nightmarish scenarios should the Wellesley plan move forward. Republicans would take over both chambers in the next election with millions of dollars pouring into the enemy's campaigns from the bottomless coffers of Wellesley's well-to-do.

Jimmy stepped into the office and interrupted Michael Blaine, the senator from Waltham and one of Corbin's Gang of Five. Blaine's family had close ties to the construction industry and managed a lot of the condo conversions in the fashionable Back Bay section of Boston, as well as the elegant brownstones along Beacon Street in Brookline.

"Excuse me, Mike. I need to remind Carl of a meeting we have before today's session."

When Blaine turned around, Jimmy got a glimpse at Hurley. He looked like one of those TV wrestlers who had been body slammed by an opponent taking leaps from the top of the ropes. Corbin was there leading his gang, and when he heard Jimmy's voice, he spun around and exploded. "I'm going to crush you, Mahoney. You'll be lucky to get a job scraping shit from hotel toilets when I finish with you."

"Throw in three weeks of vacation and a good health plan and I'll think about it, George," Jimmy said. He caught the hint of a smile from Blaine.

"You son of a bitch!" Corbin screamed at Jimmy.

"Alright, alright," Hurley said standing up and assuming a towering presence that demanded attention if not respect. "That's enough of that. You don't carry on that way in this office or on the Senate floor. I've warned you about it before, George."

Corbin managed a degree of regret. "Forgive me, Carl. You have to understand how I feel." He pointed a hand toward the west and his disturbed constituency. "A lot of people are very upset, and I'm hearing from all of them. It's a truly mad proposal. Perfectly insane."

Hurley cut him off. "We'll discuss its merits in session. That's at three o'clock. In the meantime, get a grip on yourself, George. We're not a mob. We're a legislative body."

If the discussion had to be postponed until the formal session, Corbin would manage to restrain himself. "Very well, we're finished here then," he said and left the room. The rest of the gang followed.

"Close the door, Jimmy," Hurley said and collapsed back on his chair. "What a goddamn ugly day this has been. There are a lot of people very upset by all this, and I'm afraid I have to say this is now looking like a very bad idea. The goal is supposed to be to swing some caucus votes your way. I think you've succeeded in losing some. This maneuver is stirring up a lot of people, and events might be moving beyond our control. God knows what's going to break out in session today."

Jimmy expected he was going to have a struggle pushing Hurley through the day, but now it was looking even tougher. He sounded as if he was about to give up on Jimmy's gambit. He had to get Hurley back in the fight.

"I told you yesterday that this would break like an avalanche. We were able to choose when the avalanche started, but we can't control where every rock lands."

"I know where they're landing. On Corbin's head. The man is unstable. Did you hear him on the radio this morning? He's either a very good actor or he's reached his breaking point. Was that your intention, Jimmy? To push Corbin over the edge?"

"I've tried to work with the man for years, Carl. You know that. I've gotten nothing back but animosity."

"So this is part of your strategy? I don't see how it can play out in your favor or mine."

Jimmy replied in a reassuring tone, "Look, yesterday Corbin and his gang were united by their opposition to me as a potential Senate president. That's been their purpose, their reason for being. That changed this morning. Those four are now united behind Corbin for the purpose of opposing the Wellesley plan. It's still a movement to oppose me, but now it's linked to that plan."

"You've lost me."

Jimmy explained again how he expected things to play out in session and managed to bring Hurley back on board. Jimmy left the president's office and went straight to the Senate chamber.

It was located front and center in the State House, directly beneath the gold dome, with an ornate sunburst ceiling, unchanged since the building first opened almost two centuries before. The chamber's vaulted niches held busts of statesmen including President Washington and France's Marquis de Lafayette, who paid a visit to the State House in 1825. The upper part of the high-ceilinged chamber, where the public gallery was located, had colonial-style columns and balustrades.

Thirty-nine of the forty senators sat at a circular table, with a series of desks in the middle for clerks. Below a large gilded eagle sat the president's rostrum where President Hurley, the fortieth senator, sat.

Junior sat at his officially assigned seat with a newspaper spread out in front of him, an egg salad sandwich to one side and black coffee to the other.

"Are you ready for today's ride, Jimmy?"

"Of course."

"And après le deluge?"

"Calm waters, let's hope. I've got a favor to ask, Junior."

Junior finished his sandwich and closed the newspaper, holding up the front page image of Jimmy posing beside a map with the proposed Wellesley plan. "A very good picture of you, Jimmy. I imagine Corbin enjoyed seeing your smiling face."

"Let's hope so, Junior. I'd like you to offer support for the plan during today's session. You don't have to throw yourself behind it specifically, just the concept of considering all options in searching for a regional solution."

"Easy enough," Junior said.

"Corbin will be throwing knives at you and he won't hold back, so you'll want to be wearing your thickest skin. On my cue, I want you to go to Blaine and comment that it might be time for him and the other three in the gang to reconsider their allegiance to Corbin."

The chamber began to fill as senators arrived and took their seats. At the rostrum Jimmy joined Hurley, who slammed down the gavel.

"The Senate is now in session. Please be seated. On today's agenda is debate on alternate sites for regional waste disposal. Debate will begin. The chair recognizes the senator from Dorchester."

Junior rose and thanked the president. He began by referencing the article in the *Boston Herald*. Corbin sat a few seats from Junior. On his desk he had placed a large stack of newspapers purchased from a vending machine with one quarter. As Junior spoke, Corbin held up pages of the *Herald* and slowly tore them into long strips. The ripping sound created a noisy distraction.

"As we grow as a region so does the amount of trash we produce. We have to ask ourselves … " Rip. "whether we want to create a hundred different solutions … " Rip. "or one solution that minimizes the impact on our environment … " Rip. "and makes the most efficient use of our limited resources … " Rip.

When Corbin had amassed a large enough pile of shredded newspaper in front of him, he tossed the paper strips into the air and watched the fluttering snakes fall to the floor. Some senators stared at him in amazement. Some were annoyed, some were amused. All were definitely distracted. The floor in front of Corbin began to look like a street where a ticker tape parade had passed by.

At one point, Corbin turned to the Senate's public gallery where three people sat, a pair of college exchange students from Finland and Bernie Harrington, Mayor Sullivan's adviser dispatched to take note of the waste disposal debate and report back.

"You're looking at the finest Senate money can buy," Corbin announced to the gallery.

Junior continued speaking and Corbin continued ripping. Until Junior mentioned Corbin's district. "As long as every town and city in the Commonwealth continues to produce trash, no town or city should consider itself off limits for consideration as a possible waste disposal site. That includes Wellesley."

Corbin dropped the paper from his hands and jumped to his feet. "What else are we to expect from a Mahoney crony? The man's in the pocket of the health care industry. He's raking in thousands with every patient admitted to Boston City Hospital. He's bought and paid for … "

Hurley slammed down his gavel and called out to Corbin. "The senator from Wellesley will refrain from comments that impugn the character of fellow senators."

Corbin threw a glance at the rostrum, then returned to his seat. In a low voice, he said, "I've got a refrain for you that starts with 'br' and ends with 'ibe,' my dear corruptician from Marblehead." From his stack of newspapers Corbin drew another handful and resumed his shredding.

Next to speak was Senator Michael Blaine from Waltham, a member of Corbin's gang. He raised questions about the feasibility of the Wellesley plan, pointing out that even the mayor of Boston acknowledged the need for the city to assume responsibility for the disposal of its own trash.

Other senators weighed in on either side of the issue. Those representing cities and towns beyond the metropolitan area of greater Boston voiced stiff opposition. Those from districts in and around Boston already accommodating incinerators, power plants, airports and landfills enjoyed the opportunity to criticize the wealthy suburbs.

As senators spoke, Corbin continued his shredding. He made accusations against virtually every senator present, beginning inaudibly but increasing in volume until his defamations could be heard throughout the chamber. Following the statement by the senator from Chelsea, Corbin shouted, "You want to clean up this state, you can start with loan sharks and bookmakers in Chelsea. But no, we don't want to do that. How could we finance our ski trips to the Swiss Alps if Chelsea were made clean?"

Hurley's gavel came crashing down, and Corbin was admonished once again. "The senator from Wellesley will mind his comments. There will not be another warning, and I mean that."

Corbin rolled his eyes and tossed a handful of shredded paper high in the air. A silence followed the last piece of paper touching ground, and it became clear to Jimmy that the atmosphere inside the chamber had altered. He scanned the faces of senators and found many of them looking at Corbin, no longer in amusement but in annoyance, even disgust.

Jimmy nodded to Junior, who walked over to Senator Michael Blaine. They had a brief discussion in which Junior suggested to Blaine that he might want to rethink aligning himself with Corbin on any issues, that if Corbin continued in his self-destructive behavior, then Blaine and others in the gang would likely suffer damage to their reputations and political aspirations.

Waste disposal was only one issue and not worth losing a career over, Junior counseled. On serious reflection, nobody really believed that a waste disposal site would be located in Wellesley. Junior suggested Blaine pass these thoughts on to the other gang members. Junior sat down and Jimmy watched Blaine walk over and talk to each of the three.

Corbin caught none of this. He had no idea how the mood in the chamber had shifted. Jimmy asked to speak and was granted ten minutes by the chair. He rose and thanked all of the senators who had spoken either for or against the debate. Corbin picked up the last remaining *Boston Herald*. With each tear, he let out a loud "ha!"

"I suppose," Jimmy said, "that if we are all to be taken seriously in our bid to clean up the region, we should show that we're capable of at least keeping the Senate chamber clean." Jimmy waved in the general direction of Corbin's pile of shredded paper, which had grown almost a foot high on the floor in front of him. Several senators responded with laughter.

The laughter interrupted Corbin, and he looked around the chamber to find what or who was being laughed at. He quickly understood that he was the object of ridicule. Jimmy beamed a broad grin at Corbin.

It was the smallest of sparks but enough to ignite an eruption. The last shreds of newspaper were rocketed higher and wider, like the magnificent display of a fireworks finale. As the pieces fluttered and twirled in their descent, Corbin released a burst of bile that surprised even Jimmy.

"You're a malicious maggot, Mahoney. I know what you're trying to do with your garbage scheme, and others also see it for what it is. A personal attack on me. Nobody takes it for more than that. You will never, and I mean never, succeed in working your bigoted schemes on Wellesley or Weston or Woburn or Waltham or any other of the blessed communities where you are not worthy to step and where you will never be welcome. Every decent person in this state rues the day when your blood was allowed to step onto these shores."

Jimmy listened calmly as Corbin denounced South Boston as a fortress of resistance, an enclave of hostility, an insular peninsula. His rambling speech was laced with references to busing, intended to resurrect every ill sentiment his fellow senators might have ever had about South Boston.

Instead of the intended effect, Corbin's speech produced calls of disapproval from one senator, then another. The gavel slammed down once, then again. Hurley called for order. Corbin spread his arms wide as he addressed his fellow senators.

"His brother is a gangster, a murderer allowed to live among us because of the collusion of that senator," Corbin said pointing to Jimmy. "They've created a network of espionage. They have state-of-the-art surveillance devices to listen in on all our communications. We're all compromised by their evil. The other brother circles the State House in a black bus as I speak. They are malicious. Evil and malicious. The Mahoneys aim to desecrate our city on a hill. They threaten the purity of the Commonwealth."

Senator Blaine had made his way over to Corbin and called out for him to please stop, to sit down and be quiet, and not let the discussion drift and unravel, but it had already done both. Hearing Blaine's polite suggestion, Corbin turned on him.

"I will not stop. I will not sit down. What are you, my schoolmaster? What happened to your backbone, Blaine? Are you afraid of what this will do to your relationship with the construction trade? Are you so deep in their pockets that you can no longer separate payola from principle?"

The chamber was in an uproar and neither the shouting nor the pounding of the gavel proved an effective damper. Jimmy turned to Hurley, whose face was red with a passion he had not seen in the Senate president for quite a while.

It was time to strike.

* * * * *

Buzzy had wandered through the old Combat Zone and theater district before finding someone to sell him a small bag of pot. Then he walked to Boston Common and found a secluded bench overlooking the frog pond. Empty of both frogs and water, it was a shallow cement dish where kids on rollerblades were playing street hockey.

Buzzy looked around for cops before rolling two fat joints. He smoked one and waited for his mind to rise and glide to clarity. He would be explaining himself to Jimmy soon and he wanted to reconstruct the certainty he had when he killed their father. How necessary it was, how justified. Jimmy was smart, and Buzzy knew he'd need to present the reasons to him in a clear, smart way. He also had to make Jimmy understand how crazy Francis could be.

He watched the street hockey game for a while, then decided to smoke the second joint. On the frog pond, kids were swirling around each other. They had to be about twelve, and Buzzy wondered what it would cost to buy back all the years he had wasted since he was their age. Would he have to pay with money or bargain with the years of his future? Or maybe promise to become the perfect Catholic?

"I'll dedicate my life to God. I'll do good deeds until I'm sixty-five. Or longer. Nothing but favors for everyone from the moment I wake up until the moment I go to sleep, and if I'm about to go to sleep and someone needs my bed, I'll give it to them and sleep someplace else or sleep standing up or not sleep at all. Imagine that. A life with no drugs or badness of any kind. Every decision would be one that led to something good."

Buzzy liked the idea. He let God know about it, then asked for an answer. Is it a deal, God? Tell me. I'll wait, but I can't wait very long.

Buzzy smoked the second joint down to where it burned his fingers. He closed his eyes and tried to push all distracting thoughts from his mind. His mother, his mistakes, money, coke, pussy, death, Miss Puerto Rico runner-up, sleep, food, sins, weaknesses, money again, Matthew, laziness, Miss Puerto Rico runner-up's sister, his mother again, weed, bigger sins, food again.

It wasn't working. His mind was now more cluttered than when he had started. He slowed his breathing down to relax but felt himself getting lightheaded and short of breath. One of the kids playing hockey tripped and scraped his hands while crashing to the cement. Some of them wore gloves, but this one didn't. The kid sent out a scream and it went right through Buzzy. He jumped off the park bench and tensed up as the kid howled in pain and the blood ran down his palms and over his wrists.

Buzzy felt a tingling across his palms. He also felt like he could hear his heart beating in his left ear. He looked down at the stub of the joint and flicked it away. What the fuck is in this weed, he wondered. He turned around slowly to see if a cop was watching him because it felt like the heart beating in his ear had said so.

Buzzy took a few deep breaths and shook his body, trying to get rid of whatever had crawled inside him. He spun around again, saw the golden dome of the State House and thought he better go now before he forgot why he was here. God was not getting back to him on any deals yet, so it might have to be Jimmy or nothing.

Traffic was moving slowly on Beacon Street, and as a cop car passed Buzzy noticed the cop looking at him. After a few more steps, Buzzy glanced over and saw a cab where he thought the cop car had been. The dome glowed golden in the sunshine and Buzzy smelled popcorn coming from a vendor at an entrance to Boston Common. The vendor looked familiar. When he turned around, Buzzy saw that it was Francis. Just as Buzzy began to freak out, the vendor stopped being Francis.

He climbed up the granite steps in the front of the State House, feeling like he might be getting nauseous again. Inside it was cool and the air smelled like the old library at Boston Latin School. He found the information desk and asked where he could find Senator Mahoney's office.

The woman behind the desk had thin white hair that was fluffy and high like cotton candy. Buzzy could see her scalp shining below, even the freckles and bumps on it. She looked really old and as she referred to the booklets and papers in front of her, Buzzy noticed that her head was shaking back and forth.

It was the kind of shaking old people did, something beyond their control. Buzzy thought this might be God's response to his deal. It was finally coming through all that space between heaven and earth, but the news was not good because the woman was shaking her head "no." Could a "no" somehow mean "yes" or "let's talk some more"?

"You'd have to sign in with security and they would call the senator, but I'm afraid he's not available right now. The Senate is in session. That's where he would be."

"How do I get into the session?"

The woman smiled and the subtle shaking picked up speed.

"You can't go into the session, but you can watch from the public gallery. That's at the top of that stairway." She pointed into the Hall of Flags. "Two flights up and you go to the left. At the door you'll see a guard dressed in a white uniform."

White, like an angel from heaven, Buzzy thought. "Thank you," he said. As he crossed through the Hall of Flags, he instinctively patted his pockets the way he always did before entering a place where he had to walk past anybody with a badge. He had his money, all eight bucks of it, a lighter, rolling papers and what was left of the pot. He stopped and looked around for a bathroom or a trash can where he could get rid of it.

Standing still he became a little lightheaded. Fuck it, I don't have time, he decided. He was sweating when he reached the top of the stairway, where he saw a man in uniform to his left. He was a member of the Capitol Police, not a guard but a cop with a badge and a gun, which meant he was the real deal. The cop wore a crisp white shirt and stood in the open doorway to the gallery. His attention was focused on the scene unfolding on the Senate floor below.

As Buzzy approached, he heard loud noise pouring through the doorway, the kind of shouting and banging you'd hear when you reached the end of the long ramps at Boston Garden and the explosion of a Boston Bruins hockey game really hit you. The cop was so focused that Buzzy surprised him when he tapped his shoulder. He stepped out of the doorway and gave Buzzy an up-and-down look.

"Greetings," Buzzy said as he passed through the door, and immediately wondered why the hell he had said that. He never said "greetings." I'm like the Martian visiting Earth in that Bugs Bunny cartoon, he thought.

The gallery had four rows of chairs that sloped down like the balcony in a theater. There were three other people in the gallery, all standing in the front row. Buzzy went to the opposite end of the gallery to be as far from the cop as possible.

A deafening sound rose from the floor of the Senate chamber, where the session was in chaos. People were yelling, one senator was tossing strips of newspaper into the air while another one was slamming down a gavel so hard it hurt Buzzy's ears. So this is government, Buzzy thought. He searched for Jimmy, and it took a couple of minutes to find him.

First Buzzy tried waving an arm in the air to catch Jimmy's attention and when that didn't work, he began waving both arms and then calling down to Jimmy. The three people in the gallery turned to stare at Buzzy. Up to this moment, they had been spectators to a rare public meltdown of the legislative process, and they worried whether it was something that could rise with the air and infect people in the gallery.

Soon Buzzy was screaming at the top of his lungs and he saw a few faces on the floor turn and look up. He saw Jimmy's face turn and gaze at the gallery for a moment before looking away again.

Buzzy reached into his pocket and threw his lighter at Jimmy. It struck President Hurley on the side of his head. Buzzy continued screaming as he reached into his pockets for loose change, which he threw, followed by the small bag of pot, which only made it halfway to the rostrum before falling to the floor, and finally his paper money, which made a slow fluttering descent.

A waist-high railing ran in front of the first row. Buzzy climbed onto it and pressed his hands to the ceiling. A few more faces had turned from the floor and were pointing up to the gallery. Buzzy's silhouette formed a dramatic "X" as he looked down. In his stomach he felt the space between himself and the floor, then looked to the rostrum where Hurley held the side of his head with one hand and slammed down the gavel with the other.

"Jimmy, he's going to kill me! Francis is going to kill me! Help me. God, please help me!" Buzzy screamed out. Jimmy looked up. This time he continued looking as the Capitol Police officer who had been standing in the doorway finally reached Buzzy. He grabbed hold of Buzzy's belt and pulled him down to the floor of the gallery.

"Get the fuck off me!" Buzzy swung around and punched the cop on the side of the head. He let go of Buzzy's belt. They both jumped to their feet, but Buzzy jumped faster and shoved the cop over the back of a gallery seat, which left him trapped with his head on the floor and his feet flailing in the air.

Buzzy climbed back onto the railing and his hands slipped slightly on the ceiling so that he pitched forward as if to fall before his palms finally held firm. Buzzy felt the air below him all the way to the chamber floor and a tingle ran from his back up to his scalp.

More senators had now turned to the gallery and so did President Hurley, who pointed the gavel toward Buzzy and called for the Capitol Police officer stationed at the Senate entrance to clear the gallery. The officer was already on his radio calling more officers to the scene. At the same time, Bernie Harrington was climbing over the Finnish exchange students to enter the fray.

Buzzy heard footsteps behind him rushing down the gallery steps. He looked below to the floor, and felt the tingle rise. Nothing is something and something is nothing. My nothingness.

Buzzy let go of the ceiling and leaned forward into space. He heard a scream below and felt himself jerked back by his belt once again as Bernie pulled him to the gallery floor. The officers arrived.

Buzzy lunged for one of their guns. He tried pulling it from its holster, but it was locked in there solid. When he tried to pull on the trigger, it wouldn't move. His hand was pulled away from the gun and his arm was twisted behind him so violently, it felt like he had received an electric shock to his shoulder.

Two officers pinned Buzzy down and pressed his face onto the gallery floor. They handcuffed him, tied plastic strips around his ankles to keep him from kicking and carried him from the gallery as if he were a rolled-up rug.

Up the gallery steps and down the hallway, Buzzy watched the floor passing beneath him. His eyes were bulging out from the pressure in his head and a long line of spit trailed from his mouth to the floor. Over and over he thought, I have no father, I have no brothers, I have no God. All I had left was my nothing, and now they've taken that from me.

* * * * *

The disturbance in the public gallery had distracted the senators from their own drama on the chamber floor. Many had gone silent. It left Corbin, who was so focused in denouncing his former ally Blaine that he was unaware of the gallery disturbance, the only voice still blasting away. Hurley's gavel arm lay slack for the moment as he drew a hand across the side of his head. His hand showed no blood, but the spot where Buzzy's lighter struck home was goddamn sore.

Jimmy thought he recognized the lunatic in the gallery as Buzzy, but he couldn't be sure. Climbing onto the gallery railing and threatening to jump was not the act of someone in their right mind. Jimmy knew about Buzzy's involvement in drugs, and it would not have surprised him if Buzzy had been under their influence. None of Buzzy's words had reached Jimmy however, and the reason why he would pull such a stunt would have to remain a mystery until Jimmy could finish dealing with his own crisis.

The general sense in the chamber was that the disturbance in the gallery was either linked to Corbin's own outburst or caused by it. Corbin rambled on, denouncing the three remaining members of the Gang of Five despite the fact that they had said nothing against him.

Rather than responding directly to Corbin, senators began calling on President Hurley to take action.

"And let's not forget the games that Senator Bornstein likes to play when his wife assumes he is working late at the State House," Corbin said. "It's at the Haymarket where she would likely find him, and we're not talking about the famous square downtown where patriots gave their lives for this great city, but the Haymarket Bar in the Combat Zone where young men dress as Farrah Fawcett and Tina Turner and dance across a stage all aglitter."

Jimmy stood close to Hurley and spoke into his ear.

Hurley slammed down the gavel. It struck with a cracking sound that resonated in the chamber. "George Corbin!" Hurley boomed.

Some senators did not immediately recognize the significance of the two words. Those who did were stunned. This was a historic moment, albeit a sad one. According to the rules of the Massachusetts State Senate, laid down in a century when herds of cattle and sheep grazed on Boston Common, a senator must always be addressed by the chair as "the senator from" their district.

If a senator was addressed by his own name, it meant that he was, as of that moment, expelled from the Senate and could not return unless voted back by a majority. In the history of the Massachusetts Senate, only one member had ever been expelled, but Corbin was the first to be expelled by having his name called in the chamber during formal session.

Hurley continued, "George Corbin, you are expelled from the Senate. Gather your personal effects and leave." There were three Capitol Police officers at the entrance to the Senate. Hurley instructed them, "Prepare to assist Mr. Corbin should he fail to vacate the chamber as soon as possible."

At long last, Corbin was speechless. He stared at Hurley and swayed where he stood. A smattering of claps could be heard, but most present were either too shocked or saddened by the moment to display their approval of the president's action. Hurley stared back at Corbin, confident that the crisis had passed and that maybe the monkey clinging so tenaciously to his back had finally lost its grip.

It took a moment for Corbin to distinguish his possessions from the debris in front of him. When he did, he marched toward the chamber door, where the officers stood ready. It was a long silent walk and when Corbin was a mere five steps from leaving the world of politics forever, he turned and sent a parting shot. "I gladly leave the filth of this Senate. Getting thrown out of this place is like being thrown out of a whorehouse."

The chamber fell silent before a voice called from the other side of the Senate floor, "How dare you." It was Senator Reid Manning of Easton, the head of the Republican minority in the Senate and among the legislature's most respected members, if not the most. Manning was a scholar of Senate history and one of the brightest ever to serve in the body. The esteem everyone held him in, including Corbin, and the obvious distress in Manning's voice, held Corbin frozen to the floor five steps from oblivion.

Manning rose to his feet and spoke with even more gravitas than usual. "How dare you refer to this institution so crudely. You ought to be ashamed of yourself. I've listened to you malign nearly every senator present. You've said things that are unfair, untrue and cruel. Perhaps on your way out, you'll notice all the portraits, statues, busts and murals. John Hancock, John Quincy Adams, James Otis, Paul Revere, Samuel Adams and all the other patriots who devoted their lives to governing this state from its infancy into the complicated world we live in today. You couldn't possibly appreciate their sacrifices or you would never have revealed such fathomless ignorance before us today."

A silence intervened with every senator captive to Manning's devastating rebuke. He continued, "Do people make mistakes here? Yes. That's a symptom of being human and we are fated to fail ourselves and each other no matter how hard we try not to. As flawed as we may be, we are not flawed as you have charged us. And you make your charges knowing full well that they are not true. I'm afraid the only reputation you have succeeded in tarnishing today is your own."

Manning turned to address Hurley. "This is a difficult step to take, but it's unavoidable. This institution cannot function if it is eaten away from within by abusive conduct among its members. Mr. President, you have my full endorsement and you'll receive the support of my party for the difficult measure you've been forced to take."

It was a defining moment. Had the mood not been so somber, there would have been applause. Hurley thanked Senator Manning and turned to the doorway where Corbin had stood. He was gone, and with him Hurley's problems. Aside from the commotion in the public gallery, Jimmy's gambit had played out as he hoped it would. The four remaining members of the Gang of Five were now discredited by their association with Corbin, an alliance they all regretted having made. As a result, Jimmy expected them all to abandon their resistance to his candidacy when it was brought up in caucus.

Hurley brought down the gavel. "The Senate will now stand in recess for approximately one hour." He checked his watch. "The session will resume promptly at six-thirty. At this time, I would like to direct all Democratic members of the Senate to the president's office, where we'll convene a caucus in twenty minutes. Please do not be late."

The chamber emptied as senators dashed off to make phone calls, grab a bite to eat or a cup of coffee, and put all that had transpired into some context that made sense. What remained of the Gang of Five—Senators Blaine, Chester, Stevenson and Adams—was left trying to figure out how to avoid any publicity fallout that might come their way because of their affiliation with Corbin. They strategized apart from one another, knowing that any appearance that they were still in league would do their cases no good.

Jimmy caught up with Junior in his office. "You were a champ out there, Junior. Thank you."

Junior had emptied a bag of M&Ms onto his desk and was separating them into smaller piles based on color: tan, green, orange, red, yellow and brown. It was a mindless activity that provided a distraction. "I'll tell you, Jimmy. I haven't had an experience like that since the Bruins won the Stanley Cup in '72. You planned it all nicely. Blaine stepped right into it as well. I don't think we'll have any trouble with any of them."

"Let's hope not."

"What a sight that was. Corbin at the door. Manning shellacking him. I don't remember Corbin actually leaving. I think the molecules of his body rebelled against their biological imperative to remain united and he simply vaporized. Tell me something, Jimmy. Do you feel sorry for him?"

Jimmy was preoccupied with concern for Buzzy. As soon as they took care of business in the caucus and hopefully a vote in the full

Senate, he intended to go to the Capitol Police office to find out how much trouble Buzzy could be in.

When Junior asked the question, Jimmy thought at first he was referring to Buzzy. "Corbin? Do I feel sorry for Corbin? I do. Believe it or not, I do. I can't say how much of it was a mental condition with him and how much was a failure of character. And I admit I used it to my advantage. I wouldn't be surprised if his family checks him into an institution."

Junior selected the pile of red M&Ms and began popping them into his mouth. "You know they stopped making red M&Ms for a while because of concern over the dye amaranth, which is supposed to cause cancer. The funny thing is that the red M&M's weren't dyed with amaranth. People just thought they were. Still, red M&M's had to go away for a while to calm consumers.

"Yes, Corbin's family will no doubt manage his mental recovery. Although it won't be in an institution. The wealthy go to programs now, Jimmy. Corbin's program will probably be run by some Hollywood doctor who employs a radical vitamin regimen and a sonic wave treatment that swizzles the brainpan."

When twenty-eight of the day's original twenty-nine Democrats were present in the Senate president's office, the door was closed. Hurley explained to all that, as had been known, he was stepping down from his position and retiring from the Senate. He had considered offering many names as his replacement, and he made it clear that there was no perfect choice for the job. In his many years in the Senate, he had never known any Senate president who was considered the perfect choice in his time.

Everyone had formed a circle around Hurley's desk where he stood. Some sat in chairs, most stood behind them. Jimmy noticed that Blaine, Chester, Stevenson and Adams were standing a great distance apart, with Adams barely visible in a shadowed recess beside the doorway.

"There are a number of you here who may yet prove to be perfect for the job. When your time comes, may the times be better than they are right now. I have decided on who would be the best replacement for me at this time. He is Senator Jimmy Mahoney, and I would like an up-or-down vote on him. So I officially nominate him. Do I have a second?"

"I second," said Junior.

Hurley continued, "Before we vote, I would like to make a couple of things known. First, Jimmy has told me that after hearing from a number of you, he has decided that a regional waste disposal site in Wellesley is not a workable plan. He'll get into the specifics if we happen to hold a Saturday session or next week if not. He also tells me that no similar communities need feel threatened by the same or a similar plan. Now don't ask for specifics at this time. Accept it as a matter of trust. He respects your comments, and he has dropped the plan to accommodate them. Is that more or less accurate, Jimmy?"

"It is," said Jimmy.

"Second, I've just received news that will soon be known to the public. Our very own Capitol Police are holding a man who has confessed that he is the one who murdered Salty Mahoney. He's the same man who caused a disturbance in the Senate gallery earlier. The son of a bitch hit me with a cigarette lighter. Anyway, he is not the one who many in the press, and I'm sad to say many within these walls, had speculated was responsible for the killing. I think you all understand what I'm referring to. I suggest to anyone who found themselves distracted by it, or concerned by it, to put your minds at ease."

When Hurley made the connection to the murder, Jimmy was stunned. It sounded absurd at first. As Hurley spoke, Jimmy sought for a way to come up with a plausible reason why Buzzy would do such a thing. Yes, he was involved in the world of drugs and supposedly the world of Francis. Jimmy had speculated that if there was any family connection to the murder, it would not be Francis but perhaps someone involved with him, someone who wanted to harm Francis by harming his father.

Just as Jimmy began to wrap his mind around those possibilities, another thought entered his mind. A memory of a rumor that he could never really believe. He heard it for the first time almost fifteen years before. Just as he could never fully believe it, he had also been unable to fully dismiss it.

It had come from Feebie Butler, a woman who lived in Old Colony and worked at the Oscar Meyer plant in South Boston. Feebie lived next door to the Driscoll apartment and was good friends with Buzzy's mother. She told Feebie that Buzzy's real father was Salty Mahoney. It was a puzzle piece that had sat by the side of the table, so to speak, for fifteen years, and Jimmy had never been able to find a picture into which it would fit. This might just be the one.

"Very good," Hurley called. "Let's have a vote. A show of hands will be fine unless someone objects."

There was no objection. The hands went up and Hurley counted the votes. "I count nineteen. Does anyone count different?"

Nobody spoke.

"Well, there it is. We'll make it official with a full Senate vote when the session resumes. You understand that regardless of how you just voted here, all of you are bound by this caucus vote to cast affirmatively in the chamber. It's been a good twenty-seven years but I'd be lying if I didn't say that I'm glad they're coming to an end."

Senators congratulated Jimmy. He noticed a couple of faces he wouldn't have expected to support him, adversaries from the days of busing.

"Nice work today, Jimmy," Hurley said when only the two of them were left in the office. "Machiavelli would be proud of you. Forgive me for breaking the news about the murder confession without telling you first. I received it literally seconds before you arrived. To be honest, I think it was better that I delivered it before the vote. You don't know how many were hesitant because of speculation about your brother's connection to the murder."

"I'm fine with that, but you mentioned it was the man causing the ruckus in the gallery. He's the one who confessed?"

"The Capitol Police are holding him in the basement. Apparently they have a medieval torture chamber down there. That's just a joke, by the way."

"I think I know him. He's from the Old Colony housing project in South Boston, and an old friend of my brother Matthew." Jimmy checked the time. The Senate resumed in ten minutes and he needed to be there. "As soon as our session ends, I'm going to go downstairs and see if I can speak with him."

"They said they'd be handing him over to the Boston Police and taking him downtown, but that might not be for a while. By the way, I told the stations we might have some news for them this evening. If you have a favorite tie tucked away in your office, now's the time to put it on."

* * * * *

The Capitol Police rarely made an arrest. Walter Cook couldn't think of a time the Capitol Police ever detained someone for any length of time. When he was tasked with locking up Buzzy Driscoll, his first question was "where?"

The need to hold him came from Buzzy himself. After being hauled from the public gallery down to the guard station, he told the Capitol Police that he had committed a murder and wanted to make a full confession. Buzzy would do it under one condition—that he not be handed over to the Boston Police Department.

Captain Gallagher, the officer in command, agreed. He brought in a tape recorder and pressed the record button. He advised Buzzy that he had the right to an attorney, which Buzzy declined. Then he asked Buzzy to speak.

What the captain heard shocked him. Not the graphic details about how the murder was committed but the fact that the victim was Salty Mahoney. Captain Gallagher stopped Buzzy several times during his taped confession to ask Buzzy to elaborate, to include absolutely everything about the planning of the murder, the preparation, the act itself and exactly what Buzzy did in the hours after the deed.

It was all recorded and, once transcribed, the document was signed by Buzzy and witnessed by clerks working for President Hurley. Captain Gallagher then called Boston Police Headquarters on Berkeley Street and asked for the detective in charge of the Mahoney murder.

Buzzy passed his time in a storage room in the State House basement. It once had been a lunchroom for those who worked the least glamorous jobs at the State House, like the cleaning staff. The long cafeteria-style tables now held cardboard boxes filled with legislative documents whose journey to the state archive had been held up until space could be made for them at the overcrowded building.

Buzzy sat alone in the room in handcuffs and an ankle chain locked to a nearby steam pipe. The overhead fluorescent lights emitted a steady hum, and the air was thick with vintage mustiness. On one wall hung a large institutional clock that announced the separation of seconds with a loud tick. The cop sitting outside the room had a direct view of Buzzy to ensure he wasn't setting the place on fire or trying to kill himself, but for the moment Buzzy had put that possibility aside.

He understood finally what his life was all about. He was the man in the middle. The balance between good and evil. Between Jimmy and Francis. Just like the scales he used to portion out pot, cocaine and heroin.

Jimmy had his cops, the Capitol Police. They were in white. The angels. Francis had friends in the Boston Police Department, who wore dark blue uniforms. Francis was the devil and they were the devil's helpers. Just like the flying monkeys in the *Wizard of Oz*. Right now he was in the house of the good. Jimmy was protecting him. It wouldn't be long however, before the dark blue devil sent the monkeys after Buzzy.

He had been allowed to wear his handcuffs in front so he could hold a can of Coke on the table in front of him. He had finished the Coke and one of the Yankee Doodle chocolate cakes that the captain had gotten from a vending machine upstairs.

He would have eaten more, but he had pains in his stomach from being kicked during the scuffle and from an anxiety, a dread that he was falling into a hole that would grow much darker and into which he had only just begun to fall. His right shoulder hurt as well, and he couldn't raise his right arm at all without feeling sharp pains.

From the distant end of the basement hallway came the footsteps of Detective Cory Maniscalco, who greeted the cop outside before entering the storage space and taking a seat across from Buzzy. He was young for a detective, and had a confidence and the kind of healthy good looks that drew people in. The detective wore a grey suit that was well tailored but seemed to cover his slender frame rather than fit it.

Maniscalco had brought a tape recorder of his own, a much smaller one. He told Buzzy he was going to turn it on and did so.

"Hello, Bradley. I'm Detective Cory Maniscalco." Like the captain, the detective advised Buzzy of his rights and asked if he willingly waived his right to an attorney. Buzzy said yes.

"Bradley Driscoll, I've read the statement you gave a short time ago. I'd like to ask some questions that will fill in a few missing gaps. Are you willing to answer?"

Buzzy nodded, but he didn't care either way. What difference did it make what he told them? All that mattered was what they were saying behind their voices that let Buzzy know whose side they were on. This one, he decided, was in disguise. An agent, but for the white angels or the blue devils?

Maniscalco asked about where the gun had been placed in the trunk of Francis' old car after Buzzy drove it back to Charlestown. It wasn't in the trunk, Buzzy told him, it was under the front seat. What kind of box was it in? It wasn't in a box. It was in a bag. A clear plastic bag or a white plastic bag? A paper bag, the thick kind supermarkets used for ice cream.

It went on for fifteen minutes with Maniscalco trying his best to get Buzzy to give a wrong answer to his questions. Buzzy was getting them all right. After asking every question he had written down or had come up with on the spot, Maniscalco was convinced beyond any doubt that Buzzy had committed the murder.

He left the room and returned a moment later with two Boston Police officers in uniform.

"The officers will transfer you for booking. You still have the right to an attorney if you change your mind." The cops unlocked the ankle chain and moved in to get ahold of Buzzy's arms, but he recoiled from their grip.

"What are you talking about? You're not taking me anywhere. I'm staying here with the Capitol Police. With Jimmy."

They grabbed hold of Buzzy and when he resisted, the two large cops lifted him and carried him out of the room. On passing Maniscalco, Buzzy hocked a large gob of spit that struck the knee of his grey trousers and cast a long tentacle down to the detective's impeccably shined shoe.

Despite the pain in his shoulder, Buzzy twisted and wriggled as hard as he could. His shouts filled the hallway and echoed back to Maniscalco.

"I know you now!" Buzzy screamed. "You're on the devil's team. You're a monkey with wings and you fly in disguise."

* * * * *

Frank Abbott returned to City Hall at seven o'clock as Mayor Sullivan was finishing his shower. Sullivan had added a small locker room as part of the renovations to the mayor's space on the top floor. He used it after going for a run along the Charles River with his chief of police.

By the time Sullivan had dressed, Frank was waiting for him in the conference room and had selected a deviled ham sandwich from a tray of food delivered by a shop in Quincy Market. Bernie Harrington had not yet arrived, but one other person had. Suds D'Isidoro, a friend of the mayor. Suds had no connection to the world of politics other than the fact that he was the mayor's official driver. He was there because he and Sullivan had arranged to lift several pints at The Stumbling Monk, a Back Bay bar near the intersection of Mass Avenue and Beacon Street.

Suds had been eyeing the sandwiches since first arriving in the conference room. Taking his cue from Frank, he reached for a ham and cheese sandwich and added a backup of sliced turkey and Swiss along with a Coke. Mayor Sullivan joined them at the table looking relaxed and refreshed. He took an egg salad sandwich and Diet Coke and ripped open a bag of chips.

"We've got a doubleheader against the Birds tonight," Sullivan said, referring to the Baltimore Orioles. "The first game has already started, so I'd like to take care of things here within the hour."

"So what do you think, Suds, is this gonna be the year?" Frank liked to tease Suds about his perennial optimism that the Red Sox would break the Curse of the Bambino, which began when the Red Sox traded Babe Ruth to the Yankees in 1918. At the end of every season, Suds explained the failure of the team with reasons that grew more convoluted and mythical.

Suds addressed Sullivan like a coach addressing his star pitcher before the decisive seventh game. "The math is against us this year, but in eighty-eight, Your Honor, we shall kiss the curse goodbye. That's why Billy Buckner missed that easy grounder last year. The Fates said, oh no you don't, Billy. Not until next year will we lift the fog of failure from Fenway Park. They pulled a little string in Billy's shoulder and up goes the glove just an inch or so and boop! Go home and cry in your pillow another year."

"Isn't that a wet dream?" Sullivan said. "Being mayor when the Red Sox win the World Series. And maybe beating the Yankees four games straight to get there. Ah, that might be too much for any mortal to hope for, Suds."

Bernie Harrington arrived and joined them at the table. He had just jogged from the State House and was a little out of breath. After hanging up his jacket and loosening his tie, he grabbed a paper napkin and wiped the sweat from his brow.

"If you want to join me and Suds, Bernie, we're going to the Monk to watch the Sox tonight. You too, Frank," Sullivan said, but Frank knew all too well what a trip to the Stumbling Monk meant. He'd be a designated dragger, one of two men selected to prop up the mayor at closing time and pour him into the backseat of the car, then deposit him onto the front stoop of the Sullivan home on East Second Street. The trick was to ring the bell and dash out of sight before Sullivan's wife hit the porch light.

"I don't think I can make it tonight, Mayor."

"So what happened on the hill today, Bernie?" Sullivan asked.

A fresh layer of sweat had already broken out on Bernie's forehead, and he wiped it off with another napkin. He stared across the room at nothing at all as he began. "Well, let's see. As of about thirty minutes ago, the Commonwealth has a new Senate president. And yes, it's Mahoney."

Bernie let that sink in before continuing.

"Oh, fuck," Frank said.

"Goddamnit," Sullivan said with a sweep of his hand, which unintentionally sent the Yaz bobblehead flying off the table and skittering across the floor. "I thought he didn't have enough votes."

Suds ran to the fallen Yaz, picked him up and inspected the doll for damage.

"You told us he was short, Bernie," Frank said, knowing that he was piling on but considered it payback for Bernie not supporting his plan for yesterday's conference in front of the State House.

Bernie responded, "He went from being three votes short to being five or six over, and it all occurred in the most bizarre Senate session I have ever witnessed or could even imagine. A senator was expelled from the chamber when he was addressed by his full name, which might be a first in Senate history."

"Corbin?" Frank asked.

"Yes."

"I knew he was losing it."

"Oh, he lost it alright. Then there was a fight in the gallery, and I barely kept some nutcase from taking a dive onto the Senate floor.

Don't ask me to describe how it all came about. I'll just say it was like watching the third act of *Rigoletto* over and over."

While the others were experiencing a sudden loss of appetite, Suds polished off the turkey and Swiss and reached for a bologna sandwich, which he playfully offered to Yaz first. "Mahoney's full of boloney," he said, repeating a slogan used by pretty much every candidate who ran against either Salty or Jimmy in the last half century.

Sullivan turned to Frank. "We have to get to the governor, and he has to confirm his support for our South Bay plan. Mahoney can be crowned king of the planet, but he's not going to beat us with his Wellesley plan."

"That's another thing," Bernie continued. "He's killed the Wellesley plan."

Frank was perplexed. "Killed it?"

Sullivan was irritated by the news. "Killed it? The Wellesley plan is the Mahoney plan. Mahoney can't kill the Mahoney plan."

"It's dead and buried."

As Sullivan sulked, Frank's wheels were turning. "So that means we're back to square one. South Bay is the only plan on the table and Mahoney's shown that he's incapable of offering an alternative."

"Frank, you were supposed to get ahold of the governor today," Sullivan said.

"I tried," Frank said. "But I couldn't find him."

"Couldn't find him? Where the hell is he?"

"He was supposed to be in Chicago. When I called his Chicago hotel, they said the governor's team had checked out. I left a message for him six hours ago at his office here. The staff assured me they'd pass it on immediately. I said Mayor Sullivan needs the governor to denounce the Wellesley plan, reiterate his support for the South Bay site, and he needs to do it quickly before the whole thing unravels. I left a string of messages for him yesterday and last night, but he's not returning any of my calls."

Sullivan was incredulous. "Does anybody know when this guy was last seen in his own state? He's like a fucking rock star on tour. Where's he gonna show up next? Tokyo? London?"

"He governs best who governs from a distance," Bernie said solemnly.

"He's flying back tonight on a red-eye. That I know for sure," Frank said.

Sullivan was quite worked up and considered getting on the phone himself, calling the governor's staff at their homes. Even calling the governor's wife. "Jesus Christ, is it too much to ask that he make a ten-word statement to the Boston press? The people of the state have a right to know where the governor stands on trash."

* * * * *

They had waited for hours in the emergency room at Boston City Hospital without Matthew being treated by a doctor. Other people were called into the examination area, and ambulances continued to arrive with victims of car crashes, heart attacks and one man with a piece of wrought iron fence protruding from his chest. The wait was making Anne nervous. She had gone back to the admitting station twice and had been told to wait her turn and be patient.

She grabbed a blanket from the Subaru and rolled it into a pillow for Matthew. He had been drifting in and out since they got there. That seemed a good thing at first, but now it began to worry Anne. She had heard that a person with a concussion could slide from sleep into a coma.

The crowd in the waiting room was about the same or maybe a little larger, but as Anne looked around she didn't recognize anybody from when they first arrived. She checked the time and was shocked. It had been three hours since they'd arrived.

She went to the admitting desk for the third time and waited in line while the staff changed shifts. She spoke to a young Latino named Reese, whose musky cologne hit Anne like a shock wave. She explained how long they had been waiting to see a doctor and how everyone here before them seemed to have been taken care of.

At first Reese showed the same professional disinterest Anne had received on her two previous visits, but when he was unable to locate Matthew's admitting forms, his attitude changed and Reese, a thin man barely over five feet tall, called out to the rest of the admitting staff in a sharp voice "Attention, everyone! We have these people waiting three hours and the forms run away. They run away lost." Reese already had the staff's attention, but now he clapped his hands like an irate movie director, "Everyone look! It's Mahoney. Matthew Mahoney. Find it. Now!"

Within a minute, the forms were handed to Reese. He held the forms up and strode from behind the counter. Taking Anne's hand, he marched with forms held high toward the doorway leading into the examination area. Before they got there, Anne said. "My husband."

Reese stopped. "Oh yes, the man. Where is he?"

She woke Matthew and walked him into the back.

"He waits three hours. Please." Reese handed over the forms and said to Anne. "I am so sorry about this."

The nurse who accepted the forms from Reese led them to a small room. In the hallway outside was a line of double-parked gurneys. Some were hidden by hanging curtains that spared people from the images of pain but not its sounds.

The cuts on Matthew's hands and face were cleaned up a little too hastily for Anne's liking. Then a doctor examined him, ordering a series of head X-rays. Matthew lay on a gurney and was given an injection that made him even more relaxed than before and relieved the aching in his elbow and the back of his head where it had hit the barroom floor.

The head X-rays revealed no bleeding in the cranium and no major fractures, but they did show a hairline break around Matthew's left orbital bone. For this, the doctor told them to expect possible numbness to accompany the spreading black eyes, and to see a doctor if Matthew developed any paralysis on that side of his face.

Anne had explained that they were visiting from Seattle, and the doctor told them to schedule a visit with their doctor as soon as they got home to check on Matthew's concussion. It was a serious one, he said, not just your typical concussion and Matthew needed to be watched closely, particularly in the next twelve to twenty-four hours.

The doctor sounded like he was almost too young to have graduated from medical school, but his thick black beard made up for the gravitas his voice lacked. "He'll want to sleep, then sleep some more, but you'll need to wake him every couple of hours to make sure he hasn't gone into a coma. If you can't wake him, call an ambulance right away. I don't say this to alarm you. I think he's going to be fine. It's been almost four hours now since his injury, and he's tired but he's awake. I just want you to know what to do should the unlikely occur.

"Whenever he feels like sleeping, he should. Some people never recover from their concussions because they don't allow themselves the rest they need to heal. He won't really be his old self for eight to ten weeks, and he should not even think about playing hockey or rugby, particularly rugby. In fact, nobody should be playing rugby in my opinion, even if they're in perfect health. Finally, the worst thing you can do when recovering from a concussion is to get another one. That would be very serious."

Matthew was awake and standing as he listened to the doctor, but he wasn't fully there. In years of playing hockey he had at least two minor concussions, but they felt nothing like this. Matthew looked at the doctor's name tag several times. It said Dr. Sternschein. After looking away for a minute, Matthew was unable to remember the doctor's name. He did this a few times and each time the name would slip from his mind. Thinking of the ride from the bar to the hospital, Matthew could only remember giving Connor the finger, getting into the car, then Anne having her knife taken by security in the waiting area. How had Anne known how to get to the hospital without directions?

Time seemed to be passing without gaps now. When they walked out to the parking lot, the day was slipping into dusk and Matthew had that sad feeling that came after being sick or hungover and finding that a whole morning or afternoon had passed unlived and unaccounted for.

Despite the sound of sirens and car horns, there was a calmness to everything. The evening sky had grey clouds very high up, the way it got when fall arrived. It was time to say goodbye to summer and surrender any hope that behind another losing Red Sox season there would be anything better than shorter days and the cold bleak harshness of a New England winter.

His mind drifted to Buzzy and where he might be. On the run somewhere, probably. He would have to run fast and far to escape Francis. For the first time, Matthew wondered whether it would even make any difference to Francis if he knew that Buzzy was his brother. To think Francis could kill Buzzy anyway was too upsetting to dwell on, so Matthew thought of the other possibility. That knowing it would matter to Francis.

Other than returning to the bar and facing another beating, how could Matthew let Francis know? He felt he was now helpless to do anything. It was a feeling he hated, but one he had to accept. He was out of the fight now.

He fell sound asleep on the drive back to Ipswich. When they reached Plum Point Road, it was dark and a chilling fog was drifting in from the ocean. Matthew woke as they entered the circular gravel driveway, where footlights lined the way. The fog gave each light a vaporous halo and seeing them through the windshield added to Matthew's confusion.

"Where are we?" he asked.

"Ipswich," Anne said as she gathered their things from the backseat. Matthew struggled to pull himself out of the car. The passing fog laced him with a damp chill as he stood unsteadily on the gravel. Joan was out for the evening, so the house was dark. The way the fog wrapped slowly around it gave the house a haunted look.

"I have some good news," Anne said as they sat at the kitchen table sharing an omelet that Anne had whipped up quickly. "I heard on the radio that Buzzy went to the police. Or the police went to him might be more like it. He told them he did it. He confessed."

"My God." Matthew's thoughts moved slowly as he searched for the bottom line of it all. "He'll go to prison if he's lucky. Or get the death penalty. What's so good about that?"

"He's in police custody, so he's safe from Francis. That's what's good about it. You don't have to worry about protecting him anymore."

"I get your point," Matthew said, but he felt depressed about it all. While Anne cleaned up the kitchen, Matthew took a quick shower upstairs. It involved a series of painful movements. Not only did his head and elbow hurt, but now so did pretty much every other part of his body.

When he stepped out of the shower, he caught a reflection of himself in the bathroom mirror and was stunned by how terrible he looked. His face was cut and discolored with bruises. His black eyes were so swollen he could barely see the pupils. "Jesus, did I get a beating," he said to his reflection.

He climbed right into bed. As he drifted off, he heard Anne cleaning up downstairs, then Joan arriving home to stories of yet another dramatic day.

What seemed like a moment later Matthew was woken by Anne. "What is it?" he mumbled.

"Nothing," she whispered, "Go back to sleep. I'm just checking on you."

He shut his eyes.

Anne woke him again. This time she was climbing into bed and the house was silent. Matthew saw something bright outside the window. It was the moon showing through the fog. He drifted back into a dreamless sleep.

* * * * *

The cops threw Buzzy into the backseat of a cruiser for the ride to police headquarters on Berkeley Street, less than a mile away. As they drove out of the tunnel at the back of the State House, Buzzy leaned over to look up at the golden dome, its precious metal still shining in the darkness of evening. From this close, the surface showed all of its bumps and ripples.

This was where Buzzy had gotten his first ride in a police car when he and Matthew had been caught trying to steal the gold from the dome. The Capitol Police had handed him over to the Boston cops that time as well. He remembered riding to the police station with Matthew and thinking that the whole thing was one big joke, that getting caught in the act was even more satisfying than if they had snuck away with twenty pounds of gold. He had a smile on his face that the cops couldn't slap off, and he turned to Matthew beside him and said, "Isn't this fucking cool?"

Matthew sat as silent as a stone. He told Buzzy how pissed off his father would be when he found out about the stunt. And how it would upset his mother, who had just been diagnosed with breast cancer and was scheduled for a series of painful treatments.

On that first ride, the blue lights were flashing and the siren wailing, but this time there was no fanfare for Buzzy. The cruiser moved with the slow traffic and waited at red lights. This time Buzzy was alone, and he was the one feeling the dread that Matthew had felt fifteen years before.

Buzzy had not been to mass since he was eleven or twelve, but the lines of a prayer came to him the way bad disco lyrics would surprise him with their ability to stay fresh in his memory while more important things escaped him.

"Because I dread the loss of heaven and the pains of hell." That was the line from the prayer. With all he had lost, was there anything left to dread losing? Heaven, if it existed, was a chance for him to see his mother again, but Buzzy doubted he would be welcome there. He had asked God for help today and he would have accepted anything. All Buzzy was offered was nothing, and it was hard to say just how deep and wide nothing was and whether it lasted as long as heaven, but with his luck it probably would.

At the police station, Buzzy was fingerprinted and photographed, the third time in his life he went through the drill. The station was fairly crowded and full of blue uniforms. Some glanced at him indifferently before looking away.

After the booking, Buzzy was brought to an interrogation room on the second floor, where he was questioned again by Maniscalco while two other detectives listened in. They were the same questions he had answered at the State House, and they made Buzzy relive the scene at E. Third Street over and over again. At the State House, he had been numb, watching the events from outer space like a visiting Martian, but now he was coming back into his body and the drugs that had protected him before were fading.

This time he was living the event, and it seemed even more intense than when he committed the murder. Getting the key from the garage, sneaking up the dark stairway where he could hear his father gasping on his own snores. The sound of the neighbor's dog, the smell of the smoke after he had fired all five shots, and the sound of the blood as it poured from his father's head and onto the back wall, a loud trickling that went on and on as if there were hundreds of gallons of it and the room would soon be ankle deep in its warmth.

"Why only five bullets?" one of the other detectives asked. "The clip held six. Why didn't you fire the sixth?"

"My nothing," Buzzy said.

"Your what?"

"I don't want to talk anymore."

"We're almost done," Maniscalco said.

"We are done," Buzzy said.

They brought him to the first floor where there were two large holding cells with a dozen men in each. Women were kept in a different area. Buzzy was placed in his own small cell at the far end of the hall.

A half hour passed and he received a visitor. Starchie Doyle was on duty but came for personal reasons. Starchie had grown up in Old Harbor, the project next to Old Colony. Starchie had tipped off Buzzy many times about impending drug raids in the projects, and Buzzy had returned the favors with many of his own, including several free inspection stickers for Starchie's extended family earlier that week.

"Jesus, Buzzy," Starchie said and reached through the bars with his right hand. Buzzy took it and began weeping. He was feeling it all for the first time, and it was almost too much after a week of numbness. He had finally come out on the other side of his horrible act and was able to see what others were seeing. He really did do it, and he could see how bad it had been.

Buzzy dropped down to the metal bench. Starchie bent low and talked to him. "I'm worried, Buzzy. I'm hearing some of the guys talking about you, and it doesn't sound good."

"If I plead guilty, can they still give me the death penalty?"

"I'm talking something worse, Buzzy. These guys are saying they want to take care of you right here. I gotta be honest, I don't think you'll survive the night in this place."

"Holy fuck." Buzzy leaned back against the cold metal bars and put his face in his hands. "I knew it, I knew it, I knew it. I am so fucked now, Starchie. I am so fucked!" He finished with a shout.

"Sshh. Keep your shit together, Buzzy. I'm gonna try and help you out. What you did was bad, really bad, but nobody has the right to do what these guys are talking about. Hey, are you listening to me?"

Buzzy had his face buried in his hands and was rocking slowly back and forth.

Starchie spoke in a low voice. "Pay attention to me, Buzzy. This is what I'm gonna do. I'll make it so they move you to a room on the other side of the building. It's like the interrogation room upstairs and it has bars over the outside of the windows, but at the side of the room is another door. It'll be locked. Buzzy, are you listening to me?"

Buzzy lowered his hands and nodded. His eyes were red and wet.

"Good. Now they'll put you in a chair and leave you there alone. Underneath one of the chairs will be a key for your handcuffs along with two other keys. They'll be taped to the bottom of the chair. It might be difficult with your handcuffs, so what you want to do is this. If the cuffs are in back, sit down, tuck your knees up and pull the cuffs over your feet so they're in front of you."

Starchie demonstrated what he meant and Buzzy nodded. "That'll make it a lot easier for you to reach the keys. When you get the keys, be sure to pull all the tape off the bottom of the seat and take it with you. Take the keys and the cuffs with you, too. OK? Don't leave any trace of things behind.

"Now, the other two keys. One is for the door at the side of the room. You go out that door and you'll be in a hallway. To your left will be another door. It's unlocked and opens onto an alley behind the station. Go out the door, then go to your right down the alley and before you get to the end you'll see a doorway on the left. It'll take you into a parking garage. Go down two levels to level C and look for a yellow Datsun. It's one of the cars you got a sticker for the other day. The last key is for the yellow Datsun.

"The parking is paid for so you don't have to stop at a booth or anything on your way out, but be careful pulling onto the street so no cops see you. The car's got a full tank of gas, and I put five hundred dollars in the glove compartment. It's my sister's car and it's an old piece of shit, so I don't care if we never see it again. Take it and go wherever you want, but go somewhere far away from here. Don't stay in hotels. Don't call anybody. Do you understand me?"

Buzzy nodded. A half hour passed, and two cops came to Buzzy's cell, unlocked it and walked him down a series of hallways and into a small room that looked just as Starchie had described it. The cops said nothing the whole time and locked the door behind them, leaving Buzzy alone in the room.

The metal arms of the chair were cold against Buzzy's skin. He began to worry that this might all be a trap, that the cops might want him to do something that would let them shoot him in the back while trying to escape. It had happened that way before, that was for damn sure. Buzzy made a decision. Fuck it, what have I got to lose?

He brought his handcuffed wrists to the front and reached under his chair. He couldn't feel anything and reached further back. There was nothing on the bottom of the chair. Nothing. Buzzy heard footsteps in the hallway, and he jumped back into the chair until the sound trailed off down the other end of the hall.

There were three other chairs in the room. He went to the first and turned it over. There was nothing there either. He turned over the next and there they were. Three keys held to the bottom of the seat with duct tape. He tore them free and rolled the tape into a ball that he shoved into his pocket. He took the small handcuff key and began angling it with some difficulty into the left cuff when he heard more footsteps approaching. Buzzy looked around. Three chairs were overturned and he knelt with three keys before him. If anyone came in now he'd be fucked and so would Starchie.

The footsteps passed and Buzzy went back to the handcuffs. He dropped the key three times but managed to get both cuffs off. He tucked them into the pocket with the tape and the handcuff key. After righting all the chairs, he unlocked the side door and stepped into a dark hallway.

To his left was the door Starchie described. Buzzy pushed down on a bar covered in dust, and the door yielded with a squeak that made him freeze. He waited and listened. When he didn't hear anybody coming, he burst into the dark alley, turned right and ran as fast as he could. When he reached the doorway to the garage, he leapt through it and bolted two levels down the dimly lit stairway, grabbing the rusty handrail to keep his balance.

Many of the lights on level C had burned out, so it was hard to see. There were very few cars parked there. He spotted the yellow Datsun at the far end.

The Datsun was parked so that a pole blocked the driver's door. On the passenger side, a cargo van was parked so close that Buzzy had to squeeze his way into the narrow space and lean back against the dark blue van as he tried the key. It went in easily but wouldn't turn. Buzzy pulled it out and turned it upside down and tried again. Still no good.

He was about to try it a third time when the side door of the van slid open quickly. Buzzy was yanked forcefully into the back. The door slammed shut, the van started up and sped toward the exit ramp. In the back of the van, Buzzy had the chance for one good scream before his face was slammed into the floor and his mouth wrapped with duct tape. His feet and hands were hog-tied behind him.

As the van spiraled up the exit ramp, Buzzy felt a heavy weight rolling into him. It had a smell like old garbage. The van slowed as it reached the exit to the garage and pulled cautiously into the traffic on Stuart Street. Buzzy lay on his stomach, trying to push himself away from the rolling weight that had come to rest against him like a log.

When he was able to draw himself away from it, he turned and saw that the log was something bound up tight in clear shrink-wrap plastic. Streetlights illuminated the bundle for brief moments as the van sped down Tremont Street. As it came to a stop beneath a streetlight, Buzzy realized that inside the clear wrapping was a body.

He saw the face with its lips pressed wide by the plastic, its open eyes distorted like some Japanese movie character that had special X-ray powers. When the light turned green and the van made a turn, the face rolled toward Buzzy and he saw that it belonged to Mikey.

At the next red light, the van came to a stop. Buzzy craned his neck to see who sat in front. Connor turned around and looked at Buzzy, then Francis turned as well and gave Buzzy a smile.

"Well, lookie, lookie, lookie. Who have we here? I believe it's the prodigal son who has taken his inheritance and his precious youth and squandered it all on riotous living. But now he has returned and we shall celebrate his homecoming. Yes, dear brother, we shall have us a mighty feast."

* * * * *

After the full Senate voted to confirm Jimmy Mahoney as its new president, he spoke briefly to thank those who supported him. He then repeated what Hurley had mentioned in his office for the benefit of the full Senate. That in light of the comments made to him in and out of session, the concerns raised about a possible incinerator site in Wellesley had caused him to rule it out as an option. Although the suburbs needed to play their part in contributing to a solution, it was clear that Boston had to play the central role. Beyond that he offered no details and adjourned the session, thanking the senators for their civility during a day that tested the patience of all.

It was a while before Jimmy could conclude official business. When he finally did, he went directly to the Capitol Police office and found Walter, who was still on duty. He told Jimmy that Buzzy had indeed confessed to the murder of Salty and that the Boston Police detective in charge of the case had questioned Buzzy at length. He had provided details that only the killer would know. Along with other information, this convinced the detective beyond any doubt that Buzzy was guilty of the crime.

Jimmy was interested in hearing this, and that Buzzy had been taken to police headquarters. He had already phoned his wife, Peg, and asked her to wrap up his dinner in foil and tuck it in the oven.

It was almost ten o'clock when Jimmy arrived at police headquarters. He explained that he was not representing Bradley Driscoll in a legal capacity, but that as his state senator and an old friend of the Driscoll family, Jimmy should be allowed to meet with him. He waited patiently while his request was sent to the captain on duty. Several minutes passed before Officer Hynes returned to speak with Jimmy.

"We have a problem," Officer Hynes said.

"A problem?" Jimmy's suspicions were immediately raised. If he had been told his request was denied that would be one thing, but this was an evasive answer. "A problem getting approval for my visit?"

"I'm not at liberty to say, Mr. Mahoney. Captain Bernard instructed me to tell you that it won't be possible for you to visit tonight. That's all there is to it."

"No," Jimmy said. "I think there's more to it than that." Jimmy's relationship with the Boston Police Department had never been good. Like most people in South Boston, he'd grown up with an instinctive distrust of the police. It grew stronger during the busing crisis when cops, whether provoked or not, were busting a lot of heads in his community.

More than once Jimmy had seen the TPF beat people who were perfectly innocent. In the years since, Jimmy's anger had cooled, but his distrust remained and he made it clear to Officer Hynes that he would not be brushed aside by bullshit.

"You go back and tell Captain Bernard that either I am allowed a visit with Bradley Driscoll or the Senate will launch an investigation into charges that Boston Police officers are blackmailing prostitutes for sexual favors while on patrol in the Back Bay and Beacon Hill. Tell him the Senate will turn over every single rock it can find."

Officer Hynes grew bug-eyed as Jimmy continued, "Tell him that his name just might surface somehow during this investigation. Now you go tell him that."

"Right. OK." Officer Hynes left. He returned moments later.

"The captain apologizes, Mr. Mahoney. He said he's in the middle of an emergency right now. The emergency is that it appears Bradley Driscoll is missing. He had been locked up, but now he's not there. Or anywhere that we can find him."

"Missing. Do you mean escaped?"

"He may still be in the building."

"Or he may no longer be in the building?" Jimmy asked. He sensed something very wrong about the situation.

"That's a possibility. The captain asks that you please not make this news public until we can get a clear picture. You know, why say someone's escaped, only to find him hiding in a bathroom or something? We should know one way or the other within a half hour. If he has escaped, we'll of course make the public aware of that fact."

Jimmy considered his options, which were two at this point. The first was to stay and wait for the police to either find Buzzy or admit he'd escaped. The second was to go home and have the police call when they figured things out. He wrote down his home number for Officer Hynes, then made his way home.

At the kitchen table Jimmy sat down with a glass of milk, along with a baked potato and chicken that Peg had kept warm in the oven. She joined him, and they talked about the news that the police had arrested Buzzy and charged him with the murder. After a few minutes, Jimmy found that he had talked himself out. There wasn't much to say except that it was one tragedy heaped upon another, and that it was a sad waste of life.

When he had finished, Jimmy went upstairs and read *Doctor Dolittle* to Kyle, who was feeling better and full of energy at eleven o'clock because he had spent the whole day sleeping.

One chapter turned into two, then three. It wasn't until almost midnight that Kyle finally grew tired. Jimmy kissed him goodnight and went down to the basement. The repairman had come to fix the dryer that day but instead had issued its death warrant, so Jimmy

357

folded all the clothes he had hung earlier on his makeshift clothesline.

At twelve-thirty he finally crawled into bed. Peg was reading a magazine. She turned and gave Jimmy a kiss.

"Let's not forget the good news today. You got a new job."

"Finally. It took one hell of a day to make it happen."

"But it all turned out well in the end."

"Yes, it did." Jimmy paused. "Almost everything did." Jimmy was quiet for a while. He closed his eyes and Peg turned off the reading light. They lay in the dark for a while, Peg drifting off, Jimmy thinking about his actions earlier that week. Sending Matthew to the house to help Francis. It was a selfish thing to do, and Jimmy was feeling guilty about it. He had kept it from Peg since coming up with the idea on the night of the wake. That should have been enough to tell him it was wrong to do.

The phone rang. Jimmy reached to his night table and fumbled for the receiver. It was Officer Hynes calling to say that Bradley Driscoll had definitely escaped and was at large. The police had issued a public alert.

"Thank you," Jimmy said. "No, nothing else," he said before hanging up.

"Bad news?" Peg asked.

"Do you remember that story I told you about Buzzy a long time ago?"

"You mean the rumor about your dad?"

"I never knew whether to believe it, but I think I do now. Buzzy was at the State House today, acting crazy in the public gallery. That's how they caught him. The Boston Police brought him downtown, but that call just told me that he's escaped."

"Escaped? My goodness, how do you escape from police headquarters? That doesn't make sense."

"That's the problem, Peg. I'm afraid I only know one way to make sense of it and I pray I'm wrong. We know what business Buzzy is in, and we know he has connections to Francis' world."

"How could Francis be involved? He's long gone. Isn't he?"

"Let me just put it this way," Jimmy began, knowing that Peg wouldn't press him for details if it involved anything about Francis. "I have reason to believe that he might not be long gone. That's what I'm going to have to confirm tomorrow."

"Well, it's already tomorrow," Peg said, "and you're not going to wake up rested if you worry about it now."

Chapter Ten
Last Suppers

It may have been an hour that Buzzy lay alone in the back of the van, or it may have been three or four. He wasn't able to judge time anymore. He only knew it was still dark. From the sounds Buzzy could hear, he was somewhere near a main street, but his senses were focused inside the van, where he lay on his side with his arms and legs tied behind him.

He had drifted in and out of a light nervous sleep, woken either by a burning pain in his wrists and shoulder, or by the stench of Mikey's body. At first Buzzy had been facing the shrink-wrapped corpse with his nose no more than two inches away, but he had managed to roll himself over so he was facing away from Mikey. The smell was still so overpowering that Buzzy was afraid he might puke, and he knew that if he did he could suffocate because his mouth was sealed with duct tape.

He had kept himself busy trying to get the tape off his mouth. It was attached too securely for him to push it off with his tongue, but one of the corners of the tape had peeled away a little. Twisting his head awkwardly, he tried to press the exposed corner onto the floor of the van and make it stick, so he could then pull it off his mouth, even if it was just enough to breathe a little easier.

With each attempt his neck ached. Buzzy would give up and drift off for a while. He tried many times before he felt the exposed tape finally catch on the floor. He would manage to pull it away a fraction of an inch before the tape would pull off the floor. Over and over he did this, and bit by bit it was working.

When he had the tape halfway off his mouth, Buzzy was satisfied. Now he had nothing else to concentrate on except his fate. He began with the wildly optimistic hope that it was all a big game Francis was playing, and soon he'd come back to the van and cut Buzzy free.

From there he slid into a despair so deep that he wanted to die. He asked to die, prayed to die, if only to end the pain in his wrists and shoulder. His definition of death had been reduced to an end of pain, all pain, and nothing more.

The need to piss had been bothering him for a while. Finally the urge became so overwhelming that he let it go and pissed his pants. Buzzy drifted off, then woke to the sound of voices.

The doors of the van opened, and Francis and Connor climbed inside. It surprised Buzzy at how relieved he was to hear them and to have their company, even though it was surely crazy to welcome the return of people who might be about to kill you.

"Jesus Christ, you stink!" Connor said, looking at Buzzy. Then turning to Francis, "He pissed his pants."

They rolled down their windows and Francis started the van. Once they were rolling along, the two men chatted about an ongoing scheme to launder cash by investing in condominiums and townhouses owned by friends, buying very low, paying their friends the difference in drug money and reselling the next day at market rates. All as if Buzzy were not there.

A thick fog had settled over Boston, giving the lights along Blue Hill Avenue an eerie glow. It was almost two o'clock in the morning and the streets were nearly deserted. Francis stayed on alert for cops who would prey on speeders or someone too anxious to wait twenty seconds for a red light to change. Now that Buzzy had confessed to the murder, Francis was in the clear as far as that went, but he didn't want to get pulled over with a dead body and an escaped prisoner in the back of the van.

They drove into Roslindale and around to the far side of the Forest Hills cemetery, where Connor jumped out of the van with a walkie-talkie and a bolt cutter to remove the chain at the cemetery's back gate. Connor stayed there to radio Francis if cops showed up.

The odds of being spotted were slim, but Francis took the precaution of turning off the van lights before driving through the open gate and creeping along the winding road. The secluded cemetery was beyond the congestion of downtown, and its three hundred acres of hilly ground were thickly wooded in places.

His parents' plots were near the center of the cemetery, where trees blocked the sight, if not the sound, of the city beyond. The granite headstone showed a freshly engraved year of death beneath the name of Thomas "Salty" Mahoney. Salty's grave, which had been filled with dirt on the day of the burial, had not yet been covered with sod.

Francis parked the van and shut off the engine. He slid the cargo door open and cut the rope that hogtied Buzzy. Cool damp air washed into the van. As the blood flowed normally into his hands and feet, Buzzy felt a tingling and stinging on his wrists and ankles. Francis pulled him into a sitting position and removed the duct tape dangling from one side of Buzzy's mouth.

"You think I'm going to kill you, don't you?" Francis asked in a voice that was almost caring.

Buzzy was afraid to give the wrong answer, so he said nothing.

"And maybe you think I don't know who your father is. Or was." Francis pointed to the patch of dirt behind him. "Why do you think I let you work for me all these years? You're like Mikey. You're a fuckup. I can't stand fuckups, but I put up with you all this time because I knew we shared the same father. If that isn't love, I don't know what is."

The confession surprised Buzzy. He was touched and almost began to cry, but when he looked into Francis' eyes they were as cold and grey as the granite of their father's headstone.

"C'mon, get up," Francis said. "You've got some digging to do. I missed the funeral, and I have a few words for our dear father before he has my permission to go to hell."

Francis took a stretch of rope and tied the ends around Buzzy's ankles, so that his feet could be no further apart than twenty-four inches. It made it impossible for him to run on Francis, who remembered that Buzzy had once been on a cross-country team.

From the back of the van, Francis retrieved a shovel and a lantern that he placed beside the grave. As Buzzy began shoveling,

Francis walked over to the headstone. His father's name was to the right, his mother's to the left.

He ran his fingers across the letters that spelled Nora Margaret Mahoney and gave the cold granite a kiss before seating himself upon the headstone to watch Buzzy dig. He said nothing, not when Buzzy stopped occasionally, nor when he sat down in the dirt for a few minutes with his head between his knees.

An hour into the digging, Francis walked over to the van and brought back a package of Twinkies and a can of grape soda, which he knew was Buzzy's favorite. He put them on the ground beside Buzzy, who was chest deep in the hole. When Buzzy opened the can, he was shot in the face by a spray of sticky soda. A purple froth bubbled over his hand.

After his meal, Buzzy resumed his task, trying to minimize the strain on his aching right shoulder. He shoveled carefully and dutifully, like a man working off his sins in purgatory. His shirt was soaked in sweat, so he couldn't rest for more than a minute without getting a chill.

The digging went on for almost two hours. When it seemed Buzzy might never reach the casket, they both heard a thud. Francis jumped from the headstone and walked to the edge of the hole, where Buzzy stood neck deep.

A flashlight from the van provided more illumination. When Buzzy had fully exposed the casket, he leaned against the wall of the pit and closed his eyes. His breath sent out puffs of vapor rising into the clammy night air. He was exhausted. As his wet shirt cooled, he began to shiver. "Am I done?" he asked.

"Almost," Francis said. "I have something to say to him, and I'd like to say it to his face, or whatever's left of it thanks to you."

The casket had a split lid, and Francis instructed Buzzy to dig into the sides of the hole, so there would be enough room to open the top half of the lid. When he was done, Buzzy tossed the shovel out of the hole and got onto his knees.

He worked his fingers into the dirt, feeling for the edge to the section of the lid closest to the gravestone. Clawing in the cool soil, he finally managed to secure a grip and yanked on the lid a few times before it swung open.

Loose dirt tumbled into the casket and soiled the pearly white lining. Salty's dark grey suit was visible from his chest up along

363

with his white shirt and striped tie. A dark cloth had been draped across his face. On seeing the body, Buzzy felt a sudden panic that the corpse might reach up and seize him.

"Let me see his face," Francis said.

Buzzy reached forward slowly to pull away the cloth. It was tucked beneath the back of the head and didn't yield at first. He pulled harder, then harder still. Slowly the head rose up and the cloth whipped free, allowing the head to drop back onto the silk-covered pillow.

Francis cast the light onto his father's face. It was like an illustration from an anatomy book. Pieces of skin were pulled away, revealing the skeletal structure beneath. The left eye was gone. Part of the lower lip was also missing, along with a few teeth that had been shattered by a bullet. The exposed muscle was a dull red and stiff from desiccation. The intact eye peeked from beneath its partially closed lid.

The sight filled Buzzy with far more horror than his memory of the murder. He fell away from the accusing eye and tumbled backward against the dirt wall. He tried climbing out of the hole, but Francis kicked him back in.

"Let me go!" Buzzy yelled. "I did it for you, Francis. I did it for you! Now just let me go!" He kept trying to climb out and Francis kept knocking him down. Buzzy eventually gave up and fell exhausted against the wall of the pit with his face turned away from his father's. He began to cry.

"Now I want you to get up," Francis said. "And I want you to apologize to him."

Buzzy shook his head but wouldn't look up at Francis.

"Let's get on with the show, Buzzy. This is your big act."

Buzzy stopped his sobbing and looked up at Francis. "Take me out of here and shoot me."

In a singsong voice, Francis responded. "You can't leave the hole until you say you're sorry."

"I'm sorry," Buzzy said.

"Stand up and look him in the face. Remember, it's got to come from the heart, brother. It don't mean a thing if it ain't got that swing."

Buzzy pulled himself up and pressed against the dirt walls for balance. Francis illuminated the face, which was now strewn with dirt. Buzzy bent his head down in the direction of his father's face, but he kept his eyes closed. "I'm sorry, I'm sorry, I'm sorry."

"That wasn't so hard, was it? Now I want you to say a prayer to seal the deal."

Buzzy looked up at Francis. "What prayer?"

"Any prayer. Whichever one is your favorite. This is the freestyle portion of the program."

Buzzy closed his eyes once again and thought of a prayer. He tried the "Our Father," but he could only get a few lines before he forgot what came next. He backed up and tried it again with no luck. His mind drifted up, so that he seemed to be in a tree above, looking down at himself in the dirt hole with his dead father.

There was no longer anyone or anything in the universe that Buzzy was connected to. He felt so abandoned, so desperately alone. He wanted to have his life back again the way it was just a week ago, but he knew that wasn't going to happen. It was all lost and gone forever.

Then it came to him. The first line of a prayer. He spoke it, and the next line came, and there it was, the word "dread" that had come to him on the ride to the police station. It made sense now.

"O my God, I am heartily sorry for having offended Thee, and I detest all my sins, because I dread the loss of heaven, and the pains of hell, but most of all because they offend Thee, my God, Who art all good and deserving of all my love. I firmly resolve, with the help of Thy grace, to confess my sins, to do penance, and to amend my life. Amen."

Like his relatives on the Flynn side, Francis had swallowed everything he was taught about the Catholic Church when he was young. At the age of ten, he spit it out whole, but he still knew all the prayers, including Buzzy's Act of Contrition, and he knew where it ended.

As Buzzy approached the final word, there was a faint whistling sound as the shovel cut through the air. It cracked Buzzy square on the back of his skull. He dropped immediately and fell with his face pressing deep into his father's shoulder, the way a child will do when he has had a nightmare and must be walked around the house by his father until the peace of sleep once again descends.

* * * * *

"Wake up."

Matthew opened his eyes to darkness. Anne had been waking him every two hours throughout the night to ensure that his concussion had not caused him to slip into a coma. He assumed this was just another check-in.

"It's OK. I'm still alive," he mumbled and pulled the sheet over his eyes.

Anne turned on the bedroom lights and nudged him. "Matt, you have to wake up."

Matthew rolled over and squinted at her. "I'm fine. Now can you turn out that light?"

Anne was fully dressed, and on the chair behind her Matthew saw an outfit of his clothes spread out like this was his first day of school. Beside the chair were their bags, all packed.

"We're leaving, Matt. I called and got us tickets last night. A cab will be here in twenty minutes to take us to the airport."

He was in a state of deep grogginess and slowly pushed himself up. One side of his face was tender and his eyes partly swollen. One of his cheeks had a patch of numbness. Matthew looked out the window into darkness, then looked for a clock or his watch. "What time is it?"

"It's a little before five. Our flight leaves at seven."

"To Ireland? Jesus, where are we going?"

"We're going home," Anne said. "We're going home to Seattle. I know you're tired, Matt, but you'll be able to sleep on the flight."

Matthew stood up with one hand against the wall for balance. "Is something wrong?"

She kissed him. "Everything's fine. It's just time for us to go, that's all."

In fifteen minutes they were standing in the gravel driveway, still shrouded in darkness and a chilling fog. When the lights of the taxi could be seen approaching, they said their goodbyes to Joan and thanked her. The luggage was loaded into the trunk of the cab, and they drove south for the airport.

In the back of the warm taxi, Matthew fell back to sleep. What seemed like the next moment, he was being woken again by Anne at the airport. The sky had turned a lifeless grey and the fog had broken into scattered patches. They moved quickly from the taxi and through the airport lobby, where it seemed to Matthew that everyone and everything was moving twice as quickly as he was.

They moved through security and down a long corridor where coffee shops and newsstands were beginning to open. Matthew looked at rows and rows of empty seats and wanted to stretch himself out on one of them and sleep for hours.

He always picked out an assortment of snacks and drinks before they flew, and as they passed a convenience stand Matthew pointed and started to say something to Anne, but she cut him off. "I packed a bunch of stuff, Matt."

When they reached their gate, Matthew headed straight for a seat and dozed off. Anne spoke to an agent at the desk, so that they were allowed to board early with the children and elderly. The flight was only half full, and they had a row to themselves. Anne gathered enough blankets and pillows to keep Matthew comfortable.

With his head resting against the window, he gazed out at the new day. On the southern edge of the airport was Boston Harbor, and across the water Matthew could see the smokestack of the Edison plant and the stone fort on Castle Island. He tried to reconnect himself to who he and Anne had been before the wedding and before this terrible week. Matthew turned to Anne.

"It seems like we've been here forever, doesn't it?"

She latched their seatbelts, then rested against him. "I don't want to come back here for a long time."

He put his arm around her and closed his eyes. Soon the flight attendants were doing their seatbelt checks and safety demonstrations. The plane rolled onto the runway. It paused for a moment before the engines throttled up, hurtling the plane along the tarmac and into the sky over South Boston, where Disco Callahan's Saturday morning sleep was being disturbed by a ringing phone.

* * * * *

All Disco was told was that he needed to come into the office as soon as was humanly possible, a dramatic phrase that Boston's new FBI Field Director was not prone to use unless it was very important. He showered, shaved and dressed as fast as humanly possible, stopped for a coffee and scone at the Broadway Bakery and was pulling into his underground parking spot at 7:40.

Disco had enjoyed a cozy working relationship with Patrick Shea, his former director, who had recently concluded a career considered very successful after the highly publicized Operation Beanpot.

Shea's illustrious career had been looking a little less so to Virgil Bunker, the new director. Bunker had been examining the relationship between Special Agents Callahan and Anderson and informants Francis Mahoney and Larry D'Amico. Bunker's investigation had only recently begun, but already he had uncovered a number of instances where the two agents seemed to have crossed more than one line. The informants' value to the bureau also looked as if it had been intentionally inflated.

These were top echelon informants, which typically meant they were high up in the structure of a criminal organization, but it appeared Mahoney and D'Amico were at the very top. The FBI didn't protect people at the top. They targeted them. That was only one of the many concerns that Bunker had.

He hoped both informants would have been off the street by this point because of the grand jury convened to investigate extortion charges connected with Global Jai Alai. They were close, but the suicide of one key witness and the disappearance of the other ended that possibility, at least for the present.

A new hope had emerged the evening before. Late on Friday, Bunker was contacted by his counterpart in the British SIS, the Secret Intelligence Service, who informed the FBI that a fishing vessel bound for Ireland would soon be delivering a large cache of arms intended for the IRA. The arms, including sophisticated surface-to-air weapons, would be unloaded onto smaller boats that would be seized by the British Navy once they entered Irish waters.

A British informant on the IRA's leading council had tipped off British intelligence to the gun-running scheme. The informant was also providing the FBI, via the SIS, with documentation and testimony proving that Francis Mahoney and Larry D'Amico had acquired the weapons, some of which had been stolen from military bases in the U.S., and had financed the purchases with a massive drug-running operation that implicated an admiral in the U.S. Coast Guard.

On the ride up to the 21st floor of the federal office building, Disco checked the centering of his tie in the shiny elevator doors. Director Bunker and two other agents met him in the lobby.

"What have we got?" Disco asked to break the silence as they headed for a conference room down the hall.

The phone call had made him a little suspicious, and now the quiet walk with a field director he didn't particularly care for was making Disco uncomfortable.

"Something from British intelligence," Bunker said in a casual tone. He was raised in Idaho and had a very laid-back manner, so laid-back that it grated some locals in the field office who were openly proud of the gritty, tense way Bostonians interacted with the world. Bunker also had something else rarely seen in an East Coast FBI office. A drooping grey mustache waxed at the ends for a little curl and twirl.

In the conference room, Disco took a seat on one side of the table, Bunker on the other flanked by the two agents. Disco knew one of them. Andy Finnegan had recently returned to the Boston office from New Jersey. Finnegan had grown up in the Savin Hill neighborhood adjacent to South Boston. He and Disco had gone to high school together at Catholic Memorial.

Finnegan was not the most ambitious or successful agent in Boston, but he was known for his integrity, which made him one of only a few agents who Director Bunker trusted. The other agent was Alexander Quinn, who Bunker had brought with him from his previous assignment out west.

"Have you heard about the Avalon, Terry?" Bunker began.

Disco knew what it was and he grew immediately anxious. "I don't think so, unless you mean Frankie Avalon."

"Cute," Bunker said with a disappointed smile.

Bunker then brought Disco up to date on what had happened, and the fact that evidence, if verified, proved conclusively that the operation had been overseen by informants Mahoney and D'Amico.

"We keep Mahoney and D'Amico on a pretty tight leash," Disco began. "We … I mean Anderson and I … haven't picked up on any of that, and I think I'd want to question the source of that information before I took it as gospel."

"We haven't received all of it," Bunker said, "and we haven't had a chance to verify it, but it's not looking too good for those two.

As soon as I corroborate the information we're receiving, we're taking those two off the street. And it could be real soon."

The announcement stunned Disco. It meant that Francis had to run again. If Disco could track him down and tell him. It also meant that Disco would no longer be seen as the agent who managed two very valuable informants, but the one who had mismanaged them. And what about Anderson? Technically he was Disco's supervisor, so if there were repercussions it should be Anderson who felt them first.

"Have you talked to Anderson about this yet?" Disco asked.

"He'll be here in about an hour. He tells me he's got some information he's ready to share concerning those two. A lot. Which has me very curious. Do you know what kind of information he could be talking about?"

"No, but I'm curious myself now," Disco said. He masked his fear. It was more of a panic, really, because his gut told him that Anderson was going to talk. About everything. All the ways in which the two agents had acted as business partners to Francis Mahoney and Larry D'Amico. There had been kickbacks over the years. Cash payments reaching into the tens of thousands of dollars. Gifts ranging from cases of wine and refrigerators to a diamond ring that Disco had given his first wife. They were divorced now, so she could be forced to testify against him in court. And there was more, so much more.

Disco had lately considered Anderson the type who could turn on him. Is that what he would be doing? Handing over Disco to save his own skin?

"I'd like to see what you've received on those two, if that's OK," Disco said.

"Let's wait until I have a chance to speak with Anderson. Why don't you come back this afternoon. Let's say four o'clock. That'll give me a chance to go over everything. In the meantime, I don't want you to have any contact with those two."

* * * * *

After the meeting with Disco downtown, agents Finnegan and Quinn drove to the Mahoney home on N Street to have a discussion with Jimmy. They were given a cold reception by Peg, who told them that her husband was doing the people's business at the State House and that she herself had five children to attend to and no time for idle chitchat. As soon as they left, she phoned Jimmy at the State House to warn him that visitors from the FBI would be arriving soon.

The visit was no surprise to Jimmy. He had been expecting it all week. Word had gotten around about Director Bunker taking over for Shea, and it was only a matter of time before the new law enforcement kid on the block began shaking all the trees in town to see what kind of overlooked fruit might fall into his hands. Jimmy always made it onto the guest list because it was suspected that he sat down with Francis to plot what sort of legislation might aid his brother in the underworld.

Jimmy had grown tired of it, but he also knew the worst thing he could do was to throw a tantrum. Then they'd really think there was something going on. Instead, he gave honest but terse answers to all questions. He was in the Senate president's office receiving a handoff of all the items Hurley had on the legislative agenda and discussing how best to shift them onto Jimmy's plate. Hurley's hope was to spend less than a week transitioning into retirement.

They had paused in their work to read an editorial in the Saturday morning *Boston Globe*. The editorial wagged an admonishing finger in the direction of the senator from South Boston, saying that in his new role as Senate president he should maintain the dignity of the institution and put aside the incendiary and divisive tactics employed during school desegregation.

When the FBI agents arrived, Hurley greeted them with a big smile and warm introduction. Jimmy had explained they were coming and Hurley offered them his office to talk, then he excused himself for a coffee break.

Off to the side of the office were a small table and circle of chairs, but Jimmy was not about to set such a cordial tone. He took his seat behind the president's desk for the first time and offered Finnegan and Quinn the somewhat lower chairs facing the desk, the same chairs Jimmy had sat in many a time while pleading a case before Hurley.

"So, Andy, welcome home," Jimmy said addressing Agent Finnegan. "I hear that you did a good job in New Jersey. Congratulations. I also hear that you and your wife have found a place in Roslindale, which I'm sure your parents were happy to hear."

Finnegan smiled. His father had risen to be a captain in the Boston Fire Department, and Jimmy had always gotten a kick out of it because all six Finnegan kids had the kind of bright red hair that made it look like flames were shooting from the tops of their heads. "Thank you, Jimmy. Yes, my folks were pleased. We're just on the other side of Roslindale Square from them. Close enough so they can walk over to babysit once the baby arrives. Leslie is six months pregnant."

"That's wonderful. Just wonderful," Jimmy said. He had been watching Agent Quinn out of the corner of his eye, and the serious young man with his three-piece suit and military crew cut was growing uncomfortable with the familiar tone shared by his partner and the man they were sent to question. Jimmy would have kept it up a bit longer, but Quinn jumped in.

"Excuse me, Senator Mahoney. It would be nice if we could all spend the rest of the morning catching up and getting to know each other," Quinn said, shooting Finnegan a glance. "But we've been sent over to discuss an urgent matter with you, and we have questions we'd like to have answered."

"Oh, please forgive me," Jimmy said with just enough exaggeration. "You gentlemen are on the front line of federal law enforcement, and I certainly want to do all I can to help you accomplish your goals, particularly the urgent ones."

Quinn began. "First of all, we'd like to know exactly … "

Jimmy interrupted, "Forgive me, please. You are … "

Quinn looked puzzled. "Excuse me?"

"You know who I am. I'm Jimmy Mahoney, but I'm afraid you've failed to introduce yourself."

"I'm Special Agent Quinn."

"Wonderful. And your first name, Special Agent Quinn?"

Quinn suspected he was being played and shot Finnegan another look. "Alexander. My name is Alexander Quinn."

"Alexander. That's marvelous. As in Alexander the Great. Brave warrior and conqueror of distant lands, leading his men into battle and vanquishing the enemy. That's a wonderful name, and I think it fits you like a glove, Special Agent Quinn. Now you were saying?"

"When did you last see your brother Francis Mahoney?"

"At the wedding reception of my youngest brother, Matthew. A week ago today in Ipswich, Massachusetts."

Quinn had been holding an open notepad and pen in front of him since sitting down. He wrote Jimmy's answer below a question composed earlier. Turning the page, Quinn continued, "Have you had any contact with your brother Francis Mahoney since that time? Have you seen him or spoken to him? Has he contacted you or have you contacted him?"

"The answer is no to all of those questions."

On the next page, "Do you have any knowledge of the whereabouts of your brother Francis Mahoney at this present time or since the wedding reception last Saturday?"

"No."

"Has anybody you know informed you of any contact they've had with your brother Francis Mahoney since the wedding reception last Saturday?"

"No. Nobody I know has told me of any contact they've had with my brother Francis Mahoney since last Saturday."

The questions suggested to Jimmy that Francis was, in fact, going to be indicted. He continued to answer Agent Quinn's questions patiently and honestly. Quinn then looped back to question one, which was obvious because he flipped to page one of his notepad, and began asking all the same questions with a slightly different phrasing. He was hoping to catch Jimmy in an inconsistency, but Jimmy had no patience for the tired tactic.

He stood up and walked to the coatrack by the door and pulled off his coat. "Gentlemen, let's go."

Finnegan and Quinn were both confused, and despite the fact that Jimmy was putting on his coat, Quinn suspected that Jimmy was trying to throw them out of the office. "We're not finished with our questions, Senator Mahoney."

"I know you're not, but I'm doing you the favor of giving you what you want without boring me to tears in the process. You want honest answers. You want the truth. I've given you exactly that, and now you want to waste my time by asking the same questions all over again in the hope of catching me in a lie. And, Special Agent Quinn, the fact that you are asking them again suggests you believe I've lied to you in the way I answered the question the first time."

"I'm suggesting no such thing."

"Of course you are, but I'm going to do you a favor, Alexander. I'll walk down to the federal building with you right now. I'm sure you boys have a polygraph machine down there, don't you? You can hook me up to it and ask me the basic questions you keep coming back to. Have I seen or heard from my brother Francis since last Saturday? Do I know the whereabouts of my brother Francis since last Saturday? Has anybody informed me that they have seen or heard from him or that they know of his whereabouts since last Saturday? So what do you say, shall we take a refreshing walk down School Street?"

Quinn was even more suspicious now, but he was about to take Jimmy up on the offer when Finnegan tapped him on the arm and shook his head. Finnegan knew that you didn't march a member of the state Senate, particularly the Senate president, downtown to take a polygraph unless he himself were under suspicion of a serious crime. When the rest of the Senate and House of Representatives, as well as the governor, found out about it they'd become outraged.

It wouldn't matter that Jimmy had volunteered for the test. There were too many cynical minds on Beacon Hill who would assume that Jimmy had been threatened, blackmailed or somehow coerced to take the polygraph. If it could happen to the Senate president, then it could happen to all of them, which would expose every skeleton in their political closet. In the Commonwealth of Massachusetts, the political closets were bursting with skeletons.

Collectively, this mob of politicians could bring down a major shit storm on the FBI, and they had the power to write and sign the legislation that would make it all legal.

This was why Director Bunker had sent Finnegan. He wanted Quinn to conduct the questioning, but he wanted Finnegan there in case Quinn got in over his head or missed a local nuance. This was not quite a nuance but rather a big trap that Quinn almost stepped into.

It was because Matthew had kept Jimmy insulated that he could pull off such a ploy. If they called Jimmy on his bluff and hooked him up to a polygraph, he could answer honestly that nobody had mentioned Francis' whereabouts to him.

"I take that as a no, gentleman. Very well." Jimmy checked his watch. "I've got a meeting with the governor in ten minutes, and I believe we're all done here. Special Agent Alexander Quinn, it was interesting to meet you and I'm sure you're destined for many heroic conquests. Andy, good to see you again. Give my best to Leslie and your parents."

Quinn seemed reluctant to give up his chair, but Finnegan stood up, shook Jimmy's hand and went for the coatrack. Finally, Quinn stood and thanked Jimmy for his time. "Please thank the Senate president for letting us use his office."

"That man in here earlier is the former Senate president. I'm the new Senate president," Jimmy said with a smile. "Make sure your boss understands that when you deliver your report."

* * * * *

From Macedonia to Greece, Jimmy thought as he walked to the other side of the State House for his meeting with Governor Peter Kostakos. The governor's reputation as the honest, hard-working son of a Greek immigrant had gotten him elected to his first term as governor in 1976. That and the fact that he promised to clean up corruption in state government and overturn the age-old patronage system that handed out jobs in return for favors. Appointments made by Governor Kostakos would be based on merit alone.

Kostakos proved to be the consummate technocrat, able to hold vast amounts of statistics and studies in his head and use them to build cases for reform. Corruption was targeted and attacked. Decisions were made on the basis of what was in the best public interest, not on backroom deals for personal gain. From 1976 to 1980, he governed the state in a no-nonsense, practical way that made life difficult for traditional politicians.

It was an ambitious approach. However, many soon viewed it as arrogant for Kostakos to hold himself above the world of the unwashed politicians who, he soon discovered, held much of his fate in their hands. They hindered his legislative agenda and later outright defied him. They also succeeded in painting a picture in the media of Kostakos as smug and self-righteous.

As Jimmy often said, reformers in Massachusetts politics were one-act plays. The voters gave Kostakos the boot after his first term. In 1980 they turned over the job to a governor who, by contrast, became known for his lavish lifestyle, which included having lobster salad lunches delivered to his office on the Commonwealth's tab.

In those four years out of office, Kostakos underwent a political makeover. He exchanged his righteous scowl for a smile that could remain stretched across his face for several minutes without diminishing. He also began riding the subway downtown with the masses. A dose of self-deprecation during the next gubernatorial campaign was sufficient for the Democratic Party to endorse his candidacy, if not embrace it. In 1984, the voters forgave him as well and sent him back for a second nonconsecutive term.

It was to this reborn politician that Jimmy now brought a deal that, he believed, Kostakos would not be able to refuse. The governor's meeting coordinator announced Jimmy's arrival, and he entered the large office. It was tastefully decorated with mementos dating back to colonial times, including a portrait of Samuel Adams that hung behind the governor's desk.

The setting could dwarf any man, but at five feet four inches, Kostakos seemed almost lost in the space. Along with his short stature, he stood with a slight hunch that seemed to have increased during his time out of office. Kostakos emerged from behind his desk wearing a white dress shirt with sleeves rolled up to the elbow.

The two men sat down in comfortable armchairs near the windows overlooking Boston Common. Jimmy congratulated the governor on his strenuous schedule of presidential campaigning in key battleground states. Kostakos congratulated Jimmy on his election to the Senate presidency.

"May the term 'president' apply to both our job titles in the near future, Governor," Jimmy said.

The governor nodded his head slowly and gave Jimmy a long ponderous blink. "That's what I hope too, Jimmy. God willing, if we work hard enough and smart enough, I think our side will have what it takes to take back the White House. If I'm lucky enough to be chosen for the battle, I certainly will give it every ounce of energy I've got."

Now it was time for business. Jimmy knew he'd have to be careful in how he presented his deal, so it wouldn't appear too much like arm twisting. "Governor, I appreciate your meeting with me this morning on such short notice, and I promise not to take much of your time. To the point, I'd like to propose a solution to a situation … no, a problem really, for all of us. The waste disposal site for the city of Boston."

Kostakos gave another ponderous blink while tilting his head slowly left, then right. "Ah, yes, it's a mess that needs fixing. Frankly, I was hoping you and the mayor would have this worked out by now."

"I as well, governor. Which is why I have a compromise proposal. And not one that involves Wellesley or any other Boston suburbs."

Kostakos smiled. "Well, that's good to hear. I have to say, I was a bit surprised when I heard about that proposal in Chicago. My office received a number of phone calls."

The two men shared a nervous laugh. Jimmy continued, "No, this proposal keeps the business in Boston. You know that an incinerator in South Bay is simply unacceptable to me. I prefer to find a site that's large enough to handle all the region's waste, whether for recycling or for energy conversion. However, I'm willing to accept the continued sorting of waste at South Bay with a modest increase in the handling of recycled materials."

Jimmy went on to describe a plan that made few changes to the existing situation. The plan prohibited the construction or use of an incinerator at South Bay. While some recycling would take place, most of Boston's trash would continue to be trucked to out-of-state landfills.

For Jimmy, the most important part of the plan was that it meant no trash would be burned near his community. Because he was agreeing to maintain any sort of facility at South Bay, it could be viewed as a concession on his part. However, it was a plan that would not make Sullivan particularly happy.

The governor drew in a deep breath and shook his head. "I don't know, Jimmy. The mayor might still have a problem with that. I'm not opposed to it myself. It seems reasonable, I guess, as all compromises must be."

Kostakos was making it clear that he preferred to stay out of the fray on this and any other battles that might make any enemies among the politicians who he would be relying on heavily to help him win the big battle for the White House.

"Honestly, Governor, this won't be put behind us unless you endorse it yourself in a very public way. I know that you've got many of your resources focused on the presidential campaign and you don't need distractions in the coming months. If you'd be willing to publicly endorse my compromise, I will promise that in my role as Senate president I will fully back you in conducting a legislative agenda that substantiates the claims you might want to make on the campaign trail about this state's progressive social agenda, and our ability to cultivate a productive, thriving and forward-looking business climate. I will do everything I can to make you and the Commonwealth of Massachusetts look good to a nation of voters trying to decide whether to place their trust in you … " Jimmy paused before finishing, " … or someone else."

The governor began nodding his head toward the end of Jimmy's statement, signaling that Kostakos understood the subtext of it as well. If he supported Jimmy's proposal, the Senate would pass legislation that would make Kostakos look good. If he didn't, the Senate could embarrass the governor on the campaign trail, even torpedo his quest before the Democratic convention. As such, the threat was bold and brash enough to make some politicians respond with one of their own, but Kostakos' time out of office had tempered him. He knew that his presidential hopes required that the home waters be kept calm.

The governor crossed his legs and clasped his hands over his knee as he raised his considerable eyebrows. "Yes, I suppose your support is worth my taking a little flak from the mayor. He can be a very willful man, as you well know."

They both laughed, which helped to dissipate some of the tension from the governor having swallowed Jimmy's bitter pill.

Jimmy continued. "If you'd like, Governor, I'll announce it as I described it to you, and I'll frame it as a compromise that you helped broker. One which I'm not thoroughly satisfied with, but one that I, like the mayor, must simply live with as it's in the best interests of the state and the city of Boston. At some point in the next few days, you can make your statement in support. I'll send over the details of the new plan, in case you're asked about any of the specifics. And certainly feel free to make any adjustments to the plan that you believe are necessary as long as they don't alter the general structure. In two or three weeks it'll be behind us both, and you can campaign knowing that I'm back home keeping your best interests in mind."

The two men shook hands and Jimmy rose to leave. "Happy trails," Jimmy said, and the governor smiled at the lame joke.

* * * * *

It was only ten o'clock and Jimmy had already accomplished quite a bit, but one problem remained and it was far more challenging than the FBI or the governor. Jimmy had stayed awake the night before wondering about it and had woken to it as well. What to do about Buzzy Driscoll.

He had taken it on as a personal worry not only because he had known Buzzy since he was a child and because of the possibility they shared the same father, but also because of Buzzy's suspicious escape from police custody. It was something that simply didn't happen no matter how incompetent the police guarding him were. It was an exceptional prisoner who even speculated on how he might escape a police station after arrest, unless the specific idea is planted by someone willing to assist.

Behind his incredulity about the escape was the nagging concern that Francis might be the architect of Buzzy's disappearance, if Francis was indeed still in town. There was no evidence to support Jimmy's concern. It was merely a hunch. No matter how separate Jimmy's world might be from that of Francis', the two tended to plot strategy in a remarkably similar fashion. On one occasion when Jimmy discussed a political conundrum with his brother, he found that Francis' armchair solution was almost identical to Jimmy's. The reverse scenario, where Jimmy imagined what he'd do if he were Francis, might produce similar results.

Francis' world was a place where Jimmy rarely let his mind wander, because he had long ago given up trying to get Francis to live an honest life. There were some things Jimmy just tried but couldn't make his brother do, and once he'd exhausted his reform efforts, he had to choose whether to abandon Francis or to love him and pray that someday he would mend his ways. Love the sinner, hate the sin, as St. Augustine preached.

As Jimmy allowed himself to speculate, his guess was that the murder of their father and Francis' implication in it was Buzzy's doing. Once this was discovered or suspected by Francis, he'd seek revenge. He had friends in the Boston Police Department, Jimmy knew, and they might have been encouraged to deliver Buzzy in some way to Francis.

What Francis would then do was what troubled Jimmy the most. Francis almost certainly had killed other men in carrying out his business, but Jimmy had always discounted that, if only for his own peace of mind, as a hazard specific to the world of crime and contained there.

With Buzzy, it had crossed into the world of family and friends. The worst, Jimmy knew, would be for Francis to kill Buzzy, and the implications of that were such that Jimmy couldn't contemplate them for long.

This was hardly the best time to call for one of the social meetings the two brothers would occasionally have outside of the public eye, but Jimmy felt that Buzzy's situation was a crisis where time to do something, or prevent something, was limited.

In action there is redemption, Jimmy thought. He picked up the phone and called his wife. When she answered, Jimmy heard the sound of running water and knew she was in the kitchen.

"Peg, have you seen Mrs. D'Amico this morning?"

"She's in her backyard right now. I'm looking at her."

"What's she doing?"

"She's tearing up some bread and tossing it to the birds." There was a pause. "Now she's yelling at the cat."

Jimmy smiled. "Could you do me a favor, and go over and ask her a question for me? Could you find out if she's available for lunch?"

"For a family lunch?" Peg asked. This was what meetings between Jimmy and Francis were called, and many of them had been held discreetly at Mrs. D'Amico's house.

"Yes, a family lunch. Twelve-thirty is probably the earliest I can do it. And she'll have to contact the family," Jimmy said, meaning that it would be up to Mrs. D'Amico to contact someone who knew Francis. Jimmy could in fact be there in a half hour, but he knew it might take time to get ahold of Francis.

Peg sighed audibly. "Jimmy, are you sure you want to do this now? Maybe it could wait."

"I wish it could, love, but I'm afraid it can't. Don't worry."

Peg called back twenty minutes later. "She said one-thirty is better. She's getting her hair done, then she needs to do a little shopping, but she says she's got some veal that you'll like. She'll bread it and sauté it with butter, lemon and capers."

"Oh heavens, the woman could turn a box of Saltines into a gourmet meal. Tell her whatever she wants to make is fine and not to go through any extra trouble or stress on my account, or anyone's account. I'll be home by one."

"OK, don't forget to pick up the diapers on your way. Oh, and I finished reading *Dr. Dolittle's Post Office* to Tommy, so you better find the next one and bring it home or he'll make you read this one again and I know that drives you crazy."

The morning fog had broken, and outside it was turning into one of those beautiful days that signaled the approach of fall. The air was crisp, the sky was a brilliant clear blue, and a cool breeze blew through the trees on Boston Common and sent leaves tumbling across the grass.

Jimmy took a stroll down School Street, where the tall buildings blocked the sun and made for a chilly walk. At City Hall Plaza the sun shone brightly on the vast expanse of red bricks. Jimmy paused at the Government Center subway entrance to let the sun warm his face. He closed his eyes and listened to the sounds of the city around him. The ever-present blasting of car horns in the distance, a jet flying overhead, the clicking of heels along the brick plaza, the subway turnstiles spinning with a sound like roulette wheels.

Cigarette smoke mixed with the smell of fresh popcorn from a cart whose vendor was cooking the first batch of the day. It was a melting pot of smells and sounds that made Jimmy feel very much alive. He might have sat down on a bench and enjoyed it for another five minutes, but one more sound entered the mix and caught his attention.

It was a familiar voice speaking with passion and irritation on the other end of the plaza. Jimmy opened his eyes and saw a cluster of reporters around a podium at the entrance to City Hall. He intended to pass by the very spot on his way to the bookstore in Quincy Market, but he decided to take a different route.

* * * * *

As he addressed the reporters, Mayor Sullivan thrust a finger in the air, pointing in the direction of the State House. "Governor Kostakos is running for the highest office in the republic. He has a responsibility to step forward and make his position clear. We have a right to know where the governor stands on the trash issue!"

Sullivan generally spoke in a conciliatory tone, but his frustration had gotten the better of him Saturday morning. He had intended to bring the press up to date on the progress he had made with the governor that morning, but Kostakos had cancelled their meeting with a very lame excuse, as Sullivan saw it. The mayor's mood was not helped by a lingering hangover from a night of drinking at the Stumbling Monk.

With the throbbing behind his eyes growing more intense, Sullivan wrapped up his statement with a demand that the governor respond within twenty-four hours. The mayor answered no questions before leaving the scene. He went down to the parking garage where Suds, his driver, sat waiting in the mayor's limousine eating his third honey-dipped donut of the morning and reading the *Boston Herald,* the front page of which had a story about Jimmy Mahoney being elected the new Senate president alongside a piece about Francis Mahoney no longer being wanted for questioning in the murder of his father with the confession of Bradley "Buzzy" Driscoll.

"Home to the ranch, Captain?" Suds asked, calling Sullivan by the name from his days as captain of his college basketball team.

"Swing by Flanagan's on the way."

Suds drove the shiny black car to the underground garage exit across from Quincy Market. He spied Jimmy Mahoney crossing Federal Street to his right. "There's President Baloney now. Should I run him over, Captain?"

"No, Suds. This beautiful car doesn't deserve such abuse."

The two shared a laugh as Suds pulled slowly into traffic and steered the car with a grace that suggested somebody important was on board, someone worthy of being held in high esteem by all of the city, and to hell with the governor if he wants to play political games.

Sullivan let his thoughts slip into a stream of indifference. He had taken his parting shot at the governor, and he knew in his political bones that this battle was lost. Mahoney had almost certainly gotten to the governor and twisted his arm. Sullivan already had plans for paying Kostakos back though.

The governor prided himself on the progressive agenda that had brought about the so-called Massachusetts Miracle. Improvements to the business and social climates, and the environment. Mayor Sullivan happened to know a dirty little secret that could turn the miracle into mud. As soon as it became clear who the Republican Party would choose to run for president, Sullivan would give him an inside story about pollution in Boston Harbor. It was the Achilles' heel of the Massachusetts Miracle. Enough to embarrass the governor and cost him heavily on the campaign trail.

Until then, Sullivan would content himself with his work at healing the city's racial wounds and moving it toward a more enlightened future. Jimmy Mahoney belonged to the old Boston, and no matter how much power he might hold as Senate president, Jimmy's point of view had an ever-diminishing relevance. It was an island that would continue to shrink every day until Jimmy Mahoney was relegated to a short passage in the history of Boston politics.

* * * * *

Saturday was the busiest day of the week at the Hair & Beyond. Kathleen had Debbie come in early because the salon was booked solid through six o'clock. At eleven-thirty, all three chairs were full. At the far end sat Maria D'Amico with the chair extended so she could tilt her head back into the sink. Her hair would soon be reborn in platinum blond. She had come in for a simple trim but spontaneously decided to return to the color that best complemented her complexion. The auburn was nice, but it was beginning to make her feel a little rusty.

Two more appointments were sitting in the waiting area when the front door opened. Not Mrs. Norton already, Kathleen prayed. She was busy finishing a cut so she didn't look up. In the mirror, she noticed a tremendous bundle of roses but not the person carrying them.

"Red rover, red rover, send Kathleen right over."

Kathleen spun around and dropped her comb at the sound of the voice. It was Francis. She saw his face when he shifted the roses to one side.

"Tribute to the most beautiful woman in the world," Francis said.

Kathleen froze. "Jesus, Mary and Joseph," she muttered. A TV was positioned in the back corner of the salon, and it was tuned to a show about New England's top ten romantic getaways.

Debbie knew Francis and was equally surprised by his appearance at the salon. She found her vision filled with a bush of roses moving toward her.

"Hold these, hon'," Francis said. Debbie's face disappeared from view as she accepted the thorny gift.

Francis reached into his jacket pocket and pulled out a small jewelry box. He approached Kathleen, but she stopped him with an accusing pair of scissors. "You get out of my salon right now, Francis."

"It's been a rough week, Kathleen, but everything's solid now. I'm a free man and I don't have to run anywhere. I'm here to show you that I'm ready for a new start, right here in town. Let's talk about terms. "

"I've only got one term for you, Francis, but I won't say it in present company. Now you take your rose bush and get out of here."

Francis laughed. "Or what? You're gonna give me a crew cut?"

Like many smokers, Kathleen was constantly misplacing her lighter so she always had extras lying around everywhere. She reached for one on the counter by the mirror and turned up its jet, then grabbed a can of highly flammable hair spray.

She stepped up to Francis, and with a flick, the lighter shot up a three-inch flame. The can of hair spray was poised behind the flame and aimed at Francis' face. "I swear to God, I'll do it if you don't leave now." Kathleen's hand trembled on the spray button.

Suddenly New England's top ten romantic getaways was no longer the most compelling drama in the salon, and all eyes were turned to Kathleen and Francis. Debbie was struggling to free herself from the roses, while Maria lay with her ears partially immersed in water. Out of the corner of her eye, she saw a flickering flame and turned to catch a sideways view of the scene.

Francis slowly returned the jewelry box to his jacket pocket before raising both hands. He said, "OK, I get the point. This isn't quite the best time or place."

Through the leaping flame, Kathleen spoke in an angry, shaking voice, "There won't ever be another good time, here or any place else."

Francis took two steps back to the door. "I know there's a lot to adjust to, Kathleen, but we're going to adjust to it together. There's no other future for us except together. I'll check in later. Try to show better manners when I do."

When Francis left and the door closed behind him, the salon let out a collective sigh. Kathleen let the flame die and lowered her visibly trembling hands. Debbie gave up trying to get a grip on the wild bunch of roses and let them fall en masse to the floor.

Maria had risen slightly from her reclined position in time to see Debbie struggling with the roses and Kathleen holding a jet of flame in front of her. She tried to make sense of the scene as rivulets of water fell from her hair and dripped onto the floor.

"Maria, you're dripping all over the place!" said Brenda Ahern in the next chair.

Maria ignored Brenda, and in her booming voice asked, "What did I miss? What happened?"

* * * * *

What happened in the salon didn't affect Francis' mood in the least. The murder had created a number of problems for him, but it came with a silver lining. His father could no longer stand between him and Kathleen. It might take a few days or a few weeks, but he'd break down her resistance. He knew all the ways to do it. Then they would be a couple again. It would be fine. Everything would be fine.

After burying the last of his problems at the cemetery, Francis received the news that he officially was no longer being sought for questioning in his father's murder. For three hours, he enjoyed the peaceful sleep of a free man at his Quincy condo, then a long hot shower.

After his stop at the Hair & Beyond, Francis planned to meet up with Larry D'Amico so they could bring their whole organization back to the surface. He called Larry and arranged to meet him for a one o'clock lunch downtown at a restaurant owned by Larry's cousin.

Then word came that Jimmy wanted to meet him, so Francis left a message for Larry to sit tight downtown and he'd be there as soon as he could. Seeing Jimmy took precedence, and after reading about his older brother's promotion, Francis felt it was fitting that the two toast to their good fortunes.

As he walked down Broadway, the crisp air carried a suggestion of salt from the sea and added a lightness to Francis' steps. People he passed gave him a look of surprise, followed by a smile. Others shook his hand and had trouble letting go.

"Good to see you, Francis. I knew you didn't do it, Francis. I'm glad you're back. We're all glad you're back," they said.

Buster Benson limped up to Francis in front of Flanagan's and gave his best military salute. "Son of a bitch, Francis, you showed them, didn't you? You showed them a Mahoney is better than that, by God. South Boston is better than that. God in heaven watches over this special place. They'll never lay a finger on you again."

A smile spread across Francis' face as Buster began dancing some sort of jig.

"God help any bastard that ever tries it again, Buster."

A small crowd formed. One woman held up a copy of the *Boston Herald* with a headline proclaiming Francis' innocence and another congratulating Jimmy. She called out to him, "It's the luck of the Irish, Francis!"

It went on like that as he continued his celebratory walk up and down Broadway. He handed out hundred-dollar bills, two or three to older women he knew from the projects. One woman on the other side of the street heard what was going and was almost hit by a car as she dashed across Broadway to get her share of the largesse.

Not everybody knew Francis and not everybody wanted to shake his hand or give him a kiss, but most did, and they did so with a fiery spirit. It had been as if they themselves had been accused of committing murder, of committing the ultimate act of disloyalty to one's father. Now they saw it for what it was. Just one more attempt by the outside world to screw with South Boston, but it didn't work this time.

Now that Francis had been vindicated, they felt vindicated as well. He was the embodiment of their hopes, a reflection of their adventurous inner selves, and he had proven the outside world wrong. As long as Francis and Jimmy Mahoney looked after South Boston, there was nothing in the world they needed to fear.

* * * * *

Maria D'Amico lingered at Kathleen's salon to get the whole story, so she was running a little behind in the kitchen when Jimmy arrived. He had changed out of his suit into jeans and a sweater. As a special treat for Maria, he brought homemade bread. The recipe had been carried over by the Donovans of Roscommon, Ireland, and Peg baked two or three loaves every week.

Full of raisins, dried fruit and spices, the bread was more of a cake and versatile enough to be eaten at breakfast, as an afternoon snack or for dessert with ice cream.

"Jimmy, good to see you," Maria called from the kitchen. "Give me another two minutes while I finish in here." Maria had the veal laid out on a cutting board and was ready to tenderize it. In her right hand she held a tenderizing mallet with a head almost as big as a sledgehammer's.

Maria brought the heavy mallet down on the veal with such force that Jimmy flinched. She continued with a series of rapid blows that made the cutting board jump across the counter. For a woman of sixty-four, Maria still had the strength to knock a misbehaving teenager across the room.

When she paused, Jimmy said, "Good heavens, I hope the veal did something to deserve that punishment."

Maria laughed and wiped her brow. "This is how you tenderize veal the right way. You can't be shy about it." She held the mallet up proudly. "This thing works wonders. I've had it for years." Maria looked at the mallet's shaft, which curved slightly. "Although it got a little bent at some point. I don't know how."

"I've brought you some of Peg's wonderful bread. I know you're crazy about it, Maria. She sends her love too, of course."

"Oh, that's so nice of Peg. You can put it in the fridge and help yourself to a glass of wine in the dining room. Everything's in there, including some antipasto. I'll join you in a jiffy."

Maria watched Jimmy making a place in the fridge for the heavy bread, which was wrapped in foil. God, what am I going to do with another one of those bricks, Maria thought. The things were worse than Christmas fruitcakes. Totally inedible. She had just fed the last loaf Peg gave her to the birds that morning.

The poor Irish. They just didn't know food. They cooked their meat until it was all grey and dried out. They steamed their vegetables into mush. No marinades, no proper oils and every other bite was some form of potato.

Maria didn't blame them personally. They had the big famine, after all, and that made everything get *disperato*. Although you'd think somebody would have saved a few recipes so they could start making proper food once the good times returned.

Jimmy poured a glass of burgundy. He couldn't see Maria in the kitchen, but he could see her shadow so he was able to anticipate each blow and brace himself.

When the tenderizing was complete, Maria dipped the pieces of veal in lemon juice, breaded them and placed them along with some capers in a buttered pan to sauté at low heat. She joined Jimmy in the dining room, where he poured her a glass of wine.

"This is a new burgundy I'm trying. I got it from Francis' store at the rotary and it's not too bad, although definitely more expensive than it was over in East Boston last week. He needs to keep his prices competitive. You should tell him, Jimmy. It's a thing one brother can say to another."

Jimmy agreed and was about to expand on the topic when he heard the back door open. A moment later, Francis appeared in the dining room doorway wearing a blissful grin. "Jimmy, you beat me," he said and slapped his brother on the back.

"Don't you look like the Cheshire cat," Jimmy said with a smile that had spread quickly between the brothers.

Maria was immune, however. When Francis turned to greet her, she gave him a stern look and wagged a finger in his direction. "I have a little advice for you, mister, after your performance down at the salon earlier."

Francis raised his hands in protest. "Hey, I brought her roses. Kathleen was the one who pulled the act."

"I won't lecture you, Francis. I'll just give you this one piece of advice, and you can do with it what you will. In a successful relationship, timing is everything, in more ways than one. You don't pick the busiest time of the week to show up unannounced and expect all sweetness and light from a girl who's traveled a rocky road with you. OK? That's all I'm going to say. You know I love you to death."

Maria gave Francis a kiss on the cheek. Turning to Jimmy, she said, "Your brother came this close to becoming a burning rose bush today. OK, boys, you know the drill. Time for me to flip the veal and give it another minute. The pasta's boiling and will be done soon. Gravy's on the stove and the garlic bread's in the oven. Jimmy, I forgot to ask how the kids are doing, but from the way their voices carry I can tell they're all healthy. Thank Peg for the bread. Be sure to put any leftovers in the fridge."

Once she finished preparing the meal, Maria disappeared out the back door with a bag of library books that were almost due. Francis and Jimmy filled their plates and brought them back to the dining room along with the loaf of garlic bread that was crusty on the outside, soft and hot inside, and soaked with melted butter and crushed garlic.

Within minutes they fell into the easy kind of conversation that brothers have even if they haven't seen each other for a long time. It could have been twenty years earlier with the two of them sitting in the dining room on E. Third Street with Jimmy telling Francis that he better take military discipline seriously if he wanted to come back alive from Vietnam, or Francis telling Jimmy not to be so foolish as to follow their father into the fucked-up world of Boston politics. Advice which neither one of them took.

"You are one happy son of a bitch today," Jimmy said when he noticed Francis' smile still peeking out between bites.

"I'll tell you, Jimmy, it feels good to be back and living as a free man. Nothing can touch me. I haven't been too busy to read the papers, so I know all about your good news, too. Congratulations, *el presidente*. Or *salute* as Maria might say."

They clinked glasses and drank some wine.

Francis looked at his glass. "Maria's wine is usually better than this."

"She bought it at your place, and she says your prices are way too high."

"She's forgetting about all the service that comes with the product. The love behind it. Hey, I saw your buddy Sullivan at Flanagan's looking like a head of wilted lettuce. I hope you take advantage of your new position to stick it to the bastard. He's really going through with this forced housing shit and people around The Town are not too pleased about it. You've got to make him remember where he comes from."

389

Jimmy took it all in and nodded his head to each of his brother's remarks. At this point, he would usually ask Francis how everything was, and Francis would carefully carve out those parts of his life that were safe to share and leave out the rest. However, what Jimmy had to say was probably not going to please his brother, so he said nothing much until Francis had talked himself out.

Finally Jimmy said, "I was up at the State House this morning and had a visit from the FBI. It was Finnegan, who you know, and some smart-ass kid. Anyway, they were asking about you, whether I had seen you since the wedding, heard from you. I know you were telling people a week ago you were about to be indicted..."

"It's not gonna happen. It's over."

"Well, what I was about to say is that it didn't sound like it was over this morning. If anything, it sounds like these guys are working up to something. You know they've got a new director. He's bound to try some kind of move to make a name for himself in Boston."

"Disco told me about him. He's a jerk, but Disco's on top of things. Believe me, the storm has passed."

There was a pause as Francis poured out more wine for himself, then Jimmy.

"I wanted to ask you about something else, Francis, and I hope you don't mind where the question leads," Jimmy said.

Francis suddenly had a feeling where Jimmy's question might go and he didn't like it, but he wasn't about to stop him. "Go ahead."

"Two things really," Jimmy began. "You know about Buzzy and the stories about Dad, you know..." He had never spoken about the rumors to Francis and putting them into words caused Jimmy to cast a momentary doubt on them. Regardless, he continued, "...that he had an affair with Mrs. Driscoll, Buzzy's mom, and that, well, Buzzy is the result."

"That Buzzy was our half brother?"

Jimmy paused to register something. "Exactly. Yes. You've heard that."

Francis sipped his wine, then said, "It doesn't matter whether I heard it. It's not true."

"So you know it's not true?"

"You don't know if something's not true, Jimmy. You know if it is true, and nobody has proven that rumor true. Not Buzzy, not his mom. Buzzy would have said something to me, I'm sure. If I were you, I wouldn't pay it any attention. I never have."

Jimmy had eaten several pieces of garlic bread and there were lots of crumbs on the table in front of him. With one finger, he drew a sideways eight over and over. "I'm asking you, Francis, because of what happened to Buzzy at the police station."

"He escaped."

"That's the thing. You don't escape from Boston Police headquarters unless you're very brilliant. Or unless somebody wants you to escape."

"You'd be surprised how stupid some cops can be, Jimmy."

"Buzzy worked for you, didn't he? Or let me put it this way—the two of you had friends in common."

The words from his brother gave Francis an odd sensation of being trespassed upon. Like when two dogs live for years at peace because of an agreement about where the territory of one ends and the other begins. Now, for the first time, the boundary was being challenged.

"Sure we did," Francis responded tersely.

"I'm not comfortable talking to you about this, Francis, and I'll make it brief for both our sakes. Dad didn't like Buzzy, and I can't remember him ever passing up an opportunity to insult the kid. If the rumors about Dad are true, or if they aren't and Buzzy believed them, then that would certainly be part of his motive for committing the murder."

Francis responded with a flush of anger. "There's no excusing what he did." He paused to raise a finger. "Never mind that he set me up, which I would never forgive anybody for, but what he did was against all of us. You, me, Matt, our dead mother."

The tone of Francis' voice told Jimmy that his brother was taking this as poorly as he suspected he would. Still, Jimmy continued. He had to if he was to sleep with anything close to a clear conscience.

"You're right, Francis. There is no excuse for what he did. Understanding why he did it is another matter entirely."

Francis was losing patience with the whole discussion. "What's your fucking point, Jimmy?"

"I would hope that because you knew Buzzy well, you wouldn't feel yourself privileged to take action once you found out that he killed Dad. Particularly since he might be related to us."

Francis let out a deep sigh to vent some of the anger that had risen inside him so rapidly. "The cops know he's guilty, and they know I'm not. That's good enough for me. Alright, Jimmy? As long as Buzzy and I don't bump into each other on Broadway, I have no reason to go looking for the fuckup."

Francis waited for Jimmy to respond, but he didn't. Instead Jimmy lowered his eyes to the table.

"What do you want from me, Jimmy?"

"Nothing. I said what I had to say. I'm sorry I made us both uncomfortable." Jimmy raised his eyes and looked at his brother. "I'm glad I got to see you today, Francis. I really am." Jimmy rose and brushed the crumbs from the table to his plate. He gathered the dishes in front of him and brought them to the kitchen.

Francis watched him pass and knew there was something unfinished. Something Jimmy held back, something unspoken, and it was unnerving Francis. He remained seated and called into the kitchen. "You're accusing me of something, Jimmy. Spit it out."

Jimmy returned to the dining room and patted his brother on the shoulder. "I'm not accusing you of anything, Francis. I'm just thinking about what you said a few minutes ago."

Francis looked up at him, quizzically at first, then suspiciously.

Jimmy continued, "When I asked you about the rumor, you said it would mean that Buzzy was our half brother. Not is our half brother, but was our half brother. You referred to Buzzy as if he weren't alive anymore."

Francis was silent, and he showed nothing on his face. He let a moment pass before standing up to clear the table. "It's an expression, Jimmy. He's gone who-knows-where, and I think there's a good chance that we'll never see him again. OK?"

"OK," Jimmy said. They went into the kitchen, where Jimmy wrapped up the leftovers while Francis loaded the dishwasher and soaked the pans in the sink. When they were done, they locked the back door and shook hands.

"It's good seeing you, Jimmy. And congratulations. I mean it."

"I know you do. Be careful, Francis."

"If there's one thing I'm full of, brother, it's careful."

Jimmy watched Francis walk down the driveway and waited a few minutes so nobody would see them leaving at the same time. Then he walked home wondering if he had gone too far by accusing

Francis because they both knew that's what Jimmy had done. He had crossed a line he had never crossed since they were kids.

What if he was wrong in his suspicion? Jimmy still had some doubt, but more of him felt that his hunch was correct, and he wouldn't apologize for the accusation because if he had to bet his life on it, he would say Francis had killed Buzzy, or had somebody else kill him.

There was nothing the law required of a person if he had a suspicion that was not backed by evidence, so Jimmy wasn't legally bound to say anything to anybody.

Rather than legal, Jimmy's burden was a moral one. Believing your brother had committed murder yet doing nothing about it. Because of the business Francis was in and because Jimmy was bound to hear stories of alleged deeds committed by Francis, this was not the first time he felt himself somehow complicit in the acts of his brother. If only because he continued to love Francis without conditions.

Whether or not Buzzy shared Mahoney blood, he had been part of the Mahoney family and a best friend to Matthew. This one would not wash from his conscience easily, Jimmy knew. It would not fade with the passing of a week, a month or a year.

And it had been such a week, Jimmy thought as he climbed the front steps to his house and heard young, vocal Brendan waking from his nap. They'd have an easy night. Order pizzas and rent a movie with a happy ending, but before that there would be a visit to St. Monica's Church in a couple of hours. This was no week to skip confession.

* * * * *

On the sidewalks of Broadway people were still waving at Francis, giving him a thumbs-up or a pat on the back, but now it was different. Francis was disconnected from them, returning only a nod or weak smile. He stared over their heads, at the distant skyline of downtown Boston, at nothing in particular.

Fucking Jimmy, pissing on my parade, he thought. Francis had gone to lunch in the best of spirits and now he was upset in a way that only Jimmy could make him. What would it be next time? If Jimmy is willing to trespass once, why not do it every time they meet? Didn't Jimmy realize the peace between them, the sense of trust they both cherished, depended on him staying out of Francis' business?

A car honked on Broadway. Francis heard his name called. He waved a hand in response but didn't look over. The car horn blasted again. "Wake up!" a voice screamed.

Francis turned and saw Disco rolling alongside him in his car. The passenger window was down and Disco was glaring at Francis with bug eyes. "Get over here," Disco called.

Francis took his time walking over to the car, the way he would do when he was a teenager, showing a casual defiance whenever a cop insisted he do something right that goddamn minute.

"You're all pissy," Francis said. "Are you starting a new diet?"

"Get in the car."

Francis got in, and Disco drove down Broadway until he found an open spot to park.

"We've got problems, Francis. I had a meeting downtown this morning and the new director tells me British intelligence tracked the Avalon. When it unloads onto smaller boats and they enter Irish waters, the British navy is going to nab them."

Francis let his head fall back against the headrest and closed his eyes. "This day is turning into a real fucking picnic."

"The IRA has a snitch on its council, and the guy spilled everything."

Someone passing on the sidewalk noticed Francis and waved. Francis waved back. "The IRA is full of stupid fucks, Larry. They can get an admiral in our Coast Guard to play on our team, but they can't keep the rats out of their own house." He raised his head. "Oh, well. Their money, their guns, their loss."

Disco was breathing rapidly and seemed on the verge of panic. "Yes, but that's not the fucking point..."

"It's OK, Disco. Calm down."

Finally Disco burst out, "Listen to me! They know about you and Larry making it happen. Bringing in the dope, buying the guns, everything."

Francis rolled his head. "Oh, man." There was a moment of silence as Francis looked out the window, thinking.

"And I think Anderson's gonna flip. They said he was coming in today with lots of information to share with the director." Disco's hands held the steering wheel in a death grip. "That cocksucker." Disco gritted his teeth and twisted his hands around the wheel. "I knew way back we couldn't trust him. Fucking Wellesley cocksucker."

"Disco, I've got tapes," Francis said. Disco hadn't heard Francis, so he repeated, "Disco, pay attention now. You know all those meetings Larry and I had with you and Anderson? Well, I wired myself for a lot of them, and I've got tapes of him getting shitfaced and saying exactly what he was doing for Larry and me. We've got tapes on him."

Disco wasn't sure how to take this. "What do you mean, you wired yourself when you met with me? What the fuck?"

"When Anderson was there, Disco. I've got tapes with just me, him and Larry, too. We can use the tapes that make him look bad. We blackmail the motherfucker." Francis let Disco take in the idea. "I never trusted him either, Disco. He's not one of us. That's why I taped him."

Disco relaxed his grip on the wheel and slumped over. The energy of his anger had been exhausted, and he felt a dark cloud of resignation falling around him. "The tapes don't matter, Francis. Nothing matters. They'll give him immunity. It'll keep him from being prosecuted for all of this. We're fucked." Disco looked at Francis with sad, self-pitying eyes that Francis couldn't stand.

He wanted to slap Disco on the face but instead hit him hard on the shoulder. "C'mon, get up! We're still in this game as long as we can think, Disco. Use that Machiavellian brain of yours."

Francis' words had little effect on Disco. "It's not safe for you and Larry again. I don't know how much time you've got."

"Enough of that defeatist shit. I'm not giving up. And I'm not going anywhere. Do me a favor and drop me at O'Brien's."

Neither one of them was in the mood to talk on the two-mile drive that brought Francis back along the same Broadway where two hours before he had been lighter on his feet than he had been since he was a teenager. Past the Hair & Beyond, Donnelley's Pub and Old Colony.

The short drive was all Francis needed to realize that there was no fighting the situation. As much as he hated to admit it, Disco was right. It wasn't safe anymore. He'd have to leave. And soon. The fact that Francis knew all this was something he owed, like so much of his success, to Disco standing by him.

As they approached O'Brien's, Francis reached over and patted Disco on the back. "I understand everything you told me, and you're right. I appreciate it, Disco. Thanks for tracking me down and telling me. I don't know when I'll see you next, amigo, but I'll always owe you."

Disco pulled into the glass-strewn parking lot and let Francis out. Jackie stood in the bar's open doorway, decorating his cast with a magic marker. When he saw Francis, he ran inside.

"They'll look for you here eventually, Francis," Disco said. "Somebody will mention your name and O'Brien's Tavern in the same sentence. They'll swarm this place. Get rid of those tapes that you made without telling me, please. If they show up in the wrong hands, they'll only be used against me, not Anderson."

As Francis watched Disco drive away, he thought—I'm blind now. He had contacts in the Boston Police department, the DEA and various other law enforcement agencies, but if anything came at him from the FBI now, he wouldn't know it until it was too late.

He heard footsteps behind him. Connor was running across the parking lot in a panic. When he reached Francis he blurted out, "They got Larry!"

"Who got Larry?"

"FBI. The black cars surrounded him as he was driving away from his cousin's restaurant in Quincy Market. Jesus, I thought you were with him, Francis."

"I was supposed to be. I postponed it because Jimmy wanted to meet me for lunch."

"Thank God for Jimmy."

Connor was right. If it wasn't for Jimmy, Francis would be handcuffed in the backseat of an unmarked car on his way to a fitting for an orange jumpsuit right now.

"Here we go again," Francis said. "Fucking déjà vu. Disco just dropped me off. He said it's all over. For me and Larry anyway. How are you doing?"

"I'm good. Same deal as last Saturday?" Connor asked.

"Except this time I'll need you to take me away before you take off yourself. Grab my duffel upstairs and get the box of tapes in the basement safe. Then bring the blue van around."

"Let's hope nobody's figured out that we're driving it around. Otherwise they'll put out an APB, and we're screwed," Connor said.

"We're only driving it a few miles. I have another vehicle we can use." Francis shook his head and let out a bitter laugh. "And I thought I was being paranoid." Looking at Connor, he said, "Go ahead. I'll wait out here so I can see if the feebs are coming. No fucking way am I joining Larry, no matter what I have to do."

The crowd at Jolly Donuts across the street was light, and there was no traffic visible in either direction along Dorchester Avenue. In fact, the whole scene was strangely quiet. As he waited for Connor to return, Francis looked slowly around the bar's empty parking lot. The sun seemed particularly bright, and it lit up the many shards of glass in twinkles of brown, white and green.

There was something almost magical about it, something that made Francis imagine that this was what a truly sacred place looked like. A place where people came to be cured of their afflictions. Or maybe it was how the road was paved to the afterlife and why the thousands of sparkles were almost too painful to stare at, yet too entrancing to look away from.

Was he seeing it the way it would be for him when he died, or was this what people saw when they reached the point in their lives where the possibility of redemption had finally passed? A quick glimpse into what would be denied them forever. A priest said something like that when Francis went to church, when he was young and dumb enough to believe that the words from a priest's mouth were the words of God.

* * * * *

Because Anne had purchased their tickets at the last minute, a direct flight to Seattle, or even an itinerary with one stop, was too expensive. From Boston they went to Charlotte. After a layover, they boarded a plane that took them to Denver, where they had almost two hours to kill before their flight to Seattle.

Matthew slept most of the way to Charlotte. On the flight to Denver, when he wasn't sleeping, he stared out the window at the ground far below. He wondered what his life would have been like if he had grown up in one of the anonymous towns they passed over.

Several times he woke with his forehead pressed against the cool window.

When they landed in Denver, he felt the most awake he had been since getting knocked out the day before, but after fifteen minutes of wandering around the spacious airport, Matthew felt the fatigue beginning to return. They sat down at a pizza parlor that had a café arrangement of tables extending into the terminal. It was a good place to watch people passing by and guess where they might be from.

Outside the large windows of the terminal, Matthew could see beyond the runways to distant mountains where the late afternoon sunshine lit up patches of snow across the jagged peaks. Such a different landscape, he thought.

They ordered glasses of red wine and a pizza. The wine arrived with a basket of garlic bread. Anne tore off pieces for both of them, and they toasted to the fact that they were now closer to Seattle than to Boston.

Matthew looked at his watch, which was still on Boston time two hours earlier.

"It's six o'clock in Boston," Matthew said.

"Dinnertime," Anne said.

"You mean suppertime," Matthew said. It was one of their differences. Growing up, Matthew only knew of the evening meal as supper. Dinner was what you had on Sunday afternoon, a meal that included roast beef and peeled roasted potatoes, a traditional weekly feast signifying that this particular Boston Irish family had made it in the new world.

He broke off more bread and passed a piece to Anne. Matthew felt his appetite coming back and wondered if they should have ordered a large pizza instead of medium. A group of children approached the restaurant. Several of them stared at Matthew, and as they came closer he noticed that they were still staring.

"What's their problem?" Matthew wondered.

"It's your bruises," Anne said.

"Oh, right." Matthew had forgotten how beat up his face looked. The bruises were in full blossom. Both eyes and his lower lip were swollen. The skin around his left eye was itching and he reached up to scratch it.

The waitress brought two warm plates and put the pizza between them. Anne's half had spinach and goat cheese; Matthew's had sausage and hot peppers. Looking at the pizza, smelling the garlic and the sweetness of the sauce, they could tell they had made the right choice, or maybe a lucky choice, in stopping at this café.

They pulled slices onto their plates. Before taking a bite Matthew said, "You know, I can't remember the last time I prayed, and I can't think of a time when I might want to pray again, but I think I should say how grateful I am that we survived this week."

"Not your typical honeymoon," Anne said before taking her first bite.

"I'm sorry about losing the ring, Anne," Matthew said. "And for putting you through a painful week. I did some really stupid things."

"It's alright, Matt," she said.

"No, it isn't," he said.

Anne picked up a napkin and wiped a patch of sauce from the corner of her mouth. It had been a painful week. Their first week of marriage. She looked at her husband's face and wondered how long it would take him to heal.

Then she thought of her father. Maybe surviving a terrible loss or a terrible week was the best you could do. Anne's wine glass was still half full, but she reached across the table and picked up Matthew's glass. He tried to retrieve it but was too slow.

"Hey, pain is for sharing, Mahoney. Didn't anyone ever teach you that?"

Matthew remembered something Anne had said at the wedding reception, which seemed so long ago. He smiled. "Like champagne?"

"Yes," Anne said, returning the smile. "Like champagne."

About the Book

To learn more about the novel, the inspiration for some of the characters and the history of South Boston, please visit www.chieftainsofsouthboston.com

You can also find Stephen Burke on Facebook (search under "The Chieftains of South Boston") and Twitter: @WriterBurke